MAYHEM ON MULBERRY

ALSO BY VINCENT DEFILIPPO

The Leftovers Club
Book One: JoJo's Story

Catch a Falling Knife

Braking Point: *How Escalation of Commitment is Destroying the World (and How You Can Save Yourself)*

Nine Seconds

MAYHEM ON MULBERRY

Vincent deFilippo

Mayhem on Mulberry
Book One: Rise of the East
First Edition
Copyright © 2024 by Vincent DeFilippo

ViennaRose Publishing

All rights reserved. No part of this publication may be reproduced, distributed, or transmitted in any form or by any means, including photocopying, recording, or other electronic or mechanical methods, without the prior written permission of the publisher, except as permitted by U.S. copyright law.

The story, all names, characters, and incidents portrayed in this production are fictitious. No identification with actual persons (living or deceased), places, buildings, and products is intended or should be inferred.

Paperback ISBN #: 978-1-960299-56-7
Printed in the United States of America

ACT ONE: WORLDS COLLIDE

CHAPTER ONE

September 1991

JEN MO-LI EYED THE FAMILY OF THREE WHO STOOD IN nervous silence before her in the captain's cabin as the ship rocked gently with the gentle rise and swell of the Hudson River. Jen tapped her pen on their names printed neatly on the list attached to her clipboard. The pen, a black Montegrappa from its signature class, had been a twenty-fifth birthday gift from her father. She'd used it constantly since he'd presented her with it the previous December; not because she particularly liked the pen—in fact, she hated the thing because of its significance as a pat on the head—but because it made Father happy. Even for all the wealth he'd accumulated since arriving penniless in the States in the sixties, Jen struggled to imagine how on earth he could ever justify spending over $10,000 on a pen when so many people needed help.

It served as a stark reminder to Jen that, given only slightly different circumstances, she could have easily been in this family's shoes. Were it not for the wealth her father had accumulated, it might be her name attached to a clipboard, earmarked for some grubby Chinatown apartment instead of her gilded cage.

"You will have to learn how to speak English," Jen informed the Cho family with kindness in her tone. The mother—Cho Hu—smiled and nodded as if she understood what was being said to her, when clearly she did not. To spare the woman's feelings, Jen repeated herself in Chinese; it was lucky for the Cho family she was fluent in her mother tongue. "I'm guessing you have not memorized your American names yet, either?" Jen added.

Cho Hu, her short, painfully thin husband, and virtually skeletal teenaged daughter bowed their heads in shame.

"We are so sorry, Ms. Mo-Li," Hu's husband—Feng, according to the list—spoke without lifting his eyes to meet Jen's. "We have not had the opportunity to learn."

"It's okay." Jen put a reassuring arm around Hu's shoulders. "I understand three months aboard this ship has not been conducive to learning a new language. But one of the first things you must accustom yourself to is that here, your family name is spoken and written last."

The Cho family, along with so many others, had paid out $35,000 for their passage to America in what was little more than a floating hell hole. If she had her way, Jen would have gladly sacrificed a portion of the Mo-Li family's profit for a more dignified and safer voyage.

Jen was beginning to feel the tiredness of her day, and she felt for her charges. It was getting close to midnight, and she had a bunch of undocumented immigrants still to process; she was as eager to be off the boat as they were. She and Eddie had been stuck in the captain's cabin of the *Bright Horizon* since 9 p.m. with those who'd set sail from Hong Kong in search of the American Dream. There were showers on board, but Jen had seen for herself why her clients more often than not chose not to use them. They were horrifically rusted, grimy, cold, and crawling with rats and cockroaches. Jen, too, reckoned she would have preferred to stay dirty.

The boat, a decommissioned trawler, made the grueling trip to the United States three times a year; it was little more than an old rust bucket and was ill-suited to journeying halfway around the globe. The owners, who had Triad connections back in mainland China, had *Bright Horizon* registered in the Bahamas to avoid some of the more rigorous American maritime laws. Had it been a U.S. vessel, Jen knew the antiquated boat would have been scrapped or scuppered years ago. All that considered, Jen took some solace in the fact that she provided far better passage than most other Chinese traffickers; so many people died at the hands of her rivals during their voyage, although it was impossible to know exact numbers since bodies were simply thrown into the sea and ship records altered.

"Hao de," Jen said, her Mandarin word perfect. "You are David, Cynthia, and Lucy Chin. Your accommodation address on Mott Street is listed here. You start work at Lo Sin Fat Dry Cleaners at 7 a.m., Monday morning. I will call you in two weeks to collect your first payment." She pulled a crisp sheet of paper from behind her passenger manifest and thrust it into Cho Feng's hands.

The Chos, having paid half of their passage to America back in Hong Kong, would work off the remainder they owed to Jen over the next few years—all at an extortionately high interest rate set by Jen's father and infinitely favorable to the Mo-Li family. That was another bone of contention between Jen and her father.

Jen continued, "There is also the address of the Chinese Christian church you are required to attend. We shall look forward to seeing you there every Sunday."

Cho Hu, who would take an age to learn how to pronounce her assigned name of Cynthia, grasped Jen's right hand and squeezed it tight. Finally, she dared look her benefactor in the eye. "Thank you so much for this opportunity, Mother Mo-Li. We will *all* work very hard." She cast a glance at her daughter's miserable face. "And we will not let you down."

Smiling, Jen dismissed the family with a nod and a wave. While she was in no mood for cursory niceties, she knew the Chos were good people who wouldn't let her down. For starters, they had a great work ethic and had spent their entire life savings to build a better life for themselves. The very least the weary travelers deserved was a friendly smile.

As the newly christened Chin family filed out of the cramped cabin, another family, equally unkempt and smelling to high heaven of sweat and desperation, filed in. They were accompanied by Jen's ever-unsmiling bodyguard, Eddie Sun.

"Thank you, Eddie." Jen forced a smile as he ushered the family of four—father, mother, pre-adolescent son, and younger daughter—into the cabin and had them line up like contestants on some particularly cheesy game show.

Eddie had been a constant presence by Jen's side since she turned fifteen and her father had deemed it time for her to be indoctrinated into the family business. Eddie was a tall, broad man with unreadable eyes and a gleaming, smooth-shaven head. Jen had teased him from the start that no one would ever mistake him for a child's cuddly toy. But she knew that Eddie Sun had a soft spot and that she lived in the heart of it.

Her *bà* had given Eddie to her as a protector. It was perhaps the only act that had hinted the Mo-Li patriarch cared for her as more than someone he could trust implicitly to run the immigration side of the family business. Jen initially suspected that Bà Mo-Li had assigned Eddie to spy on her; over time that suspicion had evaporated. Eddie had never given her reason not to trust what her bà had told her he was—her guardian angel. Or perhaps her guardian demon.

The patriarch of the odd-looking family, Po Jinping, stood ramrod straight before Jen, beaming as if she were the personification of Bodhisattva Guan Yin for taking their life savings so they could endure seven or eight weeks of hell at sea. "We are so humbled by your benevolence, Madam Mo-Li." The man had obviously spent a long time rehearsing the line. Jen was grateful he had conquered the language; it was far easier to integrate her immigrants when they knew at least the rudiments.

As for the man's young son, Jen wondered how the hell he'd managed to get fat during the voyage. Food on the *Bright Horizon* was tightly rationed, designed to provide only the bare minimum to keep costs and the boat's weight down. It was especially not nutritious—certainly not fattening. But there he was, not-so-little Po Zhung, with his chubby cheeks and fat belly protruding from beneath his ill-fitting shirt.

"We are looking forward very much to living in the America States," Jinping's wife threw in with a forced smile. Her body and face were painfully thin, her complexion waxen; the trip hadn't been as kind to her as it had to her corpulent son. Resting a hand on her daughter's head, Jinping's wife continued, "This will so much be a better life for her. Thank you, Mother Mo-Li."

As tired as she was, Jen couldn't help but be moved by the family's gratitude and that they deemed her worthy of the epithet. If only her father had been there to see just how well she did the job he'd deemed the only one in his whole empire suitable for a mere woman. Jen gave sanctuary to people marginalized by her birth country; she gave hope to those falsely accused of heinous crimes, and a new life to those for whom the oppressive Communist regime had become unlivable. It was that which gave Jen the most pride in her work. She supposed she might be doing the work of the compassionate manifestation of Buddha. God knew many of these people—especially women and girls—faced a fate worse than death in their homeland. America was their land of dreams, and Jen could not help but be honored to be part of them realizing those dreams. If only her father would care enough to see that, he might afford her better, faster ships.

Jen advised the Po family their new surname was Yang, and that it would be pronounced and written last when they identified themselves and sent them on their way with their battered suitcases in hand.

Next up was a tall, wiry-looking guy who wore a loose, dark gray suit that had most likely fit him in Hong Kong. It was accompanied by a red power tie. Jen was impressed; this was New York Harbor in the middle of a warm, early-autumn night, but the guy was still determined to make a good first impression in his new home country. Jen noticed a distinct sparkle of purpose in Ma Lim's eyes. She now knew he'd do well in the land of opportunity. Jen had seen that same glint in her father's eyes; it showed up in every photograph of him in his early days in America when he, too, had arrived to make his fortune.

Jen scribbled a barely legible note on her list next to Ma's name. She'd be sure to keep a close eye on him over the coming months, as young men like him came in handy in her line of business. He left the room as Mu Yin.

"Where is Gong Shu Li?" Jen asked Eddie as the ex-Ma Lim made his way out of the cabin. "Her name is not on the second manifest." Jen lifted the top sheet on the clipboard to double-check the one below it.

7

There were only two names on that particular list—the two deaths on this voyage. She strove for no deaths and little illness, but the weeks at sea without adequate food and water meant some occasionally occurred. There were also sometimes accidents at sea or fights.

"There is no one waiting," Eddie said. He took an exaggerated look out of the cabin door as if expecting Ms. Gong to have magically appeared while his back was turned.

Jen shook her head; the night was about to get longer. "Get me the captain. We shall have to look belowdecks."

Eddie's shrill two-finger whistle resounded about the cramped cabin so loud it physically hurt Jen's ears. "I wish you wouldn't do that, Eddie," she chastised with a touch more curtness to her tone than intended. "I'd much rather you go *fetch* Captain He."

Eddie gave an apologetic grin and pointed his sweat-sheened forehead toward the narrow passageway beyond the door. From there, loud and rhythmic against the steel floor, came the sound of the captain's quickened footsteps.

"We're missing a passenger. You were instructed to have them all assembled and ready to check out." Jen waved the clipboard under the captain's nose for emphasis. She checked her watch and huffed. "I'm assuming the other list is accurate?"

"Yes, Miss Mo-Li." The captain spoke quietly, eyes ever so slightly downcast. "There were only two on the deceased list this time."

"Then you're going to have to take us to the lower cabins to look for Gong Shu Li, Captain."

Captain He fiddled nervously with his thin excuse for a mustache and shuffled from foot to foot. He was a dull, skittish little man whose salt and pepper crew-cut hair belied his youth.

Without further explanation or room to allow the captain to argue, Jen made her way out through the cabin door with Eddie hot on her heels.

As they walked, Jen sensed He's hesitance. She knew the captains of the immigrant ships she chartered didn't like her snooping around belowdecks, as they didn't pay too much attention to the welfare of their passengers and had no desire for their paymaster to see the squalor in which their charges traveled. Nonetheless, as the three walked toward the staircase that led to the bowels of the old boat, Jen knew there was more to the captain's reluctance than just that.

"Has anyone *else* boarded since you docked?" Eddie asked Jen's question before her. This was far from his first outing with her on the passenger boats.

Captain He's silence spoke volumes.

"You stay here," Jen growled at the captain when they reached the hatch to the lower decks. There was no point dragging the guy down there when he was so clearly scared half to death of what awaited them —he looked like he was about to throw up. "I'll find Gong Shu Li myself." With that said, Jen yanked open the hatch and had Eddie follow her belowdecks.

CHAPTER TWO

Donnie Wu may well have been a cheap, lowlife sleazeball, but he was damn good at what he did. That's why Storm and Charlie Boy kept him around. Donnie had been a member of the Black Dragons for six years and had risen high in the ranks despite his penchant for interfering with the merchandise. As a result, Storm trusted Donnie with the highly lucrative sex side of the gang's operations and was prepared to overlook his unsavory habits.

"A pretty young bitch like you can make a lot of money here in America," Donnie told the girl who cowered all but naked on the metal bunk before him—one of six beds just like it in the dimly lit cabin. Remaining silent, the girl looked up at Donnie with tears brimming in her wide, brown eyes as her body rocked gently with the tireless motion of the boat.

Donnie stared back at her and wrinkled his nose. The foul, sour stink of dirty bodies and waste permeated the entirety of the lower deck, and, for as many years as he'd spent picking out the prettiest of the immigrants from the boats, Donnie knew he'd never get used to it. He'd learned early in his career that the best pickings were to be had before the unaccompanied girls got off the ships, even if there were risks involved in his sneaking aboard. There had been plenty of fights over the years with disgruntled traffickers who objected to the Black Dragons taking the most attractive girls for their brothels and street corner trade. Still, Donnie Wu could hold his own and was always prepared to defend himself whenever necessary. Tall, lean, second-generation Chinese, Donnie wore his hair short, spiked up, and was never without his trademark Saint Laurent polo, 501s, and sports jacket—an image he thought suited both his physical stature and high position in the Dragons.

"You want to come work for me?" Donnie slapped a hand against his chest. He wasn't sure if he was getting through to the girl or not, although she'd surely gotten the message when he ripped open her grimy, sweat-stained shirt and yanked off her shabby underpants. Donnie reckoned she was from the Fujian Province and spoke no English as far as he could ascertain as his grasp of the Fuzhou dialect was rusty, to say the least. "You will make good money." He told her, rubbing his thumb and forefinger together for the universal sign of wealth.

As the girl scooted backward on the bunk, the thin, soiled mattress curled up at the bottom. She tried her best to hold her torn shirt around her torso and clamped her skinny, bare legs together as she recoiled beneath the gangster's scrutiny.

Clean the girl up, give her a decent haircut, trim the black, wiry bush that sprouted out, wild and unkempt, between her legs, and Donnie reckoned she'd fetch top dollar in the Dragons' more select massage parlors. The long voyage from Hong Kong and meager rations had left her emaciated and had shrunken her breasts down to barely discernible nubs, but she had a sweet, round face, smooth, pale complexion, and wide, brown, cow eyes, which gave her a look of youthful innocence. There were rich, regular clients at the Flushing parlors who would pay handsomely for such youthful beauty.

Seeing that there was little chance of getting the girl to understand what he was trying to tell her, Donnie figured the best thing would be to drag her out before anyone came looking for her. He carried his cleaver in a modified gun holster hidden inside his jacket and had made sure the girl saw it so she wouldn't put up too much of a fight.

"You come with me now," Donnie instructed as he tucked his softening dick, sticky with her blood, back into his Wranglers. He nodded toward the single, leatherette suitcase by the foot of her bed. "Bring that, and let's go." He pointed at the cabin door and stepped forward, hand outstretched, to help Gong Shu Li off the bunk.

"What are you doing in here?!"

Jen Mo-Li stormed into the cabin with such force that the heavy steel door clanged loud and hard against the bulkhead. Her anger rose as she saw what was going on in the cramped steel room. *"Get away from her!"* Donnie flinched at the sound of Jen's voice but stood his ground as if to protect the territory he'd marked by force.

Eddie appeared at the doorway, his bulk almost filling it. "You heard her," he said, deadpan. "Get the fuck away from the girl."

Donnie reacted to Eddie's command with a grimace. It was dishonorable to use such language, and it spoke volumes about the muscle behind Jen and her clipboard and signaled that Eddie Sun was not a man to be messed with.

Jen eyed Donnie as he took a hasty step away from the young girl. She'd not crossed paths with the gangster before now but deduced from his tattoos he was most likely to be a member of the Mott Street Tigers or Black Dragons; none of the other gangs would have the audacity to try stealing Mo-Li's clients right from under her nose. This was the first instance Jen knew of the gangs boarding boats to purloin young women for their parlors. She was all too aware of them making approaches once they were on land, which was why she did everything she could to settle her clients in secure, respectable jobs. Of course, that was not to say it was by any means the first time—Captain He may well have had some arrangement going with the gangs. Both the Tigers and Dragons seemed to have seized the monopoly in populating their parlors with fresh immigrants, and Jen had heard rumors of both gangs picking up piecework for the Italians, too, which made them traitorous scum in her eyes.

"I'm Donnie Wu; pleased to meet you." The gangster dared to smile at Jen. "Look, she's only one girl," he said with his arms outstretched in a *you can trust me* gesture. "What's just one little illegal girl to you people? You have your money from her already." He glanced across at

Gong Shu Li, who huddled tight against the damp steel wall at the corner of her bunk bed. She pulled her ruined clothes across her exposed body and looked down with shame at the blue and white stripes of her grubby bare mattress.

"She has nothing to do with you, and you have no business here, or with us," Jen replied. "You should not even be on our boat. I suggest you leave now, while you can."

As Donnie Wu stood his ground with arrogant defiance, the young girl looked up and across at Jen with a glimmer of hope in her eyes, as if the woman with the clipboard and shiny pen were her savior.

Jen glanced at the manifest and asked, "Gong Shu Li?" She tapped her pen on the top sheet of paper. Of course, it had to be Shu, since that was the only name left unchecked.

Lifting her head a little more, the girl nodded, and a thin smile curled her lips.

"Look ... maybe we can do some kind of deal here?"

Donnie took a tentative step toward Jen. Protective, Eddie bristled and maneuvered himself to stand at her right shoulder.

"A *changji* like her comes along only once in every few shipments," Donnie explained. "She is the only one I want; you should be pleased." He offered a smile, as if Jen and Gong Shu Li were supposed to be flattered by the admission. "You know I am Black Dragon, yes?"

"As I suspected. That is none of my concern, and it changes nothing," said Jen. "I have told you—you have no business here."

"We would be more than prepared to pay you well for her." Donnie took another step forward. "What is the girl worth to you? Maybe $10–15,000 in owed payments? The Dragons will compensate you well . . . unless you'd prefer to take a cut of her future earnings. Such a young one will make us all a lot of money before her looks begin to fade."

Jen checked off Shu Li's name on her manifest with a single swipe of the pen. The young woman's allocated new name was Amy Wong, and she was to commence work at a Cantonese restaurant near the corner of Mott Street and Bleeker. She was *not* going to become a common prostitute for one of the Chinatown gangs.

"I am not interested in anything you have to offer," Jen growled. The gangster intimidated her, but she would not show it; her job was to ensure the safety of her client. "I shouldn't have to tell you again to leave."

Eddie shuffled closer—so close Jen could hear the snort of his breath through his flared nostrils.

"I will not leave empty-handed." Quickly covering the space between them, Donnie reached inside his jacket and pulled out his cleaver. Jen always considered it an odd weapon of choice for the Chinatown gangs in times of readily available firearms, but it was a tradition that went back to the Tongs and the Triads, one that was as quaint as it was deadly.

At the first glint of the cleaver's steel, Eddie stepped around Jen with a shielding arm outstretched.

Donnie in return threw Eddie a dummy. He raised the cleaver over his head as if making ready to take a swipe at the bodyguard's head, which elicited a reflex reaction. Jen saw Eddie counter, and the moment he reached out to grab at the gangster's wrist, Donnie deftly sidestepped and grabbed hold of her, his arm wrapping around her neck. The clipboard slipped from Jen's hand and clattered loudly to the cabin floor. The terrified and newly named Amy squealed and pressed herself harder against the bulkhead.

The pressure of Donnie Wu's arm on her throat had Jen fighting for breath. He held her tight to his wiry body, using her as a buffer against Eddie, who was angrily looking for a way to get to the gangster without hurting Jen. The fact that he'd gotten her in this position at all was galling.

"Stay back, big man," Donnie snarled, his breath hot on Jen's cheek. He waved his cleaver at Eddie as a warning, the steel blade inches from Jen's face to ensure her compliance. "I'll cut her if you don't back off!"

As Eddie took a step back, Jen saw in his face just how angry he was at himself for allowing the gangster to deke him so easily. He'd be beating himself up for weeks afterward.

Donnie then proceeded to maneuver himself toward Amy's bunk, pulling Jen along with him. All the while, his arm increased its pressure on Jen's throat, making her vision go gray and fuzzy around the edges.

"I'm taking the girl, and if you get in my way, I'll kill your bitch."

Donnie rested the flat edge of the cleaver against Jen's cheek; the steel was ice cold, unyielding, and menacing.

Jen tensed against the gangster's grip, her lungs aching as they struggled for air. She knew how the Black Dragons operated. Donnie Wu was not intending to leave any witnesses behind.

A rush of adrenaline coated with pure fear flared in Jen Mo-Li's breast. What she did, she did without thinking, whipping both fists up, intending to pound the sides of his head. But her right hand wasn't empty. It still clutched the Montegrappa pen like a knife, and like a knife, the sharp point buried itself in Donnie Wu's carotid artery. She felt the warm spray of blood on her right cheek and temple, then felt Donnie's arm spasm then release her as he staggered back a step. His free hand clawed at the black, ludicrously expensive pen protruding from his neck. Thick, scarlet gouts of blood pumped out through his fingers, soaking his shirt through in an instant. Donnie let out a strained, gurgling cry. He brandished the cleaver with fear and hatred blazing in his eyes.

Eddie was not to be sidelined again. In a decisive motion, he swept Jen to the side with one hand and delivered a haymaker punch to Donnie Wu's head. It was enough. Donnie went down like a felled tree. The cleaver hit the deck before he did.

Horrified, with a scream stuck in her aching throat, Jen stepped back as the spreading pool of Donnie's blood crept toward her, propelled by the gangster's weakening pulse. The whole room reeked of the stuff—a cloying, metallic stink that reminded Jen of wet pennies. In moments, the flow of blood from the gangster's punctured artery petered out until it finally stopped. Donnie's bladder and bowels let go, and the Black Dragon let out one last sigh of breath before lying still.

Jen turned her gaze to Eddie. She had no idea what her face looked like, but Eddie Sun's expression told her everything. He quickly moved to her with arms extended and caught her before she fell, helping her to Amy's bed and depositing her gently.

"Are you okay?" he asked Jen. "Did he hurt you?" His big hand barely touched the blood on her cheek.

Jen didn't answer Eddie's question, but the one she was now silently demanding of herself. "I had no choice," she said, hating that her voice trembled and sounded as if it came from someone else's throat. "He was going to kill us both; you know that. What was I supposed to do? What?"

Eddie shook his head. "What you did. But you shouldn't have had to do it. Protecting you is my job. I am ashamed to have failed you."

She looked up and met his eyes. "You have never failed me, Eddie Sun. And you never will. He would have cut me if you'd attacked him. I did what I had to do." She said it more for her benefit than Eddie's.

Eddie scowled at the dead gangster. "You shouldn't have to deal with vermin like that."

Jen tried to smile at her bodyguard's protectiveness. "I am willing to admit, I would rather not."

Trying to act tough, to save face in front of Eddie, Jen prodded Donnie's foot with her own. Her stomach threatened to rebel, so she pulled away. She took a deep breath, turned to Amy, and addressed the girl in Fuzhou, which was her own family's dialect. "You're safe now. I'll take you to your new home and we'll get you some new clothes."

Amy Wong at last dared to peel herself from the bulkhead and clasped Jen's hands in hers. Between sobs and sniffles, she thanked her over and over for saving her.

But I didn't save you. I put you directly in his path.

Keeping her eyes away as best she could from the ghoulish sight on the cabin floor, Jen helped Amy from the bed and guided her to the cabin door, which Eddie moved to open.

Jen placed a hand on Eddie's arm. "Could you speak to the captain, please?" she asked. "About ... about that." Her gaze now rested on the corpse, followed by the pen—*her* pen—stuck ludicrously, horribly out of his neck.

Eddie inclined his head. "I'll let him know he must be sure it is cleaned up and that perhaps it would be best if he didn't allow such people aboard his vessel."

My vessel, Jen thought, her anger rallying. *No, not yours,* an inner voice corrected her. *Your father's.*

"And Eddie," she said aloud, "please ... don't tell Bà about this ... incident."

Again, the solemn nod. If Eddie was offended by Jen's request to hide this from her father, he didn't show it. Instead, he simply turned and went in search of Captain He.

———

While Jen escorted Amy Wong—née Gong Shu Li—out into the cool fall breeze of New York Harbor's quayside, Eddie led Captain He down to the cabin. There, he thrust a small bundle of hundred-dollar bills into the man's trembling hand and pointed at Donnie Wu's corpse. "I'll help you get him to the freezer. I assume the ship's freezer is working?"

"Yes, sir." A tremor in Captain He's voice gave away his abject unease at having to deal with the gangster's body. While he was used to handling the inevitable passenger death or two on the long voyage to America, handling a murdered Black Dragon was understandably different. Eddie knew all too well if He was implicated in the man's death, there really would be no place to hide. The Dragons had triad affiliations with the Tai Huen Chai clan, and their reach was global. Eddie, therefore trusted him to do a thorough job of cleaning up the evidence.

"Swill this cabin out before any of the others," Eddie continued. "Bleach it, too."

Bending over, he pulled Jen's Montegrappa pen from Donnie Wu's neck. It made a wet, sucking sound as it slid out of the raw, sticky flesh. While he could trust He to dispose of the dead gangster, Eddie wasn't certain he could rely on him to destroy the pen—it was far too tempting a trinket. Eddie wiped the pen off on Donnie's jeans and pocketed it. He would toss it into the harbor when he'd finished helping with the body.

"Wait 'til you're three, maybe four days at sea on your way back to China before you dump him. Make it longer if you like. Just make sure he doesn't wash up anywhere near here."

Captain He nodded, then left the room, with its reek of blood and excrement, to collect one of the body bags he stored in the cargo hold.

CHAPTER THREE

"*Fucking Chinks.*" Enzo DeCarlo growled as he shouldered his way through the bustling Pell Street crowds. "The yellow bastards are everywhere."

"Relax, Little Enzo," his companion, Rico, said. "This is Chinatown—what the fuck do you expect?"

Enzo bristled. He hated being called *Little* Enzo, it made him feel like a dumb third grader and served as a constant reminder he was destined to live forever beneath his father's shadow. Sure, being the son and heir to Vincenzo "The Don," head of the DeCarlo family, brought with it the privileges one would expect from one of New York's most powerful Italian mob families. But it also meant he'd forever be *Little Enzo*—most likely even long after his old man died. "It's not long ago this was all Italian territory—*our* territory," Enzo complained. "Now look."

Rico chose to say nothing. He followed his friend as he took the turn onto Doyers Street, dodging the jostling, unsmiling Chinese passersby who crowded the sidewalk.

Enzo DeCarlo was a stocky, well-built young man; he had a classically handsome face with a strong, smooth jawline, a long, curved nose he considered a bit on the large side, and dark auburn hair he often wore slicked back in the old style. Today, though, he wore it spiked up with gel and hid his narrow, hazel eyes behind black aviators.

By comparison, his friend and colleague, Rico "The Pox" Corozzio, was slim and short at five-seven. He had a pinched, weasel face marred by the pits and scars of the rampant acne that had plagued his high school years. Best friends since Vincenzo had employed Rico's father as consigliere back when Rico and Enzo were first graders, the two were steadily working their way up the family business as The Don had made it clear there'd be no favoritism, and they'd be expected to make their names before they got made.

They had eschewed their usual work attire of black slacks and Hugo Boss sports jackets for shabby jeans and checked, long-sleeved shirts over gray New York University T-shirts. They were, ostensibly, just another two of the myriad tourists out enjoying the mild September weather, taking in the sights, sounds, and not always pleasant smells of Chinatown.

As Enzo walked, he relished the reassuring presence of the small gun nestled in the waistband at the back of his jeans. Like Rico, he was packing a Raven Arms MP-25, one of the compact handguns more often called a Saturday Night Special, or junk gun. Stripped of their serial numbers, the weapons were untraceable, easy to conceal, and perfect for close-up work.

"It's almost one," Enzo said. "Keep your eyes peeled. And slow the fuck down." Enzo upped his pace to keep up with Rico; the guy walked too damn fast most of the time like he was always in a hurry to get someplace. They were supposed to be blending in with the tourists, not look like they were in a goddamned street race.

This was familiar territory, of course. Doyers Street and those surrounding it had long been the stomping grounds of Italian American families, although since the government relaxed the immigration laws back in the sixties, the place had become overrun with Chinese. That rankled Enzo; not only were they strangling his family's traditional racketeering livelihood, but this was supposed to be America—for Americans—not fucking China. Enzo DeCarlo, a third-generation Italian American, saw no irony in his xenophobic attitude.

The two made their way along Doyers, past the bright pinks,

yellows, and blues of the shop fascias. Each store's name was written in big, bold Chinese *hanzi* with the smaller English translation beneath it—although some businesses had begun to omit the translation, which the likes of Enzo, Rico, and their ilk saw as a deliberate snub.

"Feeling hungry?" Enzo teased as his compadre stared at a line of whole roasted ducks hanging up in the window of one of the mini-markets.

Rico shrugged and shook his head. "Why do these people leave the fucking heads on?" He pointed at the limp, swinging necks of the ducks. "It just ain't right."

Enzo grinned. "Yeah—I'm not sure how they can bring themselves to eat something that looks that pissed off." He nudged Rico with his shoulder, and they laughed together as they neared the infamous sharp bend in the street.

Out of habit, Enzo stepped from the sidewalk and into the narrow road. Traffic was sparse, mostly cabs and small business vans, and Enzo moved slowly to avoid the meandering tourists. The bend, a sudden right turn in the block-long street, was what gave Doyers its unenviable moniker, "The Bloody Angle," and the dubious honor of being the deadliest street in America. The blind corner made it the perfect place for an ambush, which was how the corner was exploited across the years by the Italians, the Chinese Tongs and Triads, the Mexicans, and anyone else bearing a grudge, with a score to settle, or business to take care of. For as many times Enzo had walked along Doyers, the street's elbow always made his hackles go up.

But better that than dead.

"There!" Rico hissed in Enzo's ear as they rounded the corner.

Up ahead, waddling his way toward them past the gaudily dressed tourists waiting patiently in line outside the Nom Wah Tea Parlor for a taste of nostalgia and a real neat photo op, was a tall, plump guy in a dark gray suit. He was in his sixties, maybe even early seventies, with thinning hair. Enzo recognized the ruddy complexion of a man who liked his scotch neat and just a little too much.

"Frankie the Nose," Enzo said as if the old Italian needed any introduction. He'd been in the protection racket for the Taccetta family since back in Vincenzo's day. He'd been made back in the sixties and remained a *caporegime*—capo—ever since. Enzo saw Frankie Nicoletti as a relic, very old school. He always did the rounds in his suit, shades, and immaculately polished black brogues; the guy's look couldn't have read mobster any louder if he'd screamed it out loud.

Enzo quickened his step as Frankie made his way through the double glass doors that accessed a beauty parlor and an empty office building. To their left, a flight of stairs led down into the Doyers Street Tunnel.

"It's time," Enzo said. "We got the asshole right where we want him."

"Sitting duck," Rico added. "Maybe we should leave *his* head on, too." He chuckled quietly at his own joke, the humor of which was lost on Enzo. Always the would-be joker, Rico's timing and audience reading definitely needed work.

With Rico close behind, Enzo made his way down the staircase. The tunnel was a narrow, commercial passage that ran beneath the larger shops at street level from Doyers to Chatham Square on Bowery. It was lined on either side with small shops that were home to a mix of businesses: hair and nail salons, knick-knack stores, acupuncturists, accountants, and lawyers—all of them Chinese-owned. The Taccetta family's protection racket stretched down into the tunnel, although they'd been getting an increasing amount of pushback from the Chinese gangs in recent months. Still, that wasn't about to deter Frankie Nicoletti from going about his regular business.

The air down here was damp and decidedly cooler than it had been above ground. The passage, lit by a line of humming strip lights, cast a stark, white glow that seemed to Enzo to add an edge to the cool air. He could hear Frankie's heavy footsteps and labored breathing up ahead. The loud wheezing and puffing had Enzo thinking maybe he and Rico should hold off the hit and let nature take its course; the old man was a heart attack waiting to happen, unless his liver got to him first. Still, Enzo knew this was not about rubbing out one of the last old-school mafia foot soldiers, it was about sending Big Joe Taccetta and his family of assholes a message: Stay the fuck out of DeCarlo business.

Frankie saw them waiting for him the moment he stepped out of the beauty parlor he'd been visiting. The place offered massages, too, and had he still been able to get his dick hard, he'd have kept them waiting a little longer. Frankie's eyes flicked to the beauty parlor's door, then across to the accountant's office opposite; a thin sheen of nervous sweat popped up on his upper lip.

"*Little* Enzo DeCarlo," he sneered, pulling off his sunglasses to squint at the two young mobsters. "And Rico Corozzio—your face ain't gotten any prettier, has it? You boys are a ways out of your jurisdiction. Either of you been made yet, you dumb pieces of shit?"

"We're working on it," Enzo told him. "And how about you, Frankie? Still shaking down dirty lawyers and cheap hookers for Big Joe?" He tried to read the guy. Did Frankie the Nose know what was coming?

"Fuck you, kid," Frankie huffed. "And tell your old man *fuck you*, too."

He knew. In a single, swift motion, Enzo stepped forward, reached behind his back, and plucked the junk gun from his waistband. Frankie was too old, too slow. By the time he'd reached inside his jacket to reciprocate, Enzo had the muzzle of his gun pressed against the fat man's sweaty forehead.

The mobster's head muffled most of the gunshot's sharp crack. Blood, brains, and shattered pink-white shards of skull sprayed out behind him like a spume from a harpooned whale. Blood poured out from Frankie's mouth and nostrils in a dark crimson torrent as his knees buckled beneath his weight; he fell face up onto the cold, white tiles of the tunnel's passageway.

"Fuck you, too, Frankie," Enzo spat as he stepped over the fat gangster's corpse. The tiles were swiftly staining red. Enzo turned to Rico and offered a grim smile.

"Don't forget to mention this at confession," Rico said dryly. "You wouldn't want to miss out on absolution."

Enzo tucked the MP-25 back into his jeans and headed back the way they'd come in. It was time to lose themselves among the crowds on Doyers. He had no fear of being reported by anyone in any of the shops along the tunnel. The denizens of the so-called "Murder Alley" were well-used to closing their ears and looking away from what happened beyond their doors.

CHAPTER FOUR

Pell Street seemed busier and more hectic than usual for a Wednesday afternoon. The narrow road was clogged with twin rows of near-stationary traffic and the thin sidewalks were crammed with hordes of jostling people going about their hurried lives. All this made for slow-going, even with Eddie walking in front of Jen to clear the way. But it was nonetheless pleasing to see her people thriving as Jen recognized so many familiar faces on her regular visits to Chinatown. After all, she was the reason a lot of them were there.

"You *knew* it was going on, Danny?" Jen hissed into her mobile phone, trying her damndest to not raise her voice. It was proving difficult as her older brother was being infuriatingly evasive, which was not like him at all. They usually enjoyed an open and honest relationship.

"So, the gangs take a few from each shipment." Danny's voice crackled through the phone's speaker. Reception was notoriously patchy around Chinatown, and Jen had mentally mapped out the streets where she could at least catch most of a conversation. "It keeps the peace between the Mo-Li family and the gangs."

"How long?"

"What?"

"Don't play dumb with me, Danny," Jen growled. "You know what

I mean. How long have we been turning a blind eye while the Black Dragons have been abducting immigrants?"

"No one is abducting anyone, Jen," Danny replied with condescension, which did nothing to alleviate his sister's anger toward him. "You're being melodramatic—they only approach single girls, and by my understanding, they go along willingly. It's a simple business agreement, that's all, and nobody gets hurt."

"This girl today most certainly was not willing. And she got hurt. The bastard *raped* her. She would have become a prostitute. How is that not getting hurt?"

Jen had heard about the lengths the gangs were prepared to go to procure fresh workers for their parlors and street corners: coercion by false promises of easy money, the withholding of passports, free drugs, and even violence should the need arise. The very thought of these girls being sold into slavery for the Dragons and the other gangs made Jen's blood boil and freeze in turns. It was not why she worked so hard to bring good Chinese people into the country and get them started on a new life that was supposedly free from oppression and fear.

"Who's to say they wouldn't choose that line of work anyway? It's good money and there are only so many waitressing and dry-cleaning jobs to go around in Chinatown." Danny's clumsy attempt at logic upset Jen more than it angered her because it made her realize just how simple and stupid her family thought she was.

"You didn't answer my question," Jen insisted. "How long has this been going on, Danny?"

"Since the beginning, Jen. I thought you knew." Danny sounded almost sorry.

"Of course, I didn't know!" Jen's raised voice caught the attention of a handful of fellow pedestrians; even Eddie turned his head to look at her. "Do you honestly think I'd bring young women into the country to be sold like cattle?"

Danny's silence said it all.

Yes, he and Jen's father thought she was perfectly happy delivering young Chinese women into the mercenary clutches of the Black Dragons and presumably any of Chinatown's other gangs they wished to placate. It sickened Jen to her stomach, as it flew in the face of every ideal she'd worked so hard for. She was far from doing God's work, no matter how many families she helped settle into their new lives.

"It has to stop, Danny." Jen managed to keep her voice low. "You have to talk to Father."

"And he will listen to me?"

"More than he ever listens to me." As long as Jen had dealt with that reality, it hurt to speak it aloud.

"It's just business, my dear sister," Danny said.

"It won't be if I shut the whole thing down, my dear *brother*." Jen was in no mood for Danny's sweet talk; this was one occasion when she wasn't going to let him talk her around. "I can very easily walk away from this."

"And Father can just as easily replace you, Jen. You know Petey has been doing his best to persuade him to step into your side of the business."

Just the sound of her younger brother's name made the hairs on the back of Jen's neck stiffen. Petey had proven himself inept at every business avenue at which Bà had allowed him to try his hand, and the thought of those immigrants being left in his hands was not one she cared to contemplate. Danny's threat rankled Jen and had her immediately on the defensive. Up until that point, she'd not thought of Petey as being a viable replacement for her but knew in her heart Father would not hesitate to put his youngest son at the helm of the trafficking side of his empire. At least while she was running things, Jen could do everything within her power to protect her charges. Knowing what the Dragons were up to, and with a little help from Eddie and extra security, she'd be able to prevent them from boarding the boats. Once the young women disembarked, there'd be little Jen could do. But while they were under her direct jurisdiction, they'd have a fighting chance of keeping out of the gang's clutches. She could also work from the inside to break whatever bond her father had with the gangs and ensure a future safe passage for her people.

"I should have been told, Danny. I think you owed me that much." That was all Jen could think to say to her brother, although she fully understood why she had not been told—they feared her reaction. Pressing the phone tight to her ear, Jen waited for a response, only to be met with more silence. Danny taking their father's side, while not a huge surprise, brought into question the special bond Jen thought she and her brother shared.

Jen broke the unnerving silence. "We shall discuss this when I get home. Goodbye, Danny." She ended the call, thrust the little antenna back into the handset, and dropped it into her purse.

"*Ni Hao*, Miss Mo-Li." A voice caught Jen's attention from the doorway of a hair salon.

She stopped.

"Good afternoon, Lucy." She made a point of enunciating each syllable. Lucy Chen had been in the country long enough to not be mixing her Cantonese with her English—Jen was a stickler for her people using correct language.

"Please, excuse me, Miss Mo-Li." Lucy cast her eyes downward. "I still forget."

"You *must* keep up with learning American," Jen told her with a smile. "It's very important if you are to be accepted here."

"Yes, Miss Mo-Li." Lucy smiled back. "Would you like me to make you an appointment?" Her eyes flicked to the long, iridescent black ponytail that hung in a straight line down the center of Jen's back.

"Next week, when I come to collect your payment," Jen told the woman. "If you can fit me in, of course."

"I will *always* fit you in, Miss Mo-Li," Lucy said with enthusiasm. "Even though we are very, very busy." She pointed through the door to the packed shop of patiently waiting customers. "You will be for free, of course." Another smile.

It went without saying that Jen wouldn't be expected to pay to have her hair trimmed. She never had to fork out for anything from her clientele, as they were all so gratefully indebted to her for their new lives. In fact, they refused to accept payment in any form, no matter how much Jen insisted. Instead, she would shave a little off what they owed for their passage and was sure to direct plenty of customers their way. Although both she and Lucy Chen knew all that, offering was the respectful thing to do.

"Thank you, Lucy," Jen said in perfectly pronounced English, "that is most kind of you." With her part of the ritual done, Jen left the hairdresser to her clientele. As she jostled her way through the crowded sidewalk, she quickly caught up with the ever-patient Eddie, who was finishing a call on his mobile phone. Like hers, it was state-of-the-art—a brand new Motorola, just small enough to fit into the inside breast pocket of a man's suit coat. Jen was forced to carry hers in her handbag.

The street was very much like its moniker, Little China, as all but a handful of the gaudy banners, pendants, and fascias were written exclusively in Chinese. A few conceded and had an English translation available. It pleased Jen to see the infusion of her culture into the Manhattan streets. Pell's proliferation of Chinese restaurants, beauty parlors, general stores, and food markets somehow made even the iron fire escapes zigzagging up the front of the buildings like ugly, green scars appear welcoming. It was wonderful to see the community her people were building taking shape—it had all the best parts of China, with the freedom of America.

Among the myriad banners, one stood out, written in English only. Thin, gold lettering on a dark green canvas background declared the office at the top of the narrow staircase squashed between Lee's Shanghai general store and a tea parlor to be that of Ruben H. Isaksen. His was the only law office left on Pell, and the old Jew's defiant stance on his English-only signage would be the end of his business there. Jen kind of liked the old boy; he'd rented out the rooms behind his offices to her clientele for as many years as she could remember. Give dear old Ruben another year, two at the most, and he'd be taking early retirement.

"There was a shooting on Doyers—in the tunnel." Eddie broke the comfortable silence between them as he followed Jen through the single glass door that opened almost immediately onto the vertiginous stairs to Ruben's office.

"Anyone we know?" The news didn't surprise Jen as murder and assault were commonplace on Doyers. After all, she'd lived through the eighties when gang violence had run rampant through Chinatown. Right now, she was more concerned it would interrupt lunch at her favorite tea parlor.

"Frankie Nicoletti," Eddie told her as they took the stairs single file. "Shot in the head—point blank. It's assumed to be a mob hit."

Jen huffed. "I suppose it's one less Italian bothering our people," she said dispassionately. "The man was a dinosaur, but I wish the Italians would take care of business on their own streets. All this does is bring the police into Chinatown, and that makes our people nervous." Jen was more than familiar with the fat old Italian, as their paths had crossed many times over the years. He had a penchant for shaking down the restaurants, parlors, and gambling dens in her territory, many of which employed her undocumented immigrants.

Still, business was business, and she'd been as prepared to tolerate him as the gangs who ran the streets around Pell, Mott, and Doyers—until he'd crossed the line and beat down one of her oldest clients. Joe Sun Chung had built up one of the most popular restaurants on Mott Street, and Nicoletti had put the poor guy in a coma over protection money he reckoned was owed to the Taccetta family. Joe pulled through but was never quite the same afterward. He ended up selling the restaurant a little over a year later. The Chinese gangs had done nothing about it, and Jen figured they were all still scared of the Italians. But a word in Frankie the Nose's ear from Eddie, and his and Jen's paths didn't cross again.

Ruben Isaksen wasn't in his office; he was either off ambulance chasing, or representing one of his many low-life, piece-of-shit clients in court. Instead, the place was manned by Ruth, a dour, dumpy old woman whom Jen had first, and wrongly, assumed to be Ruben's mother. She was, in fact, his wife, and had never forgiven Jen for the *faux pas*.

Eschewing the opportunity to stop by and pass the time of day with the monosyllabic Ruth, Jen followed Eddie to the thin, gray door at the opposite end of the hallway. There, Eddie rapped loudly on the plywood with his knuckles. The door opened and the small, round face of a young man appeared. "*Ni Hao*, Miss Mo-Li," he greeted Jen and welcomed her into his sparsely furnished apartment.

"*Hello*, Michael," Jen replied as she made her way inside.

"Sorry," Michael Xu replied with a sheepish grin. "*Hello*, Mis Mo-Li." With a sweep of his arm, he ushered Jen and Eddie into the single-room apartment, where he had them sit on a threadbare two-seater couch facing a small, portable TV perched on a fake mahogany stand.

Xu's wife, Mai Ling, busied herself in the tiny kitchenette by the window overlooking the fire escape. The damp, bland aroma of plain rice noodles filled the room. She waved hello and gave her visitors a humble smile. Xu had sent for her almost a year to the day earlier, having spent almost two years establishing himself in Chinatown and saving up enough cash to pay Jen the necessary deposit. He worked two jobs—by day at a dry cleaner, by night at a restaurant—to pay off his passage and his wife's. In another year, Jen would be paid in full, which was fortunate, given that Mai Ling's swelling belly was beginning to show.

"It is my day off today," Xu said. "My shift at the restaurant starts at six, though."

The man felt the need to explain his absence from work, although it was entirely unnecessary. Jen knew who the hard workers were, and those who chose to pay her with excuses rather than the money they owed.

"Then, we must apologize for interrupting your time off," Jen replied.

Xu shook his head. "Not at all. It is always good to see you, Miss Mo-Li." Producing a small, grubby white envelope from the back pocket of his jeans, he held it out for Jen to take. "You will stay for lunch?" He nodded toward his wife and the tiny stove.

"Thank you very much for your kind offer, but I'm afraid I have another appointment." Jen felt a tiny pang of guilt at her lie. For as much as the thought of plain noodles didn't appeal to her, accepting lunch with Xu and his sweet young wife was to be expected as a mark of respect. However, she had promised herself lunch at the Nom Wah Tea Parlor. "I will definitely join you for lunch when I visit you next month."

Her conscience assuaged, Jen stood up from the couch.

"We will be honored, Miss Mo-Li." Xu all but bowed as first Jen, and then Eddie shook his hand.

Michael Xu saw his guests out and closed the door gently behind them. As they made their way by Ruben's office and down the narrow stairs, Jen handed the envelope to Eddie, who slipped it in the inside pocket of his jacket, next to the gun he carried.

CHAPTER FIVE

"Thought this place was going bust," Rico said as he and Enzo followed the pretty young waitress through the Nom Wah Tea Parlor to the table she'd selected for them within sight of the window.

"Yeah, for as long as I can remember." Enzo was distracted by the waitress's pert butt jiggling a treat beneath her tight, black pencil skirt. "Never will, though—it's been here a million years and pulls in too much tourist money."

"Somebody's propping it up," Rico said as he sat himself down with a broad smile at the waitress. However, she kept her eyes fixed firmly on Enzo, as women like her always did. Enzo reckoned Rico was used to it after so many years of hanging together. Not that the Pox didn't get his fair share of tail, though he never attracted the same caliber. "I heard Big Joe Taccetta had his fingers in the pie here."

"You hear a lot of things, Rico," Enzo chastised his friend. "And most of it's bullshit."

"Just keeping my ear to the ground, Enzo, you know that."

"I'll take the pork on wheat." Enzo smiled at the waitress. She blushed just a little.

"Make that two." Rico's voice was flat with disinterest. He'd already given up trying to make an impression; the girl was clearly smitten by Enzo. "Iced tea—unsweet."

The waitress jotted down the order in her small, yellow pad and scurried off. Mesmerized, Enzo watched her ass jiggle some more as she disappeared into the kitchen. He liked the Nom Wah; it was okay in his book as far as Chinatown establishments. It wasn't quite Reuben on rye at the Pastrami Queen, one of his favorite Manhattan delis, but it made for a welcome rest stop when he and Rico were doing the rounds on Doyers and Pell.

Interested enough to have looked it up, Enzo knew the Nom Wah had opened for business back in 1920, in the good old days when the Tongs first ruled the roost. And, as far as Enzo could see, it hadn't done so well at keeping up with the times; the sea of small, square tables that filled the place each had a red checked tablecloth and condiment dispensers straight out of some fifties diner. They still served food at the long bar with clientele perched atop chrome, vinyl-topped stools. It all gave the place a distressed, inadvertently retro feel, which went exceptionally well with the outside yellow walls and the faded red fascia with the establishment's name hand-painted in puke-yellow in some long-forgotten font.

"They took their time," Rico pointed to the handful of uniformed cops milling around the entrance to the tunnel. They'd finally pulled everyone out of each of the underground businesses and cordoned it off —presumably at both entrances—and the odd assortment of cosmetologists, bean counters, and cheap attorneys stood around rubbernecking and chatting amongst themselves.

"It's a gang hit. What are they gonna do?" Enzo snorted. "Can't see them spending too much time scratching their heads over who whacked some fat old wop. Frankie's been a pain in the precinct's ass for longer than most of those beat cops have been alive. Every one of them out there'll be wishing they could give a medal to whoever blew the motherfucker's brains out."

"You sure it's a good idea coming in here?" Rico wasn't usually one to show his nerves, but Enzo could see having cops in such close proximity was doing a number on him. But they'd both ditched their junk guns in a dumpster and were in a restaurant filled with tourists—mostly white faces—so there was little chance they'd stand out.

Enzo nodded. "Hiding in plain sight—that's what my old man calls it," he said with a wry smile. "And besides, they ain't going to search every goddamn tourist on Doyers."

"I guess not." Rico still looked uneasy. "Look at that." With a sardonic grin, he pointed through the grimy window.

Enzo narrowed his eyes. "What?"

"There are white cops, a couple of Hispanics, and even a ni—"

"And?"

"Not one fucking Chinese cop." Rico narrowed his eyes. "This is why they'll never push us out. Nobody gives enough of a shit about what goes on here even to put a token one on the force."

"Two pork on wheat." The waitress appeared, as if from nowhere, bearing food. "And two iced teas—*unsweet*." Keeping her eyes on Enzo, she placed the plates and glasses down carefully on the table. "Would you like anything else, sir?"

Now, there was a loaded statement if Enzo had ever heard one, backed up with eyes promising a whole manner of delights. Enzo made eye contact with the girl and flashed his best Tom Cruise smile. She was his if he wanted her; that much was a given, but the question remained: Did Enzo DeCarlo want yet another quick, easy fuck to add to the multitude of notches on his bedpost?

"I'm good," Enzo told the waitress and took some gratification at the noticeable downturn in her sunny smile as she turned to go. As he craned his neck to watch her walk away, Enzo was already regretting turning down a piece of that magnificent ass.

"Sweet Mother Maria," Rico gasped through a mouthful of pork sandwich. "I'm in love." Rico's exclamation tore Enzo's attention away from the waitress's alluring rear end and across to the stunning young Chinese girl who made her way through the door.

Petite, oozing confidence, she strode through the tea parlor with some huge, bald guy in tow. Enzo figured he might be her father, an uncle perhaps, or maybe even a sugar daddy or lover. Enzo knew the guy's type—quietly cocky and only one insult away from throwing the first punch—and he dressed the part in tight jeans and a black tee to show off his muscular physique. It was all part of the intimidation act. The guy's scuffed cowboy boots drew attention as they clunked noisily on the tiled floor.

The Chinese girl was dressed casually but still looked classy. Enzo studied her as she walked, taking in the loose denim jeans, the turquoise turtleneck tucked in tight to her waistband and straining against her breasts, and the pristine fresh-out-of-the-box white Keds. She wore her long, raven-black hair in a ponytail that stretched almost to her firm, denim-clad butt, scraped so tight it gave her flawless, oval face a look more severe than Enzo figured it deserved, although it did accentuate her high cheekbones. All said, in Enzo's mind, the girl was near-perfect.

"She's *Chinese*, Enzo." Rico's habit of speaking through a mouthful of half-chewed food was not his most endearing; bread and pork sprayed onto his plate and the tablecloth as if to emphasize each word.

"No shit, Sherlock," Enzo said without taking his eyes off the girl.

"Reel your neck back in—you don't go for that type." Rico took another bite and swilled it down with a loud slurp of tea. "You always said—"

"Just look at her." Enzo all but drooled onto his plate as the girl sashayed by his table to be greeted by one of the waiters. The staff all seemed to know her and her companion. To a man and woman, they showed her the utmost respect, which Enzo thought in some casesbordered on reverence. The girl was obviously a *somebody*, which made her all the more appealing to the love-struck Italian. Enzo knew then and there he wasn't going to leave Nom Wah without introducing himself.

As the girl took her seat at a corner table, Enzo gave her trim, toned figure an admiring up and down while studying the big guy who sat down opposite her. They were obviously close, and the bald guy looked like he was some hard-ass—quite possibly Black Dragons or Ghost Shadows—so Enzo elected to wait and pick his moment carefully. Not that he was scared of the guy. He'd taken down bigger and harder in his time, but not with Frankie the Nose's corpse still warm down the street and a whole bunch of cops standing around with their hands in their pockets looking for something to do.

As it worked out, Enzo didn't have all that long to wait. He'd taken only his second bite of his pork sandwich when, across the tea parlor, the big guy excused himself and went off to the john.

"I'll be back when I get her number," Enzo said.

"What the fuck, man?" Rico sputtered. "Hitting on one of *those* in fucking *Chinatown*—you're not serious?"

With a curt nod, Enzo got to his feet; his chair scraped backward with a jarring noise that attracted the attention of their neighboring tables. "How the hell can I *not* be?"

"Because your old man will have a fucking fit." Rico stared up in disbelief at his friend. "And we're on Doyers and ain't Chinese."

Enzo shrugged. "The old man won't know. Besides, I'm only going over to say hi, not bend her over the goddamn table." He paused as if that thought were actually crossing his mind. "Quit worrying. The Chinese folk won't want to make trouble any more than we do—not with everything going on outside." Enzo's patronizing smile said it all. Defeated, Rico quit talking and tore off another chunk of his sandwich.

Weaving between the tables and chattering diners, Enzo made his way toward the girl in the corner. She seemed absorbed in her menu, as if choosing lunch was difficult. But Enzo knew she'd seen him and guessed at his intentions. In his mind, at least, the game had commenced.

"Pardon me..." Enzo stopped by the girl's table.

"Hello." The girl looked up from her laminated menu. "If you're looking for the restrooms, they're over there." She pointed an immaculately manicured finger toward the rear of the restaurant. The slightest smile played across her full, delicately pink lips. He thought it coy.

"I'm not. I came over to say..." Enzo fought hard to get the words out. His heart pounded in his ears, and he felt a growing dampness under his pits. That *never* happened to Enzo DeCarlo; his confidence with the ladies was legendary and he was rarely lost for words.

"Please sit down. Before you fall down." Another smile; a flash of perfectly straight, white teeth.

"I'm Enzo. Enzo DeCarlo. I saw you come in and thought I'd come over and say hi." Enzo reached his hand across the table.

"Jen." Taking the hand, the young woman gave it a firm shake, her eyes exploring his face. She seemed to like what she saw. "It's very nice to meet you, Enzo DeCarlo."

Jen's hand was so wonderfully warm and delicate, yet implausibly strong in Enzo's; he was reluctant to let it go. "Likewise, miss ... I mean, Jen." He gave his trademark wide, bad-boy grin that had just made the waitress weak at the knees.

Jen appeared unmoved by Enzo's well-worn pick-up routine and cheesy smile. Extricating her hand from his, she asked, "What brings you and your friend here? You don't look much like tourists to me."

"We're from Staten Island." Enzo nodded across to where Rico sat quietly stuffing his face. "Figured we'd take our day off in Chinatown—see some sights before winter sets in." Making eye contact, Enzo was mesmerized by just how brown her eyes were—deep, shiny darkness enhanced by her smooth, flawless skin. In his mind he was already caressing every inch with his lips.

"Well, I hope you're both enjoying your day." There was a dismissive tone to Jen's voice, and her eyes flicked to the restrooms. "Is there anything else I can help you with?"

"Yeah." Enzo swallowed hard to calm his nerves. His mouth felt suddenly dry, his palms clammy. Considering all the broads he'd seduced since junior high, it really shouldn't have been as difficult as he was finding it. He drew a deep breath. "I'd like to have your number—your phone number—so I can give you a call sometime." Finally, Enzo was hitting his stride; he felt his confidence creeping back. "Unless your boyfriend's going to object, of course."

Jen let out a soft, throaty laugh and her eyes twinkled in the stark glow of the fluorescent light above the table. "There will be no objections from Eddie because he is not my boyfriend." She offered Enzo no further explanation than that.

"So? Your number?"

There was the slightest hesitation before she shrugged and said, "Sure, why not?"

Going by experience, Enzo knew Jen was toying with him now; her coy act had morphed into hard-to-get. It was a good sign, and he picked up on the beginnings of an electric spark of attraction on her part, which was inexplicable. Forget what he'd said in the past about Asian women being emotionless, harsh, and particularly unattractive. She was none of those things, and she had set Enzo's hormones on fire.

Reaching into her purse, Jen pulled out a mobile phone about as wide as a deck of cards, but taller. It was like a little black chunk of plastic with a tiny rectangular window in the middle. The only feature that identified it as a phone was the visible speaker at its top.

"Only if you give me *your* number first." She flipped the handset open, revealing a little keypad. Above that, the tiny window came to life.

Enzo shook his head no. "My old man reckons mobile phones are nothing more than a fad. I mean, you pay thousands for 'em and if you drop 'em, you're out a bundle."

Jen toyed with her phone, her fingers caressing the tiny black buttons as if she were having second thoughts about divulging her number. "Your old man is wrong, you know. Like it or not, these things are the future. Soon, everyone will carry one."

Enzo laughed and shook his head at the ridiculous notion. "Why would they need to? There are pay phones everywhere and you have to have a purse to carry something that big. I'm not carrying a purse."

"I suppose that would insult your manly pride, wouldn't it? You have pockets in your jackets, don't you? I carry a purse because, for reasons I will never understand, women's jackets do not have real pockets. It seems unfair to me," she added, with outsized solemnity.

Raising her hand to a nearby waitress, she signaled her need for a pen by pretending to write on the air. In a heartbeat, a cheap ballpoint materialized in front of her. She looked up at Enzo and met his eyes. "Tell me, do you believe everything your old man tells you?"

"Not *everything*," Enzo defended himself. Jen was making him feel like a kid, which he didn't much care for. Nonetheless, he was determined not to let her slip through his fingers. "But, when what he says makes perfect sense to me, I always listen."

Folding her phone shut, Jen plucked a napkin from the tarnished metal dispenser in the center of the table. She then jotted her cell number down in large, girlish handwriting. "You can reach me anytime, day or night, on this number." She raised an eyebrow, as if she found Enzo to be fascinating rather than sexy and intriguing, which was what he was going for. "See how convenient mobile phones are?"

Before he could answer, Enzo saw a flicker of movement down the short corridor that housed the restrooms. Eddie appeared, wiping his damp hands on the ass of his jeans. Boyfriend or not, Enzo doubted the guy would take kindly to some wop muscling in on his lunch date.

"I'll call you—soon." Enzo snatched the napkin from the table and stood up to leave.

"Okay," Jen replied with nonchalance even though a playful smile danced upon her lips. A promise of things to come?

Enzo was back watching his old friend Rico polish off the remainder of his lunch before Eddie returned to Jen's table.

CHAPTER SIX

Eddie waited until they were well away from Nom Wah before quizzing Jen about the good-looking Italian guy. He'd noticed the guy had been unable to keep his eyes off her throughout lunch, and likewise, Jen took every opportunity to glance in the young man's direction.

"Your mobile phone number was on that napkin, was it not?" he observed.

"Why are you so concerned, Eddie?" There was mischief in Jen's laugh. "It's hardly the first time some random young man has asked me for my number in a tea parlor."

"Nor will it be the last," Eddie replied with a faked sigh and a grimace. He'd sent more than his fair share of Jen's would-be suitors on their way over the past ten years or so. Her rare beauty and welcoming smile seemed to attract them like moths to a flame. "But it is not the Italian gentleman's attention that concerns me. It is yours."

Jen's eyes twinkled with good cheer. "I don't know what you mean, Eddie. I barely gave that young man the time of day." Jen gave the big man a hearty, playful nudge in the ribs. She was the only one from which he would ever tolerate such contact. Eddie Sun was not known for playfulness.

"You gave him your telephone number. If you had given him only the time of day, I'd have no concerns." Eddie's face remained emotionless; if that was an attempt at humor, the guy sure as hell wasn't showing it.

"He won't call me," Jen told him. "You know they rarely do; they seem to lose interest once they have my number. Or maybe once they've seen you up close."

She knew Enzo DeCarlo's type all too well. There had been plenty of them in the years since she'd blossomed from a spindly, awkward-looking child into a shapely young woman who turned heads wherever she went. It was always the most handsome guys who dared to approach, yet rarely followed up with their promises to get in touch. Jen figured they were either intimidated by her beauty, by Eddie, or had simply moved on to their next, easier, conquest. She reckoned Enzo would most likely already be chasing some Catholic girl who'd drop her panties at the first hint of his pick-up banter.

"And if he does call?" Eddie asked as they took a left on Mott, then onto Grand Street.

"Then I shall most likely entertain the idea of a date," Jen teased her bodyguard. "If he asks for one, of course."

"Your father would never approve of such a dalliance outside of—"

"Outside of *what*, Eddie?" Jen stopped dead in her tracks on the sidewalk and spun around to face him. "Outside of my class? Or my race?"

Eddie shrugged and chose to say nothing. He knew better.

"You're sounding old beyond your years, Eddie Sun." Jen's eyes danced. "We are in the nineties now, in case you hadn't noticed. Such old-fashioned attitudes died out when our people left China—or at least I thought they had."

"You know your father is very much of the Old World," Eddie told Jen with a stern tone that reminded her of her father. "You know he wishes you to take a good Chinese man for your husband. One who has the means to take care of you as you deserve."

"As if I could forget," Jen grumbled.

Pairing her off with someone he approved of was pretty much the only thing her bà paid the slightest bit of attention to when it came to his daughter. That's because if her father had his way, Jen's marriage would be one of convenience—a business deal. Her life was just another one of Ming Sen Mo-Li's many assets.

"You are aware the young man is mafia?" Eddie pressed as Jen recommenced her quick pace along the narrow sidewalk. She'd insisted they walk from Doyers to Mulberry to work off their lunch. "I know Italian Mob when I see them. I can practically *smell* it on them."

"You don't know that for sure." Jen was skeptical; it wasn't beyond Eddie to make such a thing up to put her off. "He looked like a tourist to me."

"He was Italian, and he approached you in a public place where you were obviously having lunch with another man." Eddie appeared put out by Jen's questioning of his judgment. "He waited for me to be out of the way—only a mobster would dare to be so forward."

"And what if he is? We come across Chinese gangsters almost every day; I don't see much difference."

"I cannot allow you to put yourself in harm's way. You know that," Eddie replied mildly. "If those two *were* mafia, then they most likely had something to do with the old mobster murdered in the tunnel. Why else would they be on Doyers Street in the middle of the day?"

"I can think of lots of reasons. And I can take care of myself, thank you, Eddie." Jen was firm. It wasn't often she needed to remind her bodyguard who was boss. But then the memory of her part in Donnie Wu's death suddenly loomed over her. She felt a split second of sharp fear twist in her chest. "And I'll enjoy *dalliances* with whomever I please."

That raised an eyebrow, but if Eddie was offended by Jen's tone, he didn't show it. They took a right onto Mulberry and headed toward 232, home of Mulberry Sunshine Cleaners. The place was owned by one of Jen's clients and had the reputation of being the worst dry cleaner in what was still called Little Italy.

When Jen and Eddie arrived at the dry cleaner, there was just one customer—a middle-aged Cantonese gentleman with very little hair. He appeared to be in the middle of an angry dispute with Jack Wa, the belligerent owner of the place, who stood defiantly behind the cheap Formica counter. The customer was losing the argument as Jack intimidated him. Jack was a good seven or eight inches the taller of the two, and at least twice as wide. The customer's face paled as Jen and Eddie entered through the single glass door. He gave them a slight bow of the head, muttered something derisive in Jack Wa's direction, and scuttled out of the place like he had something embarrassing to hide.

"It is so very good to see you, Miss Mo-Li." Jack greeted his guests with a disingenuous smile, which dropped the moment Eddie locked the door behind him, flipped the sign from *open* to *closed*, and approached the counter.

"You know why I'm here, Jack." Eschewing the small talk, Jen went straight to the point. It didn't pay to play friendly with the likes of Jack Wa, as they considered it a sign of weakness and were all too quick to take advantage. "You have not paid the remainder of your passage, nor your rent—both of which you assured me would be taken care of last month."

"I'm afraid business has been slow. What can I say?" Wa took one nervous step back in perfect synch with Eddie's step closer to the counter.

Jen sniffed as she followed Eddie across the store. Judging by the thick, acrid stink hanging in the air, Jack was still using perchloroethylene to dry-clean his customers' clothes. The chemical had been declared toxic earlier in the year, and Jen had requested Jack to quit using it as it would only be a matter of time before the business started to gather Department of Health citations and fines to go along with the back rent. Jen was also aware of customer complaints about lost clothes and sheets and rumors that Jack was stealing and selling expensive items of clothing to a couple of contacts he'd made among the smaller gangs in the area. She had her suspicions but had yet to see concrete proof of that.

"What can you say? You can say you have the money." Jen rested her hands on the counter and made eye contact with Jack. The man flinched but refused to look away. "I'm sorry, but nothing else will do today, Jack." It never rested easy with Jen to act tough as it went against her nature, which was why Bà had made Eddie her shadow.

Eddie lifted the hinged countertop and made his way into the space behind it. There was a determined defiance in Jack's eyes as he stood his ground against the bodyguard; the two were an almost even match size-for-size, and it was clear the guy was foolish enough to fancy his chances.

"Maybe I will have it for you next week," Jack offered, his tone offhanded. "Then again, maybe I think I've paid you quite enough by now—everybody thinks your interest rates are extortionate."

Shaking her head at the man's insolence, Jen cast a glance to the back of the store. There, Jack's young assistant—part of the most recent batch of Jen's illegal immigrants—worked the giant shirt press. The machine belched out great, hissing clouds of scorching steam, which added to the sweat drenching her pale blue uniform shirt and pants. The girl looked over at Jen, who dismissed her with an upward tip of the chin and a widening of her eyes. Scared, Jack's assistant abandoned the press and disappeared to the rear of the store amongst the clothes hanging on racks like so many headless corpses. Somewhere out of sight, a door opened and closed.

"You have to pay what you owe, Jack. You know how my father is with debt." Jen slipped through the counter behind Eddie and lowered the raised top. "I explained to you *last* week that I expected payment in full. I even gave you an extra week because I do not wish to see your business fail. And now you're telling me you *think* you don't have to pay the remainder of your passage, let alone the rent?"

"I paid my passage off a long time ago, Miss Mo-Li, and you know it." Jack squared up to Eddie as Jen took her place next to the bodyguard. "All I owe now is interest, which just keeps adding up. I'll never pay it all off at your rates."

Jack's protest rang partially true. Jen's father's compound interest calculations were designed to not only keep profit rolling into the business but also to maintain control over the immigrants. The truth was, many were in debt their entire lives and there was nothing she could do about it. She'd tried.

"You seem to forget just how easily you could be deported," Jen told Jack, grimly toeing the line. "You know my bà would gladly make an example of you. All it takes is one call to the authorities and you'll be on your way back to Hunan before you know what day it is." The words she'd meant to say with authority sounded pleading.

As if sensing her reluctance, Jack squared his shoulders and took a step closer toward Eddie—a bold move indeed. Eddie carried neither a gun nor a cleaver, and Jack knew it. Those were gang weapons, and his size and fearsome reputation were usually more than enough to put the point across.

"Then maybe I'll tell them everything I know about your father and his illegal operation before I go. And maybe they'll give me immunity so they can prosecute all of you."

A frisson of fear wriggled down Jen's spine. "You think they'll believe you?" Jen called Jack's bluff with more steel than she felt, but it was true; her father's company was held in the highest regard in the city, and anything Jack Wa might allege about Mo-Li's business practices would be seen as little more than baseless slander. It would, however, put Jen in a bad light in Father's eyes. He already held the traditional Chinese opinion that daughters were of very little importance, especially a middle daughter between two sons.

"They might." Jack fixed Jen's hard stare with his own. "Or maybe I'll be protected from you and the authorities. I've had offers from the Tigers and the Shadows, you know. I could also accept protection from the Taccettas or the DeCarlos; they've been around here and seem to know what's what in New York."

Jen's mind flicked back to her encounter at the tea parlor; it was a weird synchronicity indeed to hear the name DeCarlo again. She had no time to ponder it, and she was genuinely unsettled, even hurt by the man's attack. "After everything my family has done for you, you threaten us with the gangs, Jack Wa? You soil our good name with your poor business, insult the customers I send your way, and refuse to pay what you legitimately owe my father for giving you this new life? Instead, you steal your customers' clothes to sell at the markets."

"I—I," Jack stammered. "I don't—"

Jen took a step toward him. "I know why you're short some months, Jack. I know that what you don't lose at the poker tables, you spend on prostitutes."

Jack's expression was one of abject guilt laced with venomous disrespect. His eyes, which had been fixed on Eddie standing less than an arm's length away, flicked to the locked front door, and then to the back of the store. "How could...?"

"You think we don't know *everything* that goes on in Chinatown?" Eddie's voice was a menacing growl. "You have a reputation around the dens and parlors, Mr. Wa."

"Okay, okay. I can get you your damn money." Desperate, playing for time, Jack stepped backward again. His back pressed up against the wall. "I have people who owe me."

"Then you can understand *our* frustration," Jen spoke calmly and clearly. Although it was not her favorite part of the job, dealing with errant debtors on behalf of her father *was* her job. "I'm sorry, but we can't give you any more time. We, too, have people to pay."

Jack's response was unexpected. He leaped away from the wall with a snarl and swung at Eddie's face. But Eddie had the instincts of a boxer; he reared back, and Jack's punch skimmed the top of his left shoulder. He countered with a swift, hard jab to Jack's solar plexus. What the dry cleaner had in bulk came nowhere near making up for what he lacked in experience. Wheezing, fighting to draw breath, Jack doubled up and collapsed into Eddie's arms. The bodyguard dragged Jack into the rear of the store and, grunting with exertion, he hauled Jack over to the hissing shirt press and yanked open its lid.

"No!" Jack and Jen cried at once.

Eddie ignored them both. He flung Jack onto the press; the heat from the felted surface reddened his face in a heartbeat.

"I'll get it!" Jack roared. *"I'll get your fucking money!"* He struggled in vain against Eddie's grip, his feet scuffling upon the smooth tiled floor.

Eddie paused with one hand on the back of Jack's neck and the other on the stainlesssteel handle of the press. He looked over at Jen, who stood paralyzed at the counter. He well knew this was part of the job she despised. She brought people into the country to give them a better life, not to have them menaced and maimed for money. Their dialogue was silent and swift. She shook her head;, he sent her a look that somehow managed to incorporate acceptance and reproach. This was why Bà had assigned the big bodyguard to her in the first place—so that things were done his way.

She nodded, swallowed, and told Jack Wa, "You have to understand we must set an example—we cannot allow..." She ended the rote recital with another shake of her head. As bile stung the back of her throat, Jen looked at Eddie, then turned away.

She heard the press lid groan as it closed on Jack Wa's head and shoulders, heard the man's screams as he fought for freedom, and smelled the thick hot undercurrent of boiled flesh. Jen pressed a hand against her mouth to stave off a wave of nausea. Then there was a thud as Jack collapsed to the floor. His muffled moans and sobs underscored Eddie's, "In the future, you would be wise not to gamble away money you owe to another."

Jen tried to take a deep breath, but her chest was tight. She knew Jack would now pay his dues—the scars of the lesson he'd been taught would remind him. She must believe that such examples must be made. No, she must believe that Ming Sen Mo-Li believed it. Believed it enough to task his daughter with it—or perhaps he meant to test her.

"Let's go, Eddie," she said, making her way out of the cloying stink of the shop and into the autumn sun.

CHAPTER SEVEN

It was an uncharacteristically quiet evening for the Venus Joy Spa. Alternate Fridays were usually a very busy time for the Mott Street parlors, as they filled up with blue and white-collar workers blowing their paychecks on Oriental pussy.

Some of the parlors on Mott and its neighboring streets did at least make some kind of an effort to appear to be reputable establishments, ostensibly providing nothing more than stress relief and relaxation to respectable clientele. They advertised hot stone massage, aromatherapy, and deep-tissue Swedish massage utilizing tastefully designed posters depicting happy, smiling young Chinese girls in pristine uniforms adorning their windows. But not so the Venus Joy Spa—that establishment blatantly offered *full service* and *full body massages,* which were luridly illustrated with barely dressed Asian girls and heavily discounted prices and weekend specials. Any remaining semblance of propriety was instantly dispelled by the presence of the young, skinny Chinese girl who hovered around the parlor's doorway clad in red satin hot pants and a skimpy halter top to lure in that Friday night money.

There was little need for the parlor to hide behind any kind of façade as the cops rarely ventured that way anymore. They knew better than to stick their noses into any business owned and protected by the

Black Dragons—except to frequent the place as customers and take advantage of the heavily discounted prices offered to law enforcement.

The manager of Venus Joy, Madam Tung Yijun, was a fearsome, statuesque woman with sharp, angled cheekbones and high breasts. She ruled the mix of young Vietnamese, Thai, and mostly Chinese girls with a firm, sometimes brutal hand. The girls were well protected and paid a little above those in the nearby parlors, and the madam expected total compliance in return. She believed in rewarding good work but was quick to quell disloyalty or dissent with violence whenever necessary.

She had eight girls working that night, seven of whom were sitting bored in the lounge area, flicking through the scattered heap of girlie magazines on the glass-topped table at its center. On any other Friday night, the lounge would be filled with horny clients, all eagerly awaiting their turn with one of the youthful Asian beauties the place had on offer. It irked Madam Tung that business was so slow, and it gave her an uneasy sensation that prickled the nape of her neck.

She peered out through the window at the busy street beyond. The last remains of the day's light were fading fast, and the sinking sun created long, stretched shadows on the sidewalk. The madam hoped the anonymity of the encroaching night, along with the allure of the skinny girl she had working the door, would bring in the clients.

As she turned away from the window, Madam Tung heard the parlor door colliding with the wall, followed by a short, shrill cry. She spun to see the girl who greeted visitors skidding across the tiled floor on her backside only to crash head-first into the reception desk.

Four—no, *five*—young men, each wielding a cleaver, burst into the parlor in single file. They were liberally adorned with tattoos that tagged them as members of a Chinese gang—the Mott Street Tigers. The last in line slammed the door closed and slid the steel bolt across the top to secure it.

"What the hell do you think you're doing?" the madam demanded of the young man she figured to be the gang's leader.

Like the others, he wore black jeans, a black shirt, and a black bandana as a mask to cover most of his round, olive-skinned face. What could be seen of his face was framed by long, black hair that covered his ears. Over the top of the mask, his dark brown eyes glowered at the madam as he barked orders at the others in Cantonese and pointed toward the cowering girls in the lounge. The madam eyed the reception desk and its phone. She willed the stupid girl who sat there wide-eyed in fear to pick the damned thing up. One call to the business's owners and the intruders would be put right back in their place.

"You can't just—"

A sharp backhand from the gang's leader silenced the madam's protest. The force of the blow knocked her clean off her feet, her face stinging.

"Qu!" The leader gave his order and the other four fanned out into the parlor. Two dashed into the lounge, which solicited shrieks of terror from the lingerie-clad girls within. The remaining two made their way into the back rooms.

With his men duly deployed, the leader then marched across to the reception desk and kicked. His foot smashed with ease through the thin plywood. He followed with more kicks and splintering wood. The terrified young girl behind it screamed and ran, but the gangster grabbed her hair, snapping her head back with such force the bones in her neck crackled. He yanked the girl back to the desk, slammed her face down on its top, and pressed his cleaver to her cheek as she sobbed and begged for mercy.

"*No!*" Outraged at the vicious intrusion and assault on her staff, the madam struggled to her feet as the gangster drew the razor-sharp edge of the cleaver down the young receptionist's cheek.

The girl squealed and wriggled to free herself from the man's grip but to no avail. All she could do was wail and kick her legs at thin air as a thick stream of blood snaked along her cheek to pool on the desk around her face.

Madam Tung Yijun fought the nausea that crawled up her throat from the pit of her stomach. As the receptionist cried and pleaded with the gangster, the madam saw a white glint of teeth through the deep gash. Terrified, fighting her heaving stomach, she peered into the lounge where two black-clad gangsters were methodically shredding the room with their cleavers. They shattered glass tables, hacked at the couches and walls, shattered the lamps, and cut the thick curtains into strips.

Then, as the madam watched in horror, they turned on the girls.

Here, their work was more artful; they cut each girl, drawing blood, screams, and cries of pain and fear. But the damage was strategically placed behind an ear, under the hairline at the nape of a neck, in the shadow of a breast, in the palm of a hand. The madam's relief was tempered with disgust; Clearly, they intended to warn, not to maim or kill. If they hoped to earn anything from her house, ruining the merchandise was an act of idiocy, and she knew the Tigers' lord was not an idiot.

A sudden commotion from the back rooms drew the madam's fearful attention. The gangsters there had located a sex worker—a pretty Vietnamese girl who looked invitingly underage—and her overweight American client. The gangsters manhandled the two, who were entirely naked, out into the front lobby. The fat man's rippling flesh glistened, slick with aromatic massage oil.

"Stop this! This is a councilman!" Madam Tung was used to demanding things of people. But now, though beyond angry, she schooled her tone to one of pleading. She was roundly ignored; everyone's attention was on the corpulent politician.

The lead gangster had released the receptionist, who curled into a protective ball on the blood-stained carpet, cradling her ruined face in her hands. Behind him, the screams of the girls in the lounge spilled out to fill the whole parlor. He then swaggered over to face the councilman, who had smoked enough or drunk enough of something that he seemed not to even half realize what was happening. He eyed the chubby fellow with amusement and contempt, a smile crinkling his eyes.

The madam felt the icy hand of dread grasp her heart. "The Dragons will kill you for this!" she snarled. If someone of his ilk—and appetites—got caught up in the aftermath of the violent raid, his career would be over, along with the long-term relationship the madam had nurtured with him.

The gang leader scoffed behind his mask. "The Dragons are weak and no longer have teeth—they don't frighten us. This is Tiger territory now." He slowly strolled around the corpulent politician. "You can give them a message for me," he told the madam. "The message is this: If they do not cede this brothel to us—and if you do not immediately begin to pay protection to us—we will return and kill everyone here." He speared her with a glance. "Everyone."

Without another word, he produced a small, silver revolver from his waistband and fired two shots: one into the center of the councilman's chest and one into his head.

"What the fuck, D?!" The outburst came from the gangster restricting the councilman. He jumped several feet, watching wide-eyed as the dead councilman collapsed into a pale, white heap. His cohorts burst into raucous laughter.

Madam Tung looked on impotently as the gangsters left. She was grateful they'd spared her but sick to her stomach at the carnage they'd left behind. She also knew her greeter would never work in a parlor again. Her parlor was destroyed, her girls were traumatized, and there was a dead councilman on her lobby floor. At least there'd be some retribution, she told herself. There was no way Storm would allow the Tigers to disrespect the Dragons in such a brutal manner, no matter what message they'd intended to send.

CHAPTER EIGHT

"If we don't hit back, Big D will think you are weak and he's beaten us!" There was anger mixed with frustration in Charlie-Boy Fok's voice.

"And if we do retaliate, this will escalate and we'll have a war on our hands," said David Cheung, his voice deceptively mild. "A war none of us want."

David, who went by "Storm" among his friends and enemies alike, was the undisputed head of the Black Dragons. He was young to hold such a position, but savvy, cool under pressure, and watchful. He knew his deputy, in contrast, was a hothead, which made him useful in a fight but which sometimes created more problems than it solved. Still, Storm liked having Charlie-Boy around. He was loyal to a fault, and always seemed to know what was going down on the streets long before anyone else. Except for the attack on the Venus Joy. No one had seen that coming.

"Perhaps a war is what we need." Charlie-Boy stood up from the long, low, forest-green couch to face his leader across the breadth of his living room.

Storm had gone into the kitchen to pull a couple of bottles of sparkling water from the fridge. Around him, the countertops and gleaming appliances gave the predominately white space an almost sterile look, but Storm liked it; it was a refreshing change from the gritty, darksome inner-city kingdom over which he ruled. He eyed his deputy over the width of the immense, quartz-topped island, thinking how much Charlie-Boy reminded him of a bulldog—he was a good five, maybe six inches shorter than Storm, but what he lacked in height, he made up for in muscle and attitude. Charlie-Boy was broad, stocky, and had that round, youthful face that had earned him his nickname. Physically, he was Storm's opposite; the Dragon leader was tall, slender, and all angles.

"And why would we want to invite war between the gangs?" Storm kept his reply calm and level. "All that will do is create chaos and encourage *everyone* to start grabbing more territory, and I don't just mean the Chinese gangs."

Charlie-Boy shook his head in frustration. "*We* could expand our territory and demand the respect from other gangs that we seem to have lost. What the Tigers did today *must* be answered. Or are you too full of yourself to see that?"

Storm bristled inwardly but outwardly did not so much as grimace. Only Charlie-Boy, his lifelong friend, would ever dare speak to him in such a disrespectful manner. Any other Dragon using such tone and words to the boss would have been swiftly removed from the gang— permanently. Storm stroked the smooth, rounded stump of his left pinkie finger. It was a habit by now, a reminder. He'd chopped the fingertip off years ago when he'd taken over as leader of the Dragons. It was proof of his strength and loyalty. Charlie-Boy could say whatever he wanted; it didn't change the fact that his fingers were all intact.

"War with any one of the gangs would not suit us right now, Charlie-Boy, let alone *all* of them." Storm rounded the island and returned to the living room to set a bottle of Perrier on the glass-topped table in front of his lieutenant. As much as he loved and respected his second-in-command, he was prone to rash impulses when his emotions were engaged. "War with *all* the gangs would mean the end of the Dragons."

"We are the most powerful gang in Manhattan," Charlie-Boy argued. "If we take a stand against Big D now, that will send a strong message to *everyone,* including the Italians!"

Storm seated himself in a low chair that matched the sofa in color and its stylish simplicity. Across from him, Charlie-Boy lowered himself back to the sofa and picked up his Perrier. Storm took a swig of his water, then smoothed down his hair with one hand. He kept it cut in a neat bowl style that cupped his neck, just like Bruce Lee. He was well aware that it dated him, but he didn't give much of a damn. Bruce had been his hero for as long as he could remember. Now, he used the "stage business" as a way of controlling the flow of the conversation.

"We are handling the Italians as well as we need to handle them. Soon, all their territory will be ours. They're so busy killing each other and using Chinese gangs to do their dirty work that they'll be too distracted to see us coming."

Stealth had always been Storm's strategy, and it had served him—and the Black Dragons—incredibly well over the past five years. Why would he wish to wage an all-out war with the Chinese, Italians, Jamaicans, Irish, and every other wannabe gangster in New York when the Dragons could steal the streets one business at a time, right from under their noses? It was not lost on him that this unexpected move by the Mott Street Tigers was an attempt to do the same thing, but with far more bloody methods.

"People will think we are weak," Charlie-Boy repeated his point with a growl. His eyes narrowed, his nostrils flared, and his thin lips cracked a half-smile. "People will think *you* are weak."

Storm stopped just short of rolling his eyes. He was growing tired of the conversation. Charlie had always debated with him, but he rarely pressed a point this aggressively. When he spoke, his voice was firm and steady, and he fixed Charlie-Boy with an unwavering stare.

"You will just have to trust me on this one. We clean up Venus Joy and open again for business tomorrow."

"Not with a full house," Charlie-Boy told him. "Madam Tung says some of the girls' wounds need time to heal before they can work again. Some are so spooked they don't want to work again. Two have already disappeared."

"Then she can recruit more to replace them."

"Yeah? That wouldn't be a problem if Donnie wasn't still AWOL."

Storm frowned. That was both surprising and worrisome. "Still nothing from him?"

Charlie-Boy shook his head. "Not a word since the night he went to meet the boat. Nothing on the street about him, either. It's like he just vanished into thin air. My guess is the Tigers wanted him out of the way."

"If it was Tigers, his body would have turned up by now. They'd *want* us to know they'd killed him. He could have run away with one of the boat girls for all we know."

Charlie-Boy laughed at the notion. "And give up the life he spent so long making for himself—all the free women he wanted? Donnie may have been an asshole and a sick pervert, but he sure as hell wasn't stupid."

"Perhaps." Storm glanced at the oversized station clock above the mantel of his outsized, gleaming black fireplace. The others would be along soon—the chosen few among the gang who were invited into his inner sanctum, and their money at his poker table. "I say until we know for sure what happened to Donnie, or his body turns up, we play it cool."

"And just how are we supposed to play it cool when the Tigers are killing our people and cutting our parlor girls?" Charlie-Boy shot to his feet again, his face flushed with anger. "There will be no respect left for the Black Dragons to lose if we continue to do nothing about this!"

"Sit down, Charlie-Boy." A flash of icy menace sliced through Storm's composed tone.

The change in Charlie-Boy's demeanor was gratifying. He sank back onto the couch, his gaze barely grazing Storm's before he lowered it. "I apologize. I meant no disrespect," he mumbled, his voice low, submissive. "I only want what is best for our interests."

"Your intentions are never in question, Charlie-Boy. But you must learn to have faith in my decisions. Have I not built the Dragons into a force to be reckoned with? Have I not expanded our empire throughout Manhattan and beyond? Soon, we will have a strong presence in Flushing, which will make all of us very rich indeed."

Charlie-Boy studied his feet for a moment or two before he met his leader's eyes. "You know I will always support your decisions, David.

Even when they are the wrong ones." A slight smile played at the corners of his mouth.

Was the humor sincere, or feigned to cover discontent? Whichever, it was not the time to explore the question. "We will have our revenge on the Dragons for the parlor soon enough," Storm said, "and for Donnie if the Tigers had a hand in his disappearance. But, in the meantime, I'm telling you there is to be absolutely no action taken." Storm returned the smile. "And that's a direct order, my old friend."

A loud rap sounded on the door of Storm's flat. The others had arrived.

"I understand," Charlie-Boy grunted as he stood to let his comrades in.

Storm eyed his deputy as he made his way through the foyer to the front door. He'd known the man long enough to doubt this would be the last he'd hear on the matter, and that it would take something more for Charlie-Boy to understand his logic, if he ever did. Gangsters like Charlie-Boy Fok understood only one guiding principle: an eye for an eye. What they all too often forgot was the old Confucian proverb: If you seek revenge, you must dig two graves.

CHAPTER NINE

The fading evening light on Doyers added to the anonymity of the three gangsters as they made their way down the street. Dressed in the gang's trademark all-black, Charlie-Boy Fok led his two Dragon soldiers along the sidewalk. No one looked their way. The citizens of Chinatown were so accustomed to living their lives alongside the gangs that their presence was nothing out of the ordinary.

The three wove their way between clumps of people keen to catch the stores still open or stop into one of the many restaurants that lit up the street with gaudy neon displays. Charlie-Boy wasn't looking for anyone specific, but he was confident they'd bump into one of Big D's foot soldiers on Doyers or Mott at some point, because this was the Tigers' stomping ground. Charlie-Boy also knew they'd have soldiers on the ground following the cowardly attack they'd launched on the Venus Joy Spa. The Mott Street Tigers were expecting a counterattack, and Charlie-Boy was going to make damn certain they weren't disappointed.

Sure, Storm had strictly forbidden reprisals of any kind, but Charlie-Boy wasn't about to allow his leader's bad decision to stop him. The Tigers had overstepped the mark one too many times, and it was up to him to deliver a loud, clear message, especially since the Dragons' leader didn't appear to have the balls to say anything to the Tigers, let alone retaliate. And besides, Storm Cheung owed him.

"Keep your eyes open," Charlie-Boy instructed the pair of sullen-looking soldiers he'd recruited for the clandestine hit. They knew they were going against the boss's explicit wishes, and the two no doubt imagined being on the receiving end of Storm's displeasure. The man may have been renowned for his ostensibly laid-back manner, but he had a fearsome reputation for swift brutality toward anyone who crossed him.

They'd already sacrificed a pinkie finger each upon making the Dragons' ranks, and neither had any desire to lose any more body parts to pacify Storm. They'd be lucky to keep their heads. That it was Charlie-Boy who'd enlisted them for the evening hit against a Tiger provided them with some comfort, as he and Storm were like brothers. They had no doubt he'd defend their actions should the need arise.

"There." Charlie-Boy pointed across the street to a young, thickset Chinese guy making his way out of one of the small restaurants. He had the air of a man well-fed, which meant his guard would be down and he'd be sluggish and slow to react. He was a Tiger. Even in the dimming light, Charlie-Boy could make out the distinctive tattoo on his neck from across the street.

"Follow him."

The three stayed on their side of the street and kept a discreet distance from their oblivious target. As he neared the Bloody Angle—the sharp, blind bend in the road—Charlie-Boy and his men closed the gap and made ready with their cleavers. There would be no guns, as this was merely a message to the Mott Street Tigers and not an assassination.

They caught up with the guy precisely on the street's bend, where visibility was at its lowest. The Tiger had made the mistake of sticking to the sidewalk to round the bend. The moment he slowed his step before making the corner, Charlie-Boy was upon him. The three gangsters then manhandled the kicking Tiger toward the open door of a nearby barbershop.

Although it was off-hours, Sung Ho's barbershop was still open; Charlie Boy had called ahead to make sure of that. The establishment was under the protection of the Dragons, so the owner had discreetly found something that needed doing in the back room and the place was devoid of clientele. And, although they dragged the struggling gangster for twenty feet, none of the people on the street saw a thing. Such was the nature of gangland Doyers Street.

Charlie-Boy knew his victim wouldn't bother to protest or plead for his life once they got him into the shop. A seasoned Tiger would know such actions were futile. In this world, what was going to happen was going to happen. The best this Tiger could do was put up at least a token fight and attempt to escape. With little finesse, they removed the gun from the Tiger's waistband, pushed him into the barbershop, and locked the door behind them.

The Tiger sprang at Charlie-Boy and his men with clenched fists and high-kicking feet. It was now clear that he was well-versed in Taekwondo. But Charlie-Boy was ready for the attack. He blocked the kick with a swiftly placed arm, knocking the Tiger off balance and sending him sprawling across the hair-strewn floor. Brandishing his cleaver, Charlie-Boy advanced on the Tiger as he fought for his breath and struggled to get to his feet. Behind Charlie-Boy, the Dragon soldiers followed suit.

The Tiger kicked at Charlie-Boy's feet as he brought the cleaver down in a swift, smooth arc. Charlie-Boy jumped to avoid the kick, which resulted in the heavy, razor-sharp blade burying itself into the meat of the Tiger's thigh. Blood splashed out from the deep wound, bright across the tiled floor. For a moment, Charlie-Boy thought he may have accidentally hit the man's femoral artery; if so, they'd be dealing with a corpse in short order. Clutching at the long gash in his leg to stem the blood flow, the Tiger screamed in pain and anger. As he scrambled to his feet, his shoes slipped in the slick smear of his own blood, and he went down hard.

Charlie-Boy stepped back to allow his soldiers to close in on the Tiger like wolves around wounded prey. *Let them have their fun*, he thought. They deserved it for not protesting too much at his underhanded plan to exact revenge on the Tigers, and in advance for their silence once the inevitable happened and Storm found out what had gone down. Maybe it had been a mistake to use a Dragon business for the hit, but what the hell would Storm do, even if he knew for certain his second in command had gone against direct orders and orchestrated it?

"Dragon scum!" The gangster shrieked as the Dragons descended on him. They had their orders. They would maim, but not kill, and knew how to inflict nonlethal pain.

Charlie-Boy listened to the tenor of the man's screams for a moment, then called off his men with a sharp whistle through the thin gap between his front teeth. "Enough!" he added for emphasis. His seniority over the others dictated it was his place to deliver the *coup de grace*. Squatting down by the gangster's head, Charlie-Boy rested his cleaver on the bridge of the Tiger's nose and leaned in as he flickered in and out of consciousness.

"I have a message for Big D. Stay the fuck away from our territory." Charlie-Boy's growled words barely registered with the Tiger. "And tell him next time, we will not be quite so lenient when he attacks our businesses." He pressed the cleaver a little harder on the Tiger's nose and smiled when the blade drew blood as it slipped through the skin.

The pain jolted the Tiger awake for a bit.

Their eyes met.

"You can also tell your asshole boss this is for Donnie Wu." With the last word, Charlie-Boy sliced the cleaver downward and took off the tip of the Tiger's nose. Then he stood, ignoring the man's renewed shrieks. "Well, damn!" Charlie-Boy grunted, glancing down at his shoes. They were soaked with the Tiger's blood. His new shoes were ruined for sure.

After a nod to his comrades, Charlie-Boy made his way to the door. The barber would have to deal with the bloody mess they left behind. His shop looked and reeked like a backstreet butcher shop. He'd also dump the gangster someplace where he'd be easy to find and patched up. Sung Ho would, of course, be compensated fairly for his time and trouble.

CHAPTER TEN

Jen held her beige Moleskine notepad close to her chest as she followed her father through the cool, minimalist vestibule of the apartment building. He, in turn, was close behind the realtor, a jolly, round-faced Korean lady in her mid-thirties Her bright, shiny name badge declared to the world that she was Janice. As Janice ushered her two clients through to the elevators with brisk efficiency, Jen contemplated her father.

Ming Sen Mo-Li had been a dour, taciturn man for as long as Jen could remember. As his sixty-first birthday fast approached, she was positive he had gotten much worse. He was a small, plump man with a shock of thick, white hair he was too stubborn to color, even though it aged him considerably. He wore thin, wire-framed spectacles, which clung precariously to the end of his nose, and sported a tidy, white beard that dangled from his pointed chin. Jen found the white hair a jarring contrast to the navy-blue Hugo Boss suit and black Rockport shoes he always wore when out on business.

"The vacant apartment is on the fifth floor," Janice declared as she thumbed the elevator button with a perfectly manicured nail. "I just *know* you're going to love it, Mr. Mo-Li."

Janice offered a broad, toothy smile, which was not returned. When introductions had been made down by the front door, Jen had thought the woman appeared a tad put out by her father for not having a Western name. While the majority of Chinese immigrants chose to adopt one, Ming Sen had eschewed the style in respect for the mother country and his wife—Jen's mother—who had been put in the ground by breast cancer a dozen or so years earlier.

"Flushing is the most up-and-coming section of northern Queens," Janice continued her rote spiel as they rode the elevator. "I am sure you're aware of the growing Chinese, Korean, and Vietnamese presence in the area; it's rapidly becoming *the* place to be for middle-income Asians. I actually have an apartment in the Pacific Towers, which is not too far from here." There, she paused, as if expecting an excited gasp of admiration from her audience of two.

Silence.

"The Sheraton LaGuardia East Hotel opens next month, of course, which will bring yet more people and money to this part of the borough—you know how we Asians like to stick together." With another vacuous smile, Janice led them from the elevator, along a narrow hallway to the empty apartment.

"Two beds, one bath, and plenty of living space," Janice gushed as she guided Jen and her father into the living area. She stood by the large window at the far end, looking out while she continued her sales pitch. "Over there is Kissena Boulevard, and just beyond that, Main Street. The subway station there is the end of the line."

As the realtor sold Jen and her father hard on the future benefits of purchasing Flushing property before the prices rocketed beyond the means of middle-income Asians, Jen plucked a pen from her pocket and jotted down the particulars. All the information and more was listed on the colorful flyer Janice had given them on the way in. But under her father's scrutiny, Jen felt the need to appear useful and attentive.

"Where is the pen I bought you?" Mo-Li's tone was sharp, accusatory.

Janice stopped mid-flow as if she'd assumed the old Chinese man was addressing her. A look of relief settled across her face when she realized Mo-Li was facing his daughter over the top of his glasses, admonishing her as if she were a naughty child.

Jen felt her face flush. There were times, such as this, when she felt like Bà could read her mind. The unfortunate fate of the pricey Montegrappa shot through Jen's mind in vivid, nauseating detail. She now wished they'd not left Eddie waiting out on the street in the car. She missed the balance her bodyguard brought to interactions with her father. Eddie was the only man in her life who didn't treat her as a second-class citizen simply because she was a Chinese woman. Strangely, she did not recall that her father had ever treated her mother that way.

"I think I left it at home," Jen replied, her voice quiet. Wilting beneath the scrutiny of both Janice and her father, Jen felt like a small child all over again. Father was never interested enough to ask Jen about the details of her job, about how her day went, or anything at all about her life. Yet there he was, perfectly happy to interrupt important business to quiz her about a pen.

"You *think* you left it at home?" Mo-Li was not about to let the subject go. "You either left it there or you did not. Which is it to be?"

Jen's eyes sought the realtor's for some kind of feminine solidarity. Janice avoided eye contact and turned to look out of the window instead.

"I left the pen at home, Bà," Jen put a firmness in her tone she hoped would squash the man's doubt.

"I bought my daughter a wonderful, expensive pen for her birthday, and she left it at home," Mo-Li told Janice. "Perhaps I ought to have known such a gift would be lost on a mere girl. Would *you* be so disrespectful to your father?"

"Let me show you the kitchen—it has only recently been refurbished." Janice dodged the loaded question and scooted between her clients. "Did I tell you what an amazing investment property these apartments are?"

Jen followed with her notepad and cheap pen in hand. Janice clearly had no idea who the girl's father was, or that he was contemplating purchasing the whole complex, not just the one apartment.

"It certainly has great potential," Jen said as she made an exaggerated point of looking around the apartment. She opened the door to one of the expansive bedrooms and peered inside. "I have read all the predictions of Flushing possibly becoming the East Coast's premier downtown for a new middle-income Asian population."

Jen had read about it in *The New York Times* a month or so back, which was why she'd done her best to encourage her father to take a look and consider adding Flushing property to his ever-growing portfolio. Even then, it had taken both her brothers' persuasion before he'd agreed to go along.

Janice nodded with enthusiasm and directed her attention to Ming Sen. "Your daughter is right, of course, Mr. Mo-Li. With the increased influx from China and Korea alone, Manhattan will not be able to accommodate everyone. This is where the spread will reach, and Flushing will attract the more affluent. My recommendation would be to take advantage of the available property while you can and watch your investment grow."

Jen watched as her father stepped away from the realtor. He was done with Janice, and his apparent interest in the place evaporated in an instant as so often happened. It was not one of his most endearing traits.

"I shall speak with my sons later," he told Janice, his lips pursed. "They will give me their guidance on the matter, and then I *may* be in touch with you." With that, Ming Sen turned on his heels and strode off in the direction of the door.

He'd come around, Jen was confident of that. She'd seen enough of her father's business dealings to recognize that he had at least a seed of interest in the apartment complex. But he would do nothing until he'd conferred with her brothers. The great property mogul Ming Sen Mo-Li could never be seen taking the advice of a woman, even if she was his own daughter, or especially because she was.

Fighting hard to hide her embarrassment, Jen smiled at the realtor as her father exited the apartment. She couldn't help but feel Janice pitied her, and that grated on Jen's pride and made her long all the more for her father's approval. Deep down, the little girl Jen regressed to was pleased she'd left the dumb pen her father had spent so much money on in some creepy gangster's neck.

"Before you go, Miss Mo-Li." Janice's voice split the awkward silence between them. "There are some people I am acquainted with who may be interested in talking to you. You have a good eye for valuable property, even if your father does not."

Here was the feminine solidarity Jen had been looking for earlier. Better late than never, she supposed. "People?"

Janice cast a furtive glance toward the door Jen's father had left swinging open. "If you would care to give me your direct number, I'd be delighted to pass it along to them." There was no offer of elaboration.

Intrigued, Jen scribbled her cell number down on the note pad and tore out the page. "Okay, have them call me." She handed over the note and Janice tucked it into the inside pocket of her gaudy blue jacket. "I'd better go after my father. He'll be trying to take the stairs if I'm not with him. He doesn't care to ride elevators alone—doesn't trust them."

"I understand," Janice said with a wry smile, which told Jen that she, too, had a father who considered his daughter to be a lowly creature worthy of little more than creating grandsons. Jen got the impression Janice wouldn't be quite so outwardly confident in the presence of her own father. "I shall look forward to hearing from you both on this apartment."

Jen shook the woman's hand. As she made her way down the hallway after her father, her mobile phone went off in her purse.

"Hello?"

"Hi. It's me."

The unmistakable accent was immediately familiar to Jen as she knew of only one Italian who had her number. Nonetheless, she replied with a curt, "Who is this?"

"Enzo. We met the other day in Chinatown."

"Hi, Enzo." Jen maintained the coldness in her voice but smiled to herself as she pictured the handsome Italian in a phone booth somewhere. His voice had the familiar tinny echo of some street corner phone, and she could make out the muffled sounds of street noise. She was surprised at just how good it was to hear from him. Perhaps because Enzo's call had tempered the anger she'd felt toward her father.

"This is your mobile phone?" Enzo asked her. "You're not at home right now?"

Jen glanced across at her father. He was standing by the elevator all but drumming his fingers on the fading brass buttons. Even above elevators, he hated mobile phones, considering them rude and intrusive. Also, Jen didn't wish to keep him waiting for too long and further incur his displeasure.

"No, I'm not at home," she told him. "That's the point of mobile phones."

Enzo didn't seem to be offended by Jen's reply. "I really gotta get myself one of those things," he said.

"It's lovely of you to call, but I'm in the middle of a business meeting right now. Was there something you wanted?"

Enzo's breathing sounded heavy through the phone's small speaker. Jen pressed the warm plastic to her ear as she walked slowly toward her father.

"Yeah," Enzo replied after an awkward pause. "I was wondering if you were busy tomorrow."

"I'm always busy," Jen quickly replied. She knew exactly what Enzo was working toward, and she'd be damned if she was going to make it easy for him. Not to mention she wasn't all that sure if she wanted to start anything with an Italian in the first place, especially one who had trouble written all over him. But Jen enjoyed the game and wanted to make the most of it while she could. Besides, she was well aware that she was going against her father's wishes by just talking to Enzo, so why not make the Italian work hard for what he wanted?

"Okay..." Enzo sounded deflated. He was not used to a girl not falling all over him at the mere click of his fingers. "Maybe you'd like to have dinner sometime?"

It was Jen's turn to pause. She didn't have much time as she was getting close to the elevator. But if she walked any slower, she'd grind to a complete stop. "Actually, I have plans tomorrow evening." She had no plans at all, but she relished the thrill of being chased, even if it was destined to lead to nothing. "And I'm really not sure it's a good idea."

"Lunch? Give me an hour." Enzo wasn't about to give up, and that gave Jen a sweet, warm sensation in her belly. "I'll be around Doyers and Pell tomorrow, and there's a great little Chinese restaurant I know—the Fung Wah Yo..."

Jen wasn't sure if Enzo was joking around or not. "And you assume because I'm Chinese, I'm *bound* to love the food?"

"We can do something else if you prefer—" Enzo was undeterred.

"Chinese food will be fine." Within earshot of her father, Jen adopted her professional tone, which went perfectly with her poker face. "I can make tomorrow lunchtime work," her tone was standoffish as if she was arranging a business meeting she really didn't want to. Jen hung up on Enzo before he had the chance to say goodbye.

"Who was that?" Ming Sen eyed his daughter with suspicion. He was annoyed at being kept waiting by the elevator for so long and made little effort to hide it.

"It was just business, Father," she replied. "An opportunity that will most likely not turn into anything, but you have taught me it's always worth exploring such matters. I'll be sure to keep you informed of any developments."

The words were definitely her father's style, which seemed to placate him a little. With that, she pressed the elevator button and watched as the illuminated numbers above the door counted down.

CHAPTER ELEVEN

"I do agree an investment in Flushing would be a wise one, Father," Danny Mo-Li echoed the proposal Ming Sen had only just revealed to him and his brother. "I've heard the whole area is about to become the must-go place for Asian immigrants. Did you know about the hotel?"

Ming Sen took a quiet sip of his green tea and nodded sagely. "That will bring in tourist and business dollars, which is another reason why it would be good for our company to own property there."

Jen stared with building resentment at her brother as he sucked up to their father. Older than Jen by a touch over three years, Danny was a strong young man who, although not classically handsome, had a special something with his narrow nose, friendly, laughing eyes, and winning smile. That he loved to play the tough-guy gangster, running with the gangs on the streets around Doyers and Mulberry, only served to add to the aura of brute strength he'd so carefully cultivated over the years. Jen had lived her entire life in awe of her older brother and had hero-worshipped him all the way through to their adulthood. In many ways, their mutual love and respect helped negate some of the hurt she felt at their father so obviously favoring Danny.

Petey, Jen's younger brother, was by direct contrast to his brother a wickedly attractive young man. His good looks earned him the unconditional trust of everyone he came across, which Jen knew from experience he was often quick to exploit. Sadly, however, Petey was the idiot child of the family. Father was often too quick to remind him of the fact when vexed. As a result, Petey spent most of his time with his head in the clouds, daydreaming of his next inevitably ill-fated, get-rich-quick scheme. Idiot brother or not, Jen's father still insisted upon involving Petey in all business discussions. Much to Jen's chagrin, Father listened to what Petey had to say, over and above anything his smarter daughter had to contribute.

But Petey withered beneath Jen's harsh gaze. She knew all too well she was expected to keep her mouth shut until Bà asked for her opinion. Even so, it didn't prevent Jen from letting her brothers see her annoyance. Their father appeared clueless as usual. He only invited Jen to business meetings about properties that she had direct involvement in and the trafficking side of his business dealings, of course. Even though he'd only involved her grudgingly, she was supposed to be eternally grateful for his generosity. The latter discussions normally involved just the two of them, as Danny and Petey had no interest whatsoever in the shipping of illegal Chinese immigrants. Like their father, they considered it women's work and far below them.

The importance of Jen's part of the company, and it had been the cornerstone of the burgeoning Mo-Li empire since the sixties and seventies, seemed to be entirely lost on her brothers and largely forgotten by her father. Ostensibly, to all three Mo-Li men, the family firm comprised only the legitimate, respectable real estate businesses Ming Sen had built up from scratch. The family firm owned residential and business property throughout Chinatown and some of the more exclusive areas of Manhattan, which included their own expansive Upper East Side apartment. Set around the block from Yorkville on Seventy-Ninth Street in what was historically known as the Silk Stocking District—now Manhattan Community District 8—the Mo-Lis' apartment block was a classic five-story beige building that wouldn't have looked out of place in a British period drama as it sported huge, bowed windows looking out onto the genteel street. The family occupied the entire top floor of the block, which provided more than enough space for just the three of them.

Jen worked hard at not letting her father and brothers' opinions of her status get to her. She placated herself with the knowledge that she was providing new lives and secure futures for good, honest people who needed a second chance. It had been enough to keep her happy, until her discovery that Danny and her father were more than aware of the gangs' cherry-picking of vulnerable young women from their shipments.

"Perhaps we should look into buying some more of the properties around the new hotel once it opens?" Ming Sen simultaneously inquired and demanded. "Is that something you could do for me, Danny?"

Aware of his sister glaring at him, Danny feigned enthusiasm. "Yes, Father," he replied with forced conviction. "But don't you think Jen would be in a better position to look into such properties? She knows the real estate market better than any of us. After all, it was her idea to look into the Flushing properties, remember?"

Ming Sen slammed his teacup down hard onto its saucer. The delicate, intricately hand-decorated porcelain cracked, forming a fine spider web in its glaze. "This is a serious business, boy!" Ming Sen's nostrils flared in anger as his eyes widened and fixed on his son's. "What we are considering here is a major investment for our company. Do *you* honestly think we should leave such decisions to the whim of a mere woman?"

Weak, crumbling under his father's wrath, Danny lowered his eyes without so much as a sideways glance at his sister. Jen knew he felt deep embarrassment on her behalf.

Ming Sen ranted, "There are tens, maybe *hundreds* of millions of dollars at stake—perhaps even the future of the company—and you want me to take your sister's word that it's *a good idea*? Perhaps I am mistaken, and you are no son of mine." He shot a glance across the room at Petey, who knew well to keep his mouth firmly shut when his father's temper was running high.

"No, Father." Danny sounded defeated.

Jen stared at her older brother with abject disappointment in her eyes. She'd been naive to think he'd ever stand up to their father on her behalf. Nonetheless, she'd allowed herself to harbor at least a grain of hope, considering she was the company's property expert and the one who'd brought the Flushing idea to the table in the first place.

"Very well," Ming Sen concluded. With a disdainful look at his broken saucer, he struggled to his feet. "The family's men will make the decisions, and your sister will do as we agree. It is as it has always been."

The acid tang of bile rose in Jen's throat. For as much as she had to say right then and there to her father and spineless brother, she knew it would only be counterproductive for her to stand up for herself. For starters, her father still harbored far too much of the old country's culture and prejudices. At times such as these they shone through loud and clear, as if Jen needed the constant reminder that, had she had the misfortune to be born when her parents lived under China's strict one-child laws, she'd have most likely been deposited into an orphanage or ended her young life in a landfill. Going through life being made to feel like a classless person, eternally grateful for her very existence, was soul-crushing, to say the least.

"We shall discuss the matter further in one week. That will give you the time you need to do your research, Danny." The man's eyes rested on his son. "I trust you will do a thorough job."

"Of course, Father," Danny said. "Thank you for placing your faith in me."

As Jen watched Ming Sen leave the room, the conflict she felt created a roiling turmoil in her mind. Jen hated her father for his constant criticism and undermining of her abilities, but he was also her father, and she was compelled to love and respect him. The little girl inside her still craved her father's unconditional acceptance and praise, although she could not remember a time when he had given either.

As the door closed behind her father, Jen rounded on her brother. "How could you, Danny?!" She unleashed her frustration and anger, feeling herself dangerously close to tears.

"I'm so sorry, Jen..." Danny visibly recoiled at his sister's obvious resentment. "What was I supposed to say?"

"You were *supposed* to tell him I'm the one who should be heading the Flushing project and making the decisions, not you!"

Danny looked at Jen as if she had finally lost her mind. "You *honestly* believed I could do that?" He fought to keep his voice low; their father had exceptionally keen hearing when it suited him. "You know what Father's like—he'd never listen to anything you had to say in a million years."

"Not while you refuse to stand up to him, he won't." Jen's voice shook. "And *you*," she turned her attention to Petey, who was surreptitiously making his way toward the door—he always appeared uncomfortable when alone with his sister and brother, especially when their emotions were running so high. "I cannot believe Father favors you over me. *You* are less than fucking useless!"

Petey's face flushed red at his sister's raised voice and use of obscenity, which hung in the air between them like something tangible. Vulgar words were considered highly disrespectful in China. But the Mo-Lis lived in America, the land of colorful expletives. The cultural contrasts between the two were often uncomfortable.

"I–I have nothing to do with any of this," Petey stammered through his embarrassment. "I don't even know why he tries to involve me in these things. I have my own business projects to work on." He paused with one hand resting upon the gilt door handle; it was blatantly obvious he wanted to be anywhere other than in that room with Jen and Danny.

"He involves you because you're a *man*." Jen spat out the last word as if it tasted foul. "And men are so obviously smarter and better at business than *mere women*." The emulation of her father's harsh, guttural voice was uncannily accurate.

Petey flinched under the barrage of his sister's irritation and pressed down on the door handle. For a moment, he appeared to be struggling to say something—an apology for his gender perhaps? But, as always, Petey's slow brain failed him, and nothing left his lips. Instead, he slipped out of the room and pulled the door gently closed behind him.

"Do you really think I want to spend my time snooping around apartment buildings and trawling through zoning plans and all that bullshit?" Danny approached Jen as Petey left.

"Actually, no. I think you'd much rather be out running with the Dragons like some pretend, cut-rate gangster," Jen snapped back. "But what the fuck does it matter what *I* think around here? This is America, and it's supposed to be 1991, not the 1800s! Yet my opinion doesn't matter just because I have a–a cunt?"

"What has gotten into you, Jen?" Danny looked shocked by his sister's repeated foul language. "The little sister I know would never dream of soiling her mouth with such nasty words. You've changed, Jen, and I do not like what you are becoming."

"Fuck you." Jen's choice of words was deliberate. She relished getting a rise out of her brother when he tried to play her down. It was a small victory, but a victory nonetheless.

"You really ought to mind your language, sister of mine. It is most unbecoming for a young Chinese lady," Danny said as he made his way across the room. "If Father ever heard you...."

"He'd what? *Disapprove*?" Jen couldn't stop the sardonic laugh that escaped her throat. "Just like he disapproves of *everything* else I say and do!"

"He doesn't...."

"I am sure he would listen to my opinions if I didn't have these!" Jen's voice rose as she clutched an ample breast in each hand as if to wrench them free of her chest.

As Danny's eyes flicked to the door, a worried expression settled across his face. "Keep your voice down, Jen." He stood in front of his sister, so close she felt the warmth of his breath in her face. He pulled her hands away from her breasts and pressed them between his own. "You should never regret how you were born. You are a strong woman who is far, far smarter than any man I know."

"After all we have meant to each other through our years together—you still can't find it in yourself to stand up to Bà on my behalf?" Jen's eyes, sparkling with fresh tears, met Danny's. From the very first time she was old enough to realize her father's aggressive disappointment in her, Jen had turned to her older brother as a substitute for his affections. Even when Eddie Sun came into her life, Jen's primary bulwark had been Danny. And he had let her down again.

"This is so difficult." Danny studied their joined hands. "Living a life between two cultures, I mean. If we were a truly American family, Father's attitude toward you would be totally different. Every day, women are becoming stronger here."

"But we are *supposed* to be Americans, Danny. Isn't that why our parents came over here in the first place?" Jen countered. "And just look at us." Her hands flew free of his; arms wide to embrace their household with its Asian sensibilities. "We busy ourselves recreating our mother country instead of embracing a whole new, free way of life. Has our father forgotten what life was like back home under the Communists? It was a life he risked everything to escape from—a life that would have had me drowned in a bucket at birth."

"Don't talk like that." Danny grasped Jen's hands again and squeezed gently, pulling them down so that they rested over her heart. "I don't even want to think about life without my baby sister. What in the world would I do without you?"

Through the blur of her tears, Jen offered her brother a sweet smile. She slipped her hands from beneath his and draped them around his neck. He wrapped his arms around her and pulled her into an embrace.

Then came a cursory knock at the door, which was followed immediately by Eddie in the threshold. "It's time to go, Miss Jen. You asked me to remind you at three."

"Thank you, Eddie," Jen said, stepping out of the embrace. "If you could give me a few minutes to get ready, I'll be right with you."

Eddie nodded. "I'll wait for you in the car," he said and exited the room.

If he had any old country reservations about proper behavior between brothers and sisters, the bodyguard's manner didn't betray them. She knew what her father thought; she'd overheard him lecturing Danny more than once: "When I was a boy in Fuzhou, I would never have touched my sisters, let alone embraced them, or worse, *confided* in them."

Well, Bà, Jen thought, *you are no longer in Fuzhou.*

CHAPTER TWELVE

Enzo knew Vincenzo "The Don" DeCarlo was never happier than when he was holding court, even when it was with his own family and associates. Leaning back in his high-backed dining chair, he rested his elbows on its arms and took a long, hard drag on the cigarette clamped between his pursed lips.

"We use the Chinese because they're more than happy to take our money and do the dirty work Italian pussies won't touch," he said. "*They* all want to be part of the family, reap the success and rewards that brings, but nobody wants to get their goddamn hands dirty." He gave Enzo and Rico an approving nod of acknowledgment. "Except these two fine young men of course. It was good to say 'Good fucking riddance' to Frankie the Nose after years of putting up with his bullshit. Yet still not a fucking peep from Big Joe Taccetta. That proves my point about the pussies."

Angel Corozzio, Rico's father and Vincenzo's trusted consigliere of over thirty years, leaned forward in his chair, rested his elbows on the pristine, white, starched tablecloth, and bridged his fingers. Between the finger and thumb of his left hand, he held the stub of his cigarette.

"I'm not saying it's a bad idea to use the Chinese gangs, Vincenzo," he responded in his usual quiet, considered manner that served him well when he represented his mob clients in court. "But the Chinese are overrunning Little Italy now. They've made more and more of Doyers, Pell, Mulberry, and beyond their own. They're hitting our core businesses hard. Last year we saw another dip in gambling and protection. If it wasn't for the general upturn in narcotics, we'd be hurting right now. We fight back with one hand, yet we encourage them with the other."

Enzo listened intently as the two men spoke. His father was old school, but a lot of what he said made sense. He also found it amusing to hear his father use such colorful language around the dinner table. That had never been allowed in all the years he and his siblings were growing up. Had Mamma been at the table right then, Vincenzo would still be checking his mouth; she was the one person in the world The Don genuinely feared.

Enzo's mother was away in the kitchen, overseeing cleanup and the washing of the dishes. She herself had prepared for them one of her famous roast beef dinners with all the trimmings, and, even though they had staff to perform such menial tasks, she took great pride in fussing over her family on the increasingly rare occasions they broke bread together. Elena DeCarlo was just as old country as her husband.

"The Italians have run Manhattan for as long as America has let us into the country." Vincenzo plucked the cigarette from his mouth and tapped the gray ash from its end into his empty coffee cup. "We saw the Tongs come and go in the twenties, and we've watched the Vietnamese and Koreans sneak the crumbs off our tables block by block. But who won those fucking wars?"

"They did, Vincenzo," the consigliere replied with a wry smile.

"Yeah, but only because we let the motherfuckers win." Vincenzo laughed loudly at his own joke; it was an old one, but it never failed to tickle him. "We'll take them all on when we're good and ready, and beat them back to wherever the fuck they came from." He paused in a moment of reflection. "If we can get two, maybe three of the families to work together, the fucking kooks wouldn't stand a chance."

"Then perhaps you shouldn't have put the hit out on Frankie the Nose?"

Enzo's ears pricked up. Was his friend's father daring to question The Don's decision to rid Little Italy of the fat old mobster? Certainly,

Angel was the only one who would ever do so but ordering Frankie Nicoletti's assassination had taken Vincenzo a hell of a lot of soul-searching. Enzo glanced across the table at Rico, who looked like he didn't want to be sitting next to his father at that particular moment in time.

Vincenzo took another pull on his cigarette. He sucked the smoke deep into his lungs and it puffed out of him as he replied to his old friend's challenge. "You know my thinking, Angel," he said. "Frankie needed to go. He was encroaching on our turf behind Big Joe's back and letting the Chinese take over some of Taccetta's protection rackets. Frankie was trying to get his numbers up and breaking the rules to do it. I'm surprised the ungrateful fuck Taccetta hasn't sent us flowers for getting rid of his goddamn problem."

Another laugh, another drag which finished the cigarette. Vincenzo reached across the table for the packet and fished out a fresh smoke. "He'll come around," he continued. "We'll have something he wants, and he'll be just *begging* to do business with the DeCarlos. Then we run the Asians off the island."

"You sure about that?" Angel asked.

"Yeah." Vincenzo lit up his smoke. "They're a bunch of little yellow rats. They act all cock-of-the-walk 'til the cats come back home. Then they scurry back into their dirty little holes like chicken shits. The fuckers ain't going to take over New York in my lifetime, not even *yours*." He looked across the table at his son.

"We take the Chinese on by ourselves," Enzo said. "We're the biggest family on the East Coast."

Vincenzo let a long, steady stream of acrid white smoke out through his nostrils; for a heartbeat or two, his face was obscured behind the thick cloud. "Now, *that's* the kind of youthful exuberance and kick-ass confidence I miss! How about you, Angel?"

The consigliere nodded his agreement. "It's been a long time, my friend," he replied.

"When you take over, you'll understand why we can't go in with all guns blazing. Not anymore." Vincenzo studied his son's face for a moment. "You might think your old man's just a sad old fart with his feet stuck in the good old days, but even I'm savvy enough to know open warfare out on the streets isn't the way to do things. Too many Italians are willing to squeal to the feds the second they get cuffs on their wrists. There's just no fucking honor anymore." Vincenzo's heavy sigh came out in the form of smoke.

Enzo contemplated the man he'd hero-worshiped and feared from the beginning of memory. Although Vincenzo was now in his mid-sixties, with his once-sleek, jet-black hair entirely silver and his face lined with age, nothing about the man's fearsome demeanor and reputation had diminished. If anything, the decades of his brutal but outwardly fair reign over the borough and beyond, and his iron grip over the unions had carried through. It meant all the other New York families looked with reverence to the DeCarlos for guidance—even if they crossed the line every-once-in-a-while like the Taccetta's big dumb ape, Frankie the Nose.

Vincenzo DeCarlo ruled his family as his business—with a rod of iron. Enzo knew in his heart he had very little hope of living up to the great man's legacy. He often doubted people would call him Don with the same amount of respect they did his father; it was a title of the highest honor and one that had to be *earned* rather than simply passed down to the heir of the throne. Just because a man was made head of the family through birth didn't automatically make him worthy of the title.

In such times of self-doubt, Enzo envied his siblings. They had pushed hard against their father and the family's strong traditions to carve out lives for themselves well away from the business. It had been easier for Lucia, of course. Enzo's sister, younger than him by five years and change, had never truly been expected to go into the family business. Vincenzo, ever the stickler for Italian tradition and traditional roles, had planned for his only daughter to marry into another family to forge strategic bonds and strengthen the business. It was the final decade of the twentieth century, and arranged marriages were still happening. But Lucia had her mamma's stubborn genes in spades, and had instead married a respectable Jewish cosmetic surgeon. She was so merrily doing the two-point-four kids and white picket fence thing in an affluent Los Angeles suburb that even her father had to be happy for her.

As for Enzo's younger brother Dominic, he was at Harvard Law School—nothing but the best for a DeCarlo kid. Rumor had it

Vincenzo had funded something ludicrously expensive at the school to get his son in there, although it was somewhat nebulous as to exactly where the DeCarlo money had gone. Nonetheless, The Don fully expected his youngest son to bring his law degree back to the family firm. He always maintained a family business such as theirs could never have too many of that rare breed—attorneys they could trust.

Dominic, however, had other ideas. He'd confided in Enzo during his first Christmas break home that he intended to stay with legitimate legal work and help the underprivileged, pro bono if necessary. Enzo pretended to view this as liberal bullshit, but there was something to Dom's earnest conviction that his family's wealth had come through the exploitation of people whose only fault had been that they were more vulnerable than the DeCarlos. Still, he'd argued that Dominic's determination to give back was just some dumbfuck, idealistic dream, probably bestowed on him by that neo-hippie chick from San Francisco he'd been seeing. In any event, Enzo had kept his brother's confession to himself; his father would blow a gasket the day he found out, and he didn't want to be anywhere near that firing line.

This left Enzo, who was forever destined to be Little Enzo, for Vincenzo DeCarlo to groom to take over the fading family business. While Enzo had enjoyed working his way up from the bottom, living his life in his father's shadow was not what he'd hoped to be doing as he rolled into his thirties. But The Don was as unlikely to slow down as he was to embrace new ways of doing business, which meant Enzo's future would be planned for him.

This brought Enzo's thoughts back to the Chinese girl. The Don would flip if he knew his son and heir was out there chasing one of the enemy. Was that why he'd set his sights on her? Heaven knew there was no shortage of Italian girls he could simply snap his fingers at and screw. But there was just something inexplicably alluring about Jen Mo-Li that went way beyond her looks. Maybe it was the simple fact that she hadn't fawned all over him at the tea parlor. Or maybe he just wanted to piss off the old man.

"What *are* we gonna do about the Chinese, Mr. DeCarlo?" Rico broke his silence. He was more often a passive observer at anything resembling business talk, and Enzo knew he'd piped up just to stir the pot. "They're fucking *everywhere* out there."

He shot a sly glance at Enzo, who furtively gave him the finger. Enzo trusted the guy with his life and knew Rico would never spill to his father about the Chinese girl. But that didn't mean Rico wasn't going to give him hell about it.

CHAPTER THIRTEEN

Pell Street and Doyers were becoming all too familiar to Rico—the stores with their crazy writing that made no sense to him, the massage and beauty parlors crawling with yellow faces, and the restaurants wafting out the stench of food that smelled like vomit to him. Why his Chinese neighbors couldn't just eat proper American food like steak, hot dogs, and pizza was way beyond him.

"We were only just here," Rico stated the obvious to Enzo. "What the fuck, Enzo?"

"I have business to take care of," Enzo replied as they made their way along the busy sidewalk. "It's not like I twisted your goddamn arm to come."

Rico grimaced and upped his pace to keep up with Enzo's forceful stride. "And have you getting into all kinds of trouble without me?" He gave Enzo a sly, knowing wink.

"Like I really need Rico the Pox looking out for my moral well-being," Enzo cracked. While Rico was a much-needed steadying influence for his friend and colleague, it was more often than not he who courted trouble, confident that Enzo was there to bail him out.

They continued down Pell, sidestepping people along the narrow sidewalk. "What *are* we doing?" Rico wasn't about to let the thing go.

"*Jesus Christ!* You're like a dog with a fucking bone, Rico," Enzo feigned exasperation. "Can't a guy do a little business without you poking your nose all the way up his ass?"

"Not us." Rico was a tad out of breath. Enzo was like a greyhound out of its trap when he had someplace he *really* needed to be. "We gotta stick together, especially after we put Frankie down. Who the fuck knows when Big Joe is going to come at us?"

Enzo gave his friend a derisory laugh. "If that dumb pussy was going to do anything, he'd have done it by now. The Taccettas are too shit scared of their own shadows now. They have no idea who the fuck did Frankie, and Big Joe won't figure we'd whack someone like Nicoletti—he was their man on the ground when Kennedy's brains were still in his skull."

That one brought a cynical curl to Rico's lips. Some days, Enzo sounded exactly like his father, and it never failed to amuse him. "It doesn't mean we can get careless," he returned. "Besides, there are the Chinese gangs to think about—their guys are everywhere." Looking around, Rico realized he'd spoken a little too loud as the eyes of his fellow pedestrians began to scrutinize him.

"Real smooth, Rico, real smooth," Enzo chastised and gave Rico a firm poke in the ribs. "Real *fucking* smooth." With that, he came to a sudden halt between the thin doorways of a small Chinese convenience store and a restaurant.

Rico checked his watch. It was just a touch past noon. "Don't tell me you're hungry already?" He wrinkled his nose at the sickly reek of grease. "Since when do you eat so early, Enzo?"

"Since I made a lunch date." Enzo gave a cryptic wink.

Rico slowly raised an eyebrow as he caught on. "With that gal, I suppose?" He didn't even try to hide his disgust at the realization. "Your old man ain't going to like it one bit."

Enzo gripped his friend's bicep hard. "My father isn't going to find out," he said firmly. "It's just lunch. I'm not planning on getting married."

"I guess you'll get bored with her the second she's dropped her panties for you like all the others."

"You know me too well, Rico." There was a hint of hesitance in

Enzo's tone that had Rico thinking otherwise. "Can you make yourself scarce for an hour?"

There was very little along Pell that appealed to Rico. He certainly wasn't about to go eat Chinese slop in one of the multitude of restaurants, and the gambling dens were predominantly Chinese-run—he'd stick out like a nun in a brothel in any one of those. Even so, there were the myriad pool halls dotted all over Chinatown. The two of them would often go to one for a beer and a few frames at the end of a busy day. The locals didn't seem to mind too much as long as they were spending money.

"Yeah," Rico said.

"You sure?"

"Fuck you," Rico laughed. "You don't see me asking you if your hot chick is really gonna show up or not."

"She will." Enzo peered past Rico and through the restaurant's glass door. His bravado slipped a little when he saw no one he recognized inside.

"She's really gotten to you." Rico's observation was quite an understatement. He'd chased women with Enzo since the day their balls dropped, and he'd never seen the guy this antsy over one. Sometimes a gal wouldn't show up for an arranged date—they were usually the ones Enzo had hit on in some late-night bar and they'd thought better of it in the cold light of day—and Enzo would just shrug it off with that toothy smile of his and make some crude comment about her being a dyke anyways. But Rico read something in Enzo's face as they stood outside the restaurant that said it *did* matter if the Chinese girl he'd spotted across a crowded restaurant turned up to eat lunch with him or not.

"Nah." Enzo visibly composed himself. Their brief scan of the restaurant had failed to locate Jen, and Rico saw in his friend's face the beginnings of doubt. "I'm just fancying some different kind of tail is all. You know it's all about variety, and I've never screwed one of those before."

"Best of luck, old boy," Rico mocked with a terrible *old English* accent he'd picked up from some cable channel. "I hope the girl of your dreams does show up."

"You're an asshole, Rico."

"Yeah, I am." With that, Rico set off along Pell, weaving his way through the jostling crowds with well-honed skill.

Enzo took in a long, deep breath and let himself into the Fung Wah Yo restaurant. Just why he was so nervous about meeting this girl, he had no idea. It was a sensation entirely alien to him, although not an unpleasant one. The Fung Wah Yo was typical of the hole-in-the-wall joints that littered Chinatown. They were mostly small, mom-and-pop establishments—absolutely no frills, good, authentic food, and invariably under the protection of the Black Dragons, Ghost Shadows, or any one of the other Chinese gangs. Back in the day, though, it would have been an Italian family ensuring the place didn't *accidentally* burn to the ground.

"You're here," Enzo greeted Jen with relief and chastised himself for ever doubting she'd turn up for their lunch date and for sounding too damned eager. She'd chosen a cozy table for two at the back of the cramped restaurant, which was a good sign in his book.

"You came." Jen studied Enzo as he sat himself down on the wobbly wooden chair.

"Of course."

"I have to confess that I had my doubts about you, Mr. DeCarlo." Jen appeared to find her phone, which sat on the table next to her tall glass of iced water, of sudden interest. "So many men I meet make arrangements, then don't show up. Most don't even call with some lame excuse. I think I intimidate them." Her eyes flicked upward to catch his by surprise. "What do you think? Are you intimidated?"

Hell, yeah. Enzo shrugged. "What I think is that I'm a man of my word. If I say I'm going to do something, I do it—especially if there's a hot broad in the mix."

The moment the words *hot broad* left his lips, Enzo regretted it. He spent far too much time around his father, Rico, and the family's Italian American employees.

Jen studied him silently for a second, her head tilted slightly to one side, then said, "I'll choose to take that as a compliment. Thank you."

"Well, it was meant as one." Enzo scanned Jen's face but realized he didn't know how to read it. Her eyes were so dark, so opaque they were like teardrop-cut onyx set in pale gold. Had he blown it already? There was no way to know.

"Shall we order?" Jen waved over a waitress who had been standing a discreet distance away with her eyes fixed firmly on their table like Jen was a big somebody who commanded personal wait staff.

Enzo played it safe and ordered the sweet and sour chicken; Jen got the kung pao pork with boiled white rice, and they made small talk while they waited for the food to arrive.

"So... you intimidate men?" Enzo said. "It must be because you're so damn beautiful."

Jen raised a perfect eyebrow. "Does that kind of talk actually work on your Italian girls?"

"Yeah. It does." Enzo had to work to hide his embarrassment. Jen's directness and ability to pick up on his moves were off-putting but did little to dampen his ardor. "Is it working on you?"

Shaking her head, Jen studied Enzo as if he amused her. "Not so much," she replied. "For me, you ought to have led with the fact that Don Vincenzo DeCarlo is your father."

Enzo was torn between being flattered and uneasy. "You checked me out?"

"Of course I did," Jen replied. "It's not difficult to find information on the DeCarlo family in New York. You're practically royalty."

"Then you know a lot more about me than I do about you." Enzo was now on his back foot and cursed himself for not having dug a little into Jen's background. Sure, she'd not told him her full name, but he knew enough people he could ask for information. Truth was, Enzo was so enchanted by the girl's *everything* that he didn't much care what her story was. "But, you know, I like a little mystery."

"There's really not too much to know," Jen told him. "I collect rent from apartments and businesses my family owns all over Chinatown and help newly arrived Chinese people fit into the community. That's pretty much me. However, I'm far more interested in hearing what it's like to be part of one of the biggest mafia families in New York."

The two fell silent as the waitress delivered their food; it looked and smelled divine. Jen ripped open the flimsy paper wrap on her chopsticks and made ready to dig in.

"Could you bring me a fork?" Enzo asked the waitress. "I don't get these damn sticks."

The waitress was more than prepared for the *gweilo's* request. She plucked a napkin-wrapped fork from her apron pocket and placed it in front of Enzo. "Enjoy your meal, sir."

Jen watched her go. "So… spill."

"We don't say *mafia* anymore," Enzo told her. "Or *mob*. We're just businesspeople. Many of the families have legitimate interests now." He stabbed at his chicken with the fork.

"Your father isn't the one who walks around outside in his bathrobe and slippers, is he?" Jen teased.

"Nah. That's *Vincent* Gigante." Enzo laughed. "Vincent the Chin—word is, he's only playing being cuckoo to avoid racketeering charges they brought against him last year. The man's as sane as you and me; the papers call him the Oddfather, though. All the New York families distanced themselves from Gigante the minute the indictment came down. Nobody needs that amount of FBI shit floating to their doorstep."

"That's good to know … that you don't come from a *crazy* family."

Jen then toyed with her food and poked it around the plate with her chopsticks. When a bite finally made it to her mouth, she chewed with an abstracted look in her eyes.

What the hell did I say? "You okay? Did I offend you?"

She didn't answer right away, so he studied her, taking in her natural beauty, which seemed to have grown since he first met her. She was radiant, though she wore little makeup and had her hair tied back in a long ponytail. For a second, he imagined tugging the scrunchy in the throes of heated passion and how her hair would cascade over her naked shoulders. He cleared his throat and his head.

"No, you haven't offended me," Jen said quietly. "I was just wondering what your family would say if they knew you were here with me right now."

Enzo pretended to have missed Jen's point. "We have business interests all over Chinatown," he said. "My family knows I'm here."

"With *me*?" Jen reiterated. "I'm not exactly your ... your usual type. Am I?"

"My folks might have something to say about me stepping outside the culture, but that doesn't mean I gotta listen. I'm tired of their old-fashioned bullshit. I'm a grown-ass man. I make my own decisions." It was a lie, of course, but Enzo wasn't about to tell Jen that his father pulled every one of his strings and that the very thought of his son marrying *outside* would likely give the old man a heart attack.

Jen looked directly at him again—or rather, looked *into* him. "Well, *my* father would not be pleased at all. I'm afraid his roots are still very much buried in Fujian Province—its values still govern his life, and that of his family. He would consider my purity ruined should I consort with anyone outside of my race."

Looks like we're in the same boat. "So, why agree to meet me?"

Her frank, assessing regard made him itchy, but he kept his chin up and his eyes on hers as she took his measure—again.

"When you came over to introduce yourself at the tea parlor, you intrigued me, Enzo DeCarlo. A lot. I mean, that's not something that happens to me. At least, not with men who are not Chinese. I was even more intrigued when I found out who you were." Her sweet, full lips turned up at the corners. "I can honestly say I have never met a real-life mobster in person before."

"*Businessman*," Enzo corrected her, smiling to soften the insistence in his voice.

She smiled in return—a sudden, bright flash of perfect white, like the sun on a dove's wings.

He felt his breath stop in his throat. "So, my, uh, my professional background is what's putting you off?"

"If that put me off, I would never have agreed to meet you in the first place." Jen took a sip of her steaming tea—oolong. She held the little cup between her thumb and pinky. "But it is important that I consider my father's wishes, and what my community expects of me."

Well, that was some formal shit. She sounded like a princess explaining why she dared not break bread with a peasant. Enzo DeCarlo was no damned peasant.

"To marry some nice Chinese boy?" Angry now, Enzo didn't try to mask his sarcasm.

Jen's eyes met his. "Something like that."

"Okay, so, where do we go from here? Assuming you want this to go somewhere." Enzo set down his fork. His appetite had waned; the date with his dream girl wasn't going the way he'd planned. But still, Jen had agreed to meet, and he *knew* she felt the electricity between them. There was absolutely no way he was going to give up on her so easily.

With a soft sigh, Jen looked up at Enzo. "My heart tells me we should be content with this moment," she told him. "So, I am pleased I got to spend this moment with you, Enzo DeCarlo."

"Shouldn't we give it a chance—see how things go?" Enzo hoped he didn't sound *too* desperate. If this was all part of Jen's game to ensnare his interest, it sure as hell was working.

"I'm sorry. I really don't think that would be such a good idea." Jen waved over the waitress and asked for the check.

"I *have* to see you again, Jen. Lunch?" Enzo said as Jen got to her feet; her meal was barely touched.

"We are too different, Enzo." She stood looking down at him through those onyx teardrops with sorrow in her voice. "We're from different places and destined to different ends. Whatever might be between us, our families would sever." She fished out a couple of twenties from her purse and laid them down on the table by her plate.

"No. No, I'll get this." Enzo just couldn't help himself with the macho act.

"You're very sweet, Enzo." Jen bent over and kissed Enzo's lips and, for him, the world came to a full stop.

The soft, sweet sensation of Jen's warm lips on his stayed with Enzo long after she'd left the restaurant. He sat there by himself awhile in quiet contemplation, unable to eat, and unable to believe she'd just walked away from him. There *was* something between them, of that he was positive, and he'd be damned if he was going to simply give up on her.

CHAPTER FOURTEEN

Jen made her way out of the Fung Wah Yo and headed along Pell Street in the direction of Doyers. She had no business there that afternoon but needed the walk to clear her head. She'd agreed to have lunch with the Italian mobster because she'd felt something the first time they'd met. Something new. Something magnetic, electric.

When she'd seen Enzo DeCarlo walk into the restaurant just now, that feeling had returned, and Jen realized how easily she could have fallen for the guy, though he was nowhere even close to her type. Enzo's anachronistic charm, cheesy lines, good looks, and over-confidence had gotten to her, yet all she could think of was her family's abject disapproval should she follow her heart. What would Danny say were she to announce she'd fallen in love with an Italian, let alone one from a New York crime family? Her older brother was so fiercely protective of her at the best of times. Danny had scared off more of her potential Chinese suitors over the years than she cared to remember, and he had an inherent hatred of the Italians, which grew as he spent more time around the street gangs.

Then there was her father. Despite the way he viewed Jen—as his property—or maybe because of it, she didn't have to think too hard to imagine just how he'd react to her consorting with anyone who was not from good Chinese stock and preferably from the same province. All of which might have made for a much-needed distraction and release from the constant frustration and disappointment of her everyday life. The anarchistic joy of rebellion against her family and culture, the exhilarating, tingling fear of getting caught.... Yes, an affair with Enzo DeCarlo might have been the perfect expression of freedom for Jen, and it was one she'd played out in her head most nights since she had first met the man.

Yet, when she'd seen him again in the flesh that afternoon, Jen had known in her heart the trouble it would cause and the danger it could bring. It was for the best that she'd parted from him with a lingering, tender kiss and resigned herself to just thinking of what could have been between her and the handsome son of the mafia don. *My how dramatic.*

A shrill, tinny trill rang inside her purse and jarred her wandering mind back from its reverie. Without breaking her stride—Jen was keen to be out of sight of the Fung Wah Yo in case Enzo decided to play the romantic hero and chase after her with his heart on his sleeve—Jen fished out the phone and picked up the call.

"Miss Jen Mo-Li?" The voice was not one she recognized.

"Speaking. Who is this, please?"

"My name is Charles," the voice was deliberate, clear, and had a distinct Hong Kong accent. "We were given your number by Janice Pak."

"*We?*" Jen recalled the brassy Korean real estate agent and realized the woman had never actually offered her surname.

"I represent a Manhattan business consortium, Miss Mo-Li, and we would very much like the opportunity to meet with you."

"I'm actually busy right now," Jen lied. "When were you thinking of meeting? I could—"

"Now." If this Charles guy was trying not to sound menacing, he was doing it very poorly.

Jen glanced around. She had the distinct impression she was being watched. She quickened her step and wished she'd not insisted Eddie not accompany her to lunch. She didn't want her bodyguard to know whom she'd arranged to meet; Eddie's disapproval was something she could do without.

"I can assure you this is all aboveboard, Miss Mo-Li," the voice soothed as if her unease had translated itself through the phone. "We are interested in doing business with you, and we have a proposal to put to you that we think you will find most satisfactory. I promise you are not in any danger. May I suggest we meet at the Gung Choi convenience store, 202 Mott Street, in, say, ten minutes?"

Jen fought hard against the dull, gnawing sensation in the pit of her stomach. Her every instinct told her this was gang business, and she'd do well to turn tail and head to one of the safe apartments she kept in Chinatown as quickly as she could. She'd had dealings with some of the Chinese gangs across the years, but such dealings had always been indirect, and Eddie had been the perfect barrier between her and any potential unpleasantness.

However, Jen told herself, it wasn't as if this Charles was suggesting they meet in some shadow-filled alleyway or backstreet massage parlor, and she knew the Gung Choi store well. It was about as public as it could get without them actually holding a business meeting out on the street.

"Alright, I'll be there." Jen hung up the call. She'd handed over her number at the realtor's request because she'd truly been flattered by the woman saying she knew people who would want to talk with her, and Jen's business instinct knew it would be foolish to pass on any potential opportunity.

She knew well the convenience store with its bright red awning and equally garish yellow lettering, and its owner, Larry Choi. He and his family had settled in New York a little over four years ago, all thanks to Jen. At the time of the Chois' arrival, the store was owned by an ancient Cantonese man by the name of An Baixing. Having had no family to pass the business down to, he'd bequeathed the place to Larry Choi when he passed away three years later.

It wasn't too much of a stretch for Jen to assume her mystery caller knew the store was a familiar setting for her, and that was precisely why he'd chosen the location for their impromptu meeting. She was almost certain this was a gang representative she was on her way to meet and not a legitimate businessman. The question was, which gang, and why had she been singled out?

As she contemplated the possibilities, she felt a rising exhilaration. But it was an exhilaration stained with dread.

———

The man Jen deduced to be Charles was waiting patiently for her at the rear of the store. Flanked by two short, wiry young men, he leaned against a long chest freezer, which sat at the end of a narrow aisle between shelves crammed full of canned lychees, water chestnuts, bean sprouts, and bulging, oversized bags of rice and dried noodles. The guy's appearance said it all. He was not wearing a business suit, and his tattoos told her he was Black Dragon, relatively high-ranking.

"I'm Charles Fok—you can call me Charlie-Bo—uh, Charlie. Thank you so much for coming, Miss Mo-Li. Please accept my sincere apologies for the less than salubrious meeting place." Charlie-Boy shook Jen's hand and looked around the store. As he did so, his two unsmiling sidekicks stepped into the aisle, blocking it off.

Jen raised an eyebrow. That was quite a vocabulary for a street punk of any rank. "Thank you for suggesting we meet somewhere public," she replied. It did concern her a little, however, that the store was uncharacteristically empty. Even the ubiquitous Mr. Choi was nowhere to be seen. "Honestly, I wasn't quite sure what to expect." Extricating her hand from his, Jen absently eyed Charlie-Boy's colleagues, and the menacing bulges beneath their jackets.

"Again, please let me assure you that you are perfectly safe, Miss Mo-Li," Charlie-Boy said with a smile. "I have come to talk business with you—nothing more."

"What business could you possibly wish to discuss with *me*?" Jen replied. "I'm not sure how I could be of any interest to...."

"A vicious street gang like the Black Dragons?" Charlie-Boy laughed, and his companions smiled. "I'm afraid our unsavory reputation is somewhat exaggerated. We are merely businesspeople—like yourself."

Jen studied the guy's face for a hint of irony. She found none. He'd told her on the phone he was from a business consortium, which, in her eyes, was akin to Enzo insisting he was merely involved in a family business. Gangs were gangs, no matter how much they glossed over the fact. "So...?" Jen prompted.

"My co-leader would like me to arrange for you to meet with him," Charlie-Boy told her. He stood up straight and puffed out his chest with self-importance. "He asked that I make the initial contact to sound you out."

"Sound me out about what, exactly?" While Jen wasn't afraid he'd do something to harm her, there was just something about Charlie-Boy that made her uneasy.

"We would like to utilize your expertise in real estate ... and trafficking."

Did he know or was he fishing? "I think you're mistaken...."

"Let's not play games, Miss Mo-Li." The gangster's pleasant demeanor changed in an instant. His smile vanished. "You are a *fuk ching*, and your activities are well known to us. In fact, we have found work for some of your clientele in the past."

Jen was taken aback at his use of the term "fuk ching." It translated to snakehead—Fujian slang for people smuggler. Jen recoiled, remembering the sleazy gangster on the boat, the one she'd accidentally killed with her pen, and began to wonder if the meeting might just be an excuse for the Dragons to exact their revenge.

Charlie-Boy continued, "You are also most knowledgeable about the New York real estate markets, especially in and around the Queens borough. That is specialist knowledge we would like to employ."

Jen decided against arguing the snakehead point with the man. She was a trafficker, no matter how much she liked to gloss over the fact and how much she disliked the term. That Jen chose to assuage her conscience by telling herself she was doing good by helping people find better lives was clearly of no interest to Charlie-Boy Fok.

"Just *how* would you like to *employ* me?" It was Jen's turn to be blunt. "You obviously know who my father is, and his business interests."

"Of course, we know Ming Sen Mo-Li, and we are also well-aquainted with your brother Danny. We *always* do our homework, Miss Mo-Li." Charlie-Boy managed to patronize her and ogle her breasts at the same time. "We are not all simply thugs, you know."

It shook Jen to hear her brother's name on the gangster's lips. She chose to ignore Danny's love of gang life, but that certainly drove it home. She squirmed under Charlie-Boy's hot gaze, wishing she'd worn a sweater or a suit coat instead of the clingy jade-green blouse.

"You must understand," she said, "I couldn't possibly do anything to compromise my father—including choosing whom I associate with. I think I'm going to have to pass on this opportunity. Thank you, though."

Charlie-Boy took her rebuttal without emotion. "Very well. I shall advise Mr. Cheung that you are thinking about it."

Of course, Jen knew of the Black Dragons' leader, but hearing his name spoken out loud and in person prickled the skin at the back of her head. "There is nothing for me to think about," she said with firmness. "But please do thank him anyway."

"You have my number in your phone now," Charlie-Boy reminded Jen as the soldiers stepped aside to allow her to leave the back of the store. "Put it in memory and call me when you've considered my proposal and you're ready to meet with Mr. Cheung."

Jen gave him a stony look and a resolute goodbye and, as she walked back down the aisle, she half expected to hear footsteps following her, or maybe even the cocking of a gun. She'd just said no to the Black Dragons; she'd heard so many stories about those who'd dared to cross the gang. Her mind flashed to Doyers Street's Bloody Angle and all the lives lost there across the decades. She decided to take an alternate route home.

Heart pounding, Jen exited the store and stepped out into the cool sunshine by the crates of packaged noodles and fresh fruit and vegetables on Mott Street. Already, her mind was busy teasing her with all the possibilities Charlie-Boy's proposal could offer. Whatever the Dragons had in mind for her, there could be no doubt it would be most lucrative. They wouldn't have wasted their time otherwise.

She should tell her father, she supposed. Tell him the real estate agent had set the Black Dragons on her. Tell him she didn't know what to do because she was a weak woman. Anger swept through her and sent her thoughts down another path. What if she could work with the gang without her father finding out? If she could shield his business empire from any less-than-lawful activities, it might just allow her to break out from under his shadow and prove to him, once and for all, the capabilities she possessed that he chose to ignore. Meeting with Cheung was a fifty-fifty gamble: it would either incur her father's wrath or gain his approval.

Making her way through the Chinatown streets, Jen considered her territory. She then turned Charlie Fok's proposal over in her head, knowing she should reject it, and knowing, with equal certainty that she couldn't.

ACT TWO: CONTROL

CHAPTER FIFTEEN

"Are you fucking kidding me?" Rico voiced his protest as he trailed behind Enzo by the Nom Wah Tea Parlor. "It's closed, Enzo, and even if it wasn't, it'd be a million to one chance *she* would be in there."

Peering through the grimy window, Enzo ignored his friend and studied the still darkness of the tea parlor, the empty tables with chairs stacked neatly on top, and the table where Jen had been sitting when he'd first seen her. Of course, he knew it was highly unlikely she would be there, just as he knew in his heart she wouldn't be at the Fung Wah Yo restaurant when they'd checked out Pell Street earlier. But he'd had to at least try.

"It's been over a month, buddy." Rico pulled his jacket around his chest as they made their way along Doyers. With Halloween just around the corner, the air was stiff with October chill, but he was too macho to zip up; it just wasn't the done thing. "Face facts—the gal just doesn't want to know. If she did, she'd have taken your calls. It's not like she's out and you just happened to miss her a thousand damn times—she's got one of those cellular phones."

"You don't know shit," Enzo snapped. "Maybe her phone is broken. Maybe it's just shit; I heard the coverage on those things is crappy."

"Yeah, from The Don."

"What's that?" Enzo spun around to face his friend.

"Nothing."

They walked on.

"I know you need a challenge, Enzo, but you're taking it too far with this one. Let her go," Rico persisted, his breath puffing out in small, white clouds. "I've never seen you this cut up about a fucking chick before, especially one you've not even *shtupped*. It's Friday night—we should be trawling the Lower East Side or the Meatpacking District for hot tail, not stalking Chinatown for a piece of ass you only met twice."

Enzo ground his teeth. Even though he would never admit it to the guy's face, Rico was dead right. Somehow, Jen had gotten to him—to the point of driving him to distraction. There was something about the girl that had wormed its way deep into his psyche, and he just couldn't let her go. It also pissed him off to hear Rico referring to her as a hot piece of ass.

"Whaddya say, buddy?" Rico made an exaggerated show of blowing into his hands. "I'm freezing my fucking ass off here!"

Stopping abruptly, Enzo turned on Rico again. "Will you quit your fucking whining? Nobody forced you to come with me tonight—we're not joined at the goddamn hip!"

Heads turned in the direction of Enzo's raised voice. The street was busy as always, but with an entirely different crowd from the daytime—younger people out for thrills, booze, and sex, married couples out to dinner, and groups of young men on the hunt for illicit gambling and the best prices at the massage parlors.

Rico recoiled and took a step backward. There was a glint of fear in his eyes; he knew Enzo's temper well. "Sweet Mother Mary," he said, crossing himself. "We *really* do need to get you laid!"

"I'm fine," Enzo hissed between gritted teeth. "Just fucking leave it."

"How can I when you've dragged me around Chinatown two, three times a week for the last month? The Don is gonna start asking just how much business we're doing in Chinatown to warrant so much of your time. What are you going to tell him?"

"I'll tell him to mind his own goddamn business," Enzo growled.

"Yeah, right." Rico all but laughed in his friend's face, the subliminal message clear: Little Enzo wouldn't dare do such a thing. "Look how crazy you're being," he forged on. "I'm worried about you, Enzo."

For a split second, Enzo thought he'd answer with a punch to Rico's jaw. It certainly wouldn't be the first time the two had hammered out their differences with fists, but it would be the first time over some woman. Enzo instead forced himself to relax, unclench his fists, and let go of just enough of his anger to let Rico know he was in no immediate danger.

"You're right," Enzo gave in with a sigh. "You think I don't know I'm acting like a teenager chasing the first chick to offer a fucking hand job?" A cynical smile. "I don't know what it is about Jen, but it sure as hell ain't healthy."

"Amen." Rico crossed himself again; a good Catholic upbringing will do that to a guy. "Can we give up the wild goose chase and go find women who actually *want* to fuck us?"

"Sure," Enzo replied without a trace of humor. "We do have some business to attend to first, though."

"Business?" A look of concern flashed across Rico's face.

"Family business," Enzo replied. "There's a bar on Mulberry owing protection money." Turning away from Rico, Enzo began to walk with a purpose.

Clutching his jacket against the cold, Rico trotted on behind. "We don't have to do this tonight," he protested. "It's Friday; it can wait 'til next week."

Enzo shook his head as his mood darkened still further. "We're just around the fucking corner, Rico."

"Bud, this is not the time to be doing any kind of business."

Enzo knew he hadn't fooled Rico; his friend knew him all too well. He had to know Enzo was looking to take his blue-balls frustration out on some poor *schmuck*. He balled his fists in his pockets and dropped his head against the cold air chilling his nostrils. Enzo found it best to tune Rico out when he was off on one of his whining rants. It was either that or kick the crap out of him until he shut the fuck up.

The main drag through Little Italy was heaving with twilight revelers. Enzo, with Rico hot on his heels, had to weave and shoulder his way through the crowds, which did very little to lift his mood. He figured maybe he'd hit the Lower East Side with Rico once he'd shown the bar owner the error of his ways, even if it was only to shut the guy up.

"They renamed it." Rico stared up at the sign above the dive bar's entrance. "The *Italia-China*? That's one big fucking insult."

Enzo frowned. "The Chinese take over a joint and figure they can still draw the old crowd." He cast a glance at the burly, stone-faced Chinese bouncer who stood sentry at the door as if daring him to react to the comment he'd said plenty loud enough for him to hear.

The bouncer didn't so much as look at him.

"You sure about this?" Rico's voice telegraphed fear. "We should have backup. Are you carrying?"

"Nah," Enzo replied. "We're just gonna take the guy to one side and lean on him—remind him to be prompt with his payments. No need for guns."

Rico went silent.

Enzo pulled open the heavy, steel-framed door and waved Rico inside, all the while staring the bouncer down like he was just daring him to try stopping them. The bar was much the same as many of the others along Mulberry and in the surrounding neighborhoods. It was teeming with young people of mainly Asian origin, it was loud, and its air was thick with cigarette smoke. As far as Enzo could tell, the majority of Italia-China's clientele were well under the drinking age.

"What is it with these freakin' people?" Rico shouted above the hubbub. He pointed over the sea of heads to the tiny stage in the corner by the DJ booth.

Enzo looked across and there, a skinny young Chinese guy was murdering "Everything I Do" by Bryan Adams with everything he had. The soppy ballad had been in the charts for what had seemed forever, and he was sick to his back teeth of it.

"Yeah. Why the fuck can't they just listen to a jukebox? Who the hell wants to listen to that bullshit?" Curling his lip at the tuneless cacophony, Enzo made his way through the crowd toward the bar.

"Watch it, asshole," a voice growled in Enzo's ear as he brushed by a pair of young Chinese guys in black pants and tees. Snapping his head around, he found himself facing the shorter of the two, a guy with light brown eyes that glared from beneath thick eyebrows, a brush cut, and a flat, broad nose.

"You say something?" As Enzo squared up to the guy, he noticed the tattoos on his forearms and neck. He was definitely with one of the gangs, although Enzo couldn't recall which one—they all looked the damned same to him.

His taller companion stepped forward, his expression as cold as his eyes. They were a brown so dark they were almost purple. He had only one tat that Enzo could see, peeking out from beneath his T-shirt. I looked like a snake's tale.

The guy got right up in Enzo's grill and growled, "He *said* you need to watch where you're going, wop, especially when you're someplace you don't belong."

"Leave it, Danny," said his friend, putting a hand on his arm. "We came here for fun, not trouble."

Judging by Danny's expression, trouble was precisely why he was there. Who knew, maybe to him fun and trouble were the same thing.

"You should listen to your boyfriend," Enzo goaded.

"C'mon, Enzo. Remember why we're here." Rico gave a push in the middle of Enzo's back to usher him toward the bar. He sounded a little desperate to Enzo's ears.

Not without reason, Enzo had to admit. So, with some reluctance, Enzo stood down. They were pretty much the only Caucasian faces in an Asian bar, and even he wasn't bull-headed enough to pick a fight if it wasn't entirely necessary.

"You're lucky this time, wop," the Danny guy snarled as Enzo turned away. "Next time, I'll put your white ass down."

"*Enzo.*"

Rico's stern voice above the karaoke singer wailing the song's refrain was all that prevented Enzo from rounding on his adversary. Instead, he allowed himself to be led to the bar, where a cute Asian girl in a white, scoop-necked minidress greeted them with a curious smile. He figured she didn't see too many white folks on a working night.

"Two Buds?" the barmaid made the obvious assumption.

With a perfunctory nod, Enzo leaned across the bar to make himself heard; its top was unpleasantly sticky and covered with cigarette ash. "We're looking for the owner, Andy—Andy Xi," he said.

The girl's eyes flicked toward a narrow, yellow metal door at the rear of the bar. "He's not in tonight," she lied as she popped the caps on a pair of cold beers before setting them down in front of Enzo.

In a heartbeat, Enzo grabbed her slender wrist, so delicate he could snap it with a sharp twist. Fixing the shocked girl with a menacing smile, he said, "Tell him Enzo DeCarlo needs to talk to him."

"We can come back, Enzo." Rico was getting nervous. The two guys in black had not taken their eyes off them since their brief altercation. "If the guy's not in, he's not in."

"The fucker's in," Enzo growled. "And Miss Barkeep is going to go let him know we're here." A space had formed on either side of the Italians as the others at the bar shuffled away.

"I'll see if he's available." The barmaid yanked her arm away from Enzo as he relaxed his grip.

"Thank you." Enzo smiled at the young woman, handed Rico his beer, and took a hearty swig of his own. He watched the barmaid's round ass jiggle beneath her flimsy nylon dress and tried his damnedest to make out if she was wearing panties or not. The young woman then rapped on the yellow door, eased it open, and stuck her head through the gap.

"I ain't got time for this bullshit." Riding an inexplicable wave of sudden rage, Enzo slammed his beer down on the counter with such force it fizzed up and frothed out to add to the mess on the bar. "Asshole doesn't know who he's dealing with."

Ignoring Rico's protests, Enzo lifted the counter and made his way behind the bar. A quick look over his shoulder let him know almost everyone in the place was deliberately not seeing a thing. They had their beer, got to drink underage, and it was none of their goddamned business.

Perfect.

Rico had no option but to follow, catching up with Enzo just as he reached the door. Enzo yanked the barmaid out of the way, pushed open the door, and barged into the spacious office beyond.

"What the fuck?!" Andy Xi jumped up from his chair to confront the Italians. "You can't just—"

"You've been avoiding us, Andy." Enzo crossed the room in a few strides. "*Not* a wise move for someone owing two months' money."

Andy shook his head. "I owe you people nothing." The defiance in his voice carried a tremor of the fear that shone in his eyes.

"You know how this goes, Andy," Rico threw in as he pulled the door closed behind him; its thick steel muffled the dreadful amateur singing in the bar. He stepped gracefully into the role of the good guy. "Pay your dues and we leave you in peace."

"I have paid my dues already." Andy studied his battered old desk. "I can show you the receipt." Stooping, he reached down into the open desk drawer.

Before Andy could pull his hand from the drawer, Enzo kicked it shut with such force the cheap laminated wood cracked. Andy yowled as his fingers were crushed along with the splintering wood. He collapsed to his knees as blood oozed out from the front of the drawer. "You broke my fucking hand!" He wailed at Enzo.

"I'm gonna break more than your goddamned hand," Enzo snarled just inches from the guy's face.

"I already paid the Dragons," Andy croaked. His hand remained trapped in the broken drawer as he cowered like a cornered animal at Enzo's feet. "I thought you knew—I pay the Dragons now."

"You pay *us*, asshole!" Enzo delivered a hefty kick into the man's ribs.

"Enzo!" Rico yanked his friend away as Andy sobbed and struggled for breath. "Quit taking it out on Andy—you'll fucking kill him!"

"Damn right, I will!" Enzo's face blazed red as all reason left him.

The door swung open behind them. In perfect synch, Enzo and Rico turned to find themselves facing down the two black-clad Chinese guys for the second time that night.

"What the fuck do you think you're doing?" The younger gangster named Danny hissed. "This is not your turf anymore, wop."

"Bullshit!" Enzo pulled his arm from Rico's grasp. "Mulberry was ours when you were still on the goddamned boat."

Danny's hand slipped behind his back.

Enzo tensed.

A flash of silver and Danny lurched forward, cleaver in hand. Enzo ducked, the cleaver whispered by his ear, and he delivered a vicious uppercut to the gangster's gut. Winded, Danny staggered backward and collided with his colleague. The two rounded on Enzo, cleavers held high.

As Enzo moved back, Rico sprang forward to meet the gangsters' assault. He aimed a quick punch at the shorter guy's face, but the gangster twisted his head at the last second. Rico's fist deflected off his cheek, but not without the heavy ring he wore leaving a gouge. With a loud, pained grunt, the Dragon swung his cleaver at Rico, who jumped back, arm instinctively raised to protect his head. The blade bit deep into the soft flesh of Rico's forearm and a bright arc of blood shot across Xi's office.

"Bastard!" Rico snarled and grabbed the gangster's wrist with his other hand. A deft twist and the cleaver dropped from his grasp.

What happened next, Enzo didn't see as Danny came at him with the cleaver raised above his head. Enzo lurched toward him, grabbed his arm with one hand, and delivered a flurry of ferocious punches to his face. They jerked the gangster's back and mashed his lips against his teeth. Danny struggled against Enzo's vise-like grip, as he tried to hack at his head with the cleaver, but Enzo, by far the stronger of the two, kept it at bay with ease.

Danny changed his tactics. He stopped attacking and pulled away instead, breaking Enzo's grip. The second he regained his balance, he pounced, brandishing the cleaver. Enzo evaded him by vaulting over Andy's desk, and Andy himself, who was now cowering on the floor behind it. Danny paused to wipe at the blood around his mouth. Anger blazed in his eyes. Behind him, Rico got the shorter gangster in a clutch and grappled for his cleaver. Enzo lunged out from behind the desk opposite where Danny stood mopping at his face. If he could help Rico take out his guy, it'd be two against one. But faster than Enzo could track, the gangster closed the distance between them and lashed out at Enzo with a high kick that connected solidly and painfully with the mobster's chest, sending him reeling backward.

The breath knocked from his lungs, Enzo fought to stay on his feet. He knew if he went down, that would be the end of him. Danny was clearly pissed beyond all reason and out for blood. Enzo hit the wall at the back of the office and raised his fists as Danny came at him, that mean-looking cleaver slicing the air. It was like something out of an old martial arts film, which would've been awesome under other circumstances.

Danny's foot then connected with the corner of the cheap carpet beneath Andy's desk and instead of sinking the keen blade into the Italian's head, he stumbled and fell to his knees; his weapon jolted from his hand and slid across the cheap linoleum. It came to rest at Enzo's feet.

In a heartbeat, Enzo snatched up the cleaver, held it high, and was on Danny before he could scramble to his feet.

"Fucking Chink bastard!"

Danny threw himself backward, but Andy's desk was in his way. He hit the corner of it and went down, twisting away from Enzo's blow. The cleaver missed his skull by a fraction of an inch, but it sliced off most of his left ear and embedded itself in his collarbone. He let out a sound somewhere between a roar and a scream.

Enzo barely held onto the cleaver's handle as a gush of hot blood soaked his hand and poured down the gangster's shoulder and chest. The blade had hit the artery at the base of Danny's neck. Danny stared dumbfounded at the thick stream of red flowing down his body. The fight drained out of him in an instant.

"Fucker!" Enzo snarled as he attempted to extract the cleaver to deliver the coup de grace. But the blade was stuck fast, and each attempt to wrench it free brought forth a fresh spurt of blood and another scream. Finally, Enzo let go of the slippery handle and straightened, noting with immense satisfaction that this Chinese thug was actually crying.

"Well, damn. Some gangster you are, crybaby."

A sound to his right prompted Enzo to turn toward the center of the room where Rico stood over Danny's compadre with a hand clamped to the fresh wound in his arm. The gangster lay face down and limp on the office floor, his back rising and falling with each shallow breath. Rico was a master of the choke hold, so Enzo was more pleased than surprised. Slowly, deliberately, Rico placed his foot on the back of the unconscious man's neck. Then, with a grunt of exertion, he stomped down hard with all his strength and body weight.

The sharp crackle of snapping bones made Enzo jump. "What the fuck, Rico?"

"No witnesses, Enzo," Rico replied as he prodded the fresh corpse with the bloodied toe of his shoe. He then turned his attention to Danny. "Now, you deal with your fucking mess, Enzo." There was frustration in Rico's voice, the frustration of a man who had gone out for a night on the town and instead gotten dragged into a fight he hadn't wanted.

"No ... please, *no*." The voice was weak but thick with pain.

Enzo looked down. Danny had pressed himself against the desk, his black shirt stained maroon with his blood. Behind him, Andy Xi whimpered.

"*Please,*" Danny croaked. "I can pay you—I have money. My family...."

"He's bleeding out, Rico. He'll be gone in minutes. We need to get the fuck out of here before somebody calls the cops."

"We can't take the chance." Grimacing at the pain in his arm, Rico made his way across the office to Enzo.

"There's a bar full of witnesses out there," Enzo stated the obvious. "We can't kill all of them."

"Even if some of them were dumb enough to talk to the cops, what are they gonna say? A pair of white guys did it? No one is going to finger us. Most likely they'll blame it on the Koreans or Vietnamese. They hate cops around here because they're all fucking white. Isn't that right, Andy?"

From under the desk, Andy's trembling voice said, "Yes, yes."

"Andy knows that if he says anything to anyone, he'll get his ass deported. Isn't that so, Andy?"

Again, the trembling, half-whispered assurance.

Rico picked up the dead gangster's cleaver and held it out to Enzo. "Your mess."

With a shrug, Enzo took the cleaver from his friend's hand and took a short step toward Danny, who, sitting in a growing puddle of his own blood and piss, stared at the weapon with horror etched upon his face.

"Please, don't do this...." Danny begged. "*Please—*"

Enzo didn't miss the gangster's skull a second time.

CHAPTER SIXTEEN

The cold, cruelly persistent drizzle made Cypress Hills Cemetery appear all the more grim to Jen and exacerbated her misery a thousandfold. Along with the wisp-thin mist that clung to the white stone pillars of the abbey standing proud in the graveyard grounds, it made for a fitting underscore to the raw emotions of the morning.

Jen had visited the cemetery many times over the years since her mother passed away. She had spent much contemplative time wandering the verdant grounds and enjoying the quiet of the grand mausoleum. But she had never once thought she'd be burying her oldest brother in the family plot next to their mother so long before his time.

The Mo-Li burial plot stood at the corner of the Chinese section of the vast cemetery, not too far from the main Jamaica Avenue entrance, which was bridged by a tall, imposing stone archway. Cypress Hills was favored by New York's Chinese community as it was non-sectarian and non-denominational. As the Chinese population had grown in Brooklyn, Queens, and Manhattan, so had their part of the two-hundred-and-some-acre cemetery.

Ming Sen had added to the plot over the years following his beloved wife's passing with the understanding the whole family could one day rest together in eternal peace. It was now cold comfort for Jen, knowing Danny was gone from her life, and that was the only thing occupying Jen's thoughts as she stared blankly at his coffin.

Father had not permitted her to see Danny's body the night the police called at the apartment to deliver the terrible news. He had taken Petey along to the morgue to officially identify the body, although his younger son had been barely capable of dealing with the situation—he'd gotten himself into such a state upon hearing of his brother's death that he was hardly coherent. Nevertheless, Ming Sen had insisted Jen stay home, and she had been too grief-stricken to argue. The mortician did a wonderful job of patching Danny's shattered face back together, and when Jen finally got to say her final goodbyes, her dear brother looked peaceful, as if he were simply asleep.

The cops said Danny's death had all the hallmarks of a gangland killing. The two victims were Black Dragons, and there had been no witnesses despite a bar full of people. Fortunately for him, the bar owner hadn't been there. He'd spent the evening in the emergency room, having smashed his hand in a kitchen accident at home. He was shocked that such mayhem had taken place at his establishment. Now, standing by his grave, Jen thought that Danny would have been so very proud to have been identified as a Black Dragon.

The gathering at the cemetery had been sparse. With Ming Sen, Jen, and Petey the only Mo-Li family living in the States, the majority of the mourners were employees and business associates eager to curry favor with the deceased's grieving father. Huddled beneath black umbrellas against the fine rain, they'd quickly drifted away once Danny's polished oak coffin was lowered into the darkness of the neatly dug grave.

"It's time to go." Petey's voice broke into Jen's thoughts. "We've said our goodbyes." He took hold of his sister's elbow and tried to steer her away from the graveside.

Jen pulled away from his grip. "How can you be so heartless, Petey? Our brother is dead."

"I'm as devastated as you are, Jen." Petey's false sentiments were given away by the indifference on his face. "But you can't tell me this wasn't expected. Danny loved living the life of a gangster, and he died as one. He's probably somewhere in the spirit realm laughing his ass off."

"For God's sake, don't you dare stand there and tell me this is what Danny would have wanted." Tears welled up in Jen's eyes and her voice choked with emotion. She stared down at the sickly-sweet scented flowers piled high on top of the casket—lily of the valley. "Don't you *fucking* dare."

"He's gone, Jen," Petey took his sister's elbow once more. "I know how much you loved Danny, and just how much you'll miss him—we *both* will. But you have *me* to take his place now."

Something about her brother's tone made Jen look up at him. He had a strange, almost hungry look in his eyes that turned Jen's stomach.

"I'll take good care of you," he went on. "Maybe even find you a better role within the company. Father will listen to me now I'm heir to the throne. I'm his lieutenant."

"*What?*" Jen turned her attention from the dead brother to the dumb one. Did he mean—

"We were going to tell you when we got home," Petey told her. "I realize it's a big disappointment for you, but surely you didn't expect to take Danny's place? I mean, you're—"

He didn't have to say, "just a woman." The derision in his voice said it all for her. A wash of anger swept through Jen, brushing away the sense of profound loss that gnawed at her soul. She was the one with business experience, the one who had built up one of the most profitable divisions of the family business. *She* was the one who should take Danny's place at their father's side, not Petey. Petey was a rudderless daydreamer with no business savvy whatsoever. Petey was an absolute idiot.

Disappointment didn't even begin to describe the way she felt at that moment. Along with that emotion came a not-so-subtle switch inside her as the futility of fighting against the lowly position in which Father had stuck her lodged at her core.

"Your brother will make a worthy successor." Jen's father had appeared, ghost-like, a few feet away. Perhaps he'd waited until just that point in their conversation to add insult to injury. "Peter is a Mo-Li man. He is also my son. As such, he will learn to be strong and decisive. And he has no delusions of being a damned gangster."

"I am far more qualified than Petey to take Danny's place, Bà. You know this. The evidence is in the financial statements that you pore over so obsessively."

Jen knew she should hold her tongue in front of her father, especially since he'd just lost his firstborn son. But, what else did she have to lose? Ming Sen had all but shunned her in his grief, seemingly preferring Petey's false condolences to her unfeigned and shared sorrow. Jen was grateful she had Eddie to rely on. He'd been her absolute rock from the moment she'd heard the news of Danny's death. To have Father turn away from her so resolutely now was a dagger to the heart.

The Mo-Li patriarch raised a hand to silence his daughter. "I have made my decision, and you are in no position to question that—especially not now. I have no desire to discuss business with you here, at his grave."

He looked down into his son's grave for a moment, his dark eyes unreadable. When he raised them to Jen's face again, they were filled with unnamable sorrow—something Jen had not seen since her mother's death.

"You," he said, and Jen held her breath. As he struggled with whatever emotions hid behind those eyes, they turned to black chips of obsidian, cold as a hard winter freeze. "*You* should be the one in that grave, not my son."

Jen could say nothing. Feel nothing.

Even Petey was shocked by their father's cruelty. Letting go of Jen's arm, he moved swiftly to usher the Mo-Li patriarch away from the graveside. "We'll meet you back at the car," Petey told his stunned sister.

"I'll get a cab," was all Jen could manage to say. She was not sharing a car with a man who had just wished her dead. A *father* who had just wished her dead. She glanced at her mother's grave, which was just to the left of Danny's. *If you had lived, would it have changed all this?* She couldn't help but believe it would. But the past was past and could not be clawed back and relived.

Nor could Jen's future be reclaimed. There were no words she could speak that would change her father and none he could speak that would win her forgiveness.

"Goodbye, Danny," she said softly and left her brother's grave to the rain.

Walking toward the cemetery's chapel, Jen fished the cell phone from her purse. She fumbled Charlie-Boy Fok's number on the little screen, thumbed the dial button, and held the phone up to her ear.

"This is Jen Mo-Li," she said when the call was answered. "I've decided I would like to talk with Mr. Cheung."

CHAPTER SEVENTEEN

To Jen, Charlie-Boy Fok seemed nervous, which was a far cry from the self-assured, cocky persona he'd presented at their first meeting. That could well be because this was more than a meeting to arrange a meeting, or perhaps it was the presence of the gangster's boss, the infamous David "Storm" Cheung.

The venue was a large office room which amazed her as much for its location as for its appointments. The walls were naked brick, artistically distressed, and hung with surprisingly tasteful art—prints mostly, some in classic Chinese styles, some abstract. There was a seating group on one side of the room and a small conference table to the left. In the middle of the room, toward the back wall, was a silk, hand-knotted carpet much like the one that graced her bà's office at home. Atop it was a large teak desk. She had been seated in one of two leather-upholstered side chairs placed on a second carpet before the desk, behind which sat the man, himself, in a matching executive chair. This luxury was all the more jarring for being hidden behind the noise and chaos of a smoke-filled gambling club and a dented, half-unpainted metal door—a door whose secret opposite surface was paneled in thick, dark wood.

"My condolences for the loss of your brother, Miss Mo-Li," Storm said, his tone formal, his voice mild. As he spoke, he rubbed at the shiny pink stump of his left pinkie finger. "Danny was a good man and would have made a brave Dragon. He will be missed."

"Thank you, Mr. Cheung." Jen studied the guy's face for any trace of disingenuousness. She found none. While the Dragons had not sent anyone to Danny's funeral, they had sent a tasteful wreath comprised of white lilies and greenery, which had appeared at the graveside before most of the mourners. Jen figured that was doubtless for the best. Had her father found out there was a Black Dragon at his son's funeral, God only knew what he'd have done.

As if he just had to say something, Charlie-Boy declared, "I promise you that we will hunt down Danny's killers like the animals they are. Your brother shall be avenged."

Now, *there* was the unsubtle aroma of machismo Jen had scented at the grocery store.

Storm shot his deputy down with a withering look. "We are not here to discuss such unpleasant matters as revenge and murder, Charlie-Boy. That is Dragon business and Dragon business alone. We will deal with what happened to Danny in our own way and in our own time."

Jen eyed Charlie-Boy Fok, who appeared to be on the verge of a retort. Another narrow-eyed glance from Storm closed the guy's mouth. She would have to be blind and deaf not to catch the low thrum of tension between the two men.

She glanced over her shoulder at Eddie, whose narrowed gaze and nod assured her that he'd observed the same subtext. At least he was no longer bristling with disapproval. She had never done anything quite as dangerous as entering into direct parlay with Chinese gangsters. When she'd first told him where they were going, he had dared argue that she really should not be meeting with the likes of Storm Cheung and his notorious "rabble of violent psychopaths" in the backroom of some godforsaken gambling den. And if she was considering doing business with them—well, even *he* could not guarantee her safety. Naturally, the more vehement Eddie's dissent, the more determined Jen was to learn what the Dragons thought she could do for them and what they might do for her.

Catching Jen's backward glance, the Black Dragon leader seemed to notice Eddie for the first time. "Who is this?" he asked. "And why is he here?"

"This is my bodyguard, Eddie Sun. He never leaves my side." She smiled, hoping to send the message that she was protected.

Cheung's brows tilted wryly. "Eddie, eh? As in ladies' lingerie or a stuffed toy?"

"As in *bear*," said Eddie, deadpan.

Cheung gave him a moment more of appraisal, then turned his full attention back to Jen. "We understand the Mo-Li Company is taking an active interest in Flushing—somewhere close to the Kissenna Boulevard apartments, I believe."

"My father and I viewed an apartment there, yes." Knowing how to play her cards close to her chest, Jen offered nothing more. Of course, Storm knew that much already—after all, it had been his contact, the inimitable Janice, who had reached out to her. Storm also knew *precisely* where she and her father had been looking, and what her interest in Flushing was; this preamble was all part of the gangster's game.

As Storm leaned back in his chair, he wrinkled his nose at the smell of cigarette and cigar smoke creeping in from the gambling den along with a low rumble of noise. It made Jen doubt that he did all his business here. Somewhere, she was sure, he had a real office—some glass-walled, chromed affair with scenic views across his territory. Not that the leader of the Black Dragons would ever be so stupid as to invite the daughter of Ming Sen Mo-Li to his actual place of business.

"I'd be right in saying you were interested in far more than that one apartment?" Storm's question was rhetorical, of course.

Nodding, Jen crossed her legs. She wore a tailored pantsuit of a subtle shade of warm gray—business camo. It seemed appropriate; it was not lost on her that the guest chairs were somewhat lower than his executive swivel, which gave Storm the psychological advantage of peering at her from behind a wall.

As if sensing her thoughts, he rose and rounded the desk nonchalantly to half-lean, half-sit against it, looking down on her. Jen now saw the man in all his glory—tall, with a slender frame; long, toned legs; and sockless feet clad in white Converse Chuck Taylor canvas shoes. He had a sharp, angular face—attractive, but devoid of humor—absurdly framed by a bowl haircut.

Judging by the cut, Jen figured the guy for a Bruce Lee fan, which was all well and good, but the star had been dead for almost twenty years. It was men such as Storm Cheung who perpetuated their people's anachronistic stereotypes, which led to other Americans' less-than-flattering opinions of them.

Nonetheless, he was powerful, and Jen made sure to make plenty of eye contact as she sat in the leather chair, pretending to be relaxed.

"You are considering buying the entire complex?" Storm pressed. Again, he gave out the air of knowing the answer before Jen replied.

"We *were*," Jen said. "Right up until...." She fought to keep her emotions in check. Danny's death was still very raw, but she could not afford to show even the slightest sign of weakness in front of the gangsters. She merely tilted her head to one side and glanced toward the far wall.

"Of course." Storm's hands were folded over his fly, his thumb endlessly circling his maimed pinkie. "I do understand."

"Are you still in the market for the property, though?" Charlie-Boy couldn't resist adding his two cents' worth. There was an unsettling hardness to his plump, boyish face that sent a crawling prickle of unease up the back of Jen's skull.

"It is still very much under consideration," Jen told him. "If you have brought me here to warn me off the property, please say so." She glanced at Eddie for support, and to remind Storm that he was there. Her to-the-point manner could often grate on business associates, especially new ones. "If that is the case, you really could have saved yourselves a lot of time and trouble."

Storm forced a small, wry laugh. "If I had wanted to dissuade you from the apartments, Miss Mo-Li, I wouldn't have done it in person." There was no hint of menace in the gangster's tone, although his words spoke volumes.

"So, what ... you want to work with me?" Jen's eyes flicked over to Charlie-Boy who had moved to stand at his boss's right shoulder with arms folded across his broad chest.

"Why else would we be having this meeting?" Storm smiled.

"You tell me," Jen met his gaze with growing confidence. The Dragons wanted something from her and had been prepared to step outside their usual modus operandi to get it. "This is an entirely new situation for me—I'm not sure why you're interested in me."

Storm leaned forward a little. "You are a snakehead with a unique and intimate knowledge of the real estate market in and around the borough—not to mention access to one of the biggest property companies in the eastern United States."

There was that word again. Jen didn't hide her distaste for it, though her protest was mild. "I bring Chinese people into the country to give them a better life."

"As I said, you are a *snakehead*." Storm's insistence upon the word was final. "It is nothing to be ashamed of. I admire everything you do for our people. Your experience and contacts in real estate are a combination of factors that make you attractive to the Dragons."

Jen wasn't sure if she was supposed to be flattered or intimidated by the gangster's astute observations. She pursed her lips, trying to look thoughtful.

"We've been looking at expanding our operations into Flushing," Charlie-Boy blurted out their plans with all the finesse of a spoiled brat ratting out his mates. "When the hotel opens—"

"It will bring in new money," Jen finished the guy's sentence, much to his obvious annoyance. "You *did* mention that before." She gave Storm a sly, conspiratorial smile, which served only to piss off his deputy.

"What Charlie-Boy didn't explain to you, though," Storm said, "is that the business we wish to expand in that particular area is our massage parlors."

"By that, I assume you mean brothels?" Jen heard the sudden chill in her voice, a chill that rose out of her soul. She felt perverse pleasure as both gangsters recoiled at her bluntness. Well, why shouldn't she call a spade a spade?

Storm eased his scarecrow frame back onto the desktop and smoothed down his hair with both hands. "Please forgive me, Miss Mo-Li, I am not accustomed to discussing such ... *indelicate* matters with a woman."

Jen stifled a groan. Storm Cheung was beginning to sound every bit as sexist as her father and every other man she'd come across—Eddie Sun excluded, of course.

It was her turn to lean forward. Jen brought both her feet to the floor and rested her hands on her knees. "Look. If you have brought me here to discuss your sex trade, then let's not waste our time pussyfooting around which words make either one of us feel uncomfortable. Sex is sex, and business is business, Mr. Cheung."

"I'm most impressed with your professionalism, Miss Mo-Li." Storm still appeared to be somewhat perturbed by Jen's directness. "I am Chinese. I was raised to respect women and never discuss sex in front of a woman who was not my wife. So, *this* is all very new to me."

Jen all but threw herself back in the chair and uttered a surprised bark of laughter. "Respect for women? The women you're so happy to whore out for profit, Mr. Cheung?" Jen regretted the retort the moment it left her mouth.

To her surprise, Storm cracked a smile and allowed himself a chuckle "Touché. I can see you and I are going to get along well." The smile vanished as quickly as it had appeared. "Here's our proposition. We want you to purchase real estate in Flushing that will be appropriate for our parlors."

Jen let herself relax. Was that it? But before she could breathe a sigh of relief, Storm added, "And we want you to populate them with fresh merchandise from your immigration business that will appeal to the middle-class money the area will be attracting."

Jen felt as if the temperature in the room had plummeted. "You want me to recruit prostitutes for the Black Dragons?" Jen couldn't keep the incredulity out of her tone. "I have neither the experience nor the inclination for that, Mr. Cheung. If you have been as thorough in your research on me, you will know that perfectly well."

"Ah, but you *do* have the experience," Storm insisted. "You have been responsible for bringing a great many young Chinese women and girls into the United States over the years, some of which we have employed in our parlors."

"I don't bring our people into the country to be whores."

"No, you bring them in for their money, and with very little thought as to how they will earn enough to pay back the extortionate rates you charge them for the privilege."

Hearing the word *extortionate* coming from a gangster's mouth with such venom was jarring, but it raised a question: Was that a ploy or did Storm Cheung have something resembling a conscience? If so, it was certainly something she'd be able to exploit should she ever need to do so.

"I have to turn a profit. That's business," she said. "But the immigration fees are negotiable and according to capacity. And I do have jobs lined up for the people I bring here. Or interviews for jobs at the very least."

"That's business. Precisely." He rose from the desk and went back around to sit in his chair. "We will give you virtually free rein on purchasing the real estate—I'm sure you know all the right people to make that happen with relative ease—and recruiting the staff required to run the parlors. You will be paid a good salary, of course, as well as a percentage of the takings from each of *your* parlors."

Behind her shuttered expression, Jen scrambled to find a way through this apparent job interview intact. In her courtship by the Black Dragons, she'd seen a way to prove herself to her father or, failing that, to throw her achievements back in his face. She'd hoped to find a way to free herself from him and make him regret his hurtful words. But this unexpected request and demand challenged her—threatened her beliefs, her values, her hopes of accomplishment. She was stranded on an island between two alligator-infested channels. She couldn't say yes but she wasn't sure Storm would let her say no and live.

"I can certainly make the real estate happen," she told Storm, willing her voice to sound matter-of-fact. "But, recruiting prostitutes…?" She shook her head.

A wry smile lifted the corner of Storm's mouth. "How does that change anything? You simply do what you've been doing all along—bring young attractive women to America. The mother country contains an almost infinite supply. Your contacts over there can acquire just the merchandise we need. The only difference will be that you'll select according to looks and age instead of whatever measure you use now. The girls will pay only a nominal amount—for appearances' sake—and then the remainder will come from their earnings."

Acquire, merchandise. Jen wanted to spit in the man's face and storm from the room. But she didn't. That might get her killed or worse.

"I assure you, this is a sound business venture," Storm added.

Oh yes indeed, it was as if women were mere property and not human beings. Still stranded, she stalled, trying to sound glib. "So, I'm to recruit whores for you in China?"

Charlie-Boy rolled his eyes at her. "Of course, in China," he said. "You're the one with all the contacts over there."

She turned her head to look at the gangster. Had he just let slip a weakness in the Black Dragon's empire—a lack of ties in the old country? "What makes you think beautiful, young Chinese women will be eager to sign up for a life of sexual slavery in America?"

Charlie-Boy rolled his eyes again. "America is the land of opportunity. Most Chinese would do just about *anything* to get away from the iron grip of the Communists. But, hey, we don't have to tell them the precise nature of the way they'll be working off their passage. You're a smart woman, Miss Mo-Li—spin them a fantasy and they'll be fighting amongst themselves to get on the boat. Is that not obvious?"

Jen turned her full attention back to the Dragon leader. "Do you share Mr. Fok's simplistic views?"

Storm glanced at Charlie-Boy's reddening face and smiled. "We're only asking you to increase a certain segment of your clientele. We've had an agent selecting women from the immigrants you and the other snakeheads were bringing in for some time. We merely wish to increase their numbers."

Jen threw a glance at Eddie. He could only have been talking about the man who'd dared to rape "Amy" Gong Shu Li on her ship—the man she had killed. "An agent?"

Storm shrugged. "An agent who's gone AWOL, apparently. But now we have you. We can acquire precisely what we need directly at the source."

Jen smoothed an imaginary crease in the smooth linen of her trousers. If the gang leader had built his plans around her, perhaps she held the advantage. Perhaps the head of the Black Dragon needed Jen Mo-Li more than she needed him. Maybe she could cut a deal; she'd handle the real estate, but not the requirement.

"You're making a sweeping assumption there, Mr. Cheung. You're laboring under the assumption that I *want* to build brothels for you, despite everything I've said to disabuse you of the idea."

Storm dismissed her with a wave of his hand. "If you weren't interested in working with us in the first place, you wouldn't be here, Miss Mo-Li. I know for a fact your considerable talents are wasted working for your father. With the Dragons, you will have all the autonomy you need to make everything happen, *and* make a great deal of money in the process."

"I don't know what my big brother told you about me. I know he had terribly loose lips." And Danny had been desperate to ingratiate himself with the Dragons. "Apparently, he did not tell you how I felt about your prostitution racket."

She saw the subtle change in the Dragon leader's expression—the eyes going cold, the flexing of the jaw.

"You're right," she said. "I am interested in working with you, but only on the real estate end of things. I can acquire for you—"

"Perhaps you misunderstand me, Ms. Mo-Li," Storm interrupted. "This is a package deal. All … or nothing. Am I clear?" He smiled, showing perfect teeth, and leaned back in his chair. "Now, then. Why don't you just name your price, and we will get started. What do you say?"

Jen said nothing. She could only stare at him, hating him for putting her in this position. For putting in her head flashes of desire to leave New York, change her name, and disappear from everything familiar. *Better the devil you know….*

Rising with all the dignity she could muster, Jen lifted her chin and fixed the Dragon King with what she hoped was an unreadable gaze. "Please, let me give this proposal some serious thought, Mr. Cheung. This will be a considerable step away from the business I'm involved in right now. Determining the worth of that shift will require some calculation. I have to consider my father's wishes, too, of course," she added to remind him that she was not alone in the world, but part of a powerful family.

"Just as he considers yours?"

Jen winced as the comment hit home. She supposed she had Danny to thank for that, too. She gave him a close-lipped smile and turned. Eddie was already at her side and ushered her to the door before opening it for her.

Between the secret lair and the noisome club, Jen turned to make eye contact with the gangster one last time. "I will let you know very soon, Mr. Cheung. Thank you for sharing your proposal with me."

Jen was surprised to read desire in Cheung's eyes as they swept the length of her body. That could prove useful. She gave him just the hint of a smile before pulling the door closed behind her.

CHAPTER EIGHTEEN

They'd walked a little way along Mott Street before Eddie broke the silence that had settled between them since leaving the meeting with Storm and Charlie-Boy. "Surely you are not going to consider their ridiculous proposal?"

"Do I have a choice?" Jen wrapped her arms around herself, feeling cold though the temperature was mild. "You heard his threats. I made a counterproposal. He rejected it."

"A counterproposal that would still have you doing business with a common gang. What do you think your father will have to say about you throwing your lot in with people like that? Especially so soon after Danny."

She turned to face him, tears coming to her eyes. "Should I care? Should I care what a man thinks who wishes me dead and told me so to my face?"

Eddie looked down at her, puzzlement wrinkling his brow. "What are you saying?"

"After the funeral, Bà told me, in very plain English, that I should be the one in the casket, not Danny." She grimaced. "Danny, who flirted with gang life and thought it was just one big Jackie Chan movie. I guess he found out in the end that it wasn't all that fun."

"Jen!" Eddie was stunned by her words.

She pressed her hands to her mouth to stop any more from coming out. She'd pooh-poohed her brother's delusions—built upon a sheltered life with few boundaries—when she should have fought tooth and nail against them. But she hadn't, and neither had Bà. To him it was just a phase. And here was the sobering fact: Danny had died playing gangsters. He'd brought his brutal demise upon himself, and was likely responsible, in part, for the decision she faced.

Do I have a choice?

"Jen," said Eddie, reaching a big paw out to lightly cup her shoulder. "Your father was grieving—"

She pulled away. "You make excuses for him."

"No. What he said to you was wicked and wrong and you are right to be angry and hurt. But don't let it drive you to do something that is both foolish and illegal." Eddie fixed her with his most serious face.

"And the business we are already involved in is not? I may choose to assuage my conscience by thinking what we do is helping people, but I'm well aware we are also exploiting them for our gain. The Dragons' way is more honest if you think about it, Eddie. There's no pretense or faked altruism, and it's no more illegal."

"You've made up your mind?"

Jen laughed. "You heard Storm. All or nothing. If I do nothing, I get nothing, and Father gets his wish—another casket with a Mo-Li in it. But this time, the Mo-Li he *wants* dead."

"He didn't mean—"

"What he meant is fucking irrelevant, Eddie," Jen spat. "I've ceased to care what the old bastard meant."

Eddie visibly recoiled at Jen's language. He held both hands up in a gesture of surrender. "Look, it's lunchtime. Why don't we go to Nom Wah and get something to eat?"

Jen checked her watch—it was almost one. She shook her head. "Not today, Eddie," she told him. "I have a promise I need to keep."

———

If Michael Yip was startled to find Jen and Eddie on his doorstep, he hid it well. "Is everything okay, Miss Mo-Li?" he asked as he ushered the two into his tiny apartment. "Rent is not due until next week."

"Everything is just fine, Michael," Jen reassured him. "It's not about rent. This is a social visit." She took an exaggerated sniff of the warm, damp air with her pert nose pointed toward the kitchen. "That smells delicious, Mai Ling, may we impose and join you for lunch?"

Yip's wife, whose swollen belly appeared to have doubled in size in under a month, beamed from ear to ear. "We would be honored to share our food with you, Miss Mo-Li," she gushed as she prodded at the pot of rice noodles that bubbled and spat on the old, pockmarked stove.

Jen found herself able to relax and make small talk with the young couple. She found their company soothing. They worked damned hard to earn just enough to pay their rent and what they owed to Jen for their passage. After all that, they barely had two cents to rub together, but they were undoubtedly happy together. And Jen envied that.

Jen was pleased to see Eddie also relaxing a tad in the presence of the Yips. His bristly demeanor quickly evaporated as he slurped up the seemingly endless bowls of noodles Mai Ling scooped from the pot. She had added a few spices and some finely diced chicken, and though it fell short of the culinary delights of the Nom Wah Tea Parlor, it was good comfort food.

Jen thoroughly enjoyed herself. Michael was charming and naively optimistic, which provided much-needed relief from the cynicism she felt creeping up on her, given the non-decision she faced. Was this what Jack Wa had felt when he found himself beholden to not one master, but two? Her conscience pricked her for her part in Jack's injury. It dug deeper when she found herself looking at Mai Ling Yip and wondering how welcoming the lovely young woman would be had Jen lured her to America for a life of cheap sex for cash. She shook herself free of the image. Storm Cheung was not the collaborator or master she would have chosen, but he was the one she had.

For the time being, Jen promised herself that if she could use Storm to free herself from her father, she could find a way to free herself from Storm. But for now, she would have to weather the storm. She smiled at her play on words and sipped oolong from a tiny, flowered cup.

After a pleasant hour or so in good company, Jen and Eddie once more found themselves on Mott Street. It was a gray afternoon that had turned cold. The sidewalks were busy, and Jen had one more stop before she went home.

"You can go grab yourself a coffee," she told Eddie as they made their way onto Pell Street. "I'm sure you don't want to spend your afternoon with a bunch of gossiping old women while I get these done." She held up both hands to show Eddie her fingernails. "It's been far too long since I treated myself." A manicure was one of the few indulgences Jen allowed herself. There was something incredibly relaxing about having someone take charge of your hands, stroking and currying them, bathing them in warm liquid. She had the pick of the salons on Pell, Mott, and Doyers. Most of them were staffed by women she had brought into the country, so she was always well looked after.

Eddie nodded. "I believe I will do just that." He seemed to have moved from his concern over her collaboration with the Black Dragons, but Jen knew a façade when she saw one.

"I'll call you when I'm done," she said, smiling and patting his arm. "Enjoy some time away from your problem child."

Eddie shot her a reproachful look, then shook his head and trundled up the street. Jen pushed open the door to the nail bar and was met by the cloying, chemical stink of acrylic and benzene.

The nail technician—a pretty girl of barely eighteen, whose chosen Western name was Jessica Sing—babbled incoherently in at least two languages as she worked diligently on Jen's fingernails. In tandem, her colleague, an older, plump Korean woman with a friendly, wrinkled face, soaked Jen's feet in a soothing, warm foot bath infused with jasmine, lavender, and rose oil. The day's stresses and thoughts of gangsters, hookers, and Flushing melted away soon enough. Jen no longer gave thought to her father or brothers, alive or dead, or Dragon lords or cocky, asshole sidekicks. She simply let herself be in the moment.

"You like, Miss Mo-Li?" Jessica's chirpy voice broke through Jen's reverie.

Jen looked down at the young girl's eager face, then at her brand-new nails. They were perfect—a work of art, shimmering with baby pink lacquer with a tiny hand-painted daisy at the center of each pinky nail. The little flowers were so perfectly done that they appeared to be almost three-dimensional. And for reasons, she couldn't have articulated if she'd tried, they made Jen want to cry.

"Is something wrong, Ms. Mo-Li?" Jessica asked.

Jen glanced at her—the fading smile, the beginnings of fear in her eyes, the puckered brow. She hated to have that look directed at her and it made her even more unhappy. She started to deny that there was anything wrong when the older woman who was busy putting the bright scarlet finishing touches to Jen's toenails, looked up, glaring at the teenager.

"What have you done, stupid girl?" she demanded. "How have you made Ms. Mo-Li sad?" To Jen, she said, "She will do your nails again. And if she does not make you happy, I will send her to the Venus Joy Spa and let the Tigers deal with her."

The older woman raised her hand as if she meant to strike the girl, but Jen grasped her wrist.

"Please, no! I'm not unhappy with her work. It's beautiful and I–I wish always to have Jessica do my nails when I come here. It's just that my brother, Danny ... daisies were a favorite of his and so, they reminded me...." She felt a tear roll down her cheek. She was punting. Danny had given little notice to any flower, but she had to give some reason for her tears.

Both women's eyes grew large with swift empathy. "Of course, Miss Mo-Li," said the shop owner. "We heard the awful news. We mourn with you."

Jen managed a smile. "Thank you for understanding."

She went away from the nail salon feeling off-balance. She wasn't sure what had prompted the tears, but the irony of the situation hit her right between the eyes. When the shop owner had spoken of sending Jessica to a brothel, Jen ought to have signed the girl up for her new line of business. But she didn't. Couldn't. Well, she would have to learn. And she would have to find a way to protect the lives she disrupted.

Jen made a quick call to Eddie's mobile to instruct him to make his way over to meet her. He didn't pick up, so she left a message and ventured out along Mott Street. She was relieved he didn't answer, as she was enjoying her time alone, especially without Eddie's judgmental glances and worried expressions. Then a cold ripple of unease cascaded down her spine as a troubling thought crossed her mind: Would Eddie Sun prove to be one more man in her life who thought he could tell her what she could and couldn't do?

You mean, like David "Storm" Cheung? whispered a tiny hesitant voice. She turned a deaf and angry ear to it. If David Cheung thought he was using her, she would use him as a rung on her ladder to autonomy.

Before Jen had the chance to shove her phone back into her purse, it went off in her hand, attracting the attention of everyone around her.

"Oh, for Christ's sake, Enzo!" Rico groaned out loud, not caring who heard him. "I thought you cut the chick loose." Stuffing his hands deep into his pockets, he huffed at Enzo's brimming excitement.

"It *is* her!" Enzo pointed like some over-excited kid. "Coming out of that nail salon!"

"Which one? They all look the fucking same to me," Rico grunted.

Enzo flashed him a scowl.

"What if it *is* her? Didn't she blow you off?"

Ignoring Rico's sour countenance, Enzo scanned the street. "C'mon, Pox." He set off at a brisk pace along Mott, heading in the direction of a small convenience store that had a sorry-looking display of wilting flowers in squat green buckets by its double glass doors.

"What the fuck?" Rico protested as he trotted to keep up. "We have business. We don't have time to chase random pussy all over Chinatown."

"We are *not*," Enzo growled, "chasing random pussy." Grabbing a bunch of limp red roses that had seen better days, he pushed open the convenience store's door and went inside. Above the door, a small, brass bell announced his arrival with a dull tinkle.

"Sure looks like it from where I'm standing," Rico countered. "You gonna let her humiliate you again?"

Enzo glanced out between the assortment of flyers and advertisements plastered all over the store's windows to check if Jen was still out on the street. He was delighted to see she had turned away from the salon and was making her way slowly in the direction of the convenience store. As he watched, she made a call on her cell phone.

"Will that be all?" The old Chinese guy behind the counter asked with a woeful glance at the sad bunch of roses Enzo clutched in his hand.

Enzo pulled out his wallet and slapped a twenty on the counter.

"Payphone?"

Fumbling, he plucked out a grubby slip of napkin folded into a tight square packed snugly in his wallet.

"Over by the door." The storekeeper pointed to the front of his establishment. There, hanging on the wall, was an antiquated payphone, complete with a shiny black, Bakelite receiver.

As Enzo waited with impatience for his change—he needed the quarters—he kept a nervous eye on the street outside. Jen was but a small shape in the crowd now, and his anxiety grew.

"You need to get a grip," Rico chastised. "And what's with the roses? Like she's gonna throw her panties at you the second she sees *those*. You're a fucking walking cliché, Enzo."

"Leave it," Enzo growled. He snatched up his change from the counter and dashed to the payphone.

"I don't want to see you getting hurt, buddy!" Rico shouted after him, his words dripping sarcasm. He stayed put by the counter, distancing himself from Enzo's zeal.

Enzo waved a dismissive hand over his head as he snatched up the payphone's sticky receiver and dialed Jen's number.

"Hello?" She picked up on the second ring.

"Jen?" Enzo said. "It's me...."

"Who is this?"

"Enzo. We met—"

"Enzo?"

His heart sank at the tone of her voice. Had she forgotten him? "Yeah—you remember me?"

"Of course I do. It wasn't all that long ago." Jen's voice was a thrill for Enzo to hear, even though there was no hint of warmth to it. "Did you get a mobile phone?"

"Nah," Enzo tried his best to sound nonchalant. The truth was, he'd not even dared to broach the subject again with his father. "I'm on a payphone in some shitty old store. I saw you walking out of the nail bar...." It didn't occur to Enzo until much later just how creepy that sentence sounded.

"What do you want, Enzo?"

Enzo struggled to read her voice. Was that intrigue or puzzlement ... or wariness? He pressed on. He had nothing to lose, right?

"Want to grab a coffee?"

In the pause following the question, all Enzo could hear was the thump of his heartbeat and a faint, high-pitched ringing in his ears. He watched intently as Jen got closer to the store with each step, her phone pressed tight to her ear. Her head was tilted to one side and the look on her beautiful face was kind of sad. Slipping another couple of quarters into the payphone's slot, Enzo echoed Rico's sentiments and questioned his sanity: Why the hell was he feeling like some lovelorn teenager over a gal he'd only met twice?

"No."

"No?"

"I made myself clear the last time we met, Enzo." Jen was firm and to the point. "Nothing could come of it. It would be foolish to start something that will cause so many problems."

Enzo's stomach sank. He couldn't remember the last time a woman had told him no. "I've been thinking about you a lot this past month, Jen," he said. "I just want to talk."

"We have nothing to talk about. Goodbye, Enzo."

"Don't hang up!" Enzo blurted out, so loud, that heads turned in the store. The line fell silent, and Enzo pressed the receiver hard to his ear.

"Okay." Jen's voice broke the quiet, startling Enzo.

"What's that?"

"I said okay." For the first time since she'd picked up his call, Enzo thought Jen's voice sounded warm. "I'll have a coffee with you, Enzo. I guess it won't hurt to catch up." There was a wry sarcasm in her voice. Enzo ignored it.

"It won't hurt at all." He knew his wide, toothy smile was the one Rico called his shit-eating grin.

"So … when would you like to meet up?" Jen was almost at the door.

"Now?"

"It's a little short notice, Enzo."

"You can show me your new manicure."

"What?" Stopping dead outside the convenience store, Jen scanned the street. Now she looked like a startled deer.

"Turn around."

"What is this, Enzo? Some kind of sick joke?" Then, as she spun around, Jen caught sight of Enzo smiling at her through the store's window.

He waved.

Seeing Jen's face light up the moment she saw him told Enzo all he needed to know about his decision to make that call. She was delighted to see him—that was evident. There was warmth in the depths of her beautiful eyes and a sweet smile playing across the full, curving lips he'd kissed once what felt like a lifetime ago.

Enzo hung up.

"You're *really* doing this?" Rico called after him as he bustled from the store, flaccid roses in hand, to meet Jen Mo-Li out on the street. "You're fucking batshit crazy, Enzo."

Enzo shrugged and gave his friend a lop-sided *what-are-ya-gonna-do?* smile. "You love me, though."

"You're lucky I do," Rico huffed. "I'll make myself scarce again. Don't forget we got to be someplace later."

"Quit worrying, Rico." And with nothing more to say, Enzo stepped outside to greet Jen with the roses he'd just bought.

CHAPTER NINETEEN

She'd done her level best to forget about Enzo since she'd fobbed him off with her excuses the last time they'd met. She'd known then that getting into any sort of relationship with an Italian—a DeCarlo, no less—would mean nothing but trouble should her father ever find out. And, if he wasn't to find out, she could only begin to imagine just how much sneaking around and covering her tracks it would entail. At the time, she had been perfectly convinced she didn't want any of that crap in her life. Of course, she hadn't wanted to deal with the Black Dragons either, but there she was, looking that circumstance in the face. That was on her father and, if she was honest, on Danny as well.

Now she found herself sitting across the table from Enzo DeCarlo at the Fung Wah Yo, thinking of it as *their* restaurant. Maybe that was on her father, too.

"I couldn't resist," Enzo said, his face alight. "I'd given up after you ignored all my calls. Then I saw you coming out of the salon...."

Jen studied Enzo as he talked, punctuating his sentences with excited hand motions. It was as if they were long-lost lovers and not two random people who had just happened to be in the same tea parlor one afternoon.

"I'm pleased you didn't resist," Jen confessed. "I've been thinking about you."

"So ... why didn't you answer my calls?"

"I've had ... a lot on my plate," Jen replied. Her mind slipped back to the cold, miserable day of Danny's funeral. It was not a subject she wished to enter into with Enzo as her brother's death was still raw and the memories fresh. "I also made my feelings about getting into anything with you very clear. Or at least I tried." She softened the words with a smile.

"You still agreed to meet up."

"You were stalking me, Enzo," Jen told him. She couldn't help but laugh. "Flattering and all that, but I'm pretty sure Ann Landers would say it was a big red flag."

"Who cares what Ann Landers says?"

"Millions of people. What if she's right? What if I'm at the mercy of a man who was literally *watching* me walk down the street?"

Enzo threw up his hands in mock surrender. "You caught me. I'm just some weird stalker dude who follows cute chicks around Chinatown."

Jen laughed at that; it had old-school romantic connotations that resonated with her. "Yeah, I had you pegged as a creep the first time I saw you." She nursed her coffee cup between both hands. Its warmth made her fingers tingle. "So, why are *you* in Chinatown?"

"Business," Enzo said. He took a sip of his coffee and fiddled with the plastic-wrapped fortune cookie the waitress had left on the table. "It honestly was a total coincidence running into you again."

"Just like the first time we met."

"Yeah," Enzo replied. "Maybe it's God, or fate, or something like that?"

"I don't believe in fate. But I do believe God ... puts people and situations in front of us that we're supposed to use to shape our destiny, and that we must become the masters of it."

Enzo whistled through his teeth. "That's deep." He flashed a grin. "I was brought up a good Catholic boy and to accept God as the maker of all our plans."

"And I was brought up to believe my father was the one who would mold my future, the one who would dictate every path my life would take. And yet, here I am, making my own decisions and my own way in life."

Enzo looked perplexed. "Meaning?"

"Meaning, if I can push against the indoctrination of thousands of years of oppressive culture, then so can you."

Enzo studied her for a moment, then said, "All I'm trying to say here is I think we're *meant* to be."

Jen raised an eyebrow and set her dainty China cup back in its saucer. "Does that line ever work on any of your Italian girls?"

"You'd be surprised."

"Ah. So, underneath all this destiny nonsense, you're just looking to get laid."

He stared at her for a good ten seconds, his face going red, then white, then red again. Finally, he shook his head. "No. I mean, yeah, I find you really, really sexy. But I dunno, there's just *something*...."

Yes, there was *something*, and Jen wished she knew what it was. The guy was damn good-looking, that was for sure, and his shockingly blue eyes seemed preternaturally bright framed by his thick dark brows and lashes and lock of burgundy-black hair that fell over one brow. His looks kind of made up for his rough edges. So did his enthusiasm for her company, she had to admit. Enzo, unlike other men in her life, found her worthy of his attention, and more than a pawn in a business scheme. But Jen was smart enough to realize it was entirely possible that a considerable part of her attraction to Enzo DeCarlo was because even the most casual of flings with him would cause ructions not only with her family and Eddie but among the Chinese community in which she worked.

And just how would it affect her burgeoning association with the Black Dragons? It was common knowledge on the streets that there was little love lost between the Chinese and Italian gangs. Jen could now possibly wreck that business connection before it even got off the ground. She was loathe to admit there was a part of her that wouldn't mourn that eventuality.

It had taken every ounce of Jen's resolve to turn Enzo away at the Fung Wah Yo the month before. She'd felt an irrefutably potent attraction coursing through her, one she'd never experienced with any of the nice young men her father had deemed suitable for dating. Was it raw attraction, anger, or the void left by her brother's death that had made Jen say yes when Enzo's call came through out there on the street? Was it all of those things?

"So....?" Enzo prompted.

"So....?"

"Us?" Enzo had the air of a man who'd come so far and wasn't about to give up on something he so badly wanted. "We should give it a try." He reached across the table and took hold of her freshly manicured hand.

Images came in lightning speed—Storm Cheung, literally lording it over her; Mai Ling Yip, the little nail tech; and Gong Shu Li in her wretched cabin aboard the freighter. Dead Donnie Wu bleeding at her feet. And then, her father's rage at finding out she was having a relationship with the son of Don Vincenzo DeCarlo. How he'd berate her for turning her back on so many centuries of Chinese culture. How he'd say she had betrayed her entire family, and how he was so bitterly disappointed in her. Then she heard his coldhearted voice in her head: *You should be the one in that grave, not my son.*

She would enjoy his rage, relish his disappointment. "Okay," Jen said.

Enzo opened his mouth as if to say something, but nothing came out. Jen felt his fingers tighten on hers and saw the edges of his cool demeanor crumble just a fraction. If nothing else, she was certain they'd have fun together. Secrets were the spice of life.

"Shit." Enzo found his voice as his eyes moved from Jen's to the restaurant's door.

Jen twisted around to follow his gaze. She saw the guy who'd been at the Nom Wah Tea Parlor with Enzo that first time, standing at the door with his jacket sleeve pushed up and pointing at what appeared to be a gold TAG Heuer wristwatch.

"I guess that's your cue?" she said.

"It's business—*honestly.*"

"Of course it is," Jen teased. "And you weren't prowling the streets looking for me to stalk." The flicker of embarrassment in Enzo's eyes,

135

the slightest flush of his cheeks, told Jen she wasn't all that wide off the mark.

With great reluctance, Enzo relinquished Jen's hand and got to his feet. "We can pick this up later?"

"Of course," Jen lifted her coffee cup and took a delicate sip. "Give me a call next time you're in Chinatown."

A smile.

Enzo leaned over Jen's upturned face and planted a warm, firm kiss on her lips. Jen closed her eyes and melted into the moment.

As she watched Enzo go, Jen could practically see the added spring in the guy's step, it paired nicely with the blossoming warmth in her heart at the thought of seeing him again ... and the heat of a desire she knew she shouldn't feel. Really, what was he but a thug in a sharp suit? And there was a small, niggling chirp at the back of Jen's mind that warned she was making a monumental mistake—perhaps not the first one she'd made that day.

CHAPTER TWENTY

"Big D or Mr. Luen Dang or….?" Enzo kept a respectful tone. It was just him and Rico meeting with the head of the Mott Street Tigers, and they had to tread carefully. As it was, having come straight from his rendezvous with Jen, the taste of her lips lingering on his, Enzo had to work hard to keep his mind focused.

"Jonathon. Please, take a seat." Big D perched himself on one of the sturdy, green-topped card tables and gestured at some club chairs scattered about. The gang lord was a thin, wiry guy of average height who wore his gleaming black hair shoulder-length. His eyes were dark and watchful.

"Thank you for this meeting," Enzo said politely. He decided against sitting on the edge of the nearby roulette table, electing to remain standing instead. Beside him, Rico followed suit.

"Of course. We're always open to fresh opportunities," Big D replied. "Even with our old adversaries."

In the presence of the Chinese gang leader, Enzo felt vulnerable, *naked* without his gun. The two henchmen standing over by the door had relieved both Italians of their weapons before allowing them into the meeting. The room itself was a gambling den devoid of clientele. Whether it had been closed down for their meeting or not, Enzo had no way of telling. It was situated above a Chinese attorney's office, which was pretty much the last place the authorities would look for illegal gambling, even if they chose to. Much of Mulberry was under protection by the gangs, who had most of the police bought, paid for, and in their pockets.

"My father Vincenzo sends his warmest regards," Enzo said, "and hopes we can put any bad blood behind us."

"Let's cut through the bullshit, Mr. DeCarlo. You're here to talk to me about running Italian drugs in Chinatown. So, let's talk."

Enzo admired the guy's bluntness as he'd never been much for making chitchat either, although his father had always instilled in him that it was an essential part of the negotiation process to put both parties at ease. Enzo thought the gangster looked much too young to be the leader of anything, let alone Chinatown's most up-and-coming gang. He had a baby face and thick, bushy eyebrows that blended into one another at the bridge of his nose; they reminded Enzo of Margaret O'Leary, the fat Irish girl he'd finger-banged on his eighth-grade field trip to the Statue of Liberty. Hell, even the Chinese guy's thin excuse for a mustache reminded him of the unfortunate O'Leary girl.

"We can supply you with as many narcotics as you can handle," Enzo explained. "Class A and B."

"And why would we peddle your merchandise when we have more than enough of our own?" Big D plucked a card—a six of hearts—from the green baize tabletop and flipped it with skill over and between the fingers of his left hand.

"It's simple enough," Enzo said. "We sub-contract street-level distribution in Little Italy, and you expand your operations."

"The Italians are moving away from selling on the streets? Is the mafia above the dirty end of the business now?"

The word *mafia* jarred Enzo and he stopped himself short of saying, *No, but you people do it so much better*. Enzo gave the gang leader a cynical smile instead and replied, "Your people are more efficient, especially in your own territory."

"So, I'll ask you again, Mr. DeCarlo," Big D crumpled the playing card up in his clenched fist, "why am I even speaking to you about this right now?"

"The families still have clout here," Enzo replied with confidence. "Plus, cops on the payroll and a strong presence in neighborhoods you want to spread into. We can make the process smoother and faster."

"With your drugs?"

"With our *merchandise*."

Enzo and Big D contemplated one another for what seemed an age. It was clear neither one wished to break the silence, the unspoken law of negotiation being he who spoke first was on his back foot. Rico, too, maintained his silence. His role was nothing more than backup for Enzo, a show of strength, although just what he could do *sans* gun should things turn nasty was not entirely apparent.

It was Enzo who broke the silence—a calculated tactic to allow his opponent to think he'd gained the upper hand. "Remember, the Italian families have the muscle and hard cash to take down Chinese gangs and reclaim our territory—should we wish to do so."

"Is that a threat, Mr. DeCarlo?"

Enzo shook his head no and locked eyes with Big D. "Just a statement of fact."

"If we do agree to distribute for you, we shall expect a percentage that will make it worth our while—along with the backing of the DeCarlo family, of course."

"We'll finalize percentages and volumes once we have a deal, Jonathon." Enzo held out a hand ready to shake. "Do we? Or do you need time to discuss it with your people first?" Enzo shot straight to the heart of the gangster's vanity with a master stroke. Big D Luen Dang answered to nobody, and to intimate otherwise was a slight against his authority.

Big D eased himself down from the card table and took Enzo's hand. "We have a deal, Mr. DeCarlo," he said without a glimmer of emotion.

"Enzo." Enzo gave his hand a long, firm shake.

"I don't think I will call you that, Mr. DeCarlo." Big D's expression gave Enzo the feeling he found the very idea distasteful.

Enzo shrugged the rebuttal off as he broke the handshake. He really didn't give a shit what the Chinese called him, as long as he stuck to their deal. "There is the matter of the Taccetta family. They're muscling in on the territory you want to expand, and—"

"You want the Tigers to take care of them?"

"It's in your interests now," Enzo said.

"You failed to contain them with your hit on Nicoletti?" Big D's lips curved in a half-smile.

"We thought they'd take the hint after we iced Frankie, but Big Joe stuck his dumbfuck head in the sand and played business as usual."

"Why not eliminate him?"

Enzo spread his arms to his sides, palms up. "It's a family thing," he explained. "We whack the guy at the top, and there's an all-out war between the five families. Nobody wants that—not again. But, if their operation on the ground is taken out...."

"I don't think it would cause us too much trouble to sort out your issue," Big D replied. "Provided the price is right and given our new-found ... *understanding*."

"Good." Once again, Enzo offered his hand for the shaking.

This time, though, Big D declined, turning away in a silent dismissal.

CHAPTER TWENTY-ONE

The reek of raw, uncut heroin permeated the entire room. It carried with it a tart, faintly acidic smell that reminded Johnny "Freckles" Taccetta of the homemade vinaigrette his mother insisted on drenching every one of her barely palatable salads with. He'd gotten used to the pungent odor, having worked with the stuff for so many years, as it vied with the sickly-sweet aroma of pastries and strong coffee from the business establishment below.

The Napoli House of Pastries had occupied the corner of Mulberry and Hester for nigh on twenty years. Italian-owned and run since day one, protected by Big Joe Taccetta's family, it was struggling to stay afloat against the relentless creep of the Chinese. Had it not housed the headquarters of the Taccetta's drug distribution operation on the floor above it, the Napoli would have become just another Chinese restaurant or pool hall five or six years ago.

"We gotta bag all this up by ourselves?" asked Johnny's sidekick, Tony "The Blade" Ruggerio, as he eyed with disdain the neatly stacked piles of tightly packaged heroin and cocaine taking up three of the five desks. Each of the rudimentary desks was surrounded by a half dozen white plastic lawn chairs; otherwise, the room was unfurnished. As he spoke, Tony fiddled with the four-inch switchblade he always carried, which had given rise to his nickname. Nervously, over and over, he flicked the thing open before snapping it shut again with one fat, meaty hand.

"Sure as hell looks that way," Johnny Taccetta replied with a grunt. He checked his watch. "They should all be here by now; it's not like the Chinese to be so goddamned unreliable." His father, Big Joe, had organized a crew of Asians—Korean and Vietnamese, but mostly Chinese—to bag up the merchandise. They worked for a lot cheaper than the Italians, didn't help themselves to the drugs they were cutting, and could generally be relied upon to keep their mouths shut.

Tony flicked open his blade once more and stroked the underside of his chin with its keenly honed tip. "I guess we'll have to replace 'em then. Maybe even make an example of one or two. Nothing broadcasts that the Taccettas are pissed better than a few broken fingers."

"Maybe we should make one of them marry my goddamn sister." Johnny laughed. The joke was rooted in some truth. His older-by-two-years sister Gabriella was the spoiled brat of the Taccetta family and had a stinking attitude toward pretty much everyone. She was not exceptionally blessed in the looks department, either.

"I'd say that'd be way too cruel a punishment just for not turning up to work," Tony threw in with a knowing chuckle. "I'd say fingers—or maybe even ankles—would be the way to go. Save the poor bastards from a fate worse than death."

"Yeah, but that won't help us tonight, will it, Tony?" Johnny snapped, his mood darkening in an instant. "Makes me wonder why the hell the families bother working with these fucking assholes."

"Ain't that what *we're* doing here, Johnny?" The Ruggerios were not renowned for their brains.

Tony took in a deep breath to calm himself down. "We use them for packaging and selling to kids on the streets," he explained slowly. "But I heard the DeCarlos and Gambinos are dealing with the Asian gangs for distribution now. What the fuck happened to keeping business between the goddamned families?"

Tony shrugged. Family politics wasn't his forte until it came to busting heads and making people disappear—then he came into his own.

"Like I said, none of this bull crap is gonna help us. This lot was supposed to have been packed up and out on the street before it got dark," Johnny reiterated with a sour glance through the curtains at the encroaching night out on Mulberry. "So, grab yourself a mask and a bag of powdered milk and get to work, Tony." He nodded across the room to the ceiling-high stack of bulk-bought, dirt-cheap powdered milk, sucrose, and starch they used to cut the drugs with. Some suppliers chose to cut with laundry detergent and rat poison to save a few bucks. There was nothing quite like killing off your customer base.

Grumbling vulgar protests beneath his breath, Tony shuffled across to the first table. There, he grabbed a plain, brown box of tiny baggies and a cloth face mask that would hopefully prevent him from getting too damned high once the Saran-wrapped Class-A narcotics were opened. Ventilation in the room above the Napoli was far from adequate for their purposes—it consisted of two large office fans; an ancient, rattling AC unit; and the only two windows in the place that weren't nailed shut.

"You got the scales?" Tony asked.

"Yeah, there's a couple over there by the coke. I just hope the batteries are still good in 'em."

The Asians never needed to use the electronic scales. That's because they'd filled so many baggies with white powder for the Taccettas that they knew the precise gram measurements purely by eye and feel. Johnny made his way across the room. His pristine Nike training shoes scuffed up pale gray eddies of dust from the wooden floorboards as he walked.

"No way on God's fucking green earth are we gonna get through this lot tonight, but we should be able to get enough packed up to at least keep our main dealers happy." He lifted the first sash window and the chill October air bit into his face.

Tony pulled up one of the lawn chairs and sat himself down at the table with a disgruntled sigh. Their job was supposed to be supervising the crew, not prepping and bagging.

"Quit your bellyaching, asshole," Johnny told him as he flicked the latch on the window adjacent to the AC unit. "We'll catch up tomorrow when we round up another bunch of arms and legs. Besides, a little hard work never hurt anyone." He yanked up the sash window with a grunt of exertion; the thing always got stuck a quarter-way up. Another hard push and the window went all the way.

At first, Johnny Taccetta didn't know what had hit him square in the chest. Iit all happened so fast. Like a haymaker punch to his sternum, the projectile had him staggering backward into the room with the breath knocked from his lungs. In the split second it took Johnny's startled brain to register the cold wetness soaking through his clothes, searing, bright yellow flames had erupted across his shirt and pants. Screaming, Johnny beat at his chest in a vain attempt to quell the flames. He succeeded only in setting his sleeves alight as his lungs filled with scorching air.

The sharp sound of shattering glass filled the room as windows imploded and fires sprang up from bottles of lit gasoline that smashed on the floorboards.

Tony stripped off his jacket as he raced across the room. A squat, green gin bottle crashed through the window to his left. Instinctively he ducked, and it narrowly missed his head. Landing atop a heap of packaged heroin, the bottle failed to smash. Instead, gas poured over the drugs, which were set alight by the flaming cloth stuffed into the bottle's neck; it looked to all the world like some bizarre flambé.

Remembering to duck and roll, Johnny screamed as he squirmed around on the floor, the skin on his cheeks and chin charring, his hair melting into one big clump. Tony sidestepped the rapidly growing flames and threw his jacket over Johnny's burning body; most of the guy's clothes were gone, yet his bare flesh still burned with the gas that had soaked him. Results were mixed; the flames on Johnny lessened, but Tony's jacket caught fire.

"*Fuck!*" Tony yelled in anger and frustration. The room was fast becoming an inferno with the build-up of years of drug dust feeding the fire and the flames sucking the oxygen from the room and licking at his clothes. Another minute at the most, and the only exit door would be blocked. Tony's every instinct screamed at him to get out of the burning room before the flames consumed him. But Johnny was the boss's kid, and there was no way he could leave him. If he did, Tony Ruggerio might as well stay put and burn alongside him.

Tony grabbed hold of Johnny's bare feet—they were the only parts of him not on fire as the gasoline that burned away his shoes hadn't soaked through them to the flesh beneath—and dragged him toward the door. Johnny yowled in agony as clumps of his charred back left a blackened, bloody trail behind him. Choking back the acid burn of puke that rose to the back of his throat, Tony kicked open the door and heaved Johnny out into the hallway beyond.

Flames reached out for Tony through the doorway, like sinister arms beckoning him back into their scorching embrace. He kicked the door shut, which afforded a reprieve from the blistering heat. Panicked, he scanned the dimly lit hallway for an extinguisher, a fire blanket, anything that could prevent Johnny Taccetta from burning to death. Of course, he found nothing. OSHA had very little jurisdiction in the mafia drug dens.

All Tony could do was roll Johnny Taccetta around on the hard wooden floor and bat at the flames with his hands, despite the sweetly vile reek of burning flesh and the blisters erupting on his palms. He knew he had to get them both away before the fire department turned up—the last thing they needed was to be discovered in the same building as a room full of burning heroin. Tony managed to get Johnny Taccetta away before the door burned out and the fire spread through the entire floor above the Napoli House of Pastries. On the way to the hospital, they passed the fire truck speeding in the opposite direction along Mulberry. Johnny had fallen quiet by that time. Consciousness had mercifully left him.

CHAPTER TWENTY-TWO

"Hey, the Chinks did good." Vincenzo DeCarlo leaned back in his high-backed chair and took a long, welcome drag on his cigar—finest Cuban, of course. "*You* did good, Little Enzo."

Enzo grimaced at the name. As he'd gotten older, his father only wheeled it out in moments of levity, but it rankled nonetheless. "Jonathon Dang came through." He refused to call the gangster Big D—it made the guy sound too much like some Saturday morning cartoon character. "We picked the right gang to get into bed with."

"They're all pretty much the same," Angel Corozzio threw in. "No matter which one you'd chosen to approach, any one of them would have been happy to torch Taccetta's place." Puffing on his fat cigar, the consigliere tipped a wink at his son, who sat across the table from him nursing a deep glass of Glenfiddich Grand Cru. Rico smiled back as he absently swirled the rich, amber liquid around in the cut crystal.

In the three days since the DeCarlos had sanctioned the firebombing of the center of Big Joe Taccetta's drug distribution network, not one finger had been pointed in the family's direction, nor had there been any retribution from the Taccetta family.

The fire department had somehow, only by the grace of God, managed to save the Napoli and, along with it, the best red velvet donuts in Manhattan. Although, without the Taccettas' narcotics money to prop the business up, the general consensus was that its days were pretty much numbered. Upon the discovery of what remained of the heroin and coke after the fire had taken its toll, the police and feds had crawled all over the room above the shop, as well as the two stories above that. Naturally, they had found nothing to link either the place or its contents to the Taccetta family or the Mott Street Tigers.

"Pity about Big Joe's kid," Enzo said. "I heard he's gonna live, but the fire messed him up real bad. He was a good-looking kid, too."

Vincenzo exhaled heavily through flared nostrils, the white plumes of smoke pouring from him like flames from a dragon. "Wrong place, wrong time," he said without compassion. "These things happen in our line of business." Another long drag.

"And if Big Joe finds out who's behind his drug distribution being burned out of business?" Enzo asked the obvious question. The arson he'd instigated at the behest of his father had cost the Taccetta family millions of dollars in burned-up drugs and lost sales revenue. It was doubtful Big Joe's business, with its limited means, would recover.

"Taccetta knows," Vincenzo told him. "He's just too shit-scared to do anything about it—just like he knew who took Frankie the Nose out and did nothing. Maybe the stubborn old bastard will come to the table and talk about a truce before we wipe him out completely. Maybe we could even merge the two families' interests somehow."

"It would benefit Mr. Taccetta to open up a dialogue," Angel explained. "If only to avoid the fallout we all lived through back in eighty-five."

Vincenzo sat forward in his chair as if an exceptionally bad smell had wafted his way. "God forbid the likes of Rudy fucking Giuliani gets involved in our businesses again," he growled. "That asshole cost us all dear—some of the families are *still* trying to claw their way back from that goddamned shit show."

Enzo knew the story all too well. It was still fresh in the Italians' minds, the wounds unfathomably deep. Back in the day, when Giuliani was U.S. Attorney for the Southern District of New York, he'd spearheaded the round-up of mafia bosses, which had all but decimated the Italians' stranglehold on the city. Making the most of the RICO charges, they'd prosecuted eleven key players, including heads of the five families, and had been successful in putting eight of them behind bars for a hundred years apiece. Vincenzo DeCarlo had managed to wriggle free by the skin of his teeth, all thanks to his consigliere, who proved to be more conniving even than Giuliani himself. Vincenzo had watched from the sidelines as they bagged Castellano, Salerno, and Corallo, all of whom he considered to be personal friends as well as business allies.

"I hear Giuliani has plans to run for mayor sometime soon." Angel waved the red flag at Vincenzo. Enzo knew there were times the consigliere enjoyed getting a rise out of the man.

"Then may Mary, mother of Jesus Christ, have mercy upon all of us!" Vincenzo took the bait and growled through a thick cloud of smoke. "What a dark fucking day for all of New York that would be."

CHAPTER TWENTY-THREE

Jen took her time walking through the Minster Tower apartments. It was her first time back in Flushing since the trip with her father a little over a month ago, and the first outing under the auspices of the Black Dragons.

Eddie had come along for the ride, even though he refused to hide his obvious displeasure at her dealings with the gang. She'd told him there was no need for him to babysit her since she was merely viewing the property. Charlie-Boy Fok was also accompanying Jen on her maiden reconnaissance, and she knew all too well his presence would only lead to friction between the two men. It was an assumption that was borne out the first moment Charlie-Boy saw Eddie climb out of their car. Yet somehow, despite the open hostility between the two, Charlie-Boy managed to remain civil and Eddie, as always, was the model of discretion.

Trailing a stride or so behind Charlie-Boy, Eddie appeared all the more menacing with the addition of the black eye he'd acquired the day Jen had met up with Enzo DeCarlo following her visit to the nail bar. The bruise faded quickly; now it was little more than a purple-gray shadow around his left eye. Eddie had given no further explanation than saying he'd encountered a little trouble that needed taking care of. Jen had not pressed, nor had Eddie offered any more information. She did have an inkling it may well have had something to do with the underground gay bars Eddie liked to frequent, as they seemed to attract drunken troublemakers intent on a little gay-bashing. Still, Jen had learned over the years that, when Eddie Sun didn't want to talk, he sure as all hell wasn't about to be coerced into it.

"Are we sure we want to get involved in co-op investor apartments?" Charlie-Boy spoke up just to have his voice heard. The guy just seemed to hate silence. "This place was going under less than a year ago."

Jen wasn't all that impressed by the gangster's attempt at pretending to have done his homework; that particular snippet of information could easily be gleaned from any one of the sales handouts. Jen glanced over her shoulder at Charlie-Boy. "That has no bearing on whether or not we should buy. Don't forget, because they are investment properties, we will be free to sublet and do whatever we want with them."

"I guess it's a nice area," Charlie-Boy continued. "Maybe *too* nice for hookers."

"If we intend to attract a higher level of clientele, then it will pay to be where they are—and where they're prepared to visit." As much as it irked Jen to field the gangster's asinine comments, she knew he'd be reporting straight back to Storm Cheung—and *he* was the one she was out to impress.

"I don't see what's wrong with the Chinatown fuck shops," Charlie-Boy replied. "They're cheap to run and they make us good money."

"Your boss is courting a better class of clientele than those who frequent your average massage parlors," Jen explained as they let themselves into another of the apartments. "The kind of men who will pay two, three hundred dollars for an hour."

"You're fucking joking?" Charlie-Boy scoffed. "Nobody's going to pay top dollar for Chinese pussy."

Jen gritted her teeth. "Nobody will pay top dollar in *Chinatown*," she spoke slowly as if addressing a slow child. "But here in Flushing, where new money is coming in, they will—especially if we provide them with *quality*."

Charlie-Boy closed his mouth awhile, which pleased Jen. His incessant chatter was giving her a headache, as if this whole situation wasn't bad enough. She gave the large suite they were touring her full attention, picturing the walls that could so easily be put up to divide it and create additional bedrooms out of the living area. That would make any of the large apartments she'd seen so far just perfect to house four or five girls, along with a madam. Other apartments in the block could be used to give the girls a place to call home and spend their off hours. Plus, the smaller apartments would make ideal gambling dens to get their clientele to part with yet more of their hard-earned money. In all, Jen figured, Minster Tower on 160th Street was the most viable real estate for what the Black Dragons had planned.

"So?" Charlie-Boy broke his all-too-brief silence. "Are we going to buy the whole complex or not?"

"I don't think that would be a very wise business decision." It grated on Jen to have to explain everything to the fool. He was beginning to remind her of Petey.

"Why not? We have the money to buy this place, and more."

Jen offered the gangster what she hoped was a pleasant smile. "If you own the building outright, it will be difficult—impossible even—to relocate should the authorities discover you. I feel it would be best if your operations here were mixed in with regular tenants."

"Hiding in plain sight, eh?" Charlie-Boy appeared to be most delighted with his observation.

"Something like that," Jen replied. "I think it's time I spoke with the seller—you need to make an offer quickly, while the apartments are still available. I'd hate for you to miss out."

Jen then turned on her Manolo Blahnik heels and made her way back out into the hallway with Charlie-Boy and Eddie in tow.

By the time Jen returned to Storm's Chinatown office, Charlie-Boy had been with the gang leader for well over an hour.

"How did the negotiations go?" Storm greeted Jen as she walked in. Looking long and lean in a black silk long-sleeved shirt and black jeans, he leaned back against his over-large rectangular desk. "Charlie-Boy told me he talked you into making an offer on the Minster Tower co-op."

Jen was taken aback. So, that's how this was going to go, was it? She smiled. "Why would he have to talk me into my own idea?" She made a dismissive gesture. "Whatever. They accepted your offer of $50,000 per apartment for five apartments—plus first refusal on future vacancies."

Charlie-Boy shot her a warning shark smile that Jen would have gladly slapped from his sycophantic, backstabbing face.

"I'm delighted Charlie-Boy saw the potential in Flushing," Storm delivered a hearty slap to his deputy's shoulder. "Getting in on the ground floor of such an up-and-coming area will pay us long-term dividends. Buying a handful of co-op apartments instead of the whole building was a masterstroke."

"Thank you," Jen and Charlie-Boy said in perfect unison.

"It's a no-brainer when you think about it," Charlie bulled on. "We keep our exposure low and hide among regular tenants—most of whom will be Asian and easy for us to intimidate."

"The location of such an upmarket property will allow us to attract a better quality of clientele," Storm repeated Jen's words back to her. Clearly, Charlie-Boy had left nothing out while grabbing the credit for all her hard work. It was like being back in her father's office, having the rug pulled from under her yet again.

"And we make more money per girl per hour." Charlie-Boy seemed to take great delight in overshadowing Jen. She figured he must have been intimidated by her to pull a stunt like that.

Fine. Let him. For now. Jen took a seat in one of the side chairs that faced Storm's desk, crossing her slender legs and noting the way both men's eyes followed the gesture. Under other circumstances, she would have smoothed down her skirt. Here, now, she didn't bother.

"There is more than enough space to accommodate the girls, so there'll be less coming and going to attract suspicion," she explained. "Plus, you can apply the same upper-market principle to your gambling operations. A den at Minster Tower would attract bigger money—the kind of guys who won't balk at having to park their German cars outside for fear of having them broken into or stolen."

"Yeah," Storm said, "Charlie-Boy already told me."

"Of course he did—just like he told you everything else. I'm beginning to think you don't really need me at all, since he's so fucking smart." Unable to hold her tongue—or temper—any longer, Jen felt the color rush to her cheeks.

"Excuse me?" Charlie-Boy glowered at her.

Jen got to her feet, holding Storm's gaze. "Your sock puppet has everything covered, so I reckon that makes me surplus. I'm sure you'll have no problem closing the deal, Charlie-Boy." She turned to let herself out.

"Hold on." Storm rose from the edge of his desk and lifted his hands toward her. "I don't know what's going on here between you two, but I *won't* tolerate this level of disrespect."

Had Storm ended his sentence with "from a woman," Jen would have likely slapped his face before she stormed out. To hell with him being a gang leader. What was he going to do, shoot her in the back?

"Charlie-Boy." Storm turned to his second-in-command. "Could you please leave us?"

Charlie-Boy opened his mouth to protest, but something in his boss's face made him think better of it. "I have to be somewhere, anyway," he grumbled as he headed for the door.

Jen's eyes followed him, suspecting Charlie-Boy Fok's days were numbered.

CHAPTER TWENTY-FOUR

"He means well. And he's a good man," Storm told Jen as Charlie-Boy exited the office, not quite slamming the door behind him. "I never doubt his loyalty to me and the Black Dragons."

"I'm sure he's incredibly loyal," Jen observed dryly. She flipped a lock of hair back over her shoulder. She'd worn it loose today, letting it cascade around her shoulders. It was an instinctive choice, calculated to make her look more appealing. Eying her chair, she decided against sitting back down. "But, if you've brought me in to do a job, what sense does it make to allow him to undermine me like that?"

Storm fiddled with the collar of his expensive silk shirt and let his eyes slowly take Jen in from top to toe. "Charlie-Boy has been by my side for most of my life," he explained. "We made friends in sixth grade and worked the streets together once we decided school wasn't for us. We started out dealing weed for the Jamaicans and the Mexicans, and when we got a little older, we earned a decent living gun-running and strong-arming for the Chinese and Vietnamese gangs. I guess our graduation was when we finally made it into the Black Dragons."

Jen was curious. Why had Storm chosen to offload his life story on her? She didn't need any justification from him.

"He saved my life," Storm added simply. "I owe him."

"That's most admirable, but to involve him in important decisions at the expense of your business?" If there were cracks in the armor of Storm's ostensibly unwavering loyalty to his asshole friend, she was determined to expose and exploit them. Perhaps she might also exploit her gender.

"We were sixteen . . . thought we knew it all," Storm went on, ignoring Jen's question. "You know how that goes."

Jen nodded, though she'd never had that singular experience as her life had always been dictated by the men in her family. She envied the freedom Storm had enjoyed in his youth, even though it had been played out on the treacherous streets of Chinatown.

After a moment of hesitation, during which he read Jen's face, Storm said, "Back in eighty-two, eighty-three, we crossed paths with the Koreans. They were little more than unorganized thugs back in the day. But, by the time Charlie-Boy and I got involved, they'd begun to organize themselves into *Jopok*—proper gangs with the beginnings of structure. They ran some of the streets around Doyers by terrorizing the locals. They'd carve up the pimps and small-time gambling den owners for a slice of the action and beat anyone who got in their way into a few weeks' stay in a hospital bed. I guess you could say Charlie-Boy and I just happened to be in the wrong place at the wrong time."

Jen dropped her purse into her chair and stepped slowly toward the gangster. She was all too aware of the effect she had on men, and Storm was no exception. He was opening a door into his life, and she was not above exploiting that for her own cause.

"We'd got hold of some crack cocaine from one of Charlie-Boy's old contacts—the stuff was just taking hold back then and was cheap and very addictive—we reckoned we could sell it under the Koreans' noses and get away with it. We didn't." He let out a short, snorting laugh and lifted the hem of his shirt. A thin, straight, white scar ran from the shallow indent of his navel up to the lower curve of his sternum.

Jen hesitated, shocked by the violence to which the scar bore mute testimony, and that Storm showed it to her.

He ran a finger along the thin, white line. "They were about to gut me like a fish when Charlie-Boy stormed in—the madman. He snatched an iron bar from one of the Koreans and laid into all of them like he was possessed by a demon or something. There were four of them, but they didn't stand a chance against Charlie-Boy."

Under the pretense of taking a closer look at the scar, Jen moved closer and traced her finger down its entire length. "That must have really hurt," she said, making her voice soft.

Storm shrugged with exaggerated bravado. "They went deep," he said as his eyes followed the path of Jen's finger; his eyes widened as its pink nail came to rest at his waistband. "They'd have spilled my guts all over the sidewalk and left me there as an example, but Charlie-Boy busted every head and sent them running. I don't think I've ever seen anyone look quite so terrified for their lives since."

"And that's why you keep him around?" Slowly, deliberately, Jen slipped her finger a little lower. Storm drew in a breath, his muscles tensed, and she rewarded him with a seductive smile.

"Like I said, I owe my life to...." Storm's voice trailed off as he grew ever more distracted from his story. "*That's* why I keep him around."

"I find that most admirable, David." Jen hooked the waistband of the gangster's black jeans, tugging ever so slightly.

Storm's fingers tightened on the hem of his shirt; the growing bulge in his jeans was most noticeable. "Are we doing this, Miss Mo-Li?" There was a raw expectation in his voice.

Jen leaned in and pressed her lips against the gangster's, her tongue slipping between them to seek out his. When he responded, she waited for a beat, then pulled back, smiling and meeting his gaze. *Your move.*

His move was to bury his hands in the dark silken cascade of her hair and tug her downward. That was an easy signal to read. She knelt and unbuttoned Storm's jeans, pulling them down along the lean, toned thighs. She pressed her lips to the warm flesh below Storm's navel, kissing a downward trail, as she rid him of his briefs. She paused to admire his bared erection—she'd learned how much men liked that—then eased him back against the edge of his desk and took him into her mouth.

He groaned out loud, tightening his grip on her hair. It was a sound she'd heard before, but this was new—this sensation of power it bestowed. In less than a few minutes, she had rendered the powerful Chinese gang leader entirely helpless *because* she was a mere woman, not in spite of it. Had she intended to assassinate the man, she could easily have done so with a sharp knife, a razor blade, or an expensive pen, and it would have been all over for Storm Cheung. But that was not Jen's intent. No, she intended to exploit Cheung's most primal instincts to imprint herself onto his psyche and remind him just how much more useful to him she could be than Charlie-Boy Fok. She felt no specific desire. To Jen Mo-Li, this was strictly self-preservation.

Storm grunted, yanked Jen's head back and away from his groin, then grasped her upper arms in a vise grip and yanked her upward. She didn't have to be told what he wanted. Hiking up her skirt, she hitched her panties to one side and mounted the gangster, her knees on his desk. She took him in slowly, with long, measured strokes while he hissed and groaned and gasped out fragments of words in English and Chinese.

Once she had him, the sex became quick, aggressive—urgent. Jen crushed Storm's lips with hers and invaded his mouth with her tongue. His hands explored her bared thighs and slid up beneath her sweater to knead her breasts as his breath escaped him in rapid, shallow gasps.

Jen wanted to laugh out loud. This was what it felt like to be in the driver's seat. To take control. She celebrated the dark revelation, and she feared it. She hadn't striven to manipulate, merely to not be the victim of manipulation. But this....

Storm came with a sound like a cough. His body spasmed, his head lolled back, and he squeezed his eyes tight shut. Jen took pleasure in how vulnerable he'd made himself. And for what? A few moments of physical gratification. Not very smart, these men.

Any fear Jen felt guttered in the heady, white-hot sensation of empowerment that cascaded seamlessly into orgasm. Jen rode the waves of pleasure until they waned in tandem with Storm's erection, then slid from his body, smoothed down her skirt and sweater, and twitched her panties back into place so there'd be no embarrassing trickle of semen down her bare legs when she left. Then she retrieved her purse from the side chair and pulled out a hairbrush.

"Thank you," Storm said from behind her. His voice was breathy, but cool and polite, as if she'd just straightened his tie, or brought him a coffee.

She turned to look at him. He'd tucked himself back into his briefs and was pulling up his jeans. Smiling her sweetest smile, Jen smoothed her hair and considered her response. Did she admit her pleasure and let him imagine he'd forged a bond, or did she let him wonder at the expense of his considerable ego?

She decided to say nothing. Let him interpret her smile as he would.

He went around behind his desk and seated himself in the executive chair. Putting distance between them, was he? Hiding his vulnerability. He cleared his throat. When he spoke again, his voice was all business. "I want you to fly out to China—Fujian, to be precise."

Jen sat herself down in the chair facing Storm across his desk. She did not want to go to China. Did not want to pick out "livestock" for the Black Dragons' pricey brothels.

"Why?" she asked simply.

"You already know the right people in the province. We have a few contacts of our own, who should be of use to you. So, I think it's best Charlie-Boy accompany you on your first visit."

What the hell? Determined to not allow her frustration at the news to show, Jen took in a short, controlled breath. "Alright," she said, "then if you would organize passage for Eddie, too, I'd appreciate it. I'd feel safer."

"I can assure you that you will be well taken care of, Miss Mo-Li." Storm seemed a tad put out by Jen's request. "But, if it is what you want, I'll have the necessary arrangements made."

"Thank you. It will take some time for me to get used to our working arrangement," Jen said. "I am accustomed to dealing with families, not—"

"There will still be families seeking passage, although we will only select those with daughters in the required age range. You are to adhere to that requirement without deviation. Is that quite clear, Miss Mo-Li?"

"Perfectly," Jen replied. Despite the outwardly icy demeanor, she knew in her gut she'd had the desired effect on David Cheung. "What is the age range you have in mind for your new establishments?"

When Storm told her, it was all Jen could do not to scream in his face. Somewhere deep inside of her, a tiny voice asked, *What are you doing?*

CHAPTER TWENTY-FIVE

The Jīn Bāozi restaurant at the southern end of Mulberry Street was the perfect setting for Jen, Storm, Charlie-Boy, and a select handful of Black Dragons to celebrate the acquisition of the Minster Tower apartments. Sandwiched between a small butcher and a fish monger, and within easy sight of the intersection at Bayard Street, the restaurant had come under the Dragons' protection in recent months, and the new management was making a great success of the place.

The restaurant had been closed to the general public for the night so Storm and his associates could enjoy the full attention of the waitstaff and chef, and not have to watch their backs as they ate. That particular area of Mulberry was much coveted by the other Chinese gangs, as well as the infamously violent Vietnamese gang, Born to Kill or BTK.

Despite her being the only woman at the table, and without Eddie, Jen felt remarkably comfortable surrounded by the gang members. She wore a simple, white silk dress that was more modest than her usual attire for an evening out. It had a high collar that covered her neck, showed no cleavage, and was demurely knee-length. Although her choice of dress showed very little skin, it hugged her figure more than enough to engage the interest of her dining companions without giving out the wrong signals. Jen's one extravagance was her footwear—a brand new pair of black patent Christian Louboutin high-heeled open-toed shoes, which showed off her fresh pedicure to perfection. The French shoe designer was the hottest new thing that year, and Jen had fallen instantly in love with the red-soled shoes the moment she'd laid eyes on them.

"I would like to propose a toast," Storm silenced the chatter around the table, which sported a pair of Lazy Susans crammed with every type of Chinese delicacy imaginable. "To the beginning of our most lucrative association with Miss Jen Mo-Li and the Mo-Li Corporation." He held up a shot glass filled to the brim with *baijiu*—known locally as Chinese vodka—and paused a moment for everyone to follow suit.

It jarred Jen to hear her father's company mentioned in the same breath as the Black Dragons' venture. She'd gone to great pains to keep the two separate and, other than taking advantage of the contacts and business relationships she'd nurtured in Hong Kong and around the dockyards of Fujian Province, they were two entirely separate entities. Her father was never to know about her association with the Dragons, but she would not correct Storm Cheung on his assumptions, either, since he seemed so proud of linking the Mo-Li name to his gang. Lifting her glass of baijiu to her lips, Jen drank the toast with a knowing smile at the gang leader.

A loud banging on the restaurant's front door interrupted the fete. From their place at the rear of the restaurant, the view obscured by tall, fake ficus trees, it was impossible for Jen or any of the Dragons to see who was thumping to be let in. With an embarrassed glance toward Storm, the manager, Denis Wap, scurried across the room to silence the ruckus.

"We are closed! Read the sign!" As he walked, he made an exaggerated show of pointing to the neatly handwritten note on the door, which made it quite clear Jīn Bāozi was closed for a private function.

"I guess some people just can't take the hint, especially when they're drunk," Storm dismissed the rapping on the glass door with a laugh. "This is why we have the place to ourselves." With that, he returned to his conversation with Charlie-Boy as his soldiers chatted and filled their bellies.

Bristling, Jen listened as old Wap slid back the bolts at the top and bottom of the door to address the unruly would-be gatecrashers. Her instincts told her something was not quite right about the interruption, especially when she heard a voice she thought sounded eerily familiar.

"Tommy Guo?" The voice spoke in broad New York Italian. "He's overdue. We've come to collect."

"He is not here. I am manager now," Wap explained in his very best, broken English. He was a slip of a man, but he remained steadfast.

Jen then heard the sound of a bolt sliding shut before she saw Storm, Charlie-Boy, and the other Dragons pointing as all conversations muted. A scuffle could be heard as well as a cry of surprise and annoyance. Denis Wap then staggered backward into full view of everyone at the table. Despite flailing his skinny arms in an attempt to maintain his balance, Wap fell flat on his bony ass on the cream-tiled floor.

Storm and his cohort immediately got to their feet as a couple of the Dragons pulled cleavers out from beneath their jackets and stepped away from the table. The sound of chairs scraping in unison on the floor grated on Jen as she wondered what she was expected to do. She was the only female among the party, and, although she knew how to take care of herself, she wasn't sure if that would be expected should the inevitable happen.

When Enzo came into view, flanked by Rico and a trio of mean-looking Italian thugs, Jen's breath caught in her throat. Of all the places and times to see Enzo DeCarlo again. She glanced around; it was too late for retreat. All she could do was stand her ground.

When their eyes met, she felt a visceral charge of adrenaline and saw something like it mirrored in his eyes. Unfortunately, that did not keep him from advancing into the room.

"Any of you know where Tommy is?" Enzo demanded as he and his men squared up to the Black Dragons. All three of Enzo's henchmen had short iron bars in their hands, and Rico had one hand in the inside of his jacket, a less than subtle hint he was packing more than a jemmy.

"This is a private party," Storm growled. "You people have no business here."

"We *do*." Enzo eyed the cleavers and pissed off Dragons. "But not with you. Tommy Guo owes us money." He glanced over at Wap, who was back on his feet and making his way over with a defiant look on his face.

"You need to leave, wop," Storm took a couple of steps forward. His men did likewise.

"We ain't going *anywhere*," Enzo snarled. He looked over at Jen, who had gotten to her feet and was ready to fight.

Jen met Enzo's gaze with defiance. She had no desire to be involved in an altercation, but there was no doubt in her mind as to where her loyalties must lie that night. Her eyes sought out Rico, who simply stared right through her without a glimmer of acknowledgment. That was hardly surprising, she thought, since she was in a dress, had her hair up, and wore a little more makeup than usual. She also had Enzo's friend pegged as the they-all-look-the-same-to-me type.

It was Charlie-Boy who made the first move. "What the fuck are you looking at?" He surged forward and threw a punch at Enzo's face.

Deflecting the blow with a protective arm, Rico delivered a rapid flurry of punches into Charlie-Boy's face and throat until one of the Dragons returned the favor, punching him so hard in the side of the head that he toppled like a felled tree.

Jen flinched and looked on helplessly as the men with whom she'd been enjoying a celebratory dinner advanced on the Italians with cleavers raised and bloodlust in their eyes. They were met by a barrage of iron bars, and the resounding clang of metal on metal filled the restaurant as the Chinese and Italian gangsters attacked and parried in their brutal attempts to maim one another.

Storm didn't hesitate to leap into the fray; as leader of the Dragons, it was his place to show no fear and fight from the front. With an effortless jump, he kicked high at one of Enzo's men. His foot connected dead center on the guy's sternum. The Italian flew backward, hit the floor, and skidded to a stop halfway under a table, where he gasped for air, the fight knocked out of him.

Enzo bound at the Dragon who'd floored Rico, lashing at his forehead with his iron bar. The blow split the thin skin above the Dragon's right eyebrow and released a torrent of blood that obscured his eye. Still, the guy clung to his cleaver, blindly holding it out in front of him to ward off further attack. Enzo had taken one step toward the bleeding man when a short, muscular Dragon rushed at him with vicious intent, his cleaver slashing the air.

Enzo spun and met the downward arc of the gangster's arm with his jemmy. The Dragon squealed as the metal bar connected with his fingers and dashed the cleaver from his hand. It skittered away across the restaurant floor, almost slicing into Jen's unprotected toes. Jen jumped to avoid the blood-streaked blade as chaos whirled around her. Sounds of fight, fury, and pain assaulted her ears. She wanted nothing more than to flee. Jen was used to the sort of backroom violence that was a part of her world, but this—she'd never seen anything like this. It stunned her to paralysis.

A loud crash to her left made her jump and turn. Not more than four feet away, one of Enzo's gangsters, a tall, broad thug with a newly slashed face from cheek to chin, lifted one of the Dragons from his feet and slammed him down hard on the table. Food, china plates, and drinks spilled everywhere as the table buckled in the middle and folded around the hapless Dragon. The Italian then went about pummeling his victim's face as he lay dazed amidst the destruction.

Blood spattered Jen's dress and bare legs as she dodged in the opposite direction, all but colliding with Rico. He'd picked up his fight with Charlie-Boy and had his hand buried in the Dragon's hair. Face battered, Charlie-Boy was barely conscious; had Rico not had him by the hair, he would have fallen.

Jen knew she could no longer hold herself back. She had to pick a side. She aimed a jab punch at Rico's kidney, relishing the sensation of her knuckles sinking into the soft flesh of his flank. Shocked and winded, Rico relinquished his grip on Charlie-Boy's hair, leaving him to slump to the ground. As Rico spun around to Jen, her Wing Chun training kicked in as her arms instinctively went up to protect her face. Teaching her the martial art was possibly the only thing Jen's father had done right by her.

Rico raised a fist and a jemmy and stepped toward her. Jen threw a slapping block in return, thwarting his punch with one hand while the other caught him in the nose. Blood sprayed across his cheeks, but Rico stood his ground. He lashed out with his iron bar. Jen blocked him with her forearm, then rolled in beneath his arm to catch him in the chin with her elbow before she scooted out of reach. That was when their eyes met and Jen saw a glimmer of recognition in Rico's eyes just before she jabbed his throat, throwing him off balance. As he reared back, Jen swept his legs with a low roundhouse kick and knocked him clean off his feet. He went down hard. Jen raised a beautifully pedicured foot, still clad in its Louboutin stiletto heel, to deliver the final kick. But, before she could, she was wrenched backward by a strong, firm hand on her shoulder.

"Stop!" Enzo growled as he turned Jen around. "You'll fucking kill him."

Without hesitation, Jen peppered Enzo with chain punches, then finished with a high kick that caught his chin. She dropped back into a ready stance, taking in the look of sheer bewilderment on Enzo's face as he stared her down. She could see the conflict in him as he fought his every instinct—no doubt he'd been raised to never raise a hand to a woman, let alone one he was crazy about. Jen found herself praying he would back down.

He didn't. Raising his arm with an iron bar clenched tight in his fist, Enzo took a swing at Jen. She deftly sidestepped the blow and struck out with the heel of her left hand. It connected with Enzo's shoulder with far more power than he'd expected. He grunted and staggered to the right. Wishing she'd removed her shoes—the footwear had been too stupidly expensive to ruin—Jen took advantage of Enzo's hesitation and kicked out at his torso. In a flash of bright red, the ball of Jen's foot connected with Enzo's solar plexus, doubling him over. Jen's knee crushed his lips against his teeth before she hopped back and waited for him to fall.

She'd underestimated him. Enzo jacked upright and threw a punch at her face in return. His knuckles grazed her cheekbone before a second punch caught her in the mouth and drew blood. She countered Enzo's third strike by grabbing his wrist mid-air with her right hand and twisting hard. She felt bones grind, heard him grunt with pain, then brought her foot up between his legs. A kick to the balls was hardly in the spirit of Wing Chun, and Jen knew her father would have wholeheartedly disapproved, but the exposed target was far too good to pass up. Enzo crumpled to his knees in too much agony to even cry out. Jen stood, victorious, over the felled Italian, as the sounds of the mêlée swirled around her. She raised her hand once more to make sure her opponent stayed down.

The strident wail of sirens split the air. Blue and red lights flashed through the windows of Jīn Bāozi, and all eyes were drawn to the many silhouettes of police officers. In an instant, the fight was over and all the gangsters—Chinese and Italians alike—scattered like cockroaches under the harsh glare of a sudden searchlight. As the cops thumped on the front door, everyone raced out through the kitchen. Jen held out a hand to Enzo, who was still on his knees nursing his balls.

"We need to go," she said.

Wincing, Enzo took the offered hand with obvious reluctance and followed Jen behind the restaurant's narrow counter and into the kitchen beyond.

Behind them, Wap unbolted the front door to allow the police entry. He'd taken his own sweet time shuffling there to give his patrons time to make their escape. That his establishment was trashed, and blood smeared across the once-pristine tiles wouldn't matter to the cops. Whatever had gone down was Chinese business and they would have no desire to delve into it.

The cool, moist night air filling the alleyway behind the Fong Jing came as a welcome relief from the sour stink of adrenaline sweat and blood inside. As the metal door clanged shut behind them, Jen yanked on Enzo's arm and dragged him along with her to the dark shadows that pooled beneath the corroded zigzag of a fire escape. Enzo opened his mouth to protest, but Jen pressed her lips against his to silence him.

CHAPTER TWENTY-SIX

Enzo struggled to comprehend. Only a few minutes before, the girl of his dreams had been kicking his ass. But now he had the warmth of her body pressed up against him and her tongue invaded his mouth like some burrowing animal. He tasted blood on her lips, and his mouth was as sore as hell, but Jen felt good.

His first instinct upon running from the restaurant was to get as much distance between him and the scene of the crime as possible and to catch up with Rico and the others. At least two of their guys would need stitching up by one of the DeCarlo's recommended doctors, and Enzo figured he ought to be around to oversee that.

But Jen Mo-Li had her smooth, slender arms entwined around his neck and the curves of her tight and powerful body pressed against his. Her chest heaved with the exertion of fight and flight, her skin gleamed with a light sheen of sweat, and her mouth tasted of alcohol. It was all a heady combination that had Enzo's senses reeling. He'd tried to talk, but Jen's tongue filled his mouth. Instead, Enzo gave in to the moment.

Other than the faint scamper and squeak of rats, the alley was deserted. Enzo figured the cops had decided against exploring beyond the back door of the restaurant, but there was still the chance of him and Jen being caught in flagrante, which only served to inflame his desire for her and fuel the rapidly expanding erection that made the balls she'd just bruised throb painfully.

Dipping a hand below the curve of Jen's firm, shapely buttocks, Enzo inched up the hem of her white dress until he felt the heat of her bare thigh against his fingers. Jen moaned softly into his mouth and gently thrust her hips into his groin. Thus encouraged, Enzo dared his hand to move up and around, seeking her sweet spot. Jen responded with a moan and more fervent kisses. It was as if she was trying to devour him, her tongue probing at his with raw, aggressive passion. She pushed her breasts into his chest and writhed against him, panting like an animal in heat.

His questing fingers found the hot, moist well he sought.

"*No.*" In a heartbeat, Jen broke the kiss and yanked Enzo's hand away.

"What?" Enzo couldn't see Jen's eyes to gauge her intent, as it was far too dark. Surely, she wasn't going to leave him high and dry? Had their tryst been nothing more than a continuation of their fight?

"Not here. Not like this," Jen whispered, her breath warm against Enzo's face. "I have a place."

While the alleyway had held the excitement of being caught, of fucking outside in the chill fall air, Jen's place offered the cozy warmth of concealment from prying eyes and not having to concentrate on keeping their passion silent. Enzo felt more relaxed there, although he'd struggled at first with the forcefulness with which Jen had all but dragged him to an apartment above an accountant's office on Mott Street. He was always the one to make the moves, and it went against his grain to have the chick take control.

But passion soon overrode any reticence on Enzo's part. Jen stepped from her dress the moment the apartment door closed behind them. Standing in front of Enzo in just her bra, panties, and vertiginous shoes, she let down her hair to cascade over her shoulders and the bare skin of her back. Even with blood smeared up her legs, she was the absolute image of perfection.

Enzo undressed as quickly as decency would allow and was surprised to see no reaction from her when he unclipped his holster and laid his gun carefully on top of his heap of discarded clothes on the floor. Before

Enzo had the chance to kick off his underwear, Jen led him to her bed, her hands seemingly everywhere at once as she explored his body.

Although Enzo fought hard to lose himself in the moment, he found Jen's passion so intense, so forceful, he was overwhelmed. Nonetheless, his dick rose admirably to the occasion—aching balls be damned—and without pause for anything even remotely resembling foreplay, Jen mounted and engulfed him, slick, hot, and undeniably ready. As pleasure rolled through him, Enzo stroked Jen's flat stomach, breasts, thighs, and buttocks, grasping her ass as she hit her climax. Incredibly, she became even wilder in orgasm. He half-believed that if he hadn't held her to him, she'd have flown away.

Enzo's climax took a little longer; perversely, Jen's dominance had blunted his ardor. He figured she'd put it down to incredible stamina on his part and would be delighted that it afforded her another couple of orgasms. Leaning down, Jen kissed Enzo with the same passion as in the alleyway, panting in quick, short breaths as her sweat-slicked body connected with his. If Enzo had been surprised by her skill and abandon, he was stunned when he felt her hand cup his tender balls, her touch feather-light. He arched into her, thrusting deeper, and came.

The pleasure was so intense it was almost like pain shot through him in a flash flood, wringing a deep, resonant groan from his throat. He gasped at a host of new sensations and moaned at release so complete it drained him physically and emotionally. As he closed his eyes, the image of her perfect, naked body remained imprinted in his mind—the smooth, flawless ivory of her skin, the glorious dark mass of her silken hair, the glistening sheen of sweat between the twin mounds of her breasts.

Yet through the post-coital glow, Enzo harbored the faint sensation of resentment at how Jen had dominated him and taken her pleasure as if he was an afterthought. It was an altogether new experience for Enzo DeCarlo, the great seducer of so many women, the love-'em-and-leave-'em type who never allowed himself to get emotionally involved.

It was a feeling he didn't entirely dislike.

"Nice apartment. Kind of a surprise in this 'hood." Enzo was not well-versed in post-sex small talk. He usually dressed and got out of a chick's place before she had time to run to the bathroom to clean up. But he had no desire to make himself scarce with Jen. He was enjoying too much lying naked with her in the huge bed with its soft feather pillows, her body contoured to his beneath the cool, silken sheets. Enzo thought she molded well to him, liked how she'd draped her arm across his chest, and enjoyed the warmth of her legs wrapped around his.

Although the apartment was somewhat small and situated in a less than wholesome part of Chinatown, it had a sweetly feminine air to it, which Jen had coupled with a touch of luxury here and there: tasteful artwork; an expensive, distressed brown leather couch; a huge TV set; and polished hardwood floors covered by Persian rugs. It was obvious the gal liked her home comforts.

"Thank you." As Jen spoke, she stroked Enzo's chest with light touches of her fingernails, which generated gooseflesh down toward his belly and beyond. "It's my little bolt-hole—someplace to get away from it all when work gets too much."

A huge print of Klimt's *The Kiss* hung on the wall above them at the head of the bed; it was paired with the artist's *Portrait of Adele*, which hung above Jen's antique dresser. The prints were framed in gilt-edged oak wood and added to the sensual feel of the bedroom. Enzo was no expert, but he figured Jen's dark wood antique bedroom furniture was not fake, much like the pieces he'd seen in the living room as Jen had invited him forcefully to her bed. He was impressed.

"I didn't think rent collecting was a stressful job," Enzo joked as he ran Jen's silken hair through his fingers. "Unless the tenants don't pay up, of course."

"That rarely happens. And even when it does, I don't resort to the same methods as you people." Jen laughed, her breath warm against his bare skin.

"*Us* people?"

"Yeah, gangsters, mafia, mob... whatever it is you like to call yourselves these days."

"*Businesspeople.*" Enzo feigned offence. "I've seen how you handle yourself, Miss Mo-Li. I imagine your tenants don't give you too many problems."

"I didn't hurt you too much, did I?" Jen's hand trailed down beneath the sheets to cup Enzo's balls again.

"Nothing I couldn't handle," Enzo said with a wince. Her hand felt good down there, and he could feel things beginning to stir once more. "You don't hold back."

She laughed. "Should I have?"

"Maybe."

Jen kissed Enzo's chest, her lips soft and wet. "And give our dirty little secret away? That would have been immensely foolish, given the circumstances."

"We didn't *have* a secret."

Jen scoffed at that. "I think we both knew this was going to happen from the first time we met," she told him. "Although, I'd never have figured in a million years you and your henchmen would decide to shake down a restaurant on a night the Black Dragons were there for dinner."

"It wasn't my intention," Enzo said. "Can I ask what you were doing there?"

"You can *ask*," Jen teased. "Business. I occasionally help Chinese people into the United States, and the Dragons have some resources I need."

"Illegally?" Enzo found himself even more intrigued by the Chinese girl. There was clearly a lot more to her than a cute face and a body to die for.

"Unfortunately, yes," Jen lifted her face to look at Enzo. "Not everyone can get the right paperwork to enter the country, even after they eased the restrictions on Asian immigration back in the sixties. I help them out with all of that."

"For a fee?"

Jen nodded. "I do it more to give back. My father came here as an immigrant, and I know just how hard it was for him."

Enzo thought he really ought to ask about Jen's father, but couldn't muster the interest to discuss families when the touch of her breasts pressing into his side, and the heat of her hand on his balls was proving to be quite the distraction. "I didn't figure you as a philanthropist," he said.

"And just what did you have me figured as?" Jen's smile was wry. "An easy fuck?"

Enzo wasn't sure why he was shocked to hear the word tumble so easily from Jen's mouth. After all, the Italian girls he fucked all cussed like sailors. Maybe it was that she seemed so goddamn innocent? "Not after you blew me off, no."

"Then it was the challenge, the thrill of the chase?"

"Something like that." Enzo craned his neck to kiss Jen, his hand buried in her hair down to the scalp.

When their lips parted, she said, "I'm taking a trip to China," and then sat up, breaking the mood.

Enzo found himself staring at her back. "When?"

"In the next few days. I'll be gone for a few months."

Enzo detected no hint of apology in her voice; this was Jen simply letting him know how things were.

"We just got things started." It crossed Enzo's mind that she might simply be passing him off now she'd had him. Was that how all his conquests felt, too?

"It's business, Enzo. I'm sure you of all people can understand that."

"I guess I have no choice."

"No, you do not."

With that, Jen crawled from the bed and padded, unashamedly naked, across her bedroom to the dresser. Puzzled, thinking their rendezvous was over, Enzo sat up to ogle Jen in all her nude glory as she slid open the middle drawer of her dresser, bent over, and rummaged through what appeared to be a hell of a lot of underwear.

"Here." Turning around, Jen tossed something at Enzo before pushing the drawer shut with a firm nudge of her bare knee.

Enzo snatched the projectile out of the air with the expertise of a pro ball player. As Jen made her way back to bed with a wanton expression on her face, Enzo studied the small, black object. It was a mobile phone about as thick and wide as a deck of cards, but half as long. It was closed, and though he'd seen her open hers, he wasn't about to experiment in front of her and risk breaking it out of sheer clumsiness.

"What's this for?"

"For you. So I can call you when I get back from China," she said.

"Um, okay." Enzo wasn't sure what he was supposed to say—*thank you, like hell you will, I'll believe it when I see it*—because that was his line. He was secretly pleased to be presented with the phone, but the gesture gave out the clear message to him that Jen was very much in charge of where—if anywhere—their relationship was to go from here. It was the same as with the sex she'd so masterfully controlled. Enzo found Jen's domination both maddening and electrifying. Choosing to say nothing, he studied the cell phone and tugged on the little antenna.

Jen teased the bed sheets away to expose Enzo's firm, muscular body. "There's no need to look so hurt, Enzo. I *promise* I'll call." She kissed her way up along his thigh, her tongue teasing the sensitive flesh on its inner side. "And I *always* keep my promises."

Enzo felt the soft caress of Jen's breasts, the stiffness of her nipples, against his legs as she maneuvered her way upward to where he was, once again, hard and waiting for her.

CHAPTER TWENTY-SEVEN

Jen had always enjoyed the late fall in Fuzhou. The November weather in the Fujian Province was sunny and mild, with the mercury rarely straying below the mid-sixties. It certainly made for a welcome change from the encroaching bitterness of the New York winter. Even though she was in China for business, Jen did her best to allow herself at least a little time to enjoy her mother country and not spend her entire time there stuck in the drab, utilitarian dockside offices.

"This afternoon's applicants are here, Miss Mo-Li," Tang Xun bustled into the spacious office carrying a stack of paperwork. "Should I show the first ones in?"

Short, stocky, middle-aged with a stern face and cropped, salt-and-pepper hair, Tang Xun oozed efficiency. Jen knew the woman would have each one of the potential recruits sitting patiently in the reception area, all on time, all beautiful, and all more than eager for the opportunity to begin a whole new life in the great capitalist nation of the United States of America.

Jen had worked with Xun through her father's company since she'd taken over running the immigration part of the Mo-Li empire. Xun had been recommended to Jen's bà as the very best contact in China and Jen had heard rumors of links with the 14K Triad gang. The latter was not a subject the woman could ever be drawn to, even blind drunk on rice wine across a card table. Even so, such was the relationship they'd built over the years that, when Jen had approached Xun with her new proposition, she knew Xun could be trusted implicitly to hold her tongue and say nothing to Ming Sen Mo-Li. Had Jen's father so much as caught wind of the true purpose of her visit to China, the entire new venture with the Dragons would have unraveled even before it had begun and Jen would have no grand achievement to prove that she could and would build her own empire, quite apart from his.

"Thank you, Xun. I'll see the first three now," Jen said. "If you could ask Mr. Fok to join me too, I'd appreciate it." A raised eyebrow at her old friend said otherwise; the only reason Jen had entertained Charlie-Boy Fok in any part of the process was because Storm Cheung had insisted. Inevitably, Charlie-Boy's presence meant Eddie would tag along too, because he just didn't trust the guy.

Facing the three of them made for a nerve-wracking experience for all the young girls Jen was screening. Although, given the nature of the work awaiting them back in Flushing, Jen figured it would be a convenient way to weed out the nervy and feisty ones. Xun quickly reappeared with three petite, smiling young women. Behind them, Charlie-Boy and Eddie trailed in and took their places on either side of Jen.

Jen's office was an exact square, roughly twenty by twenty feet, and was furnished sparsely with six low-backed wooden chairs, a faux-teak desk, and a water cooler that churned and bubbled in the corner furthest from the door. One wall was made up entirely of windows, which looked out across the port to the estuary of the Mingjiang River. It made for a picturesque view, and reminded Jen a little of the Hudson back home.

As the three girls, dressed primly in knee-length black skirts, crisp white cotton shirts, and navy-blue jackets took their seats and Xun scurried out of the office, Jen shuffled a few papers and scrutinized each girl with a critical eye. Two looked to be perfect, but one appeared rounder about the middle than she would have preferred. A couple of months at sea was likely to sort that out.

"Thank you all for coming." Jen made her greeting as friendly as possible. Reading their names from the list she kept on the desk, she added, "Jessica, Emily, and Juliette." They had picked out their Western names before the interview; Jen much preferred it to her father's insistence on selecting names for their clientele. And she liked Juliette as a name—it reminded her of Juliette Lewis, her favorite actress, and she thought it suited the innocent, round-faced young girl who sat before her.

"We were very impressed with your credentials," Jen continued with a cursory nod to Charlie-Boy. She deliberately chose to speak only in English to the girls. She had instructed Xun to weed out any who were not entirely fluent in the language because they would take far too long to pick it up in the parlors. If she was honest with herself, she'd have to admit that it was also a way of sparing at least some of the girls a harrowing experience. "You have each been selected to apply because of your skills." The lie tripped from Jen's tongue with surprising ease. "This will enable you to become translators, teachers, secretaries, and even models."

She smiled and made eye contact with each of the girls in turn. At the word *model*, they all perked up; they had been seduced by glossy images of beautiful girls in fashion magazines and promises of sky-high earning potential by Xun's discreet advertising. Although any one of the three could easily have made it in any of the professions Jen had mentioned, they all had aspirations toward the glamor and sparkle of modeling.

"You have your passage fees ready?" Jen asked.

All three nodded.

"Should you be selected after today's interview, you will be expected to pay before the close of day tomorrow and be ready to travel at the end of this week."

"You do understand you will be expected to pay far less up front for your passage and papers than if you were not to work directly for us in America?" Jen continued.

The three nodded and smiled. Xun had been nothing if not thorough with briefing all the applicants.

"You will be expected to pay off the majority of your fees through a garnish on your wages once you arrive in America—that is to say, we will take our agreed payment from your wage *before* you are paid." The girls appeared to be just fine with that, so Jen pressed on. "Of course, we will hold onto your papers until the debt is paid in full. Was all that explained to you?"

More nods.

"Then I think we are done, unless you have any more questions?"

Charlie-Boy opened his mouth to speak, but Jen and Eddie both gave him withering glances. He'd asked a batch of girls earlier that week how they felt about nude modeling and film work, and they'd all but run away screaming. Witnessing the guy's lascivious pleasure at the distress he'd caused only served to confirm Jen's assessment of him as an irredeemable asshole. The gangster was a liability. He was lucky they were flying back to the States; Jen had a gut feeling that if they went by boat, Charlie-Boy wouldn't survive. The only question was who would murder him—Jen or Eddie? Having seen the beating he'd taken in the restaurant at Rico's hands, Jen knew it wouldn't take much for Eddie to make the guy quietly disappear.

The young girls sat in silence for what felt like an eternity to Jen. Not one of them came forward with a question, not even Juliette, which disappointed her. *Ask me something,* she thought. *Something for which I'll have to dismiss you.*

None of them did. Either Xun's briefing session with the applicants had been ludicrously detailed, or the Chinese girls were just so delighted at the prospect of their new lives that they didn't care what was going to happen to them once they reached New York Harbor.

Jen's eyes flicked down her list. The remainder of the applicants that afternoon were families. She'd insisted they incorporate enough families in their intake to make the shipment appear as much like business as usual as possible. She didn't want to raise suspicion among the girls, or those who'd helped round them up. It also provided her with plausible deniability should Father ask too many questions. Having said that, each family had been hand-selected by Xun for the potential suitability of their daughters for the Dragons' businesses. Storm had been quite explicit on some of the requirements for his Flushing parlors.

As Jen watched the three make their way out of the depressingly functional office, Charlie-Boy undressed each one in turn with his greedy eyes, while Eddie Sun gazed absently out of the window.

They'd all been invited to a card game at Xun's apartment later that evening; apparently, this was a regular event. The older woman was a bit of a mystery when it came to her extra-curricular activities, and Jen was beginning to wonder if she had a gambling problem. She'd also noted Eddie's reluctance to participate, although she put that down to her bodyguard's dislike for Charlie-Boy. Nonetheless, it was something to look forward to, and a welcome change from eating too much at the small, but incredibly good restaurants near the Fuzhou docks, then collapsing on the lumpy mattress in her hotel room.

It also provided Jen with a nice distraction from the last of her guilty thoughts regarding Enzo. She'd enjoyed her brief time with the Italian even though he'd seemed a little deer-in-headlights when it came to sex. Truth be told, that had only inflamed her desire and her sense of empowerment. It wasn't the same as the sense of power she'd derived from her swarming of Storm Cheung. She *liked* Enzo DeCarlo and found him intriguing and sexy. The kinetic attraction she felt around him was like an electric current that pulsed between them—whether they were fighting or fucking.

And, while she didn't expect the Italian to wait chastely for her return like some lovelorn sap in a romantic movie, Jen hoped to the bottom of her soul that he'd still be smitten by her when she returned from China.

CHAPTER TWENTY-EIGHT

Charlie-Boy was bored, but Jen couldn't have cared less. She had no doubt he'd been reporting back daily to Storm throughout the entire three weeks they'd been in the province, so, let the asshole sit and twiddle his thumbs just because he felt he *had* to go along to Xun's apartment for the evening. Charlie-Boy had done everything he could to make it clear to Jen—and Eddie, much to his chagrin—that he was the overseer of the recruitment trip, albeit self-proclaimed.

Eddie, on the other hand, appeared to be in his element. He was the most relaxed Jen had seen him since their arrival, and was enjoying himself drinking, smoking, laughing, and playing Chinese Poker with Xun and her myriad young male friends, a couple of whom appeared to have caught his eye. Eddie also seemed to enjoy Charlie-Boy's boredom.

Xun's modest apartment in the Antai Residential District was a stone's throw from the docks and, from her place on the third floor, within sight of the Dongxi River. The Jiayang apartment building was an unremarkable gray stone structure on Jiayang Road, although Jen knew Xun could have afforded much better on the kickbacks her father, and now the Dragons, were paying for her services. Still, the woman seemed more than happy with her lot, and Jen noted she had a great many men friends who outnumbered the women at the raucous gathering three to one.

"Another game, Miss Mo-Li?" Xun asked with a smile; she'd had more than her fill of rice wine and was way beyond tipsy.

Jen surveyed the low card table with its scuffed, green baize top and the stack of money she'd won from Xun and her inebriated friends. She didn't want to take any more cash from them. She'd grown up playing cards with her brother Danny and had cultivated one hell of a poker face, which had made winning against the drunken partygoers embarrassingly easy. "I think I'm going to call it a night, Xun," she replied. "We have another very full day tomorrow."

Xun nodded as sagely as she could, considering her intoxicated state. "I know, Miss Mo-Li, I'm the one who organized the day." She gave Jen a most uncharacteristic nudge in the ribs with her elbow—something she'd never have ventured in the cold, sober, light of day—and giggled. Pointing at the stack of bank notes on the table, and then at the shiny-faced old man perched on the couch with a beer bottle in his hand, she said, "Eng Hun would like the opportunity to win at least some of his money back. I think he has taken quite a shine to you, too."

Jen smiled across at Eng Hun, who looked to be close to her father's age and was as far from a possible suitor as she could have ever imagined. "I really think I should—"

"He is offering double or nothing and is most insistent." Xun was suddenly, completely serious. "Also, he is 14K." Xun left the word hanging in the smoke-filled air as if there was nothing more that needed to be said. There wasn't. 14K was a member of the Triad, a collective of Chinese gangs even Storm Cheung would fear, had he any sense.

"Double or nothing?" Jen acquiesced; the last people she wanted to piss off in Fujian were the Triads. "But, haven't I already won *all* his money?"

"He is offering to put one of his boats on the table," Xun replied. "It would be foolish of you to decline such a generous offer."

"Poker?"

"Dou Dizhou—Hun *insists*."

Jen was more than familiar with the traditional Chinese card game, as her mother had played it with her from as far back as she could remember. She remembered that Mother preferred to call the game Fighting the Landlord, which was the more popular Westernized translation of its name. It was more a game of chance and required only a few of the skills required by poker, which was most likely the reason for the old man's decision to switch games. Having lost in such spectacular fashion at poker, he was stacking the odds of winning back his money in his favor.

"Double or nothing it is, then." Sitting herself back down at the card table, Jen pushed her money toward its center, much to the delight of Eng Hun and his supporters. Their cheers and back-slapping filled Xun's apartment as one of the few younger ladies in the place scooped up the playing cards, slipped two jokers back into the pack, and shuffled them with all the flashy dexterity of a Vegas croupier.

Jen and Xun were each dealt seventeen cards out of the deck of fifty-four, with two Jokers included as wild cards. Eng Hun received his seventeen and placed the remaining three cards face down in front of him as stock. He'd been granted the role of landlord by a cut of the deck which, by the rules of the game, made Jen and her colleague peasants.

As the game began, Jen was skeptical of her cards; she had but a few high-value face cards and only one ace. She was going to have to rely upon her two opponents having less nerve than she did when it came to betting against the higher stakes. That's where her poker face would come in handy.

Xun had the three of hearts, and so was first to bid. She was also first out of the game. Jen had guessed it was a deliberate ploy on Xun's part to quickly pit her against Eng Hun and bow out with dignity; she'd made some high-risk bets against low cards and played it off by acting more drunk than she was.

"Your turn, Miss Mo-Li," Eng Hun said with a broad smile. They were both down to their final few cards, plus the unknown three which remained face down. The atmosphere in the room had grown tense; all eyes were on the card table and the two remaining players.

Jen bid high on a seven, which was easily beaten by Hun's nine. That put a glint in the Triad's eye as he bet high against his jack of diamonds and fixed Jen with a confident glare.

A black queen beat Eng Hun's jack, and they were down to their final card each. Hun took a big shot of rice wine and made his final bet against the ace he'd been holding back, eschewing his right to draw from the three-card stock. Finally, the boat was on the table—denoted by a napkin upon which one of Hun's friends had drawn a rudimentary cartoon and Hun had signed.

Taking her time, Jen gave a fleeting look in Eddie's direction. He looked tense as he watched the game, although some of his attention was distracted by his new young lady friend, who pressed herself up against his side with her perky breasts smooshed into his ribs. Eddie cocked an eyebrow at Jen, a little concern in his expression. She was gambling against a member of the Triad, after all.

With a heavy sigh, Jen drew a card from stock, made a pouty face, and turned it face up on the table. It was a joker. A card that could be whatever the hell she wanted it to be. A card that trumped even Eng Hun's ace. A card he would have drawn if he hadn't been quite so cocksure of the win.

Xun's apartment fell silent. Even Charlie-Boy had turned his attention to the game, although he appeared less than delighted by Jen's victory. As everyone stared down at the card, Jen pushed it delicately toward Eng Hun. She looked up and met his eyes as the façade of bonhomie slipped from his face, just for the briefest of moments. She couldn't be sure if the guy was pissed because he'd just lost a boat, or because he'd lost a simple card game to a woman. She had a hunch it was the latter.

Slowly, without breaking eye contact, Hun stood up. He flapped a hand at the croupier girl, and she got to her feet too. From the corner of her eye, Jen saw Eddie stiffen; the suddenly icy atmosphere worried him. Jen began to think maybe she ought to have let Hun win his money back. But, with a snort and a grimace, Eng Hun pushed the napkin with the boat picture across the card table to Jen. She bowed her head in acknowledgment.

"Congratulations, Miss Mo-Li." Hun spoke quietly, deliberately. "You play exceedingly well."

"Thank you," Jen replied softly with the expected humility. "The cards were certainly in my favor tonight."

Eng Hun scanned the room. A broad, toothy smile spread across his face. "Is this a party or a wake?" he said loudly. "Miss Mo-Li has won the *Xiao Hong*!"

A deafening cheer ended the awkward silence, and drinks began to flow once more. Hun reached across the table to shake Jen's hand— a gesture that showed great respect. "Take good care of her, Miss Mo-Li," he said as Jen took his hand, which felt unexpectedly small and dry in hers. "She has been very good to us over the years. I wish you many safe voyages."

While the Triad appeared to be taking his defeat with good grace, Jen couldn't quite shake the fear that there might be a subtext to Hun's words that should frighten her. Shrugging it off, she extricated her hand, got to her feet, and picked up the napkin. At the turn of a card—a joker, no less—she had become the proud owner of the *Xiao Hong*—an auspicious name that hinted at the promise of favorable voyages. The first thing she would do once she got it back home would be to have its translated name painted on its bows: *Morning Rainbow*.

ACT THREE: LOYALTY

CHAPTER TWENTY-NINE

"How many more strip joints before you quit mooning over your Chinese chick?" Rico Corozzio chastised his friend.

Enzo shrugged and fiddled with his beer. He was still only halfway down the glass, and it was flat and warm. "I'm not *mooning*, I'm bored."

Rico scoffed at his friend and sprawled out on the red, faux-velvet seat in their booth. He'd sprung for a VIP area so he and Enzo could enjoy a private dance or two, or maybe a little more—the girls at Bucks Wild Gentleman's Club were renowned for being generous with their favors and wonderfully accommodating.

"We got the most beautiful strippers this side of the Hudson, how the fuck can you be bored?" Rico pointed toward the stage where a trio of girls in transparent heels, thongs, and latex nipple covers gyrated in time to the thumping music. "See—not one C-section scar or track-mark between them!"

Enzo curled up the corners of his mouth at that one. In some of the less savory Manhattan strip clubs Rico had dragged him to, the quality of dancers had left a lot to be desired. But, peering through the smoke at Bucks' girls up on the stage, Enzo saw for himself that Rico's observation was indeed accurate. Nonetheless, not one of the three, nor any of the multitudes of barely-dressed young ladies in the club stirred much more than a cursory desire in Enzo. Sure, he'd fuck anyone of them if they offered, but Rico was right. His mind was definitely elsewhere.

It was January, three months and some since the fight at the Chinese restaurant, and since he'd bedded Jen Mo-Li. She had promised him she'd be back from her China trip within three months, so where the hell was she?

The cell phone Jen gave him had never left his pocket since that night. He'd managed to keep the phone a secret from his father, which hadn't been too difficult, since the thing had remained depressingly silent.

Rico had done his best to pull Enzo out of his funk and had taken full advantage of the Christmas and New Year season with all the alcohol-fueled parties and over-eager women letting their hair—and panties—down. Enzo had played along, even screwed a few of the floozies his friend sent his way, but his heart just wasn't in it. Enzo went along with Rico's plans for him mostly because he still felt guilty about the night at the restaurant. Rico had taken quite a beating at the hands of the Chinese gang, *and* he'd finally realized—a good two days later once his concussion symptoms faded—who the kickass chick was who'd done her best to kill him, and that Enzo had run off and fucked her fresh from the fight.

"Pick one," Rico was saying, nodding toward the strippers gallivanting on the tiny stage or acting as hostesses. The guy was well on his way to being fall-down drunk, having matched each one of Enzo's half-drunk beers with two of his own. "How about Stacy?" Leering, he pointed an unsteady hand at a thin, statuesque bleach-blonde with an all-over honey tan. "Chantelle?" Rico turned his attention to a petite black woman standing at the bar whose generous breasts spilled out from her white leatherette bikini. "She *loves* to do the dirty with Italian guys—you might not even have to pay her that much."

Feigning interest, Enzo checked out the two girls, although he knew he wasn't fooling Rico at all—the guy knew him far too well for that. "I'm not feeling it tonight."

Rico's frustration boiled over. "Oh, for fuck's sake, Enzo," he snapped. "I buy you beers all night that you don't drink, and I offer you classy pussy you can't be bothered with. Whatever kinky Asian shit that broad did with you is in the past. She's not coming back, Enzo. You're gonna have to face that fact sooner or later—preferably sooner." Raising a hand above his head, Rico motioned for the overly abundant Chantelle to bring over their no-doubt exorbitant check.

Enzo knew his friend was right. He'd enjoyed the thrill of the chase and sealed the deal with Jen, so why the hell couldn't he move on? Sure, she'd played hard to get, and she'd proven herself to be as aggressive and dominating as he was, if not more so. Was that it? Was that the allure that had him praying for the goddamned mobile phone to ring and it be Jen's voice when he picked up? Was it that his ego wouldn't be satisfied until he'd exerted his masculine dominance over the broad?

"Hold the check," Enzo said to Chantelle as she tottered to their booth in her impossibly steep patent heels.

Rico eyed his friend with suspicion. "You said—"

"I changed my mind." Enzo gave him a wry smile. "Chantelle," He reached for the girl's hand as she bent over to drop their check on the table. "How about a little private time?"

Chantelle appeared delighted by the proposition; her eyes sparkled beneath the vermillion shadow that painted her lids. "Sure thing," she said in a thick Bronx accent. "I'll go get us some champagne—sound good?"

Enzo grinned at the young woman and let go of her hand. "Invite one of your friends over."

As Chantelle made her way back to the bar, Enzo and Rico watched her ass wiggle beneath her skimpy briefs—like two pigs fighting under a blanket, as Vincenzo would have put it. "Good to see my old Enzo back in business," Rico clapped Enzo a hard one on the back.

Enzo smiled into his warm beer. "How could I let you down when there's Chantelle and her classy colleagues to sample?"

The two laughed together, and for a moment, it felt like old times.

But then the phone rang in Enzo's pocket. He *felt* it rather than heard it above the music. Startled, he fished it out and stared at the tiny strip of screen.

"Seriously?" Rico groaned as he eyed Chantelle making her way back to their booth. She carried champagne in a silver bucket in one hand, and led the tall, honey-skinned stripper, fresh from the stage, with her other.

"I've got to take this." Enzo stood up.

"Sure, you do." Rico didn't try to mask his disappointment. Instead, he greeted the two strippers with a wide smile and a wad of cash as Enzo made his way out the club's door with the phone pressed to his ear.

CHAPTER THIRTY

"I didn't think you'd call." Enzo sat naked at the edge of the bed, his back to Jen. "It's been a while."

Lying back among her messy clutter of pillows, Jen contemplated the man she'd just fucked. He'd arrived at her apartment less than a half hour after she'd called him, reeking of cigarette smoke and cheap perfume. Jen hadn't bothered to ask where he'd come from; she didn't much care and figured it was none of her business. Whatever other women he'd had, he dropped them to come to *her*. That meant something.

"I told you I'd call as soon as I returned from China." She traced down along the ridge of her lover's spine with a bare toe. "And I *always* keep my promises." Her gaze roamed across the broad expanse of Enzo's taut shoulders, admiring the toned muscle, and she realized just how much she'd been looking forward to this.

Enzo turned to face Jen, his face still shiny with the sweat of exertion. This was the first actual conversation they'd had; talking had been the last thing on her mind when he'd come through her door to find her naked and waiting.

"My mom says promises are made to be broken," he said with a wry smile, "and I've broken plenty."

Jen grinned back at Enzo and stretched her arms over her head as the Egyptian cotton sheet slipped from her body to expose her breasts and the reddening bite marks he'd left there in the heat of passion. She felt more than saw Enzo's gaze settle on them; it was a warm sensation, almost as if he had brushed them with his lips or fingertips. "I hope I was worth the wait."

Enzo's smile was boyish and frank. "More than. You're all I've thought about."

"Thought about screwing me again, you mean?" Jen massaged the small of Enzo's back with her perfectly pedicured toes.

"No," Enzo confessed; he seemed a tad shocked to hear her talking that way. "Not *just* that. I mean, it was ... the first time we...."

"Screwed?" Jen laughed.

"It's more than that for me." Enzo sobered and ran a hand through his hair.

Jen was stunned by the quiet admission ... or was it a ploy? Nothing more than post-coital small talk? She'd been with guys who thought what a girl wanted to hear as she climbed down from her orgasm was that they loved her unconditionally and wanted to marry her and have kids with her—the usual schmaltzy bullshit.

Mostly, Jen never heard from them again.

There was something different about Enzo, though. Somehow, he'd managed to worm his way into her head, even before the night they'd spent together. Why else had she agreed to see him after her lame attempt at shaking him off? The sex had been good, satisfying in a way she hadn't experienced in a hell of a long time. It had been just as good this time, though Jen had forced herself to allow Enzo to take the lead. He wasn't Storm Cheung—a dangerous ally to be controlled. Still, he was clearly used to getting his own way with the women he slept with as his quaint, old-time Italian upbringing had taught him the man took the upper hand in every aspect of life—especially in the bedroom. Well, she was fairly confident he'd begun to unlearn that the first time she'd ridden him. If it had offended his ego, he wouldn't be here now.

"I ... enjoy you, Enzo." Jen sat up in the bed and curled her arms around his neck. She enjoyed the feel of her skin against his, their faces close, the rhythm of his breathing. "More than I have enjoyed any man in a long while."

Turning around, Enzo kissed Jen's lips, his tongue playing along them as if inviting hers. His hands caressed the smooth, damp skin of her back. "I enjoy you, too, but—"

Jen pressed her lips hard against Enzo's to silence him. However he'd been intending to finish that sentence, she wasn't sure she was ready to hear it.

CHAPTER THIRTY-ONE

The first large apartment Jen procured in the Minster Tower block had taken shape in her absence. The three-bedroom space had been modified to create seven comfortable bedrooms by partitioning the large master ensuite, the family room, and part of the expansive living room. Each of the rooms had a full-sized bed and tasteful décor. The front rooms had become a comfortable reception area furnished with tan, distressed leather sofas, a small bar from which patrons would be served a selection of quality French wines, imported bottled beers, and upmarket spirits—all the better to relax the gentlemen and make it even easier to separate them from their hard-earned cash.

Next door was a second apartment Jen had set up as a dormitory. There would be no business done there, no over-eager Johns with their overflowing wallets and dirty little fantasies. That apartment, also tastefully decorated in pastels and watercolor landscapes, would serve only as a haven.

As Jen walked through the working apartment with Eddie close behind, she inspected the quality of the construction and introduced herself to the handful of young girls who were already in place, along with the fearsome, stunningly beautiful Madam Ziyi, who was to oversee the day-to-day running of the place. Charlie-Boy had tagged along, of course, although his presence was entirely unnecessary. After having spent the better part of three months in China in proximity to Jen, he knew when to make himself scarce.

Of course, it would be a month or so before the first batch of girls arrived by boat from Fuzhou; those milling about the front room had been selected from the Dragons' parlors around Mulberry and Doyers. They were all incredibly pretty. They knew their trade and were inured to it. When she'd recommended they open first with experienced girls—an idea unexpectedly upvoted by Charlie-Boy—Jen was also hopeful that the veteran hookers would help the rookies accept their circumstances.

Madam Ziyi ushered Jen and Eddie into the largest of the bedrooms. It just happened to be the biggest and was lusciously decorated in subdued reds and purples. It was also the only one of the seven with an ensuite bathroom. The bed at the room's center was a king-sized four-poster with leather restraints and shiny black latex sheets; on the wall at its head hung a huge, tastefully artistic photograph of a girl clad head-to-toe in a red PVC catsuit. And, alongside that, an array of paddles, floggers, whips, and riding crops, all of which hung from a series of wrought-iron hooks.

"This is our VIP room," Madam Ziyi announced with a dramatic sweep of her hand. The woman appeared to Jen to be not much older than her charges, yet she commanded a great deal of respect. "It is for gentlemen with more ... *unusual* tastes."

"I can see," Jen replied with a tight smile. Behind her, Eddie stirred uneasily as if the place disturbed him as much as it did her.

"There are men who will pay very good money for an hour or two in this room," Madam Ziyi continued. "And they will always come back for more."

Jen gave the woman an assessing glance. Seeing such cold calculation in one so young was discomfiting. Jen couldn't help but wonder just how old Madam Ziyi had been when she'd begun her less-than-wholesome career in Chinatown's parlors.

The ensuite door opened and a girl stepped out into the bedroom. Although she wore her off-duty wear of loose-fitting jeans, scuffed sneakers, and a plain black, baggy tee, she was still a true beauty. She seemed familiar.

"Ahh, this is one of my best girls—this is to be her room." Madam Ziyi waved the young lady over. "Come and say hello to Miss Mo-Li."

"It is a pleasure to see you again, Miss Mo-Li." Gong Shu Li held out a dainty hand for Jen to shake.

Jen heard Eddie's startled cough behind her as she struggled to hide her own surprise at finding herself faced with the girl she'd last seen over the corpse of Donnie Wu.

"Amy?" Jen asked, recalling the name she had given the girl on the boat.

"Shu Li," said the girl, her voice dove-soft. "Gong Shu Li."

"Likewise, Shu Li." As Jen shook the girl's hand, she studied her face. So, she had not taken an Americanized name. That was surprising, though not as much as finding her here. Jen was saddened that Shu Li had disappeared from her radar the moment she'd stepped off the *Bright Horizon*. She'd paid her passage in full, so Jen had no way of knowing the new life she'd chosen. She doubted a life of prostitution had been Shu Li's plan. More likely the rape had nudged her down that path. Did she feel that Donnie Wu had ruined her? Or had his big talk of easy money and riches beyond her wildest dreams lured her in? Or was the BDSM room a way of punishing the men who used her?

"It is an honor to be working for you, Miss Mo-Li," Shu Li slipped her hand from Jen's, her gaze direct, almost defiant. "I hope I will make you proud."

"I am sure you will," Jen replied with a tight smile.

The moment's awkwardness was disrupted by a slow, rhythmic bumping against the wall to the left of the expansive bed.

"What on earth? We are not doing business yet!" Madam Ziyi bustled out of the room.

Jen said a quick goodbye to Shu Li and followed the madam out into the hallway. There, she and Eddie watched as the madam barged into the adjacent bedroom without so much as a polite rap on its door, her raised voice shouting something incomprehensible in Cantonese.

Charlie-Boy, inevitably. It had been a mistake to allow him to wander off around the brothel by himself. Gritting her teeth and checking her temper, Jen made her way into the smaller room, which was painted in delicate sea green with accents of pearl.

"*What the fuck!*" Charlie-Boy snarled as he clambered from the bed. He dragged the top sheet with him to cover up his naked dick, leaving the young prostitute he'd broken off fucking entirely exposed. She squealed and attempted to cover her breasts and crotch with just her hands, her eyes downturned in shame.

"What do you think you're doing, Charlie-Boy?" Jen was across the room and in the gangster's face in no time at all.

"What does it look like?" Charlie-Boy snarled. He took a downward glance at his sheet-covered dick, which was still noticeably hard and looked like a pint-sized Halloween ghost. "I'm testing the merchandise, bitch. It's all part of the goddamned job—or did Storm not fill you in on that?" He laughed at Jen and shot a defiant look across at Eddie.

"Go clean yourself up!" Madam Ziyi ordered the terrified girl. "*Now!*" The young prostitute darted from the room.

"I am so sorry," Jen apologized to Madam Ziyi on Charlie-Boy's behalf. "I can assure you this won't happen again."

"The fuck it won't!" Charlie-Boy stepped closer, his angry breath hot on Jen's face. "I'm not going to let some prissy little realtor bitch like you get in the way of my perks."

Jen's desire to scratch the gangster's eyes out warred with her survival agenda. As much as she wanted to settle Charlie-Boy here and now, she knew she could not. If she was going to rise above this circumstance, she was going to have to choose her battles with care. So, these girls must prostitute themselves and she must facilitate that. But let them at least be treated with the respect they deserved regardless of their profession.

Instead of backing down, however, Jen pressed closer to Storm's lieutenant. So close, their noses almost touched. She kept her voice low, close to a purr ... or a growl. "This is not a candy store, Charlie-Boy, where you can expect to get free samples. And these girls are not merchandise to be tasted or tested. So, let me be perfectly clear: You will treat my girls with respect, and you will *ask*, not demand. These girls are not for you to do with as you please, you *prick*!"

The last two words came out like the scream of a mountain lion and caused Charlie-Boy to flinch. Then, as if suddenly becoming aware that there was an audience for this rebuke, he reared back and raised his fists. Eddie was at Jen's shoulder in an instant with menace burning in his eyes. Madam Ziyi made a sound that might have been laughter and slipped discreetly out through the door.

"You're way out of your jurisdiction, bitch," Charlie-Boy growled, lowering his hands.

"And you're a fucking *embarrassment*. What part of upscale do you not understand?"

Charlie-Boy's temper broke its restraints. He reached out to grab hold of Jen's upper arm, but he'd betrayed the move. She parried with a left-handed slap block, the heel of her right hand already flying toward Charlie-Boy's face. Then Eddie's strong, persuasive hands were on her, stopping her momentum and dragging her backward.

"Choose your battles," he murmured, and she knew he was right.

Charlie-Boy scoffed at her. "That's right, hide behind your bodyguard," he sneered and shook his fist at her. "You better stay scared of me, Jen Mo-Li. All I need is a fucking good reason to put you down. You might be useful to the Dragons, but that doesn't mean you can't be replaced like *that*." He snapped his fingers in front of Jen's face for emphasis.

She smiled and gestured at their surroundings. "Do you think you can't be, Charlie-Boy? If you disappeared tomorrow, all this would still go on. If I disappear, it crumbles. And *he* knows it."

There was no doubt who *he* was and no doubt that Jen's barbed comment had stung the gangster. He fixed Jen with a murderous look, his lips pressed closed, his fists flexing impotently, then turned his attention to Eddie. "You'd best get this bitch the fuck out of my sight," he growled. "Otherwise, I won't be responsible for her safety." He raised his fist to Jen's eye level to underline his threat.

Calmly, Eddie ushered Jen to the bedroom door. "It is not her safety I am afraid for, Fok," he said. "It is yours."

Jen allowed Eddie to escort her back to the parlor's reception area, where she sat awhile and sipped tea with Madam Ziyi while Charlie-Boy dressed himself and left. Eddie saw him to the door.

"He will try to kill you," he told her when they were at last back in her car. "You know this."

"Yes," she said simply.

"Something needs to be done."

"Yes," she said again. "Yes, it does."

———

Jen stopped by Storm Cheung's Chinatown office to provide her debrief on progress at Minster Tower, having successfully ditched Charlie-Boy and given Eddie the evening off. After a perfunctory chat about the upcoming opening night at the Flushing parlor, Storm simply dropped his pants and seated himself in his executive chair, making it blatantly obvious he was expecting a repeat performance of the night he'd told her he was packing her off to the mother country for three months. He said nothing, merely exposed his already inflating cock and watched her through half-closed eyes, waiting for her to make the next move. After a moment's thought, she pulled off her sweater and bra and got to work.

Jen found herself making comparisons between Enzo and Cheung, noticing that Cheung's penis was longer and thinner than the Italian's. She felt no pang of conscience as she pleasured the gang leader; it was work. Even if Enzo was ever to find out about her trysts with Storm Cheung, Jen wondered if he'd understand that this was business and he was pleasure.

After several minutes of giving the arch Dragon a blow job, Jen pulled up her skirt and started to climb into the chair to mount him. He put his hands on her shoulders to press her back down.

"Just keep on doing what you're doing," he said, his voice tight whisper. His eyes were closed, his face a picture of concentration. "I want to come in your face."

Jen was glad the gang lord couldn't see the expression on that face. She'd had a guy do that to her once and knew it for what it was—a gesture of disrespect. A way of spitting on her. A power play. The great Storm Cheung was attempting to mark his territory like a dog peeing on a hydrant. It infuriated her. And it made her wonder: Did Storm

Cheung see her as so much of a threat to his masculinity or his position within the Black Dragons, or both, that he felt the need to demean her? She thought fleetingly of biting his dick but knew that wouldn't end well for her.

She bent back to the job. In mere moments, Cheung began moaning and rocking his hips, while Jen considered, again, just how foolish he was to allow himself to be so vulnerable with a woman he didn't know. When he gasped and started to come, she pulled to one side and dodged the spew, smiling a little as it decorated his legs, his expensive trousers, and the silk carpet beneath his chair.

She rose quickly, turning her back on him to hide her silent laughter. By the time he'd recovered, she was fully dressed, had reapplied her lipstick, and was sitting casually in what she'd come to think of as her chair across from his desk. If he challenged her, she'd claim to be the victim of high heels and the bucking of his chair, but he didn't seem to have noticed that he was the only one wearing bodily fluids.

"Charlie-Boy managed to disgrace himself this afternoon," she said, watching him wipe himself down with a bundle of tissues he'd produced from one of his desk drawers. She knew all too well how suggestible men could be immediately after release.

"I heard you walked in on him interviewing one of the girls," Storm replied with a frown. "Madam Ziyi called me after you left."

She cocked an eyebrow at him. "And you're okay with that behavior? With him 'testing' the 'merchandise' as he called it?"

Shrugging, Storm pulled up his pants and tucked his dick away. "It's what he does. It's what Charlie-Boy has always done. It's kind of a—"

"Perk of the job. He told me."

"They're hookers, Jen," Storm replied matter-of-factly. "Sex is their currency—it's what they know. I really don't see what your problem is."

And now it's my currency. Maybe that's what my problem is. "My problem is they are not there to be exploited by Charlie-Boy, or anyone else who thinks they have a God-given right to take whatever they want." Jen's thoughts turned to Donnie Wu and the sickening, metallic stink of his spilled blood. "Perhaps you should leave the Flushing girls to me?"

"Flushing is as much Charlie-Boy's project as it is yours." Storm tucked in his shirt. "He's the only one I can trust to keep me informed of what's going on there—no offense meant." His smile was most insincere.

Jen said nothing.

"Besides, he'll be earning the right when he goes up against the Mott Street Tigers next week."

Jen's interest was piqued; she hid the fact, lazily crossing her legs. "You're taking on the Tigers?"

"Yeah," Storm replied absently. He fished a half-finished bottle of single malt whiskey and two tumblers out of the drawer that housed the tissue box. "They've encroached on our territory with the Sum Ying pool hall—that place has been ours for three years now. It's time we took the bastards down a rung or two." He poured out two generous glasses.

"I guess business is business." Jen took a tumbler from Storm and sipped at the amber liquid within, her mind elsewhere.

"It is, and such things need to be executed perfectly," Storm replied. "That's why Charlie-Boy is my lieutenant—I know I can trust him to do things right."

Jen sipped quietly at her whiskey, listened politely to Storm's retelling of the story of how he became so much in Charlie-Boy's debt, and began to wonder if there might be a chance Charlie-Boy Fok might not return from his battle with the rival gang.

Storm stopped talking, causing Jen to look up at him. He'd tilted his head to one side and was looking at her intently.

"What?"

"Your makeup. It's flawless."

"Is it?" She smiled, knowing that it shouldn't have been. "Thank you. I do make the effort."

He opened his mouth, possibly to press the issue, then frowned, shook his head, and said, "I have another meeting in a few minutes. You'll need to leave."

Jen watched with mild bemusement as he went back behind his desk and reseated himself in the chair. He didn't look at her again.

CHAPTER THIRTY-TWO

Joey Greco had been managing the DeCarlos' bookmaking and number-running rackets from the red-fronted apartments on Elizabeth Street for going on ten years. In all that time, the family had no reason to suspect he was anything other than whiter than white, and that if he was skimming—which all racketeers did at some point or another; it was kind of expected—it was strictly small enough numbers for them to turn a blind eye. Until the guy got greedy and took one liberty too many with DeCarlo money, that was.

It had been Angel Corozzio who'd brought to Vincenzo's attention the glaring discrepancies in Greco's books, plus the fact that takings were considerably down, despite the buoyancy elsewhere in the underground gambling businesses. He'd even checked in with a couple of the other families to be certain, which had only served to further reinforce the consigliere's suspicions about Greco.

Angel had convinced Vincenzo to let Greco go with little more than a warning that should he ever set foot in Manhattan again, he'd be getting acquainted with the flora and fauna at the bottom of the Hudson. Unfortunately, Angel had made the mistake of discussing Joey Greco's indiscretions with his son.

It was a touch after one in the morning when Rico and Enzo broke into Joey's apartment. The guy was alone and sound asleep when the two quietly jimmied open the front door and let themselves in.

"I never figured you for one to sleep naked, Greco," Rico said as he flicked on the nightstand light and prodded the guy awake with the muzzle of his revolver.

"What the fuck?" Joey was wide awake and sitting up in an instant. Enzo could see the guy's adrenaline-fueled pulse pounding in his neck even in the dimness of the small lamp. The flabby body looked pasty, his man tits wobbling grotesquely as he protested the discourteous intrusion.

"You know exactly *what the fuck.*" Rico jabbed Joey hard in the ribs with the gun, which had the man flat on his back again and struggling to sit up.

"You've been helping yourself to what belongs to The Don," Enzo chipped in. "And The Don isn't pleased, you fat fuck."

Joey's eyes flitted between the two young gangsters; a thin sheen of nervous perspiration glinted on his upper lip and quivering jowls.

"Hey, everybody skims," Joey gabbled. "It ain't no big deal in this game. And–and I'll pay it back. Just give me some ti—"

Rico smacked the gun hard against Joey's temple. He winced on Joey's behalf as the skin split and a thin line of blood trickled down to stain the pillow, which was already damp with the guy's sour sweat. Joey slumped back onto the bed, half-conscious. He no longer looked terrified; now he just looked confused.

Enzo stood over him at the edge of the bed. "You don't get to tell us what we *need* to do," he growled. "You've betrayed the family's trust and stolen money out of our pockets."

Joey could only shake his head, his mouth opening and closing like a big white flounder. In no mood for negotiating, and tired of the fat guy's pleading, Enzo snatched a pillow from beneath Joey's head and slammed it in his face.

"What the fuck, Enzo?" Rico stepped back from the bed to avoid Joey's flailing arms.

Ignoring the obvious question, Enzo pressed the pillow hard over Joey Greco's face, turning a deaf ear to his muffled cries. "Get his fucking hands!"

Rico stuck his gun into the back of his pants and took hold of Joey's hands. The guy was strong in his panic, and it took all of Rico's strength to prevent him from struggling loose and slapping Enzo's face. It took a while but soon enough, Joey's hands fell limp and his legs quit kicking. The bed was now messed up—his feet had scrunched the sheets to the bottom end and his bladder had let go sometime before he'd stopped breathing.

"*Motherfucker*." Enzo pulled the pillow away from Joey's face. He had chewed through the cotton case and the pillow's cover, and his mouth was crammed with tiny duck feathers.

"Is he dead?" Rico asked as he wrinkled his nose at the sight of Joey's limp, naked corpse and semi-erect dick. "Should we check on his pulse or something?"

"He *looks* fucking dead," Enzo said with a satisfied smile. He peered into Joey's still, glassy eyes and figured pressing his fingers against the guy's clammy, fat neck was a tad superfluous.

"Then we need to get the fuck out of here." Rico glanced nervously around as if he was expecting someone to magically appear from the gloomy shadows.

Enzo pulled a knife from his pocket; it was one of the paring knives Mamma used to skin and gut the fresh fish they received every Friday from their fishmonger business on Mott Street.

"We'll go when we're done," he said. "First, we make an example of the thieving prick and send a message to any other bookmaker thinking of lining his pockets with DeCarlo money." He lifted Joey's arm off the sweat-soaked mattress and ran the knife's keen blade across its lifeless wrist.

Angel Corozzio was less than impressed with his son and Enzo's nocturnal activities. He'd torn a strip off Rico earlier and had been about to lecture Enzo when Vincenzo walked into the office and intervened.

"Give the kids a break, Angel." Vincenzo barked. "They're out to prove themselves—they dealt with the problem on Elizabeth Street."

"They left Joey Greco in Elizabeth Street Gardens with his hands cut off!" It was only on the rarest of occasions Angel dared raise his voice to The Don, even though he was one of only two people who could do so without fear of a bullet to the head. The other, of course, was Elena DeCarlo.

"It's what we do to thieves," Vincenzo told him.

"It's what we *did*, Vincenzo." Angel's frustration was evident in his reddening cheeks. "This is not a Puzo novel. We're not living in the goddamn fifties anymore, Vincenzo, and we're definitely *not* untouchable."

Vincenzo chose to take his consigliere's slight with good humor. "Maybe if we did go back to the old ways, things would work out better for the families?"

"We have the police poking around all over Elizabeth Street. We're going to have to close down Joey's numbers racket, and where are we going to find the money to replace that?" Angel shot Rico and Enzo a blazing look. "You two jackasses just cost us two hundred grand a month!"

Rico knew better than to say anything. His father's anger still scared him, even as a grown man. Enzo, on the other hand, just couldn't keep his damn mouth shut.

"We get the Chinese gang to sell more heroin and coke," he offered. "Up the volume and we cover the shortfall overnight."

"See," Vincenzo clapped his consigliere on the back. "What were you worrying about, my old friend?" He slid open his desk drawer and pulled out four fat Cubans.

Angel dismissed the offer with a raised hand and shake of the head. "I have work to do," he said and made his way to the door.

Vincenzo thrust a cigar to both Enzo and Rico, which they eagerly accepted. He nodded at the door Angel had just exited. "He pretends he's against the old ways and thinks we should forget them. Sometimes it pays to keep tradition, especially in our line of business." He gave a rare smile as Rico and Enzo lit up their cigars and puffed out the smoke. "You boys did good last night. I'm thinking maybe it's time you were made—you're both ready to be capos."

CHAPTER THIRTY-THREE

Jen studied Eddie's face from the kitchen. The man was impossible to read at the best of times, his stony features an entirely closed book. But this time, the concern etched upon his stern features was as clear as day, even if his words sounded supportive.

"If you're going to insist on doing this, I'm coming with you," Eddie said. "It's my job to protect you."

Jen fiddled with the small, silver pocket pistol—a baby Browning that would serve its purpose well. Eddie had procured it for her without asking why. He'd simply acquired the weapon, filed off the serial number, and waited patiently for her to venture an explanation.

"I can't let you do that, Eddie," she told him. "You know this is something I have to do alone."

Eddie shifted his bulk on Jen's couch and eyed her with unease. "You could get yourself killed, Jen. I cannot allow that to happen. What would your bà say?"

Jen chuckled at that. "What, are you more worried about Ming Sen's reaction to my hypothetical demise than my actual death?"

"You know that is not—"

"Don't be. He'd be only too happy to have his embarrassment of a daughter out of the way."

Eddie rose and turned to face her. "You read him wrong, Jen. He may cling to many of the old traditions and attitudes, but he values you as a part of his family and business."

"I'm not the one who's reading him wrong, Eddie. He's *never* valued me." Jen checked the gun's clip to avoid eye contact with her bodyguard. "And when Danny died...."

"Your brother's death hit your father hard, as you well know," Eddie reminded her. "But that did nothing to diminish his love for you."

"He has no love for me," she sneered. "He puts Petey above me—and barely tolerates him. He simply sees him as a better asset, not a son."

Jen palmed the gun in her right hand; it was the perfect fit. She looked across her lounge at Eddie, the one man in her entire life she'd been able to rely upon, and who refused to treat her with anything less than respect. She could not afford to lose him.

"Petey is an idiot." Eddie's voice was flat, without emotion. He was simply stating a fact. "Ming Sen knows as much, and he feels he must protect the boy. Especially now that he is the only son and heir."

"*That* is precisely why I have to do this, and why I must build up my business with the Black Dragons."

Eddie shook his head. "You already have a good business with your father. It carries far less risk than anything you are doing with the Dragons. I never thought you would get involved in prostitution, of all things. Ming Sen would be horrified if he knew the dishonor you were bringing upon the family name."

Was Eddie judging her?

"Just like he'd be mortified if he knew about Enzo?"

"Ahh, the Italian." Eddie sighed, reseated himself, and laced his fingers together on his broad lap. "Yes, I think we both know what your father would have to say about that. And I believe that's the main reason you are attracted to Vincenzo DeCarlo's son."

"Are you *analyzing* me, Eddie?" Jen didn't know whether to laugh or grind her teeth.

"Maybe I am," Eddie said. "Have you considered what will happen when the Italian finds out who—*what*—you are?"

Of course Jen had thought about that, but it hadn't stopped her from falling for Enzo. So far, he'd not asked her anything that indicated he didn't believe she was more than a rent collector and a benefactor to Chinese fleeing their homeland, and she'd certainly not offered up any information to the contrary. In that respect, Enzo DeCarlo was much the same as her father; he didn't expect too much of a mere woman.

Jen laughed. "If I can cover my tracks from my father, I don't think I'll have too much trouble hiding anything from Enzo. Besides, Enzo has other things to distract him from what I do for a living."

"I don't doubt that for a minute." Eddie huffed; he'd seen Jen through a number of dalliances over the years, none of which had ended pleasantly.

"Once I've set up my own business with the Dragons and made it a success, then I'll show Enzo—and my father—that I am as good as any man, if not better."

"And if they decide to turn their backs on you for the path you have chosen?" Eddie seemed to relish playing the part of the growling Buddha.

Jen furrowed her brow and laid the small pistol carefully on the countertop. "Then to hell with them all. I'll still have my own business and my own wealth. I swear to you, Eddie Sun. I will never be beholden to a man again."

CHAPTER THIRTY-FOUR

The Sum Ying pool hall was at 9 Doyers Street, within sight of the old Chinese theater. As pool halls went, it didn't seem all that bad. They served a little food—mainly wings and hot dogs—and the beer was local, cheap, and watered down. It was a typical Tiger property and one that Charlie-Boy had chosen to send a message to the rival gang. It was a message Storm Cheung had not sanctioned, which made it perfect for Jen's purposes.

Dressed in black jeans and a black hoodie with a bandana over the lower half of her face, the little Browning tucked into its kangaroo pocket, she hid among the shadows at the entrance of the next-door barbershop. From there, she watched as Charlie-Boy Fok led his troops —the youngest and most cocksure of the Dragon cohort—into the pool hall. There was an exodus, of course, as players and their groupies scurried out into the night like mice flushed from hiding. Their flight was accompanied by the music of mayhem and destruction as the Dragon horde took cleavers and sledgehammers to the pool tables, liquor bottles, and any Tigers idealistic enough to think they could prevail against the unexpected and heavily armed attack force.

Through it all, Jen crouched in the darkness of the doorway, waiting, her heart beating too quickly. She steadied her breathing and willed her heart to slow down. This was something that must be done.

When the sounds of shattering glass and wood and roars of fury and pain had faded, the Dragons departed. As was customary in these situations, they separated as soon as they hit the street and disappeared in all directions. It appeared to Jen that Charlie-Boy and his newest acolyte—a starry-eyed Fok fanboy who called himself Bullet—were the last to leave. Charlie-Boy slapped his companion on the back, gave him a shove up the street, then turned and headed right toward Jen's hiding place. Heart thudding, she leaned back into the shadows, with her hand on the Browning. If he walked right past her, would Charlie-Boy see her crouched there in the darkness of the shop entrance?

Nearer he came, his footsteps quick but heavy, and growing louder. She saw him as a blur in the moonlight as he strode past ... and did not stop or hesitate. She was out of her hiding place in half a heartbeat, daring to dart after him, quiet, sure-footed, intent. The Browning was in her hand now, her index finger lying along the side of the short barrel, as she calculated when to make her move. Too long, and he would be out onto Bowery.

In the end, Charlie-Boy took that decision out of her hands. He stopped just shy of one of Doyers' two bends and turned to face her.

"C'mon, Bullet. I told you not to follow—" He stopped, staring at the small, dark figure roughly six paces behind him. "Who the fuck are you?"

Some perverse demon made her say, "Guess. You get one chance."

"Fuck you. Quit playing games, whoever the hell you are."

"One chance, Charlie." She raised the Browning, her finger now on the trigger.

"Jesus," said Fok.

Jen laughed and pulled down her mask. "Not even close. You're bad at this game."

Eyes wide, face contorted with fury, Charlie-Boy took one step toward her. She fired. The sound of the gunshot reverberated down the odd little street. The bullet caught Charlie-Boy right between the eyes. He went down slowly, his knees buckling, his body folding up like oversized origami. He slumped to the sidewalk, a dark pool spreading out from his head.

Jen pulled up her mask, pocketed her pistol, and ran. When she turned the corner onto Bowery, she slowed to a walk. Her hoodie was now tied around her waist over a vivid blue blouse, her hair loose about her shoulders, the Browning tucked into a little sparkly crossbody purse she'd worn beneath her sweatshirt. Jen no longer bore any resemblance to the ninja who'd just taken out the Black Dragons' lieutenant on the Mott Street Tigers' turf.

Storm Cheung would suppose, as he was meant to, that his deputy had been murdered in retaliation for his ill-conceived strike in the heart of Tiger territory.

CHAPTER THIRTY-FIVE

Three days after Charlie-Boy's assassination rocked the Black Dragons, Storm Cheung gathered his dozen or so soldiers together to give them some shocking news. He'd shared his intentions with Jen first, and while she'd gotten over her own surprise, she was shocked anew by the level of venom the chiefs directed toward her when Storm told them his shiny new lieutenant was a woman and an outsider.

After a profound silence, Storm's office exploded with anger, grief, and testosterone. Some of the gangsters brandished their cleavers, although not one of them would dare cause Jen any harm in the presence of their leader; this was a ritual show of strength. Even so, she wished Eddie was at her side and had not been banished to the hallway. Still, there was something humorous about a bunch of grown men waving cutlery in the air while howling impotently at their leader's sudden fit of feminism.

"Charlie-Boy is not yet cold in his grave, and you give us this bullshit?" Sonny Yee dared raise his voice to the gang lord. Understandable —he'd just been passed over for a position he must have been certain was his.

Storm eyed the angry gangster with an unreadable expression. "I have based my decision on what is best for our business interests. Jen has a stronger grasp of business than any of us. She's proven that in Flushing—"

"Flushing was Charlie...."

"Taking credit for Jen's work," Storm said, glancing at Jen.

She stood next to his executive throne behind his desk, reveling in his praise and glad to have the barrier between her and her adversary.

Sonny was an impressive specimen. He was short, buff, and probably nineteen or twenty, though he looked older. He boasted the full set of gang tattoos, some of which crept up his thick neck to adorn his smooth-shaven head. He was missing both pinkie fingers, meaning there could be no doubting his loyalty to the Black Dragons. However, it wasn't loyalty Storm had cited in giving Jen the job, it was business acumen. While he mourned the loss of his lifelong friend, Storm had no option but to be pragmatic about the future of the Dragons.

Of course, Storm had not even the slightest inkling Jen had anything to do with his deputy's untimely demise. He assumed—as did everyone else in the gang— that the murderer was a member of the Mott Street Tigers.

For her part, though Jen had hardly expected it to bear fruit, she'd made sure to spend quality time with Storm, ostensibly to comfort him, while taking full advantage of his vulnerability and openness to suggestion. She'd been light-handed in her campaigning, reminding him of her trafficking experience and contacts, which Storm assumed would provide almost unlimited cash for the gang to expand the other lucrative areas of their business—drugs and real estate.

Sex had been a key component of her strategy, of course, and whatever that physical closeness meant to Storm in his grief, she had no idea and told herself she didn't care. If he was falling for her, it only strengthened her position. The elevation to deputy had come as a surprise, as did random pangs of guilt that crept up the last time she and Storm were together. The net effect of her discomfort was that she deliberately ignored Enzo's persistent phone calls, telling herself she'd make it up to him as soon as she could.

"Okay, maybe Charlie-Boy took credit for shit he didn't do, but I don't think this is about this bitch being good at business. I think it's about her being good at something else." Sonny grabbed at his crotch and made a crude thrusting motion in Jen's direction.

Storm stood up so quickly that his chair tipped over behind him, hitting the floor with a thud. The room fell silent.

"If any one of you would like to challenge me for leadership, then please, be my guest." Storm spread his arms out to his sides—a symbolic gesture to offer his unprotected heart to the gang and anyone who cared to take their best shot at his authority.

Jen studied each one of the silenced officers in turn. Storm had told her to expect a great deal of dissent in the ranks, and that he fully anticipated at least a handful of them leaving the gang over her promotion. They'd most likely defect to the Tigers or the Ghosts to lick their wounds and complain about how Storm Cheung had gone soft over some snakehead woman he was fucking.

"*No one?*" Storm reiterated his challenge. "Then I can assume you all accept my decision to make Jen our operations officer."

"We all respect you and your decisions, Storm," Sonny spoke up. "But *she* is not worthy of taking Charlie-Boy's place as vanguard."

As he pointed accusingly at Jen, his fellow soldiers voiced their similar opinions in loud, ragged unison. Some chose to show their disapproval by waggling their cleavers in Jen's direction like angry fishwives. Sonny joined in with his eyes fixed firmly upon the gang leader.

It crossed Jen's mind to say something, but she knew there was nothing she could say that would change their view of her. This required action. Resolved as she had been the night she shot Charlie-Boy, she rounded Storm's desk before he had time to react and faced the dissenting Dragons head-on.

Squaring up to Sonny Yee, Jen snatched the cleaver from his hand with a movement so swift it was in her possession before he'd registered what was happening. Sonny took a step back as if expecting his own weapon to be used against him, but Jen pivoted and slammed her left hand down on Storm's desk, fingers splayed apart. Then, with her focus on Storm's shocked face, Jen raised the cleaver, paused for a split second, and then brought it down hard, severing the tip of her pinkie. The pain was excruciating.

As much as Jen had braced herself mentally, she could never have anticipated the white-hot, searing agony that shot up her shoulder as the razor-sharp blade hacked through the flesh, tendons, and bone just above her first knuckle. She ground her teeth hard together, striving with everything she had not to show any sign of weakness before these men. Fighting debilitating nausea, she raised her hand, leaving behind the beautifully painted tip with its delicate white daisy.

"Let this prove I *am* worthy!" Jen held up her hand for all to see a thick, steady stream of blood running down her arm, staining the sleeve of her white shirt bright scarlet. "I may be only a woman, but I am equal to any one of you." Thoughts of her father, Petey, and Danny flashed through Jen's mind; her gesture had been as much for them as for the awe-struck Dragons. "Not one of you can doubt my loyalty to the Black Dragons now. No one can doubt that I have only *our* best interests at heart."

Still holding her mutilated hand aloft, she looked into each and every face, taking in their disbelief and what she hoped was grudging respect. Last of all, she looked at Storm Cheung and saw something like pride. It warmed her, even though she knew it was merely pride in his decision and how it reflected on him. The warmth dissolved into disappointment deep in her heart as she still longed to see that look on the face of another man—her father.

CHAPTER THIRTY-SIX

Jen did her best to ignore the dull throb that lit up her hand. She'd downed a few Ibuprofen tablets in the restaurant's restroom and hoped they'd kick in before too long as she so much wanted to enjoy her time with Enzo after almost a week apart.

"Preparing fish?" Enzo repeated her explanation for the tightly bandaged stump of Jen's left pinkie finger. "What were you using, Jen, a freakin' chainsaw?" He laughed at his own joke, but his brow was furrowed, and his eyes displayed obvious concern.

Jen smiled. After immersing herself in the Dragon's strange and violent world, it felt good to be spending time with Enzo again, and the place he'd chosen for dinner, Mia Bella, was simply exquisite. She rarely ventured into the East Village and had only ever walked past the renowned First Avenue restaurant.

"The knives they use have to be sharp enough to cut through the scales and backbones of the toughest fish. It's what I get for helping out my clients, I suppose." She raised her hand and, despite the pain, wiggled what was left of her finger for emphasis. It was sad to think her hand would never be as beautiful again, no matter how skilled the technicians at her favorite salon were.

"Do you always work in your clients' kitchens?" Enzo asked.

"Not as often as I would like," Jen told him, truthfully, she realized. "I actually find the work quite cathartic—sometimes it's nice to step away from my job and work with my hands for a change. I'm sure you find that, too?"

Enzo shrugged and sipped on his cabernet. "Can't see me working *for* my clients."

"That particular restaurant takes in many of the people I help get into the country," Jen explained. "They provide employment and sometimes accommodation for my new clients—just long enough for them to find their feet. I guess I'll just have to chalk this up to a hazard of the job."

Gingerly, she picked up her wine glass with her injured hand and took a sip of the dry red wine. She spent a moment letting the cascading flavor of black cherries and burnt wood distract her from the pain. She considered, not for the first time, telling Enzo more about the real shape of her association with the Dragons. She would have relished having someone to share her trials and triumphs with, but something stopped her. Enzo was a gangster in every traditional sense of the word, so he'd understand why she had chosen to work with Storm Cheung and his gang. But she couldn't be confident he'd accept the power she now held in that relationship; there could be no guarantees he wouldn't turn his back on her, especially with his dated attitude toward women. The fact that he'd so readily accepted her lame story about gutting fish spoke volumes—he wouldn't think her capable of losing a fingertip the way she actually had.

She resigned herself to the fact that she'd have to play her cards close to her chest for as long as was necessary and let Enzo carry on in his ignorance thinking her work was limited to collecting rent and helping immigrants find work. If he ever decided to dig around and come at her with questions, then she would consider letting him into her new world just a little more.

She found herself hoping that would never happen and wondered if she had stranded herself in some sort of no-man's land between two incompatible cultures. As she laughed at Enzo's riffing on why he thought of *The Godfather* as comedy, she was surprised at how much she wanted that not to be true.

ACT FOUR: JUST BUSINESS

CHAPTER THIRTY-SEVEN

It was early morning and still dark outside. Jen stood in the cabin of the *Bright Horizon* with her clipboard in hand and Eddie by her side. The boat had docked in New York Harbor in the small hours, having spent two long months at sea bringing over Jen's very first shipment for the Black Dragons. She was eager to unload the cargo she'd so carefully selected in China.

It was hard to believe it was March already, although the New York weather remained cold and there were still the occasional snow flurries —the final vestiges of the dying winter. In Central Park and around the tree-lined city streets, a few of the trees ventured fresh green shoots, which the last of the frosts would quickly kill off.

Because she'd utilized her father's boat, Jen had ensured a realistic mix of families and young men to distract from the presence of so many young women traveling alone. Had she filled the boat with single passengers, Father would have undoubtedly been alerted and asked questions she'd have trouble answering.

For the next shipment from Fujian, which was already being prepared by the ruthlessly efficient Tang Xun, they'd be using the *Morning Rainbow*. The battered old tub had undergone a considerable amount of refurbishment after Jen won it from Eng Hun. She had only recently been informed it was finally seaworthy and capable of making the long voyage to New York. For that voyage, there was to be only a token number of families aboard, since Jen's father did not know of the boat. That meant more room for the single girls the Black Dragons required for their Flushing brothels.

"It is good to see you again, Juliette," Jen greeted her in the seemingly endless procession of passengers. She remembered well the young woman she'd interviewed back in November, although her clothes were disheveled from the weeks at sea, and her cute, once-round face was pinched and colorless.

"It is good to be in America at last," she replied with a tired smile. "Thank you again for this wonderful opportunity, Miss Mo-Li."

Jen frowned, reminding herself that after a month or so of acclimation and three square meals a day, Juliette would return to her previous fresh-faced beauty. *Yes*, added a small, nagging voice in the back of Jen's head, *but what will she look like when she discovers the sort of work you've brought her here to do? When she realizes that instead of working behind a desk, she'll be earning her living on her back and knees and taking weekly STI tests.*

Jen silenced the voice and said, "Welcome to the country, Juliette. I shall look forward to seeing your progress."

The young woman half-bowed to her and moved to the next step, waiting for the rest of the young women to be processed.

"Miss Mo-Li." Instead of the next expected girl, the boat's captain stepped into the cabin. He took off his hat as he addressed Jen, holding it with both hands at his waist.

"Captain He." Jen had been wondering just when the elusive captain would make an appearance; she'd gotten the impression he'd been actively avoiding her. She thought the man seemed to have aged considerably since their previous encounter, his hair far more salt than pepper, and he was uneasy in her presence.

"It is my duty to inform you we had a fatality at sea." The captain's eyes flitted nervously between Jen and Eddie as he spoke. "One of the single ladies..."

A chill clutched at Jen's heart. "Which one?"

The captain visibly flinched when she addressed him as if he was expecting her pen through his throat for having delivered the bad news.

"Emily Wang," Captain He replied, eyes downcast. "There was some trouble with a few of the other passengers ... the young men...."

"Trouble?"

He tilted his head, wringing his cap. "They ... confronted her—"

"You mean they raped her."

He kept his eyes on the deck between his feet but said nothing.

Jen took that as a yes and bit back a sharp retort. "And the body?"

"We buried her at sea."

Jen ground her teeth and drew a neat, thin line through Emily's name. She saw little point in interrogating the captain as to the whys and wherefores of Miss Wang's burial at sea.

"Is that all?"

"Yes, Miss Mo-Li."

Jen saw the captain's gaze settle on her left hand. It had been several months since she had parted company with the tip of her pinkie, and she had gotten quite used to the smooth stump once it healed over. Although she considered her maimed hand ugly, it had served her well as the Black Dragons were beginning to accept her, if begrudgingly, as second-in-command. That they did it because of Storm Cheung and not her personally was a given.

"Thank you, Captain He," Jen dismissed the man.

She was pleased to see the back of him and would be relieved to have a different captain on the *Morning Rainbow*. She'd left instructions with Tang Xun to be sure to recruit someone with more courage and sharper powers of observation than Captain He.

Next on the list were the Qins—one of the families Jen had booked onto the voyage under her father's aegis. As with all others for whom she'd arranged passage, they had paid half of their fee prior to leaving China and would pay off the remainder over the following few years. However, what Jen hadn't realized in Fuzhou was just how stunning the Qin daughter was; even after suffering the rigors and poor diet of the voyage, she was a rare beauty and appeared to be far younger than her eighteen years. Two thoughts struck Jen at once: the changes in Shu Li because Donnie Wu got to her before Jen could, and the fact that she had one less girl than she was supposed to have for the Minster Tower parlors. Both made her uncomfortable.

"Sarah Qin," Jen said as she ticked off the names she had allocated to the family of three on her list. "I would like you to work directly for me."

"Thank you, Miss Mo-Li." The girl's father, the newly named Steven Qui, stepped forward. "But we have work already arranged for us all at a restaurant with cousins of my wife." He pointed at the gaunt, petite woman by his side; she wore her hair up in a tight bun, which served to accentuate her thin, pale skin.

"That may be the case, Mr. Qui," Jen told him bluntly. "But I have something else in mind for Sarah." If the man's fearful expression was anything to go by, Jen figured he had a good idea what she had in store for his daughter's new career. Was it the pinkie stump that screamed *gang*?

"I *must* insist," Qui protested. "We stay together *and* work together as a family."

Jen slipped her cheap Bic pen into the metal loop at the top of her clipboard and, lowering it, gave Sarah's father her full attention. "I am offering your daughter the opportunity to make a place for herself—and you and your wife—here in America, and to earn substantially more money than she would as a waitress. It will only be temporary—until you have paid off the remainder of your passage—and I can assure you she will be very well taken care of." Jen paused to see if her assurances were having any effect on the stubborn Mr. Qui. "As a father, would you deny Sarah such an opportunity?"

"I have heard of *opportunities* like this," Qui replied with some steel in his voice. "My daughter will be ruined."

Jen feigned offense. "Just what *exactly* are you accusing me of?" she demanded. "I can assure you I have only your family's best interests at heart, Mr. Qui." She cast a glance at Mrs. Qui, who remained stony-faced and silent, then addressed the young girl. "May I remind you, Sarah, that if someone discovers that you are here illegally, they can have you and your parents on the first plane back to China? Minus the money you have already paid for your passage, of course. If you are working for me, I can protect your family from that."

Sarah nodded, frowning. "I will be happy to work for you, Miss Mo-Li."

"No!" Qui took hold of his daughter's arm. "We have family here, Miss Mo-Li, and we know what happens to pretty young girls like Bao in this city." Pulling on his daughter's arm, he took a step toward the cabin door.

Eddie stepped away from Jen's side to block him.

"I don't think you quite understand the situation here, Mr. Qui," Jen said, reaching out her hand to the man.

"I understand enough to say *no* to you and your *kind*."

Mr. Qui slapped Jen's hand away with enough force to make her yelp. Instinct and anger then kicked in. Jen dropped her clipboard and threw a lightning fist at Mr. Qui's face, dealing a blow to his chin. Mr, Qui stepped back to steady himself, and even though Eddie loomed over him, he struck back. Jen blocked the blow and jabbed at Mr. Qui's stomach, doubling him over. Then she took his feet out from under him with a sweep of her leg. He hit the deck hard but immediately struggled to rise.

Now Eddie shoved forward, trying to get between Jen and the target of her wrath, but Jen held an arm out across his broad chest to stop him. Screaming inarticulately, she kicked out at Mr. Qui in fury, catching him in the shoulder, then in the stomach. Mrs. Qui and Sarah could only watch in mute horror while Eddie barked Jen's name several times. When Jen aimed a fist at Mr. Qui's head, Sarah lunged forward and grabbed Jen's arm, pulling her off balance.

"I said I will work for you!" the girl cried, tears streaming down her cheeks. "I will work off the rest of our passage! *What more do you want?!*"

As swiftly as it had come, the hot current of rage passed, leaving Jen feeling gutted. She let the younger woman pull her away from Mr. Qui, now groaning in pain.

"You should leave now," said Eddie, stepping between Jen and Mr. Qui.

Mrs. Qui nodded, then scurried forward to help her husband from the floor and guide him out of the cabin and away from Jen. Once he was safely out of Jen's reach, Sarah let go of her arm and followed her parents into the passageway.

As Jen stood quivering in the aftermath of her rage, Eddie turned on her with a gaze that carried the full weight of his bitter disappointment.

"Not that long ago," he said, his voice a low growl, "you would have been the one protecting that girl from the life you will now force her to live. I, too, must ask you: What do you want?"

He let go of her then and left her alone in the dank room.

CHAPTER THIRTY-EIGHT

Sarah Qui stood out among the dozen recruits for the first parlor, and Jen was pleased to include her as one of the first employees at Minster Tower, even if it had drawn Eddie's ire. Jen watched Sarah carefully, looking for signs she was in distress. It seemed to her the girl had made herself very much at home—she was relaxed, chatty, and looked all the more stunning for having had her nails, hair, and makeup done by the artisans Jen brought in. If there was fear or dread or uneasiness about what her first night of work entailed, Jen didn't see it in her dark eyes.

The new girls had all had a month in which to acclimate. They had been established on birth control—mostly IUDs put in place by doctors connected to the Black Dragons—and the few who had been unable to reconcile themselves fully to their new role were given medication that would make their time there less unpleasant. They had all been tutored in manners and conversation, which a surprising number of clients desired almost as much as they did the sex.

In this, the largest of the Dragon's five parlors at Minster Tower, Sarah Qui was one of three girls whose pure, youthful beauty put them in a category apart—a category prized by a certain segment of the parlor's clientele. Madam Ziyi had also selected Jessica Ni and Juliette

Quong for their schoolgirl looks and had dressed all three girls appropriately. Jen had moved twelve of the older prostitutes back to the parlors around Doyers and Mott to make room for the new girls. None of them had been particularly happy with the move.

Except for the three labeled "schoolgirls," the women were arrayed in dresses Jen had personally selected from one of Manhattan's finest boutiques. Some were short and low-cut, others ankle-length and split to the thigh. Most displayed a good amount of cleavage; all spoke of class and were a far cry from the adult store thrift the gang had their girls wearing at the Chinatown parlors.

Only Gong Shu Li wore a unique costume—an exquisite bondage outfit made from the finest black leather—befitting the parlor's resident dominatrix. She had also been allowed to keep her real name, as Madam Ziyi thought it deliciously exotic.

Even while running with the older prostitutes for several months, the Flushing parlors had garnered a reputation for being a cut above the rest, one Jen was keen to nurture and build upon. Following Charlie-Boy's demise, she had taken it upon herself to dictate every detail of each parlor's running—from the tasteful décor and mood music to the concise rules about the treatment of the girls. Armed security guards were assigned to the parlors that Madam Ziyi could call on if a client became unpleasant or threatened to harm the girls. This, among other things, had caused Madam Ziyi to become Jen's ally, for she knew Jen was unlikely to let another Charlie-Boy Fok force himself on any of the girls under the pretense of trying them out.

Now, all thirteen of her charges were sitting attentively on the plush couches in the reception area waiting for Jen to address them.

"Tonight is your first night of work," Jen began. "And you all know what is expected of you."

The girls nodded; some smiled at Jen, and some regarded her solemnly. Shu Li's expression was completely indecipherable.

Sarah raised her hand. "When will we be able to apply for other jobs?"

"Once you have paid off your passage in full, you will be free to look elsewhere," Jen told her. "We will safeguard your paperwork until then, of course." Hold hostage was more like it. The Minster girls were going nowhere.

"Any other questions?" Madam Ziyi stepped in, the tone in her voice *daring* her girls to ask anything.

They all remained silent—even Sarah.

"Remember that your clients are paying a great deal of money for your company," Jen continued. "But if they wish to tip you, that is perfectly fine, and you do not have to declare that to Madam Ziyi. However, do bear in mind that each client must pay in full before they spend any personal time with you, so do not be offended if they do not tip."

"And remember," said Madam Ziyi, "whatever services they ask for, the answer is always...."

"Yes," the girls chanted in harmony.

Jen shot the woman a sidewise glance. "That is not to say you are to accept any form of violence or threat of violence," she said. "We will simply *not* tolerate that here. You are to use the emergency button at your bedside if you feel threatened. Madam Ziyi is here to ensure your safety at all times," Jen added, looking directly at Madam Ziyi.

The madam inclined her head demurely. The girls nodded their approval, and Jen saw a glimmer of gratitude on their pretty young faces. She knew from experience the more money a man had, the more he considered himself above society's norms. With her parlors offering younger, more exotic girls at higher prices, Jen figured it was wise to be prepared for such eventualities as some rich men got their kicks beating on young girls. That train of thought ended at her father's door. He had never lifted a finger to strike her; her scars were invisible.

You should be the one in that grave....

With nothing left to say, Jen left the young women in the capable hands of Madam Ziyi and sought out Eddie, who had secreted himself in the kitchen. Jen thought he seemed particularly uncomfortable as if the sexualized, feminine environment of the brothel was more disturbing than usual. Jen decided against inquiring; had Eddie wanted her to know what was bugging him, he would have already said something.

"Time to go?" Eddie grunted and drained his cup of green tea.

"I have a date, remember?" Jen's smile was met with a frown. "I don't want to keep Enzo waiting, Eddie."

Eddie followed Jen from the apartment and down the hallway. He'd made himself scarce while she addressed the employees, or rather, slaves. Eddie had noticed how the young girls seemed uncomfortable having him around, although he'd not once given any of them good reason to be. Perhaps, he mused, it was that the girls didn't realize they held no interest for him and expected him to behave like that Fok character.

There was a time Eddie would have shrugged that off and stuck to his place by Jen's side, but it gave him a good excuse to be somewhere else. Jen Mo-Li didn't need his constant presence within the relative safety of the parlors, and that allowed him to distance himself from the person she was becoming.

He'd noted a less than subtle change in Jen since Danny's death and had come to believe something had happened during or after the funeral that had struck her deeply. Since then, her dealings with the gangs, the trip to China, the way she'd dealt with Charlie Fok, the way she'd gone off on Sarah Qui's father—it was as if the Jen Mo-Li Eddie had known since she was a young slip of a girl was metamorphosing into something alien. Something cold. Certainly, she was more assertive and confident in her abilities, but also more ruthless. He was torn. Eddie Sun was caught between admiration and dread.

Jen rarely spent time at home with her father and Petey anymore. She was there just enough for whatever was essential to keep up the business responsibilities that allowed her to present a respectable façade to Ming Sen and her younger brother. In place of the family time Jen once grudgingly endured, she much preferred to spend time with the man she had come to think of as her Italian hoodlum—yet another subject that had become taboo between them. Jen had confided in Eddie about all the relationships in her life, from the thrilling flush of first love to the inevitable heartbreak. But since she'd taken up with Enzo DeCarlo and witnessed Eddie's disapproval, Jen had closed off the entire subject.

"Hey! *You!*" An angry voice erupted behind them.

Eddie turned in perfect synch with Jen to see a tall, slender middle-aged man standing in the doorway of one of the apartments. Hovering behind him was a petite woman of about the same age, wearing a tad too much green eye shadow and dark, plum-colored lipstick.

"Can we help you, sir?" Jen said.

"Sure, you can." The guy stepped out of his doorway, but not too far. "You can fuck off back to China. That's what you can fucking do to help me."

Eddie willed Jen to back down. He was in no mood for an altercation. But Jen bristled to such a degree that Eddie swore he could feel pinpricks of her displeasure on his skin.

She strode toward the angry resident with a growl, "Excuse me?"

"You heard me. Go the fuck back to China!" The man punctuated his words with the jab of a finger, but then seemed to see Eddie for the first time. He lowered his hand and seemed not to know what to do with it. Finally, he put both hands on his hips, perhaps trying to look more imposing than he actually was.

Eddie smelled the unmistakable sour whiff of booze on the guy from ten feet away. He imagined he could smell the heat of Jen's anger, as well.

"I didn't come from China. I was born right here in New York. You need to check your assumptions," she said, coming to a stop just beyond arms' reach of the man.

Perhaps because she seemed no more imposing than his wife, the guy scoffed directly into Jen's face. "*Should* I now?" He puffed out his chest. "We've been living here eleven years among decent folk, and all of a sudden the place is swarming with you fucking people!"

Full of alcohol-fueled bravado, the man stepped toward Jen, who didn't so much as blink but merely lifted her chin higher to maintain eye contact. Eddie maneuvered several inches away from Jen's right shoulder and scrutinized the man who was squaring up to her. He seemed respectable enough—appearance-wise at least—in his crisply pressed Chinos and stylish Ralph Lauren polo, his hair carefully tousled and his Don Johnson scruff scrupulously trimmed. Eddie glowered at the man and hoped that would be enough to get him to go back to his wife and the TV he could hear in the background.

"My father almost died in 'Nam fighting you lot." Mr. Miami Vice, far from retreating, persisted, daring to waggle his finger dangerously close to Jen's face. "And every fucking day, I open my front door and there's more of you little yellow bastards swarming all over the place. Don't think I don't know what's going on around here—I should call the cops on all the slanty-eyed sluts and johns coming and going at all fucking hours."

Eddie tensed in tandem with Jen. This was both personal and threatening to her business, and he knew she was not going to stand by and take it.

"First of all," Jen said, her voice deceptively mild, "we are Chinese, not Vietnamese, so your dad didn't fight us 'little yellow bastards.' Second, if you are not happy here, sir, then I'd suggest you move. I'm sure there are many other nice places you could live—upstate perhaps? I'd be more than happy to speak with the owners about buying you out."

"I'm going fucking *nowhere*!" The man's face turned a concerning shade of puce as spittle flew from his lips. "This is my fucking country and I'll not be pushed out by some fucking, yellow-faced bitch!" He took a swipe at Jen, which she missed, having seen it coming.

Jen slipped into her fighting stance as the guy coiled to take another swing. Eddie shot out a hand to grab the guy's arm in mid-air; his wrist felt like a collection of chicken bones in Eddie's big hand. "You need to back off, buddy," he growled.

"Take your fucking hands off me!" The guy's voice rose at least an octave. "You're breaking my arm!"

Eddie squeezed tighter and returned a malevolent smile. "Not at the moment, but I could. Now, *back off*."

"I'm calling the cops!" The guy tried in vain to squirm his wrist out of Eddie's grasp.

Jen lowered her fists, but Eddie saw the anger in her eyes replaced by something cold and reptilian. He knew what was coming next.

"Deal with this asshole," Jen snarled to Eddie. "Persuade him now would be a *very* good time to relocate—before anything untoward happens to him, leaving his lovely wife on her own."

Eddie shrugged as if the matter was unimportant. "We could just have the landlords evict him."

"Ron!" roared the little wife, in a voice twice her size. Mr. Miami Vice uttered a wild-eyed grunt in return.

"There, see," Eddie added, "he's more scared of his wife than he is of me." Besides, the police would take a white guy's complaint seriously—especially *here*. He wanted to remind Jen of that but didn't want to put ideas into Ron's head.

"I've asked you to deal with the asshole, Eddie." She spoke each word slowly, deliberately. "If you don't, I will. And I expect not to see him the next time I'm here." Jen spun on her heels and marched off along the hallway, leaving Eddie to do his job.

"Yes, ma'am," he said to her retreating back.

Eddie was torn between loyalty to Jen and doing what was prudent and right. Beating someone to a bloody mess for cause didn't bother Eddie too much, but this was sheer retaliation for personal insult, and more than just being purposeless, it was potentially dangerous to Jen's business interests. God only knew what the Dragons would do if the Minster Tower parlors were raided because Jen's henchman messed up a neighbor.

In the end, Eddie sat Ron and Mrs. Ron down and explained, graphically, the sort of things his boss meant when she demanded he "deal with" someone, starting with how easily he could have broken Ron's wrist. He was sure that they would reap a very nice amount for their condo if they were to put it up for sale at their earliest opportunity.

By the time Eddie finished his explanation, Ron and his good wife had decided a nice townhouse upstate might be more to their liking after all. He recommended they vacate ASAP and, in the unlikely event that Ron should encounter Jen again, he gave the guy a black eye.

Eddie left after that, still worrying about all the ways in which Jen Mo-Li was changing right before his eyes.

CHAPTER THIRTY-NINE

"What was *that*?" Enzo gasped as Jen toppled off him and collapsed onto her side of the bed.

"What?" She could barely breathe, let alone hold any kind of conversation.

"You beat the crap out of me." Enzo rolled onto his side so she could better see the bite marks on his chest and the red imprints of her fingernails on his shoulders and neck.

"Did you enjoy it?" Jen caressed her lover's cheek with trembling fingertips and wriggled her naked body closer as he nodded with enthusiasm.

Yes, she'd taken her frustrations out on Enzo. The white guy's disrespect, Eddie's reluctance to do as she'd ordered, and his questioning of her authority had put her in a stinking mood. In her mind, the changes in Eddie dated from her killing Donnie Wu in self-defense and had only grown since Danny's death. Jumping into bed with a Chinese gang—literally—had not been on her radar, but it was a means to an end. Yet that too had become a source of contention between them. She supposed she should be grateful that Eddie generally expressed his opinions sparely and quietly, but his silent, judgmental regard, like her father's, was wearing. He didn't seem to appreciate how much she'd managed to achieve on her own merits.

Eddie had always been there for her, through thick and thin, which made his insolence all the more unbearable. Hell, she was the only one he'd confided in about being gay—such things were *definitely* not discussed in respectable Chinese society. Okay, he disapproved of her new business associations and practices, but the least she could expect from the man was his continued respect toward her as a person and not to see her as some little woman who had overstepped. What she needed, she decided, was to make him see that she wasn't overstepping; she was completely in control. Jen knew what she was doing.

As for Enzo, Jen knew, although he protested on occasion, that he had grown to enjoy the rough sex and didn't mind too much when she used him to work out her tensions whenever they were in bed together. He'd even quit trying to maneuver himself on top of her when his instinct told him she needed to be dominant. Enzo DeCarlo was just happy to be along for the ride.

"I've never fu—*slept* with anyone like you before." Enzo leaned in to kiss Jen's damp forehead and brushed aside the strands of hair that stuck there.

"You can say fucked, Enzo." Jen laughed and draped her leg over his, enjoying the heat of him. "I think I'd describe what we just did as fucking, wouldn't you?"

"Yeah," Enzo agreed. "I get the feeling your head is someplace else when we ... fuck like that."

Jen pressed herself tight against her lover and laid her head on his chest. "I'm not imagining you as someone else, if that's what you're thinking," Jen assured him. She was still in no mood to soothe the guy's ego but reckoned she owed him at least that much of an explanation. "Sometimes it's like having an extra-vigorous workout at the gym to relieve my stress—only much more fun."

Enzo laughed and held Jen tight. "I hope it is," he said, his voice still slightly breathless, weary.

Jen allowed herself to relax. She felt safe with Enzo, *at home*, more so than with any man she had ever been with. There was just something about his old-world charm and thuggish innocence that gave her the security she craved to allow her to let her guard down. Outside the bedroom, she was in command, the driver of her own destiny. But within the intimate confines of her bed, Jen had begun to feel that it was okay to be naked and vulnerable, though it took a great deal of effort to allow herself that luxury.

As fatigue washed through her body, Jen contemplated Enzo, who was already sound asleep. In working through her anger and frustration at Eddie, she had truly worn him out. It puzzled her how Enzo had still not asked about her work, and how he seemed more than content to swallow her lies. Maybe he didn't care about who she was beyond the confines of her bed. Maybe she was just sex to him. The thought made her sadder than she expected, but wasn't that for the best? She increasingly didn't want to know how Enzo would react if he ever found out about her life beyond these walls.

That was a worry for another day, she told herself, one she would do everything within her power to avoid. As she lay against Enzo's sleeping body, his arm draped protectively about her bare shoulders, Jen was more than happy to let everything but the two of them melt into the background as she, too, succumbed to sleep.

Doyers Street was remarkably busy considering it was still a few minutes before six on a Wednesday morning. Enzo had snuck out to buy donuts, which were warm and deliciously aromatic in the brown paper bag he clutched tight in his hand. He'd had to walk a fair way to get the good ol' home-cooked variety he knew Jen had a weakness for and aimed to be back at her apartment before she woke up to an empty bed. Enzo had taken to staying the night with her, although Rico informed him The Don had noted his absence at home on more than one occasion. Enzo couldn't bring himself to just fuck Jen and leave like some heartless cad, although he'd done it countless times before with his other conquests, many of whose names he'd long forgotten.

"Hey, *Enzo*?" A voice from behind.

Startled, Enzo turned around. "Matteo?" he said once his flitting mind put a name to the grinning face; his distant cousin had been made capo a little over two years ago, and their paths rarely crossed. "I'm sorry ... I didn't expect...." He felt his face flush and knew he had guilt written all over it.

"Hey, cuz, quit panicking," Matteo laughed. "I'm not following you or anything. Looks like you had a good night." Nodding at the bag of donuts, he tipped Enzo a wink. It was meant to put him at ease.

Enzo wasn't taken in by the fake *bonhomie*. There was only one explanation for Matteo bumping into him so early in Chinatown, and it sure as all hell wasn't coincidence.

"What brings you here this early?" Enzo ventured.

"A little bit of business." Matteo was suitably vague. "Nothing worth buying donuts for, though." Another wink.

Enzo was insulted—the asshole had not even made the effort to think up a decent cover story for spying on him. Gripping the paper bag, he tried to think of what would be best. Lie and tell Matteo the donuts were for someone other than the hot Chinese girl he'd just spent the night with? Or plead with the guy to say nothing to Vincenzo?

Neither option was viable; Enzo knew that. There was no doubt in his mind his father had put the tail on him. The fact that the tail was Matteo—a family member, no matter how far removed on his mother's side—let him know the severity of the situation he was now facing. Just how much the guy knew about whom he'd been spending time with, Enzo could only guess at, but the fact that he'd broken cover was a clear signal from The Don that the game was well and truly up.

"Nice to see you, Matteo." Enzo forced himself to keep up the pretense. What else was there to do?

"We must grab a few beers and catch up some time," Matteo said with a wide, shit-eating grin. "It's been too long."

Family or not, Matteo simply wasn't the type Enzo chose to spend his downtime with; he was too fucking sneaky, for one.

"Sure," Enzo replied as he sidestepped the guy to continue along Doyers. He figured he might as well enjoy the donuts in bed with Jen before heading home to face the music.

CHAPTER FORTY

As Enzo predicted, Vincenzo was not happy, nor was he impressed with his son's attempts at explaining himself.

"I got a tip-off about a drug deal," Enzo squirmed in the leather armchair opposite his father's. They were in the upstairs study, which Vincenzo reserved for only his most serious business discussions. Had Enzo been anyone other than The Don's son, there would have been the strong likelihood of him leaving that room feet-first in a body bag.

"Don't bullshit me, *Little Enzo*," Vincenzo grunted. "We don't deal directly in Chinatown anymore. You know we leave that to the Chinese gang now; you set the fucking deal up!" He scrutinized his son's defiant face. "Let's cut to the chase, boy. I don't have time to go around the motherfucking houses. I know you were out all night in Chinatown, and not for the first time."

Enzo shrugged.

Vincenzo leaned forward and stroked his chin, the bristle making a rough, grating noise. "I don't mind if you're out chasing tail. Christ knows I did enough of that when I was your age. You're a grown man, Enzo, with DeCarlo genes, and I'm well aware of what that means. You can do better than some cheap Chinese girl. I thought I'd raised you to have *some* standards." He left that comment hanging in the sour atmosphere between them.

"Who says I'm out banging a Chinese girl?" Enzo tested the water. If The Don didn't know about Jen, then he could still bluff his way through some of it.

"Why else would you be staying overnight on Doyers?"

Enzo didn't know.

"You know my opinion of those people," Vincenzo growled.

"You like 'em well enough to do business with them," Enzo countered. He comfortably knew his father had no idea about Jen. For all Vincenzo figured, the nights spent in Chinatown had been nothing more involved than a string of one-night stands.

Vincenzo suppressed what Enzo thought was a cynical smile. "That's all they're good for—they know those streets better than we ever could. Business has never been better, but I'd very much like to keep it that way. You running around banging their women isn't the way to keep things professional."

It struck Enzo as weirdly comical that his father considered dealing with the Mott Street Tigers as being professional. Maybe that was what was wrong with the anachronistic world The Don lived in.

Vincenzo shook his head and reached into the inside pocket of his jacket for a cigarette. As a matter of courtesy, he offered the packet to Enzo, who declined. "To think I was this close to making you." Lifting a hand in front of his face, Vincenzo brought his finger and thumb within a fraction of an inch of each other to denote just how close Enzo had come. "Instead, I don't know if I can trust my own son."

Enzo read the disappointment in his father's eyes and for a split second, he felt a sharp stab of guilt. He was guilty of letting his father down by hooking up with a Chinese girl, guilty of sneaking around and hiding his indiscretions with deceit, and guilty of denying how he felt about Jen because he was too scared of what he knew his family would say.

"That's going to have to wait for the time being," Vincenzo continued. "We have an upstate casino being turned over by the management. A hell of a lot of money has gone missing—*our* money. You go spend some time up there. Find out who's got their fingers in the goddamn till."

"Then what?"

"Deal with it." Vincenzo snarled as he lit up his cigarette. "You're to stay up there until it's sorted out. There's no point trashing all the management on account of one bad apple—assuming it is just the one apple, of course."

Enzo opened his mouth to protest as thoughts of Jen and her warm, sweet body flashed through his mind.

The Don held up a hand with the smoking cigarette between his fingers. "Rico will go with you. I can trust him to keep an eye on you and report back to me. That ought to keep your dick out of Chinatown awhile and give you both the chance to chase some top-class pussy—there's nothing like the lure of the tables to loosen a posh gal's panties." He laughed at his crude joke.

Enzo pretended to laugh along, even though his heart felt unbearably heavy and there was a pit in his stomach.

"It'll do you good to learn the casino business," Vincenzo added by means of placating his son, "especially if you're planning on being more than just a thug someday. You have any objections?"

It was, of course, a rhetorical question.

CHAPTER FORTY-ONE

It had taken three months of digging deep into the business at the Empire World Casino to unearth the true scope of Billy Borgeil's thievery. The casino—offering the very best in upstate New York gambling, lodging, and nightlife, according to the flashy brochures—was the DeCarlo family's flagship, and represented a huge investment in money, time, and bribery of local officials.

This was why Enzo and Rico were under instruction to deal with the matter, and the manager, as thoroughly as possible, but only once they had all the facts, figures, and hidden bank accounts. Unlike their fatal altercation with Joey Greco, Vincenzo had sanctioned the retribution himself—via Angel Corozzio, of course—the moment concrete proof had been presented to him.

It had been Rico who'd slotted the final piece of the puzzle into place, all thanks to a snippet of careless pillow talk by one of the casino's accountants he'd bedded a handful of times. In passion's afterglow, she'd let slip something about *other accounts*, and Rico realized he and Enzo had been looking in the wrong places. Good ol' Billy had a bunch of offshore accounts set up in his ex-wife's name, as it turned out.

Billy had been seemingly helpful throughout their investigations; he'd even gone so far as to befriend Enzo and Rico and would often join them after hours at the tables or drinking in one of the resort's many bars. The guy had played it so damn cool, deftly deflecting suspicion onto his deputies, that both Rico and Enzo were genuinely surprised when they finally found him out.

"You're gonna have to do better than that, Billy," Enzo growled into the man's ruined face. His left eye was blackened and all but swollen shut, his ashen skin drenched in sweat and smeared with blood from his busted nose and split lips. "We know about the two Virgin Islands accounts. Give us the numbers and we'll make this easier for you."

Enzo's promise rang somewhat hollow. Strapped to an old, wooden chair down in the casino's boiler room, Billy Borgeil didn't look like a man who figured he was going to get out of his predicament alive. Billy had given up most of his secrets between screams and pleas for mercy. Enzo figured the guy was holding out so his family would have some kind of legacy once the inevitable happened and he never went home; Billy knew damn well he'd be leaving the casino in pieces.

Enzo gave a long, exaggerated sigh and reached for the bloodied claw hammer that rested across Billy's lap like some sinister pet. The manager's eyes widened. Rico's face fell at the prospect of them inflicting yet more pain on Billy when it was clear he was done talking.

"Maybe he's had enough, Enzo," Rico chipped in. "I think he's done; we should finish up and go get wasted."

At the suggestion of finishing up, of which there could be no misinterpretation, Billy's face slackened. To Enzo, the guy kind of looked *relieved* at the prospect of his impending death.

"You want to tell The Don we didn't get *all* this asshole's bank accounts?" Enzo snapped.

Rico said nothing.

Enzo was poised for a swipe at the manager's hand when the mobile phone in his breast pocket rang. Jen was the only one who called him on the cell phone. Enzo wanted to pick up before she hung up on him again; she'd developed the habit lately of only waiting three or four rings before giving up on him, and it was beginning to bug him. Dropping the hammer back onto Billy's legs, Enzo dug the phone out of his pocket and thumbed at the keypad to pick it up.

"Hey, baby." As he spoke, he turned away from Billy and Rico, who folded his arms across his chest and frowned his displeasure.

"I miss you, and I need to see you," Jen's voice purred quietly into Enzo's ear.

She hadn't called often while he'd been stuck at the casino and asked him to visit even less frequently. That had Enzo worried; for as little as he'd managed to sneak away from the casino to be with her, Jen seemed to be getting along just fine. Enzo was beginning to think she might be cooling off, and that was putting a strain on their relationship, at least as far as he was concerned. He hated that he allowed Jen to make him feel that way and that she was the dominant one in their relationship. Each time he dashed back to see her, Enzo promised himself he'd be more assertive. But each time, Jen turned it around and showed him who was boss.

"Actually, I was planning to come down this weekend," Enzo told her. "Rico can cover for me."

Rico's brow furrowed. Enzo turned his back on his friend, feeling a twinge of guilt. He knew he put Rico in an impossible position each time he snuck back to Manhattan, a fact Rico had brought to his attention on more than one occasion. While they were best friends, comrades, and soldiers together, Rico's ultimate loyalty had to lie with the family—Vincenzo DeCarlo in particular. Lying to The Don wouldn't do him any favors should he ever be caught out, even if it was to cover for Enzo.

"When can you get here, baby?" There was a sensual, alluring tone to Jen's voice, which had Enzo stiffening in his pants.

"I'll leave right now," Enzo told her with a backward glance at the semi-conscious casino manager. "I'm not doing anything important."

Happy with that, Jen said her goodbyes and Enzo hung up the call.

"Are you fucking kidding me?" Rico spat. "You can't just duck out of this and go play grab-ass. Not again."

Enzo gave his friend a placating smile. "I'll owe you one, Rico."

"You owe me more than fucking one," Rico replied. "I'm tired of lying to The Don. There's only so many times he's going to believe you're out chasing tail. If he finds out you've been creeping back to Chinatown, he's gonna go fucking apeshit."

Enzo studied his friend's face; there was no hint of possible betrayal there. He was confident he could rely on Rico to keep *shtum* and cover for him while he spent time with Jen. Rico was right, of course—if Vincenzo got wind of his son's dalliances after having gone to all the trouble of putting a stop to them, there'd be hell to pay.

"We'll make sure he *doesn't* find out."

"Right. What are we going to do about *this*?" Rico nodded down at Billy.

"I'd say we've got all the account numbers he's going to give us." Enzo picked up the hammer. "Let's call it a day."

CHAPTER FORTY-TWO

"Seriously?" Enzo fumed. "I drive all this way in the middle of the goddamn night, and you're going out?"

Jen glared at him. Sure, Enzo had dropped whatever it was he was doing at the casino because she'd begged him to, but that didn't mean he could talk to her like she was his tame little wifey. Now he stood in the middle of her bedroom with his shirt unbuttoned, his shoes in his hand, and the erection bulging in his jeans, gradually deflating.

"Enzo, I told you, something's come up and I need to take care of it," she said as she checked her makeup in her dresser mirror. "I got the call literally a minute before you walked in the door. You know how it goes. If it was something I could leave until morning, don't you think I would?"

"It's two in the morning, Jen." His voice raised, Enzo persisted. "What can you possibly have to do that's so fucking important it couldn't wait a few more hours?"

She stared at him in disbelief. What could she *possibly* have to do that was important? Really? It took everything she had not to snarl at him. Instead, she simply said, "It's *business*, Enzo. I have to deal with it now, and it's not going to take long. You'll get what you came for; don't worry," she added tartly.

He dropped the shoes. "Damnit, Jen, this isn't about me getting my rocks off. I mean, yeah, I want you. But I mostly just want to *be* with you for the little time I've got. And I just got here...."

Jen took a deep breath. As much as she wanted to snarl at him, she couldn't. He looked so damn sexy standing there with his shirt open to show off the thick, black hair that covered his muscular chest and stomach, and teased her by disappearing into his waistband. She was by now well aware that this wasn't just about the sex for either of them. He was her haven, and she was his. She got that. But when he was like this—demanding, self-centered....

She shook off her irritation at the need to explain herself to him and tried to get him to understand. "Enzo," she said, striving to keep her tone even, "I've gone to great pains to keep my business affairs separate from our relationship, but I still must conduct my business." She did not add that that wasn't about to change just because he pouted.

"Can't someone else in your family handle it? Your dad or brother?"

She almost wanted to tell him, then, that this had nothing to do with her family. This was *her* business. But no, he wasn't ready to hear that. At least not yet.

"No. This is on my plate. Now, I really have to go." She put on a lascivious smile and pointed to the still-impressive bulge in Enzo's pants. "Don't you dare start anything without me."

Sadly, her attempt at levity fell flat. Enzo flopped back onto her bed and grabbed for the TV remote on her nightstand.

"No promises," he said.

Jen pulled on her jacket, slipped on her shoes, and let herself out of the apartment.

———

Eddie was already at Minster Tower when she got there. She'd made it to Flushing in less than half an hour; the roads across Manhattan and off the island were a hell of a lot quieter in the small hours than in the daytime.

"What the hell is going on, Eddie?" Jen demanded as she waited for him to hold the door open for her.

"Madam Ziyi insisted we deal with the unrest immediately," Eddie replied with a stifled yawn.

Jen was well acquainted with her bodyguard's penchant for understatement. The madam wouldn't have called them both out in the middle of the night for something as trivial as a little unrest among the parlor's girls. Had that been the case, she and Eddie would have spent most of the past six months at the place.

Madam Ziyi met Jen and Eddie at the parlor's door and, as she ushered them quickly inside, she explained that it was Sarah Qui who was at the root of the trouble. "That girl has been stirring things up since day one," Ziyi told them. "She is very much in demand by our clients, so I've managed to keep her under control—until now."

The three made their way into Madam Ziyi's small side parlor, where a slim, middle-aged man in a dark blue business suit sat on the edge of a pale leather chair with an ice pack held to one eye. A quartet of angry red scratches emerged from beneath the ice pack and ran down to the blood-streaked collar of his once-crisp white shirt.

"Sarah did this?" Jen asked.

"It's not the first time she's said no to a client," Ziyi explained with a deep sigh. "But she's never actually assaulted one before now."

"How the fuck can I go home to my wife and kids looking like this?" the man snarled.

Jen looked at him with disdain, little caring that he recognized the emotion. *How the fuck can you come here when you have a wife and kids?* The words sat poised on the tip of her tongue, but she swallowed them and followed Madam Ziyi across the main lounge to Sarah's room with Eddie tagging behind. The girls relaxing in the lounge watched them pass. Jen made sure to acknowledge each one with a nod and a smile; she knew all too well the importance of exerting her authority, especially at such times as this.

Sarah Qui sat in the middle of her bed toying with a six-inch stiletto knife. She wore the archetypal schoolgirl's outfit, complete with knee-high white socks, plaid miniskirt, pigtails, and pale makeup—all at the whim of the guy who sat nursing the ice pack and others like him. Sarah looked up with an expression of blatant defiance when Jen, Eddie, and Madam Ziyi marched into her room without knocking. Her crisp white blouse had been pulled open at the top, revealing the tops of her breasts. The girl looked like some over-sexualized manga character of no more than twelve or thirteen years, and it almost threw Jen off guard.

Jen stopped several strides away from the bed—there was something about the deliberate way the girl played with the knife that gave her pause. "What's going on here, Sarah?"

"Do you *know* what that sick pervert told me to do?" Sarah said, her top lip curling up at its corner. Tears had welled in her eyes. "I don't care how much he paid. It was *wrong*."

Jen eyed the knife. "What did he want?"

"For me to cut myself." Sarah pointed at her breasts with the tip of the blade. "He said he wanted to fuck me covered in my blood. *He* brought this in!" She held the knife up for Jen to see. The narrow blade glittered in the light of the bedside lamp.

Madam Ziyi made a reproachful sound and shook her head. "That's against house rules!"

"Even so, you should not have attacked him." Jen ventured a step forward. "You should have simply refused."

"I *did* refuse!" Sarah snarled. "He tried to cut me. I defended myself."

"You should have alerted me," Madam Ziyi murmured.

"Did you not hear me? He came at me with the knife and tried to cut my breast and I couldn't reach my panic button."

"If you had screamed—" began Madam Ziyi.

"And what would you have done?" Rounding on her manager, Sarah jabbed the knife in her direction. "You *always* side with the johns! You'd have told me to suck it up, just like you always do. All these 'rules' against violence you just ignore. It's–it's bullshit, and we're sick of it! All of us!"

Jen turned to the madam. "Is this true? That you ignore the rules I have set?"

"I–I have used my discretion...."

"You've let us be beaten and bitten and have horrid, painful things done to us. And we have spoken up without relief."

Madam Ziyi opened her mouth to protest, but Jen cut her off. "From now on, you will have the parlor guards search every man who enters this place. I do not want a repeat of this. Do I understand that we have girls here who are injured?"

"Well...." said Madam Ziyi. "There are a few who...."

"Ask her where Juliette is," said Sarah.

Jen raised an eyebrow. "Where is Juliette?" she asked Madam Ziyi.

The woman paled and took a half-step back, which did not bode well for her answer. "She–she's taking a few days off to rest and—"

"Her client tried to strangle her with her own braids in the middle of sex," said Sarah. "It will be more than a few days before the bruises fade. Of course, it may be that other johns would think they are sexy."

"Is Juliette the only one?"

Sarah shook her head. "There are others who are 'resting' because of things the johns did to them. Tanya Jiang, Linda Bo—I know for sure."

Jen turned her attention back to Madam Ziyi. "How many? How many are 'out-of-service?'"

The madam returned to her usual aplomb, head high, back straight. "Five, in all. But we're covered. I restaffed from Venus Joy and will send those girls back when our regular girls can work."

"That does not change the fact that we are losing the money that those girls bring in," said Jen. "In fact, we may be losing regular clients for whom these girls are favorites. And how long will it be before a girl is hurt so badly, she can no longer work?" She gestured at Sarah. "These girls—these women—are our assets. Without them, you would not have a job."

"These girls," said Madam Ziyi, her scarlet lips curling, "are ungrateful bitches, Ms. Mo-Li. If it were not for you, *they* would have no jobs!"

"There are other brothels," said Sarah. "I've already been approached by someone from another parlor, offering more money. So have others. The Tigers are saying they will pay off our debt to you if we go with them."

Jen could barely believe what she was hearing. She'd gone to such great pains to make the Minster Tower parlors nice, safe working environments, and had ensured the girls were paid not only well, but over and above every brothel in the area. And now, through Madam Ziyi's poor oversight....

Madam Ziyi lost her composure completely. She threw herself at the younger woman with a shriek of utter rage, slashing at her with her long fingernails, leaving four bloody furrows across the top of the girl's breasts. With her free hand, she snatched the knife from Sarah's hand and turned it on her.

Shocked into action, Jen instinctively did the only thing she could do to stop Madam Ziyi from stabbing the girl. She aimed a roundhouse kick at the madam's hand, catching the knife and sending it flying. Her momentum carried her foot upward to collide with Madam Ziyi's head. The madam collapsed at the foot of the bed, holding the side of her face. But Jen wasn't done. She pinned the madam to the bed and slashed at her with her own well-manicured nails. Even Eddie gasped as she raked four deep lines down the side of Madam Ziyi's face, leaving one false fingernail embedded in the delicate flesh below the madam's left eye. As Jen stepped back, the woman curled in on herself, sobbed, and tried to stem the flow of blood.

Jen ignored her. She turned to Sarah instead. "Do you intend to go to the Tigers?"

"I intended to return to my family and their business as soon as I paid off my debt to you. But...." She looked down at the bloody tracks across the tender flesh of her breasts. "I think that will not happen now that I have no way to repay you. There may be others who will go."

"Will you encourage them?"

Sarah snorted indelicately. "Would the Tigers treat them any differently than they have been treated here?"

Jen winced inwardly. "I had no intention for that to happen. How can I make sure they stay?"

"Enforce the rules you put in place, Ms. Mo-Li, and find a madam who will protect your assets." She cast a contemptuous glance at Madam Ziyi whose sobs had become a low, keening moan.

Jen nodded and met Sarah's eyes. "I think I've found her," she said. "If you will accept the position."

Sarah was stunned. "Ms. Mo-Li, are you certain? Madam Ziyi called me a troublemaker."

"Madam Ziyi was blinded by greed. I'm not. You will be able to work off your debt more quickly and then, if you wish, you may go to your family business."

"Then, yes."

"Good." Jen reached over to the bed to snatch up the pink comforter on which she wiped the hand she'd bloodied on Madam Ziyi's face. She held the scrubbed hand out for Sarah to shake. "Now, you must go see the staff doctor and have him tend to those cuts. I'll deal with your client. Eddie, please help Madam Ziyi pack a bag and send her to a hospital."

Jen exited the room, strode down the hall, across the lounge, and into the madam's parlor where the "gentleman" had mostly cleaned up his face. The wounds were not as bad as Jen had first thought. Sarah had only broken the skin in two places, the tracks were mostly red welts that would fade in mere days.

"Well?" he asked as she entered the room. "What are you going to do for me?"

Jen folded her hands demurely. "I'm going to ban you from this establishment."

"What?"

"You broke two cardinal rules of my business—you brought a weapon into my parlor, and you attempted to maim one of my employees with it. So, get out." She turned and started to walk away.

"How am I supposed to explain this to my wife?" he wailed again.

She paused to look back at the pathetic prick over her shoulder. "I don't care. I'm sure you'll think of something."

"What was *that*, Jen?" Eddie murmured when he returned from seeing Madam Ziyi away in a cab.

Jen had gathered the available prostitutes to brief them on the change of command and left them in Sarah Qui's care. Now she and Eddie took the elevator down to the parking garage.

"What was what?"

"I agree that Madam Ziyi was not the loyal steward the girls deserve, but there was no need to do ... *that*."

"There was *every* need, Eddie." Jen's retort came out more aggressively than she'd planned. "An example had to be made, and I made it. It will be worth her loss to put a stop to abuse ... and rebellion. If they're happy in my house, then they will not plot to leave."

"You destroyed her face, Jen," Eddie persisted. "She didn't deserve—"

"She deserved every inch of it. She was allowing my girls to be maimed, to be abused by those so-called men. What's with you, Eddie? You've complained that I've stopped protecting my people. Well, I'm protecting them."

He shook his head. "I don't know you these days."

"Maybe the timid little girl in the shadows finally grew up," Jen said with a derisive smile. She knew in her heart she'd maimed Madam Ziyi out of anger and spite. She could have simply fired the woman. But it had felt good to exert her authority over the Minster Tower parlors in such an absolute way; it came with a head-spinning sensation of power.

Eddie fell silent after that, and Jen felt the gulf between them widen just a little further. Of all the men in her life, she had thought Eddie would never question her, never expect her to justify every action.

It was still dark outside as the two silently made their way out of Minster Tower and onto 160th Street. Eddie mumbled something in the way of goodbye and got into his car only once he'd seen Jen climb into hers.

She'd talk with him later in the day and smooth things over, but in the meantime, she had Enzo's unbridled Italian passion to go home to.

ACT FIVE: FAMILY

CHAPTER FORTY-THREE

It was a typical hot, humid New York August, and outside the sanctuary of the Mo-Lis' air-conditioned condominium, the Upper East Side was wilting beneath the stifling mid-afternoon sun. Jen Mo-Li didn't care how damned hot it was outside, or that her father, brother, and Eddie were holding a business meeting without her. Jen's only focus was on the small plastic strip she'd just peed on.

Wearing only her thin cotton panties, Jen perched on the edge of the bathtub, her mind trudging through the implications of a small blue line appearing in the tiny window. She'd skipped her period twice in as many months, something she'd not done since her first menstruation on Valentine's Day at age eleven, and she knew in her gut what that signified. From that day on, she had been as regular as clockwork and had been lucky enough for *the curse*, as her father so eloquently called it, to be little more than a minor inconvenience—just one more thing to remind her of the inherent weakness of being a woman. Only now, as she faced the very real prospect of being pregnant, Jen felt curiously strong. Being a creator of life was so far removed from weakness that it was no wonder men did their very best to downplay it.

Of course, Jen was all too aware of her carelessness. An outside observer might even conclude Jen had *wanted* to get pregnant as she'd been sporadic in taking her contraceptive pills and eschewed condoms with both Enzo and Storm Cheung. Even though she considered herself to be in love with Enzo, Jen had continued to entertain Storm's advances, although not with as much frequency once he'd made her his number two and she was able to exercise her influence on the gang. Not that Storm had much cause for complaint, as he'd seen the gang's fortune increase five-fold and trouble with rival gangs—the Italians included—were at an all-time low. It only flared up when Jen considered it prudent and for the good of the business. She found all the Dragons embarrassingly easy to control—not one of them suspected a woman to be capable of such manipulation.

She was 99 percent sure that if she had gotten pregnant, the child was Enzo's. The dates matched up perfectly with one of his increasingly infrequent trips to the city from the upstate casino. Still, there was a tiny grain of doubt, which Jen deftly pushed to the back of her head.

Watching in silence as the thin blue line materialized on the testing strip, Jen allowed herself a sigh of relief. At least she knew for certain what she faced and could make her plans accordingly. There was no question of her not keeping the child. Jen considered life far too precious to even contemplate an abortion.

Plucking the strip from the edge of the sink and her mobile phone from the floor, Jen padded across the room to sit on her bed and make the inevitable phone call. She realized as she listened to the phone ring, that a part of her was actually happy.

When his mobile rang, Enzo was kicking back in the casino bar with Rico and the new manager Vincenzo had appointed following the sudden disappearance of Billy Borgeil. The new guy, Jimmy Scalzo, was one of The Don's old cronies from back in the day. He was older than dirt, but Vincenzo said he could trust him to fix the mess Billy left behind him and keep his goddamned hands to himself.

As for Enzo and Rico, they had both finally been made and basked in their new capo status. Vincenzo had insisted they both stay at the Empire World Casino, ostensibly to help Jimmy find his feet and settle in, but mainly to take an extended vacation as a reward for stemming the expensive flow of Billy's extracurricular activities. Enzo also knew his father wanted to keep him away from New York—Chinatown specifically—for as long as possible.

"Hey, baby," Enzo smiled as Jen's voice greeted him through the phone. "Is it as hot in Manhattan as it is here?" He took a hearty sip of his vanilla daiquiri—he'd acquired a taste for the cocktail over the past three months or so—and listened intently to what Jen had to tell him. He felt the smile slide from his lips.

"Shit, looks like somebody died," said Rico.

Enzo's cheeks felt cold.

Rico shifted on his bar stool to face him. "What the fuck, Enzo?"

Waving a hand in Rico's face, Enzo put his drink down on the polished walnut bar, slipped off the bar stool, and made his way to the door and out into the harsh sunlight.

"How the fuck, Jen?" Enzo exclaimed once he was outside. The blistering heat prickled the back of his neck as trickles of sweat dripped down the inside of his shirt from his pits.

There was a long pause before Jen's voice came back, sounding prickly. "What the fuck is *how*, Enzo. It happens. I thought you'd be happy."

"I am," Enzo lied. "It's awesome ... *wonderful* news. Just a bit of a shock is all." His first instinct was to ask if the kid was his, but Enzo wisely decided to keep that to himself for the time being. "When? I mean, how long?"

"Two months," Jen told him. "I did the math."

Enzo struggled to find something else to say. Jen was on the pill, she'd made no secret of that, so just how the fuck did she wind up fucking pregnant? Of course, he'd heard it could happen, but never to anyone he'd ever known.

"So, are you—?"

"I'm keeping it, Enzo," Jen said, anticipating the question. "So don't—"

"I wasn't...." Another lie.

"With or without you, I'm having this baby." Jen sounded strong yet vulnerable, and Enzo could think of nothing more than being with her.

"I'm coming home," he said. "I'll tell my father I'm done here and I'm ready to come back and settle down." There was no way he could tell The Don he was about to make him the grandfather of a Chinese half-breed, but Enzo figured he'd think of something. He had seven months to come up with something, after all.

Her mood seemingly improved, Jen chattered at him about what they would do when he got back to New York, then they said their I-love-yous and see-you-soons and hung up the call. Enzo was not particularly happy to be left alone with his thoughts. He wished she'd waited to tell him until his next visit. It felt wrong to get news like this over the phone. But there it was. In just a few minutes, his entire world had been upended. Had it been some Italian chick or one of the innumerable girls he'd seduced during his time at the casino, Enzo would have thrown them a stack of money and had them escorted to the nearest clinic, Catholic or not. It was different with Jen. There was something about her unerring conviction in her decision to keep the child that made Enzo crave her even more. And strangely, he kind of wanted this baby.

Enzo returned to his room. As he walked, he ran through in his mind what he figured would be best to tell his father as to why he was returning to the city. None of the possibilities included the fact that he was going to be a grandfather.

CHAPTER FORTY-FOUR

Jen put the phone down on the bed and stared once again at the testing strip. Enzo had done little to disguise the shock and abject terror in his voice, and she knew him well enough to know he'd be panicking at the thought of not only becoming a father but also breaking the news to his family. She didn't even try to fool herself into believing Enzo would simply merrily announce he'd be starting a family with some girl he'd just knocked up in Chinatown. Still, he had said he was coming home—soon, and for good. He was not going to *ask* his father if he was ready to come home, he was going to *tell* him.

With a deep breath, Jen got up, dressed herself in her best skirt suit and gold silk shirt, and went out into the lounge. There, her father was holding court with Petey and Eddie.

"I need to talk to you, Bà." Jen sat down on the couch opposite him.

"You have already missed the meeting," Ming Sen advised her with an exaggerated look at his wristwatch. "The time is past."

"This is important, Father," Jen brushed off his clumsy attempt to dismiss her. "What I have to say cannot wait."

Appearing intrigued, Jen's father waved a hand at Petey and Eddie, and said, "We can continue our discussion later. It appears my daughter has something more important to discuss with me."

The derisive words cut Jen deep, and she fought to maintain her composure. It took every ounce of her inner strength to present herself as the strong, independent woman she was confident she had become—a woman he did not know.

"They can stay," Jen said calmly. "What I have to say concerns them, also."

Eddie shot Jen a concerned glance; no doubt he was worried she was about to land herself—and him by default—into a whole world of hurt. Petey, as usual, adopted his usual confused expression and looked to his father for support, as he found confrontation in any form most upsetting.

"I have been working with the Black Dragons," Jen began. She'd figured she might as well hit her father with everything in one go—rip off the Band-Aid, as it were. "They tasked me with purchasing properties in Flushing on their behalf and recruiting for their business interests."

Ming Sen sat forward on the couch. Jen thought he was about to say something to cut short the discussion before it had really begun. Instead, he studied her with unmoving eyes. She stopped speaking and returned his gaze, hiding her discomfort. At his barely perceptible nod, she continued.

"I have built up a considerable portfolio in the past twelve months and made large profits for the Dragons, as well as earned more money than I ever could have working for our family business."

"Working for *me*, you mean?" Ming Sen broke his silence.

"Everything I have learned from you has been invaluable, Father. I do not want you to think I am ungrateful for everything you have done for me." *Including telling me you wished I had died.*

"I am sure you do not," Ming Sen replied. "Do you not think I had an idea you were conspiring with the gangs?" He pointed at the smooth stump of Jen's pinkie finger. "I am neither blind nor stupid, daughter."

"I needed to prove myself to achieve power. Isn't that how you have always taught me?"

Ming Sen gave her a sage nod, and Jen could tell he was grudgingly impressed. How could he not be?

"It seems I have taught you *too* well," he said. "I have been unaware of your other life, blissfully so, and I have chosen to ignore the signs for my own peace of mind. So, why are you breaking your deceit now, Jen? What has been your catalyst?"

Jen swallowed hard. There were times such as this she'd swear her father was peering straight into her soul and she could keep no secrets from his prying. "You are going to be a grandfather," she spoke quickly, trying to keep her voice from cracking. "I am pregnant, Father."

"I understand the process through which one becomes a grandfather," Ming Sen stroked his thin beard. "I had always hoped for this day, and had feared it would never come after Danny's death." A withering glance at Petey, who, along with Eddie, stared at Jen in shock. "Would it be too much to ask that you were married first?"

"You would approve of my marriage to an Italian?" Jen asked quietly.

Ming Sen stood up from the couch as if it had bitten him. "You are having a child with an *Italian*?" He struggled to get the last word out as if it physically hurt him. "I have heard rumors that my son was murdered by Italians!"

"Rumors. Chances are Danny was killed by Mott Street Tigers who took him for a Black Dragon. And despite the fact that you made it clear you'd rather I was the murder victim, I have not done this in retaliation," she told him, her voice laced with sarcasm.

He stared at her, his face going pale then red in turns. Then he threw up his arms in an exaggerated gesture of pained exasperation. "Why you have done it doesn't matter. The effect is the same. You have brought disgrace upon the family and the family name. Is it not enough that you are carrying a bastard child without it being the bastard child of an *Italian*?!" He sneered as he spoke the word, as if it were something filthy.

How close she came to apologizing to him, Jen was ashamed to admit even to herself. She looked to Eddie for support but was met by an unreadable expression.

"You will leave this house," Ming Sen spoke quietly, purposefully. "Petey and Eddie will help you with your belongings."

"Pardon me?" Choking on her words, Jen defended herself. "You're throwing me out for getting pregnant? We're not in the old country anymore, Father."

"I am very well aware of where we are, thank you," Ming Sen snapped. "You have betrayed your family and your race by consorting with the enemy. You have deceived me and chosen to do business with the brutal gangs who run the streets. Therefore, you are no daughter of mine, Jen Li."

Jen could only look on, speechless and heartbroken, as her father made an exaggerated motion of turning his back on her and moved slowly toward the door. By the time he reached it, her heartbreak had solidified into implacable anger. As his hand grasped the handle, Jen found her voice.

"*No!*" She got to her feet and turned to face him.

As Ming Sen turned around, Eddie and Petey both stood.

"Everything I have done, I have done for *your* approval. But nothing I have done has ever been good enough for you. You have always favored my brothers over me—even *him*." She looked across at Petey, who stood in slack-jawed silence; no one ever spoke to their father in such a way, and certainly not a mere woman. "You claim to have loved my mother, honoring her by adopting her family name, yet you treat her daughter with contempt. After all I have done for this family, for *your* business, you turn me away for daring to love the wrong person? Or is it because I remind you too much of my mother?"

"No," said Bà Mo-Li, "I treat you with contempt because you are nothing like her."

He opened the door and left the room, leaving Jen quaking with unspent rage and anguish.

CHAPTER FORTY-FIVE

Petey Mo-Li fidgeted on his sister's couch and glanced nervously around her apartment; it was decidedly spartan in comparison to the family's luxurious condominium. Still, he looked as if he expected their father to appear at any time.

"How are you finding my job?" Jen asked as she poured tea for them both. "I hope Eddie is showing you around okay."

Petey flinched at Eddie's name; he had never enjoyed the same relationship with the bodyguard as his sister. Eddie thought Petey was a weak excuse for a man and had never bothered to hide the fact.

"It's going well," Petey told her. "Me and Eddie make quite the team."

Handing over a plain white porcelain cup of dark tea, Jen smiled at her brother. Eddie had been a regular visitor since she'd moved out of the family home, and he kept her up to date with the old clients whom she was surprised she missed so much. Eddie had done more than show Petey around. He'd prevented the fool from screwing up or falling afoul of the more unscrupulous immigrants; the kid wouldn't have lasted the two weeks since Jen left the family business without him.

"Are you okay for money?" Petey asked between sips of his steaming tea. "I can give you some if you're struggling." Placing his cup and saucer down gently on the low table, he took another look around the small apartment with a look of disdain.

"I'm managing just fine, Petey; thank you." It was sweet of Petey to offer, especially because their father would be angry at him for daring to do so. Ming Sen had no clue Petey was visiting Jen, and they both intended to keep it that way.

As it was, Jen was more than just fine for money. Between the cash she'd put aside during her years working for the family business, and the generous amounts rolling in from the Dragons' Flushing parlors, Jen was amassing a considerable fortune. As for the apartment, it had served Jen well as a bolthole when Father threw her out of the family home, but she would need somewhere bigger and less *Chinatown* for when the baby came. As such, Jen had already made plans to find someplace nice in Flushing, so she'd be close to her business interests.

"How has Father been since....?" Jen sat down next to her brother.

Petey cocked a half-smile. "You know our father," he said. "It's business as usual."

The reply hurt Jen more than she thought it would, even though she'd anticipated it. What had she expected? That her father would be bitterly lamenting his decision to ostracize the daughter he'd done nothing but use and suppress? Or perhaps taken to his bed in grief and dispatched Petey to bring her home before he died of a broken heart?

Hardly.

Jen wished she'd told her father *everything* about the father of his first grandchild—how he was not only Italian but the son and heir to one of the biggest crime families in New York. But for some reason, she'd held back on delivering that particular blow. Was it possible, even after everything, that she *still* craved her father's approval?

"You have nothing to worry about, Jen." Petey gave her his serious face and placed a reassuring hand on her knee. "I'll make sure you are well looked after, at least until Father comes to his senses."

"You know how stubborn he can be, Petey. I really can't see him going back on his decision to remove me from the family. Besides, I can look after myself."

"Right. You have your *other* work now." There was sadness in Petey's tone. "I suppose you don't really need us anymore."

"Think of it as your big opportunity to shine," Jen patted Petey's hand. It felt cold and clammy. "Impress Father and you'll have a great future in the family business."

"But I miss *you*, Jen," Petey insisted. "You belong at home with us, with *me*. I thought after Danny died, you and I would have the chance to be closer."

Jen felt Petey's fingers tighten on her knee and at once felt uncomfortable. "I love you, Petey, but you and I have a different kind of relationship."

Surprisingly, fat, watery tears sprang up in Petey's eyes. He slid his hand a little higher on Jen's leg. "With Danny gone, I hoped I could take his place, Jen—that I'd become everything he was to you." He leaned toward Jen, tilting his head as if he meant to kiss her.

"*Petey!*" Jen stood so fast she nearly spilled her tea.

"What?" Petey looked up at her in confusion.

"I think you should leave," she said, ignoring his kicked-puppy expression. "*Now*, Petey!"

He got to his feetslowly, smoothing invisible wrinkles from his tie. "You're all alone here, Jen," he grumbled. "You'll soon come crawling back, and when you do, don't think you'll have me to just pick up as you please."

Jen ushered her idiot brother to the door. She knew he'd always been jealous of the special bond she'd enjoyed with their brother but would never have guessed he'd interpreted it that way. It was obvious Petey saw her as lonely and vulnerable. She promised herself she would never be so again.

———

Enzo passed Petey Mo-Li on the stairwell leading up to Jen's apartment. Neither acknowledged the other, although Enzo turned his head away and made a mental note of the guy's flushed, tearful face. As soon as he was in the door, he asked Jen who the hell the miserable-looking man was.

"My little brother. He came to ask me to throw myself on our father's mercy and beg him to let me come home," Jen told Enzo. "He won't be back."

Enzo kissed Jen's cheek and put his hand on her belly; it was still flat and taut, but he liked to imagine he could feel the child growing inside her. "I don't like the thought of you being alone."

Jen stroked his hair. "We've talked about this, Enzo," she said firmly. "A mixed-race couple living in Chinatown? We'd be conspicuous if no one knew who you were. And if they did...."

Pulling away from Jen, Enzo sat down on the couch. She was right, of course, although he had an inkling she just didn't want him around all the time. "Maybe we should think of going away. Los Angeles? Vegas?" Sure, they'd had this conversation a dozen times before, but Enzo wasn't one to let things go.

"You know that would be impractical for *both* of us." Jen sat beside him and took his hands in hers. "We have our businesses to think about. And besides, what do you think your father would say if you left New York right now?"

Jen was ever the pragmatic one, which Enzo sometimes applauded and sometimes found a tad infuriating. Still, he had to admit she had a point. Enzo was back in the thick of running things: managing the gambling and numbers runners, the hookers, and dealing with the distribution of drugs through the Chinese gang. He was happy with his lot, comfortable within the cocoon of his family. But there was a growing part of him that wondered what it would be like if he took control of his destiny. If news of his continued relationship with Jen ever reached The Don, especially with a half-and-half baby in the mix, he might have no option but to make a life for himself and Jen elsewhere. That was a possibility Enzo didn't care to think too much about.

"I think he'd be happy if I married a nice Catholic girl, even if she wasn't 100 percent Italian," Enzo said.

"I'm 100 percent Chinese, Enzo. That's *zero* percent Italian." Jen had a habit of talking down to him at times like he was a dreamer detached from reality. "And you know my feelings about converting."

Enzo frowned. "What harm would it do?"

"I will not be a hypocrite, Enzo." Jen pulled her hand away. "Not about that. It upsets me that you persist in nagging me. I see your religion, and I see the businesses you're involved in, and the methods you employ within those businesses. You don't think I pay attention to the news, Enzo?"

"It's not all *Goodfellas*, Jen—we're *businessmen*," Enzo protested.

"I was raised with the Tao, Enzo. I can't also be Catholic, nor can I throw away my beliefs." Jen's retort hung thick in the air between them. "And as for us getting married . . . you know that would never work."

Enzo was crestfallen. In his mind, marrying Jen was the right thing to do; it was how he'd been raised as a good Catholic. But she always avoided discussing it seriously, using her being Chinese and of a different faith as a cast-iron excuse.

"We could *make* it work." Enzo was painfully aware he was beginning to sound desperate.

"Just how would you expect that to go, Enzo?" The annoyance in Jen's tone cut through him like a knife. "Your father would never accept me, no matter what. That I'm a heathen *chink* and pregnant with his grandchild sure as hell isn't going to help my case now, is it?"

"Don't use that word," Enzo reached for Jen's hand.

"Why not?" Jen allowed him to squeeze her fingers. "Everyone else does. I'm sure you have."

Enzo was about to explain how that was different but decided against it. She didn't chastise him anymore when he used racial slurs because it was just the way he was, and she accepted that. So why couldn't he accept her as she was, too?

"Your family comes first, Enzo. I do understand how that works." Jen continued. "I also understand that for you, I would only ever be second place to them, even if I was a nice Italian Catholic girl." She touched a fingertip to Enzo's lips to silence the protest that formed there. "Let's just keep things as they are. For now, at least, we are doing perfectly fine without making any drastic changes. The gods only know I've seen enough change in the past year to last me a lifetime."

As Jen leaned in and gave Enzo a slow, firm, loving kiss, any further thoughts of pressing her evaporated. He admired her ambition and while he found her stubbornness exasperating, he was confident he'd be able to change her mind given enough time.

Breaking the kiss, Jen said, "I need to shower and make myself beautiful for tonight." She remained close, her breath warm and sweet on Enzo's face.

"About that...." Enzo began, looking away from her.

"You're kidding me." Pulling away, Jen jumped to her feet. "You promised me dinner and *Miss Saigon!* Were you just wanting a quick fuck and off you go?"

It upset Enzo to see Jen so disappointed. Her anger played on his insecurities, and there was always the gripe at the back of his mind that she was out of his league and someday she'd realize it. "It's a business dinner my father set up."

Jen huffed and folded her arms over her breasts. "This is you making things work? This is how you plan to stand up to your family and merrily announce you're marrying a non-Catholic, pregnant *chink*?"

Jen's deliberate use of the insult grated on Enzo, but he chose to ignore it. He got to his feet. "If I could get out of it and spend the night with you, don't you think I would?" His eyes searched Jen's for a grain of forgiveness; she had become prone to mood swings since he'd gotten her pregnant, which did little to assuage Enzo's insecurity. "And it's not like you haven't done the same thing to me."

"Not the same," she said. "I made it up to you."

"And I'll make it up to *you*." Enzo reached for her, but she turned her back on him.

"Just go, Enzo," she growled.

"Fine. I'll see you later." He made his way to the door and stepped out into the overly warm night.

CHAPTER FORTY-SIX

"I want you to make a big effort to make nice with Big Joe's daughter," Vincenzo told his son as he greeted Enzo at the door to brief him on the way to the dining room. To The Don, this was nothing more than another business meeting, albeit dressed up as a cozy dinner. "You're a capo—you'll do the right thing. You tell me you're ready to quit chasing tail and settle down . . . Enzo, this is your chance to do something for the good of the family."

"You invited Big Joe Taccetta here?" Enzo raised a quizzical eyebrow at his father. "Are you sure that was a wise move? Meetings between the families are always on neutral ground."

"When the aim is to settle bad blood, we invite families into our homes," Vincenzo replied. "It is a sign of humility and willingness to extend the olive branch. Besides, Big Joe has his wife and daughter with him. What the fuck is he gonna do?"

Enzo smiled along with his father; he'd known for some time Vincenzo had been planning to smooth things over with the Taccetta family, ever since Johnny "Freckles" got so horribly burned up in the fire above The Napoli House of Pastries. Word on the street was Big Joe and his missus wished he'd been left to die up there; the flames had messed up their handsome son so badly he'd never be the same again. Needless to say, Johnny was not to be mentioned over dinner.

"Speaking of his daughter," Vincenzo continued, "a union between the families would build good, solid bridges."

Enzo eyed his father. So *that* was why he'd been invited to dinner with the Taccettas. He was little more than potential marriage material for Big Joe's only daughter.

"Quit looking at me like that!" Vincenzo offered a conciliatory smile. "She'll make the perfect wife. The girl's easy on the eye, not too bright, and has good child-bearing hips."

"Is that what you said about Mamma?"

"Not within earshot," Vincenzo laughed.

His father hadn't been far wrong in his assessment of Gabriella Taccetta. Enzo found her to be attractive in a homely sort of way, with a round, pudgy face that appeared fixed in a permanent, toothy smile. She was *Rubenesque*—her plump body hidden beneath a generously cut dress that showed off just enough cleavage to appear enticing. Gabriella sat quietly with a bright, expectant air, sandwiched between her parents, whom Vincenzo introduced to his son.

"Call me Giuseppe." Big Joe shook Enzo's hand. "This is my good wife, Isabella, and this is the apple of my eye, Gabriella."

As Gabriella got to her feet to shake Enzo's hand, she knocked over her full wine glass and a dark red stain bloomed across his mother's best tablecloth. Gabriella looked suitably mortified, as did her parents.

"Don't worry about it," Elena reassured with a forced smile. She beckoned over one of the hired waitresses to mop up the spilled wine; the DeCarlos had gotten caterers in for the occasion, which was more a show of strength than to give Enzo's mother the night off from running the kitchen.

Enzo gave Gabriella's hand a perfunctory shake and sat himself down in the vacant chair opposite her. The girl was undeniably pretty yet stirred nothing within him; his thoughts wandered to Jen and the baby she was carrying. As a result, he could think of nothing to say.

Picking up on the lack of enthusiasm, Big Joe shot a concerned glance at Vincenzo. Enzo wondered just what promises his father had made on his behalf, and what expectations Gabriella had of him.

"Don't you worry about the kids," Vincenzo said to Big Joe as he topped his wine glass. "They'll sort things out in their own time." Then he smiled long and hard at Enzo to make damn sure he got the message.

Jen, still livid with Enzo for canceling a rare romantic evening, paced her apartment in the short, sexy dress she'd bought especially for the occasion, her mobile phone in hand. She knew he would always put family first and was surprised at herself for taking it so badly. After all, he was right—she had stood him up more than once because of business.

Different! cried a plaintive voice within her. Enzo was part of a family that had his back and in whose business he was thoroughly involved. Perhaps it was the hormones? Perhaps it was the thought that once their baby arrived, there would be even fewer chances for them to enjoy time together? It struck her suddenly that regardless of Enzo's good intentions, she'd be raising their kid pretty much alone. That rankled. And it wasn't just the hormones talking. The hurtful fact was that she and Enzo could not live under the same roof and that a normal life with a normal family was something she could never have.

Fine, then. She knew what she *could* have. She might as well embrace it.

Stabbing at her phone's keypad, Jen brought up Storm Cheung's number, only to stand staring at it. All the reasons this was wrong clamored to be heard above Jen's anger. Why should she be alone while Enzo ran home at his father's whim? She had stood up to her bà—couldn't he do the same? The truth, she told herself, was that he didn't love her enough to stand up to the great DeCarlo Don.

Well, to hell with Enzo and his whole goddamn crime family. And to hell with what he'd say if he found her out; it wasn't as if she could get any *more* pregnant.

She waited for Storm to pick up.

ACT SIX: EMPIRE

CHAPTER FORTY-SEVEN

November 1992

Jen was reaching the limits of her endurance. The Mott Street Tigers were increasing their attacks in Black Dragon territory as Storm obstinately refused to strike back for reasons he could not articulate, and there was mounting unrest within the Dragons' ranks caused by all the above.

The three months remaining of her pregnancy stretched like some impossible jail sentence. Jen's body was bloated out of proportion, and she suffered the baby's daily onslaught on her insides. She honestly could not remember the last time she'd enjoyed a full night's sleep, uninterrupted by savage kicks to her kidneys or bladder, or nausea that would often leave her hunched over the toilet bowl.

Nevertheless, Jen refused to show any signs of weakness in front of Storm and the other Dragons. More and more over the past few months, she had seen the gang beginning to look to her as their voice of reason, and she wasn't about to throw that away to indulge her swollen ankles.

Enzo, for his part, had provided Jen with more than his fair share of stress. Although he maintained distance from her for the sake of his father, Enzo's opinions as to his child's involvement in his family's businesses leaned more and more toward the positive the larger Jen's belly swelled. While Jen had argued it was far too soon to even begin to consider their child's future career plans, Enzo had become insistent that if the kid was a boy, he be indoctrinated into the DeCarlo family as early as possible as heir to Enzo's eventual leadership. All of this despite Jen's protests that she didn't want her child to grow up as little more than a glorified street thug. On the other hand, Enzo's vehemence against their child taking part in Jen's business had also grown, so much so that it even had Jen considering that Enzo might know more about her involvement in Chinatown's gangs and sex industry than he let on.

Jen tried her damndest to avoid the subject at all costs, as it had led to more than a few rows and increasingly awkward evenings together. But Enzo was like a feral dog with a bone; he simply refused to allow the subject to drop, no matter how much Jen begged him to for the sake of her sanity. After all, there would be plenty of time to discuss the future once the baby was out of her body. And what the hell happened to allowing it to make its own choices in life?

To Jen, Enzo's short-sightedness against common sense was far too similar to Storm's refusal to retaliate against the Tigers, which she had found to be increasingly frustrating in the months following her promotion to his deputy in place of Charlie-Boy Fok. Once again, Jen found herself in the dead center of the gang's mounting dissatisfaction with their leader as she attempted to make him understand just how essential it was for the Dragons to be seen to be doing something about the latest disrespect and affront to their business interests.

"How can you just turn a blind eye to what they are doing to us?" Den Cha confronted Storm with harsh anger in his voice. "The Tigers walk in and take over our whorehouse *again* and you do nothing!"

Jen flinched at Den's choice of words. Storm had a particular dislike of the word *whorehouse*, although it puzzled her as to how it could possibly offend the sensibilities of a man whose business it was to sell women's bodies for cash. The hot, sticky, and hostile emotional atmosphere in the office was the polar opposite of Storm's air-conditioned sanctum. His sub-deputies, Den Cha and Gary Hu, stood toe-to-toe with their boss and his other two subs, Stevie Lee and Mike Ye. Jen chose to remain a silent observer. She would pick her moment wisely, as this would only be her fight when she decided to make it so.

If he was offended by Gary's deliberate word use, Storm didn't show it. He spoke calmly, firmly. "I will *not* be responsible for starting a street war. How many more times must I explain that to you?"

Gary Hu, a wiry scarecrow of a man with a mane of thick, black hair that rested on his skinny shoulders, fought to maintain an air of respect for his leader. "How can you not see there is already a war going on out there?" he demanded to know. "And that our refusal to stand our ground will ensure we have no chance of ever winning it."

"You know the Tigers and BTK are eroding our businesses, Storm," Den threw fuel onto the fire. "Not to mention the Jamaicans and the Mexicans. Now that they've taken the Venus Joy Spa from us with no repercussions, we have very little left on Mott Street."

Jen knew that to be not entirely true as the Dragons still had parlors, gambling dens, and bookmakers on and around Mott, as well as the dealers who plied their trade on the street corners. However, Den's point was a valid one—if Storm continued to do nothing, the gang would lose their hold on Chinatown. That the Tigers had finally succeeded in taking over the Venus Joy, less than a year after their initial attack, had come as a particularly hard blow, even though Storm had appeared unfazed by it. Jen knew that was partly her doing. She had provided the gang lord with a pragmatic, deliberative sounding board and it had changed the way he operated. Perhaps too much.

Storm had taken the same stance when the Tigers took over the Jīn Bāozi restaurant on Mulberry; Denis Wap had been discovered in a burned-out Toyota Corolla on a piece of waste ground by the harbor. His throat had been slit ear-to-ear and the message to the Dragons was a clear one. Within days, the Tigers had declared the restaurant under their protection and replaced all the staff. Word was that it was Big D Dang's favorite establishment, although Jen reckoned that was put out to rub Storm's nose in his loss.

"The Flushing parlors are generating more than enough income to compensate for any losses in Chinatown," Storm reminded them. "Perhaps it is a good time for us to be moving away from Mott and Doyers.

With the money we have to pay out each month to the police for their ... discretion, the parlors there are becoming less and less profitable."

"That's only because the Tigers have that prick Harrison on their payroll," Gary spat. "And along with him, the whole 109th Precinct."

Stevie Lee stepped forward in an act of defiant confrontation. "Lieutenant Harrison is not the only dirty cop in Chinatown taking handouts and free fucks for ignoring the parlors," he growled at Gary. "We have our own cops, both here *and* in Flushing."

"He's the only one who counts around Mulberry, Doyers, and Mott," Gary countered with a sneer. "With Harrison in their pocket, the Tigers think they are above the goddamned law."

"They are no more above the law than we are." Storm got to his feet. It was his clear indication that the meeting was over, and he would entertain no more discussion on the subject. He glanced at Jen and then at Eddie, who stood silently in the far corner of the office like a surly statue. "Now, if you will all excuse me, I have a card game to go to," he said politely, making his way around his desk and across to the office door.

Stevie and Mike followed Storm out, and as Den and Gary exchanged shrugs and followed suit, Jen saw a bright, clear opportunity. She stood and raised her hand. "Wait."

Eddie let out an audible grunt and moved to close the door.

"We clearly have work to do," Jen told the sub-deputies. "I believe it is time the Black Dragons sent a clear message to the Tigers and every other gang out there who think they can walk all over us."

"Storm said we were not to retaliate." Den, not the brightest member of the gang, appeared to be confused.

"Which is why he is not to know what we are doing until the job is done." Jen fixed both Den and Gary with a steely gaze. "I can rely on your silence, of course." It was not a question.

The gangsters nodded their compliance. Jen could be confident they both fully understood they'd be finished if they so much as breathed a word to Storm; she also knew they held more respect for her than they did for their leader and were frustrated with his inaction. Jen understood instinctively that this split in the Dragon's inner circle represented a chance to make a move she'd only recently realized she wanted—no, *needed*—to make. If the Mott Street Tigers were responsible for Danny's death, then she owed them. Pregnant or not, Jen couldn't allow an opportunity for payback to slip through her fingers. She felt relatively safe from Storm's wrath. She hadn't told him the child she carried was his, but neither had she told him it wasn't. She'd let him assume whatever he wanted.

Eddie, still standing by the door, cleared his throat.

She glanced at him over her shoulder. "Did you want to say something, Eddie?"

She'd had just about enough of Eddie's watchful gaze and opinions—spoken or unspoken. Her father had disowned her, her brother was too damn scared to visit her, and Enzo questioned her decisions about their child all the while being too concerned about his mafia family to even think about being a proper father. She didn't need Eddie second-guessing her too.

"No, ma'am."

Jen hated it when he called her that, and he knew it, too. She decided to ignore him. She turned to Gary. "I need you to get hold of some ammonium nitrate—discretely, of course—enough to make half a dozen devices." To Den, she said: "If you could procure 2,000 rounds of .22-caliber bullets . . . or ball bearings if you can't."

"Are you sure about this?" Den Cha's eyes were full of concern.

Jen bit back sudden anger. Why the hell couldn't these men stop questioning her? Wasn't she giving them what they wanted: action?

"When the Tigers come at us with cleavers, we retaliate with bombs and bullets," she explained. "This is war, whether Storm Cheung wants it or not."

CHAPTER FORTY-EIGHT

As Lieutenant Chad Harrison stepped out of the Venus Joy Spa into the cold night air, the gaudy lights in the parlor's window illuminated him on the sidewalk far more than he was comfortable with. Should anyone of significance, such as a colleague or member of the snooping press, witness him exiting a brothel at one in the morning, it really wouldn't do his career much good at all. Hence, the cop had always gone to a great deal of trouble to ensure even a chance encounter with anyone was unlikely. That's why Madam Tung Yijun always had a parking space vacant for him directly in front of the parlor's door when he visited; just a mere couple of strides and he'd be secure and invisible inside his Cadillac.

He reeked of cheap perfume, sweat, and scented latex condoms, and the stink offended him. He was also more than aware he'd consumed far too much scotch to drive, but who the hell was going to make the head of the 109th Precinct blow into a goddamn bag? The scotch, of course, was complimentary for him at the Venus Joy Spa, as was the sweet young thing he'd taken quite a shine to. He'd visited Li Na every Friday night when Bernice was out at her book club or poker night or whatever the hell it was she did with herself since the kids left home. Who knew? Maybe one day he'd leave his fat, frigid wife for the Chinese girl and run off to San Francisco. They were much more tolerant of mixed marriages there, or so he'd been told.

Harrison thumbed at the car's remote key fob and, as he yanked open the door, he noticed the rear passenger window had been smashed in. The beige leather seat was festooned with tiny cubes of safety glass that twinkled with myriad colors reflected from the brothel's neon sign.

"*Sonofabitch*," Harrison snarled beneath his breath. For as much as the cop needed to shout and curse to vent his anger, he fought to contain it. The last thing he needed to do was draw attention to himself outside a whorehouse. Instead, he began to ease his tall frame into the car, already rehearsing his excuses to Bernice as to where he'd been so late to get his car broken into. And Christ help whoever the fuck had smashed his beloved Caddy's window if he ever found them out. Now, there was a fatal accident in the police cells just waiting to happen.

But Lieutenant Harrison didn't spot the small bundle—about the size of a basketball—lying in the passenger-side footwell until it was too late. The bomb's blast took the roof off the Cadillac like it was made of paper, and the couple hundred small-caliber bullets contained within its metal casing shredded the cop's body almost beyond recognition. He was reduced in an instant to little more than chewed-up hamburger meat and a fine, red mist that splattered to the second floor of the Venus Joy Spa where the windows were blown out, along with those on the first floor and the adjacent convenience store.

After a few seconds of eerie silence came shrill, terrified screams from inside the parlor. It took Madam Tung Yijun minutes to gather her terrorized and wounded girls and their johns and herd them out the rear door of the brothel. When at last she made her way around to the front of the building, her eyes, wide with shock, fixed upon the twisted, smoldering wreck of the police lieutenant's car as the sound of explosions from adjacent streets filled the night. She then heard above the sobbing of her girls the faint whine of police sirens.

CHAPTER FORTY-NINE

"*How the fuck did this happen?*" Storm Cheung slammed his fists down hard on his desk, rattling his fine China teapot and toppling over his cup of fresh green tea. Fuming, he watched as the steaming liquid soaked into the morning newspapers that lay open on his desk. Both *Metro New York* and *Sing Tao Daily* led with details of the previous night's bomb attacks around Chinatown, which included the tragic death of a prominent 109th Precinct cop. And, although neither publication gave specific details of the bookmakers, gambling dens, drug houses, and brothels that had borne the brunt of the explosions, Storm knew full well each one was in Mott Street Tigers territory.

"Miss Mo-Li put out the order," Stevie Lee said with a flinch as if he expected a punch in the mouth for delivering the bad news.

"I *know* that much," Storm spat. "Do you think I am so stupid that I have no idea what is going on in my own business? What I want to know is how the hell she organized all of *this* behind my back." He slapped his hand down on the newspapers to emphasize his point.

"She gathered support among the ranks," Mike Ye ventured. "Many look to her as a leader because she listens to their calls for retaliation against our enemies."

Although Mike's explanation hardly came as a fresh revelation to

Storm, it was not something he wanted to hear out loud, and certainly not from a subordinate. He had good reasons for not wishing to fuel an all-out war with the Tigers. The main one was that while peace, albeit an uneasy one, reigned over Chinatown, he could focus on building the Dragons' business interests in Flushing and beyond. Jen Mo-Li ordering hits on the rival gang's territory behind his back was not conducive to that in the least, and Storm knew this was one thing he couldn't afford to let go of if he was to save face.

"This cannot be allowed to happen again," Storm said to Mike and Stevie. He knew he could rely upon their unerring support, and he trusted the pair to keep their mouths shut—no matter what was decided that morning within the four secure walls of his office.

"We can deal with Den and Gary," Mike offered. "We know they are loyal to Miss Mo-Li—it was they who planted the bombs."

Storm shook his head. "That will not be necessary. They are good soldiers, even if their allegiance has been split. I will allow them to remain within the ranks—for now, at least—since we are likely to need all the men we can get after...." His eyes darted to the tea-soaked newspapers, and their pictures of devastation and anger hardened his expression.

"So, what *can* we do?" Stevie asked.

Tearing his attention away from the lurid reports of ruined property and innocent lives lost, Storm addressed his sub-deputies with chilling calm. "If Jen Mo-Li is the heart of the problem, the heart must be cut out."

"The Flushing parlors," Mike said, "are entirely her operation."

"We managed without Jen Mo-Li before, and we will do so again," Storm told him with little emotion in his voice.

He had enjoyed the woman immensely, but this was business. He knew there was a chance she carried his child, but he might only be sure after it was born, if then. "I have good people in China to handle the merchandise, and Flushing is well-established. I am sure we can find people to take care of our business interests there—people I can trust."

"You can trust us to deal with this ... loyalty problem quickly and with discretion." Mike's clumsy segue was jarring.

"No," Storm cut across him. "Nothing happens to Jen Mo-Li while she is carrying ... her child," he made purposeful eye contact with both men. "We are businessmen, not monsters. Do you both understand?"

He came close to explaining that he thought Jen's bastard child might be his, then realized wryly that they likely assumed it was. Prudence suggested that he should pretend it was not his, but if it was....

"We shall wait for the right time, Storm, you have our word on that," Mike assured.

"I will tell you when it's the right time. Should anything happen to her before she has the child—and I mean *anything*—I will hold you both accountable."

The threat in the gang leader's voice was palpable, designed to leave Mike and Stevie in no doubt whatsoever as to their fate should *that* direct order be defied. Storm was not prepared to tolerate any more defiance.

"Understood," Stevie echoed his colleague's sentiment.

"Be vigilant," Storm said. "Keep a close eye on Miss Mo-Li and those loyal to her—particularly Den Cha and Gary Hu. I will keep those two away from the parlors and Miss Mo-Li until matters have been dealt with to my satisfaction."

Dismissing the two with a barely perceptible nod of the head, Storm Cheung set about clearing his desk of the ruined newspapers. It didn't brighten his mood any that both rags seemed far more concerned about the violent demise of the crooked cop than the loss of Chinese lives and destruction of Chinatown property.

CHAPTER FIFTY

February 1993

THERE WERE COPS EVERYWHERE IN NEW YORK, DAY AND night, each one of them skittish and trigger-happy following the bomb attack on the World Trade Center just two days before. Enzo had watched the aftermath on the news, astounded someone could simply drive a truck filled with explosives up to the North Tower like that and blow the place up, leaving seven dead and countless injured. It had certainly garnered global attention. Speculation was they'd used ammonium nitrate, and Enzo had made a mental note to look up who the hell supplied fertilizer in such quantities to a pair of *ragheads*, as his father called them, without squeaking to the authorities.

Nonetheless, increased cop presence or not, the streets around Flushing were as deathly quiet as they were cold at three in the morning, for which Enzo was grateful as he sped his Grand Am with skillful ease through every red light with impunity. Should any cop stop him with threats of a citation, he had the number one, age-old, cast-iron excuse to beat them all: He was about to become a father.

Swinging the car into the main lot of New York Presbyterian Hospital—nothing but the best for Jen—Enzo dashed in through the main doors of the imposing, white stone building, set on locating the maternity wing. It was all over by the time Enzo arrived at Jen's private room, for which he had to admit to being grateful, because he'd had no desire to witness the horrific, bloody mess he understood childbirth to be. His father had deliberately avoided the deliveries of all three of his children, as he had seen no merit in witnessing his beloved wife in such a state and in so much pain as she gave birth to his offspring. He had passed along that wisdom and advised both his sons to adopt a similar stance when the time came.

A plump, surly nurse with noticeable gray bags under her bloodshot eyes directed Enzo to recovery room 5B, which was at the far end of a long, brightly lit hallway. As he made his way along, wondering if he ought to have at least bought one of the limp bouquets on offer in the downstairs lobby gift shop, Enzo passed Eddie who was on his way to the restroom.

Exchanging a cursory nod with Enzo, Eddie grunted, "5B."

"Thanks," Enzo said. He had no intention of stopping to chat as his focus was very much on his newborn child. Besides, even though it had been Eddie who'd called him about the imminent birth, the two had hardly fostered a warm relationship, theirs being more a forced tolerance out of mutual respect and affection for Jen.

Enzo slipped quietly into the room. The lights were dimmed, and he couldn't be entirely sure Jen wasn't sleeping. He didn't want to wake her. The room was spacious and well-appointed with polished walnut furniture and pretty, floral curtains. It was so luxurious the hospital bed seemed small and Enzo half-expected there to be a minibar. A huge TV clung to the wall in one corner of the room, a clear liquid drip hung from a pole by the head of the bed, and a tray of what had once been a decent dinner sat untouched on the counter. Parked next to the counter was a hospital-issued wheelchair with NYPH stenciled across its back.

"Meet your daddy, Nicholas," Jen's weary voice made the introduction as Enzo crept toward the bed.

"He'll get called *Nicky*," Enzo told her with a warm smile. "Hardly traditional Chinese." Standing over the bed, he stared down at the small, peacefully sleeping pink bundle in Jen's arms and couldn't remember a time she had looked quite so beautiful.

"Take a look at him, Enzo," Jen replied and returned Enzo's smile. "I don't see that being much of a problem—do you?"

She handed the baby to Enzo, who held him like something precious and infinitely fragile. Even in the soft light of the plush private room, Enzo made out the kid's shock of black hair, olive skin, and the nose his mamma always referred to as the *DeCarlo nose*. There were definite hints of Jen's DNA too, of course, which Enzo knew would ensure his firstborn son was going to be one hell of a heartbreaker when he grew up and was unleashed on New York's unsuspecting female population.

"He's so beautiful." Jen's voice was low, weary. "Thank you for our beautiful son, Enzo."

For perhaps the first time in his life, Enzo was rendered speechless. Mixed, confusing emotions spun through him like restless spirits. The kid really was something quite special, and Enzo knew his father would be incredibly proud if the circumstances were different, and if only telling him about his new grandchild were an option. As it was, Enzo knew Vincenzo would be mortified to have a bastard in his God-fearing, Catholic family—doubly so with him being a half-breed.

"I'm tired," Jen whispered and lay back among the heaped pillows, "It's been a long day."

"Hint taken," Enzo replied. "I'll come back later. Sorry I missed—" Placing the baby in the Perspex crib by the side of the bed, Enzo covered him up with the blue cellular blanket.

Jen laughed at Enzo a little, her eyelids already drooping. "You're not *really* sorry. You didn't miss much; your son was out almost the minute they got me into the delivery room, like he couldn't wait to see the world. That's a good sign for his future—for *our* future, Enzo." Reaching up, she grabbed Enzo's hand and squeezed his fingers tightly.

Enzo returned the squeeze, then slipped his hand from Jen's. "I'll see you guys later."

Jen was asleep before Enzo left the room.

The hallway was a glaring, bright contrast to the muted light in Jen's room, and it took Enzo a moment or two of squinting for his eyes to readjust as he made his way back toward the nurses' station. A pair of doctors bustled by him with brisk purpose, their long, pristine white coats sailing out like stiff capes as they walked shoulder to shoulder. Enzo thought of their haste as they appeared not to notice his perfunctory smile in their direction. Asian doctors were ten-a-penny in and around New York. He tried to imagine how his father would take it if he met one in the OR during an emergency.

Just ahead to Enzo's left, the door to the men's restroom swung open and Eddie Sun staggered out looking like he'd been hit by a freight train. His shirt was ripped and stained red, his jeans torn and festooned with bloody footprints. His huge, round face was smeared with blood from a ragged gash in his temple. His nose was awry, his cheek split, and his right eye all but swollen shut. Fighting to stay upright on shaking legs, Eddie steadied himself on the doorjamb. When he saw Enzo, a look of mixed desperation and relief lit up his eyes. He glanced over the Italian's shoulder and said, "Jen."

Adrenaline pumping, Enzo pivoted just in time to see the two doctors pushing open the door to room 5B. He hightailed it back down the hallway toward Jen's room with Eddie limping along after him as quickly as his battered legs would allow.

Jen was awake, more or less, when Enzo burst into the room, but she didn't seem to be reacting to the two strangers approaching her bed. Enzo took in the situation at a glance: One man had a cleaver, the other, a long, thin-bladed knife. They'd shed their white coats to reveal shirts and jeans of light-sucking black, and their faces were covered by bandanas.

Cursing himself for not having brought his gun—he'd been asleep when Eddie called him, and it never occurred to him he'd need to be armed to visit with his newborn son—Enzo grabbed the abandoned dinner plate and hurled it at the assassin closest to him. The heavy china struck the guy's head as he spun to face Enzo, cleaver poised. The plate shattered, lacerating his forehead and decorating him with stale food. He staggered backward, tripped over a chair, and went down, dropping his cleaver as he hit the floor.

Jen, now fully awake, let out an animal snarl, her maternal instincts overriding her pain and fatigue. Under cover of Enzo's distraction, she pulled the drip stent from her wrist and clambered from the bed, intent on her sleeping son. She scooped her baby from his crib and darted to the far corner of the room. It was her only choice; her attackers were between her and the door.

With Jen safe for the moment, Enzo grabbed the thick plastic food tray and turned to face off against the other would-be murderer. The man stood at the foot of the bed, shoulders squared, legs braced for attack. He held the knife like the experienced street fighter Enzo had no doubt he was. Above his mask, his eyes were fixed on Enzo's. Using the food tray as a makeshift shield, Enzo rushed the guy. Bent on protecting his family at all costs, the foolishness of launching himself at someone wielding a long, sharp knife with nothing more than a food tray didn't even register.

Enzo lashed out with the tray the split-second he was within striking distance of the assassin. His intended target countered with a lightning slash of his blade, the steel glinting in the muted light of the hospital room. Enzo's reflexes were as sharp as the knife. He flipped the tray hard to one side, connecting with the knife, but not with enough force to knock it from the assassin's grasp. Instead, the blade flew sidewise and slashed through Enzo's shirt and into the soft flesh of his forearm.

"*Sonofabitch!*" Enzo snarled. A dark red stain bloomed on his white shirtsleeve as a ragged pain spread along his arm.

Now, Enzo's silent attacker lunged forward and stabbed at the Italian's chest. Enzo blocked the blade's lethal trajectory with the food tray; the hard plastic caught the blow, but the knife blade bit through, its steel tip protruding half an inch. The force slammed the tray hard into Enzo's chest and the knife—embedded in the tray—pierced Enzo's chest, just to the left of his breastbone. He gasped at the sharp, icy sensation and knew that were it not for the tray, the blade would have buried itself in his heart.

Roaring in pain and fury, Enzo delivered a hard, decisive kick to his opponent's balls and whipped the tray aside. The knife went with it, disappearing into the darkness of the room. The would-be assassin doubled over tottering backward toward the empty bed. Enzo didn't relent, but lashed out rapidly with his fists, pummeling the guy's head with a flurry of blows. Enzo didn't quit until he went down and stayed down.

Behind him, the man Enzo had floored with the plate had wiped smeared food and congealing blood from his face, retrieved his cleaver, and hauled himself to his feet. Thanks to his grunt, Enzo turned to see the assassin coming at him again with his cleaver raised. Enzo, weaponless, turned quickly to dodge the attack. But slipped on the blood-slicked tile as the second assassin pounced with a roar of victory.

Bright, white light flooded the hospital room as the door flung open and Eddie Sun's bulky silhouette appeared in the doorway. After the lightning came the thunderclap, so loud it made Enzo's head throb. The cleaver-wielding assassin collapsed in an ungainly heap at Enzo's feet, the thick blade missing his toes by less than an inch.

It took Enzo a moment or two to realize his face was spattered with blood and gore from the black-clad man who now lay twitching and bleeding out on the beige-tiled floor.

Enzo looked up at Eddie. "Where the hell was that when they jumped you in the restroom?"

Eddie glanced down at the compact Smith and Wesson in his hand. "In my jacket pocket. You try drawing a gun while you're standing at the urinal with your dick in your hand."

Enzo almost laughed. It was easily the funniest thing he'd ever heard Eddie say. He pointed down at the broken corpse. "I hope you don't think this makes us allies or anything."

Eddie shrugged. "You'd better go," he told Enzo. "You don't want to be here when the cops get here."

On cue, an alarm sounded out in the hallway; a strident noise that screamed with urgency.

Enzo looked across the room at Jen. She was still crouched down in the corner cradling his son, who was, by the sounds of things, gearing up to make some noise of his own.

"Go," Jen implored. "You can't be here."

"I'm not leaving without you." Enzo's tone left her no option.

Jen forced a weak smile and picked herself up off the floor. Stepping with care around the slippery pools of blood and the broken china, she made her way across the room toward Enzo and Eddie, pausing only to snatch the blanket from the Perspex crib.

"You're fucking crazy," Eddie groaned as he stepped aside to allow Enzo and Jen out of the room.

Enzo glanced up the hall toward the nurses' station. A harried nurse stood out in the hall with a cell phone pressed to her ear, her free hand making frantic gestures. "Not as crazy as leaving her here," he replied. "There'll be more of those gangsters on the way."

"Tigers," Eddie told him. "Got a look at the neck tattoos."

If Eddie was correct, Enzo knew the Mott Street Tigers wouldn't quit until they'd achieved their goal of killing Jen and possibly his son as well.

"You gonna help me?" Enzo grumbled at Eddie.

Without a word, Eddie reached back into the room and pulled out the wheelchair. Enzo all but pushed Jen and the baby into the thing, and the three of them raced away toward the fire exit as the nurse was joined by a trio of hospital security guards, resplendent in their navy-blue uniforms.

It seemed an eternity before the fire door closed behind them and Enzo could no longer hear either the alarms or their three pursuers shouting for them to stop where they were.

CHAPTER FIFTY-ONE

It had been less than twelve hours since she'd given birth, and Jen felt like she'd been to hell and back, but she was pleased to be back in her new apartment in Flushing. After the attempt on her life in the hospital and the abject fear she'd felt for the first time in her life for someone other than herself, Jen was relieved to have her son someplace she considered safe.

"That's going to need stitches," she told Enzo. He was stripped to the waist, his face finally clean of sticky blood, gore, and tiny white bone fragments. His injured arm was wrapped with a bandage from her medicine cabinet; dots of blood were already beginning to soak through from the wound he'd splashed with vodka and attempted to hold together with a couple of Band-Aids.

"Don't worry about it," Enzo gave Jen what she figured was supposed to be a reassuring smile. "I'll get it fixed later. I know a guy."

Jen did not doubt that at all. The DeCarlo family would likely have a whole army of doctors on call who would fix them up with no questions asked, but so did the Dragons. Whether Enzo would be able to keep the wound from his father was another matter in itself, although Jen knew he was more than capable of concocting a plausible excuse for needing his arm stitched up.

Eddie had declined Jen's offer to go back to Flushing with them. Even though he had done his best to hide his pain, Jen knew he'd taken a savage beating and, by the way he'd struggled to walk from the hospital, Jen figured her bodyguard's knees had borne the brunt of the attack. She'd seen it before, of course. It was the Chinese gang equivalent of kneecapping—a sure-fire, ruthlessly efficient means of disabling the opposition, only without the need for wasting bullets. However, the pair of assassins had underestimated Eddie's stubborn fortitude and strength; any lesser man would have been left unable to walk for months after such punishment, let alone save the day—and her skin—by taking down one of the attackers. Jen reckoned Eddie would be back on his feet within the week.

"Eddie ID'd them as Tigers." Enzo took a slug of the vodka he'd saved from sterilizing his knife wound and sat down beside Jen on the couch. Nicholas was sleeping soundly—Enzo had checked at least a dozen times in the past hour—in the nursery room Jen had painted a pale, neutral green and adorned with Disney character stickers. Her child's watchful, two-dimensional guardians included Pinocchio, Piglet, and Winnie the Pooh. Enzo had already told her he was planning what shade of blue they should change it to, now they knew they had a boy. Jen knew Enzo wanted nothing more than to shout from the rooftops that his firstborn child was a son, and that it killed him inside knowing he could not.

"That is always possible," Jen replied with a frown. "Things are volatile in Chinatown right now. Some gangs are growing their territory while others are clinging to what they have."

"Why target you?" Enzo downed the remainder of his liquor.

"I have no idea," Jen lied. "Perhaps they think I'm encroaching on their territory, or maybe it was on behalf of a disgruntled tenant. Not all of my clients are happy, Enzo."

"Is this how your people do business?" Enzo asked her. "Killing women just after they've had a kid? What kind of monster does that?"

"The kind who would only stop short of murdering a helpless child in the womb," Jen said, though she had wondered the same thing herself. While she could understand the Tigers wanting her out of the way, even if it was to make a point to Storm, she couldn't think of any who would wait until she'd delivered her baby and risk entering the hospital to do it on the same day the child was born. There was something almost ritualistic about the attempt. She would certainly do her research once she was back on her feet, and she would get Eddie to make a few discreet inquiries around Mott and Doyers. There was always somebody who knew something, and Eddie was most proficient at digging them out, especially when he was looking for revenge.

"My family has some links with the Tigers," Enzo told her matter-of-factly. "I'll ask around, get some names."

"You need to learn when to leave well enough alone, Enzo," Jen rebuked him. "You have a child now. Don't risk your life over what was likely just a matter of business." The words sounded terribly hollow. How could Jen being murdered in front of her child be part of anyone's business?

She resolved to keep Nicholas away from it all as much as she could. Even if it meant breaking Enzo's heart and getting the hell away from New York.

ACT SEVEN: 1,000 CUTS

CHAPTER FIFTY-TWO

March 1993

Less than four weeks after the birth of her son, Jen was back in the saddle. She'd hired a nanny—a sweet Mexican girl in her mid-twenties—who had come with glowing recommendations. Jen now had two offices from which to manage the Black Dragons' businesses. One was a rented office space above a tea shop on Mulberry and the other was an alcove in Madam Sarah's private lounge in the Minster Tower's primary parlor. Although she missed being with her baby, Jen welcomed getting out of the confines of her Flushing apartment. Despite its comfortable size, at times she felt like a bird in a cage.

Enzo had taken an instant dislike to Josefina and insisted they employ a nice Italian woman—someone older who could instill Italian values and culture into their young son from an early age. Jen rejected the idea and argued that Josefina was Catholic, which seemed to placate Enzo enough to make him stop insisting on something Jen was never going to go for. She had no intention whatsoever of indoctrinating Nicholas with sexist, anachronistic cultural mores—Italian or Chinese.

As much as Enzo protested that he was entitled to a say in the matter, Jen stuck by her stance that since he chose not to live with her and their child openly, she got to set the rules. Enzo's refusal to make that move had been a huge disappointment to Jen; she'd harbored hopes that the birth of their son would give him balls enough to stand up to his family—but no. They still lived their separate lives and only got together when Enzo was able to dodge out of his father's sight.

As Jen had predicted, Eddie bounced back preternaturally and was again working after the eight days of recuperation she'd insisted he take. Since the attempt on her life at the hospital, he had remained steadfast in his determination not to allow her out of his sight and had taken to carrying a gun at all times. He had become so obsessive about remaining close that Jen actually considered herself lucky the guy didn't insist on following her to the toilet.

Following Nicholas's birth, there had of course been no word or acknowledgment from her father. Jen had instructed Eddie to inform him of the arrival of his first grandchild, which he had done and which had apparently been met with cold indifference. Jen had seen in her bodyguard's eyes just how much it hurt him to have to pass that news on to her, even though she feigned apathy and told him she was okay. Even Petey had stayed away, most likely under their father's strict instruction, and that raised Jen's hackles even more than the man's stubborn refusal to acknowledge his grandson.

Absently, Jen shuffled the sparse pieces of paperwork around on the desk she shared with Sarah as she waited patiently for a connection to a call from Fuzhou. She was finally by herself in the office, enjoying a moment alone, away from the overly protective Eddie. Thankfully, he had decided the parlor was a safe enough place to leave Jen unattended for a couple of hours while he took care of some business of his own. Despite still seeming uneasy around Sarah, he showed her marked respect.

"Miss Mo-Li?" Tang Xun's distinctive voice trilled through the receiver; she sounded faint, tinny, as if she were calling from Mars instead of China.

"Tang Xun!" Jen found herself shouting, even though she had no idea if the crappy reception went both ways.

"Congratulations on your baby," Tang Xun said. "You must be very relieved it is a boy."

Jen couldn't help but smile. That one sentence pretty much summed up everything she considered to be wrong with the motherland and its culture. "Thank you, Tang Xun," she said. "Yes, I am *very* relieved that I have a healthy baby of either gender."

The line crackled and fizzed and, for a split second, Jen thought the connection had dropped.

Then, Tang Xun's voice floated back through the ether. "There has been bad weather."

"In Fuzhou?" Jen couldn't see the relevance of Tang's information, unless this was an attempt at small talk. In which case, she had neither the time nor the inclination.

"The Cape of Good Hope," Tang explained as if Jen really ought to have known what she'd meant. "There were storms, some damage to the boat. The *Morning Rainbow* will be delayed by two weeks."

"Ah, I see. Thank you for telling me." Jen did the quick mental math—the *Morning Rainbow* would now dock in New York sometime around mid-June. A two-week delay wasn't the end of the world, however inconvenient.

"There have been some deaths," Tang Xun informed her. Jen sensed reluctance in the woman's voice. Had her reputation built to such terrifying proportions that people were scared of her from thousands of miles away?

"How many?"

"Five, maybe six." A deep sigh. "There has been much diarrhea on the ship. The food, I am told, was inadequate and of poor quality."

Jen swallowed her anger; it wasn't Tang Xun's fault the inevitable had happened and it wouldn't be diplomatic to rip at her for it. This one rested firmly with Storm and his constant penny-pinching. Had he followed Jen's recommendation for more latrines and better water sanitization when they refurbished the *Rainbow*, she wouldn't be counting the dead.

Jen would raise the subject of making changes with the gang leader the minute she had the opportunity. Or better yet, persuade him to simply put her in charge of that part of the process. She hadn't seen Storm much since Nicky's birth; it almost felt as if he was avoiding her. Perhaps, she thought, he was afraid she'd insist the child was his, despite the obvious presence of Caucasian blood, and insist that he marry her or some such nonsense. He'd not so much as sent her a card and flowers when she left the hospital, which hurt Jen more than she cared to admit. Since theirs was a purely business arrangement, she chalked the man's detachment up to his being put off by the fact that she'd given birth. She'd read that a great many men were put off—a Freudian thing and had to do with suddenly perceiving a woman as a maternal rather than sexual being. Jen also had a fleeting thought that Storm might be disappointed the kid turned out not to be his but dismissed it as silly.

Dreading the reply, Jen asked Tang Xun, "Has the illness been contained?"

"The captain hopes so," the woman told her. "There are still some sick, but he has informed me they are most likely to recover. He was able to take on some fresh provisions in Cape Town and procure some medicine."

"Something he should not have had to do. I will make sure this doesn't happen again." Jen tried her best to sound optimistic. She knew they couldn't afford to lose any of the girls, whether Storm understood that fact or not. The parlors were busy, and the Dragons had plans to expand the operation throughout Flushing and beyond. "Thank you for keeping me up to date. Let's speak again next Monday."

She returned the phone's receiver to its cradle before Tang Xun could bid her a crackly goodbye. It surprised Jen to realize just how put out she was that the woman had not bothered to ask her any more than the cursory minimum about her baby.

Eddie came in without knocking before Jen had the time to switch her train of thought to the next task in hand, which was to speak with Sarah about accommodating more girls during the early morning shift. She was appalled at just how many white-collar workers rolled out of their marital beds, kissed their wives goodbye, and, instead of hitting Starbucks, made the detour to a brothel for a quick fuck on their way to the office. Still, it was all good business and something Jen intended to capitalize on at Minster Tower.

"We don't knock now, Eddie?" Jen chastised with a playful smile. She'd missed the big lug while she'd been at home with the baby. He'd visited her only a couple of times, despite his initial excitement at becoming an honorary uncle to the kid.

"I'm sorry...." Eddie sat down with a grunt; his legs were still bothering him after the ambush.

"I'm teasing. You have something for me?"

The big man nodded, his brows set in a frown. "Someone has been running his mouth off about the attack in the hospital," he said.

Jen took a deep breath to calm her suddenly pounding heart. She'd thought she'd made progress muting the panic she felt when she remembered that day. "And...."

"And he's saying he knows who put the order out to have you...." Eddie had no desire to say the word.

"Killed?"

Eddie nodded.

Jen shrugged. "It was the Tigers. We know that. Big D wants me dead." The words made her lips feel numb.

Eddie looked down at his big hands clasped between his knees. "If it was the Tigers, as reported in the newspapers, why would this guy act like he had some big secret?"

Jen suppressed a groan. That she knew who her adversaries were had given her a measure of security. Someone raising questions about who was really responsible for the hit was the last thing she and her tenuous peace of mind needed. The Mott Street Tigers had continued their pressure on the Dragons all the while she'd been out on what Storm had called her maternity leave, which was a strangely orthodox phrase, given her position within the gang. Eddie had kept her informed as best he could about the cut-price drugs the Tigers had flooded into Chinatown and their sporadic intimidation of parlor clients. Thankfully they had not dared spread out into Flushing as yet. The all-too-regular beatdowns of the Dragons' gambling den managers was becoming increasingly difficult to manage. They were either scared away or too badly beaten to even contemplate returning to work.

All this angered Jen because it meant Storm had refused to capitalize on the chaos she'd created within the Tigers' businesses with the bombings and the murder of the dirty cop. It irked her that she had been taken out of the loop before she could do more; the baby had chosen to arrive at just the wrong time. Of course, as far as she knew, Storm had no idea she had been behind the attacks, which was fine by her since she'd not done it for recognition or a pat on the back. She'd done it to push him to either act or get out of the way. That made his lack of action to fill the void all the more infuriating. The Tigers had bounced back stronger and more vicious than ever, and the Vietnamese gangs had gained yet more ground, BTK in particular.

"Okay, so who's doing the talking?" Jen asked.

"Mike Ye."

Jen allowed the information to sink in. It was surprising to hear the name of a Black Dragon in this context; she'd fully expected Eddie to have unearthed one of Big D's inner circle as the man in the know. Surprising . . . but after a moment of thought, she caught a glimmer of what it might mean. She had split the Dragons' loyalties and cut Mike Ye and Stevie Lee out of her plans to countermand their leader's express instructions. Had the scene at the hospital been payback for that? Had the men Eddie and Enzo had taken for Tigers been Ye and Lee's buddies in disguise? She'd wondered why the gangsters had shown no interest in harming Nicholas, why they'd waited until after his birth to stage a hit. That made perfect sense if they feared what would happen if they harmed a child that might be their leader's.

Anger curled in her breast. To maim or kill a new mother just to keep her in her place was extreme even for the Tigers, let alone the Black Dragons, who had a pattern of sparing non-combatants. Once again, her life had changed around her, leaving her in the dark when it came to vital information, such as from what quarter she should expect attack.

"I believe we need to have a conversation with Mr. Ye," Jen said. "Discreetly, of course."

"Of course." Eddie struggled to his feet with a low, rumbling growl.

"Storm must not find out we are talking to him." Although that much was a given, Jen felt the need to say it as the implications of what Mike might know—coupled with the fact that he thought he knew *something* about the night at the hospital—carried with it serious implications Jen had only fleetingly considered. Was it possible Storm had been involved in the attempted assassination? And if so, what was she prepared to do about it?

There was only one way to know.

CHAPTER FIFTY-THREE

Jen chose the cold storage at the rear of Mulberry Dried Beef Inc. for her confrontation with Mike Ye. The butcher shop was owned by one of her oldest, most loyal clients—someone she could trust to keep his mouth shut. The choice of venue wasn't arbitrary; Jen figured the hanging slabs of ex-cows and pigs would subtly convey a threat in case the gangster objected to her summons or took this as a chance to get at her.

He did object, as it happened. Mike greeted Eddie's unexpected appearance at his door with extreme hostility, which caused him to arrive at the butcher shop bruised, a bit bloody, and wearing only boxers, a T-shirt, and a fine sheen of sweat. Mike began the confrontation seated forcibly in a plastic chair between two sides of beef. But his first sight of Jen—all cozy and warm in a fleece-lined jacket—catapulted him out of his chair, his restrained hands itching to wrap themselves around her neck. He ended up suspended between the beef slabs, bound hand and foot, still wearing his defiance like a shield.

Jen stood directly before him where she could look into his eyes. He was not a complicated man, and easy enough for her to read; his face was eloquent with contempt. His reaction to Eddie approaching him, coupled with his stupid attempt to throttle her, sealed her suspicion that he had been party to the attack in the hospital.

"You know why you're here, don't you?" It was not really a question.

"I'm here because you're a traitorous bitch," he said.

Eddie, standing to Mike's left, poked him in the ribs with the butt of the knife he'd used to cut the rope binding the gangster's wrists.

"You're here," said Jen with a calm as chill as the room, "because you've been telling people—the wrong people—that you know something about the Tigers' attack on me and my son."

Good God, the stupid bastard actually smiled.

"Tigers, yeah. I do know something about that."

"Like, for example, that they weren't really Tigers at all? Like that?"

Mike's smile faltered. "Big D hates you after what you did on his turf."

Not a denial. Jen took a step closer. "More than you hate me, Mike Ye, for taking a position in the Dragons you thought you'd get?"

"The only position you take in the Dragons," he sneered, "is on your knees with Storm Cheung's dick in your mouth."

She slapped him before she realized her own intention, her hand flying out in reflexive fury. The force of the blow rotated him away from her. Jen reached out and pulled him back around by the front of his T-shirt.

"What's the matter, Mike? Are you jealous because you're not Storm's type?"

Eddie made a sound that could have been a grunt of surprise or a snort of laughter. Mike, hearing it, lashed out at Jen with his bound feet. He caught her in the stomach—a weak blow, barely enough to knock some of the air out of her lungs. She responded reflexively again, this time with a roundhouse kick to his groin. He roared in pain and, unable to double over, pulled his knees toward his chest. She took the opportunity to sidestep and land another kick to his unprotected balls. The roar became a shriek.

She mockingly covered her ears. "Oh, my God, Mike, you sound like an old fishwife. Doesn't he sound like an old fishwife, Eddie?"

"He does," said her guardian, deadpan.

Jen got back in Mike's face. "Don't do that again, because I can guarantee you, I will respond in the same way, only harder and with the toe of my pointy little boots. Understood? Now, please, for your own sake, tell me what you know about the hit on me and my son."

"It was just an attack on you," Mike rasped. "Your baby wouldn't have been harmed."

"Beyond losing his mother, you mean? Am I supposed to take some comfort from that?"

"I don't care what you take from that."

"All I want to know is who instigated the attack. I don't like uncertainty, you see, and the suggestion that it wasn't really the Tigers makes me feel uncertain. I need to know who my enemies are. Are you my enemy, Mikey?"

Jen was right up in his grill again, peering into his eyes. She saw the swift flash of fear that crossed Mike's face before the defiance was back. She knew exactly how to bring back the fear.

"Here's what I think," she told him, "I think your implication that the Tigers didn't call the hit is right. I think *you* called it. You and Stevie Lee and your stupid posse. And I think the best way I can take care of that threat is to tell Storm what you've done and let *him* handle it. What do you think?"

Mike's reaction was not at all what Jen expected. The fear she'd seen a moment before was completely erased, and in its place was seething scorn. "I think you fucking can't see what's right in front of your face. Storm Cheung put the hit on you, you dumb, crazy bitch."

Jen stepped back, feeling as if she'd flash-frozen to her core. She reflexively wrapped her arms around herself. "You're lying."

He shook his head, openly laughing at her now. "No, bitch, I'm not. And you know it. Storm's wanted you dead since you moved against the Tigers. He just waited until after you had the kid because—"

Jen didn't let him finish. Horror and rage at Storm's betrayal broke over her like a tsunami. Whirling, she snatched Eddie's knife from his hand and plunged it into Mike's chest—again, again, again, again— screaming in inarticulate rage. She felt the warm blood on her hands, felt it spatter her face. Then Eddie was behind her, stilling her hands and lifting the knife from them, slick and sticky with Mike Ye's blood. He turned her away from the dying gangster and wrapped his arms around her in a tight, protective embrace.

In the safety and comfort of Eddie Sun's arms, with her head against his chest, she sobbed out her anger and desolation. She had wanted to come out of this with certainty but had found none. Jen learned one thing only tonight. She didn't know her friend from her enemy.

"Let me take you home and get you cleaned up," Eddie said, the words rumbling in his chest. "I'll take care of this, Jen. I'll take care of it."

CHAPTER FIFTY-FOUR

"So ... you wanna fuck me or not?" It sounded to Enzo like Gabriella Taccetta was taunting rather than attempting to seduce him. Sprawled on her four-poster bed in a diaphanous red and black negligee like a fifties' movie star with her pale thighs slightly parted, Gabriella's more than generous breasts spilled out over the top of the half-cups. She'd played the old *let me slip into something more comfortable* line the second she'd gotten him back to her Midtown apartment. Now she was there for the taking.

Truth be told, Enzo thought she looked ridiculous—the gaudy silk designer lingerie intended to be daring but merely looked cheap and tacky, especially on someone of Gabriella's proportions. Not that she was fat; she wasn't. Hers was simply not the kind of prettiness Enzo had come to admire, and he found himself comparing her unfavorably to Jen. Her skin was too pale, her breasts too large (how was that even possible?), and her pubic hair looked like a curly doll wig she'd glued between her legs.

Their date had been set up by their fathers, both of whom were eager to cement the new-found, if somewhat uneasy, armistice between the two families. The DeCarlos and Taccettas were finally working together after so many years of bitter feuding, and all concerned considered marriage between Enzo and Gabriella to be the perfect icing on the cake.

Enzo had surprised himself by enjoying Gabriella's company over pasta and seafood at Mamma Leone's Italian restaurant over in the theater district. She was surprisingly well-read, intelligent, knew her way around a sommelier's menu, and made for a welcome change from the near-constant talk of baby behavior and Nicky's future he got from Jen. But despite them actually getting along, Enzo hadn't been looking forward to what he'd correctly assumed was to be the inevitable conclusion to their evening.

And there she was—dressed up like some two-bit whore and demanding her pound of flesh because Enzo had been gallant enough to buy her dinner. He wondered vaguely if the women he'd dated ever felt like this. He'd fucked worse, of course—hell, he never turned down the opportunity for sex. But that was before Jen had pulled him into her orbit. Enzo could believe she may well have put him off other women for good.

"Don't tell me the great Enzo DeCarlo is shy?" Gabriella rolled over and crawled across the bed to perch at its end like some predatory siren. "You need me to suck on it to get you in the mood?" Reaching out, Gabriella unbuckled Enzo's belt with expert ease.

The thought of her lips on him…. "No," Enzo all but jumped back, away from her groping fingers.

"*Pardon me?*" Gabriella's breasts jiggled as she let out a light, embarrassed laugh; clearly the daughter of Giuseppe Taccetta wasn't used to hearing the word *no*.

"I–I'm sorry," Enzo stammered. "Too much wine…."

"You got the brewer's droop?" Gabriella gave him a sly grin. "I don't believe half a bottle of Chianti Riservas has put the famous Enzo DeCarlo out of action."

Above the smile, Enzo could see hurt in the girl's eyes and was ashamed of himself. She'd obviously gone to a hell of a lot of effort to seduce him, and no doubt by her father's wishes. Enzo knew his reluctance would not just be seen as a slight on her as a young woman, but on the very honor of the Taccetta family.

"Is it something else?" Gabriella cupped her bountiful breasts and pushed them together to create the deepest, darkest cleavage Enzo had ever seen. "Don't you like what you see, Enzo? Are you....?"

Enzo's mind raced. What the hell was he supposed to do? Fuck the girl to save his family's face and the truce between the families? What was this, the 1920s?

"Don't tell me you're a goddamn faggot?" Gabriella scooted backward on her bed and covered her voluminous chest the best she could with her hands. "Oh, my God! Enzo DeCarlo is a fucking fag! Just wait 'til I tell your father. This is gonna fucking kill him! And what's your dear, sweet mamma going to say when she finds out she raised a *fag*?" She sat with her back pressed against the white velvet headboard, hands still covering her breasts, legs tightly crossed, as if she thought a purported homosexual posed a threat to her . . . what, her virtue?

Anger actually helped, Enzo found. He felt a tickle of lust at the challenge of convincing Gabby Taccetta that he wasn't a fag. But to help things along, he replayed his last encounter with Jen in the back of his mind, remembering how she looked in nothing but a black motorcycle jacket that stopped at her waist. "Let me show you," he told Gabriella, his voice a menacing growl, "how much of a faggot I am." There was a menace in Enzo's voice as he dropped his dress pants, kicked off his shoes, and scaled the bed.

"Now, that's more like it, Mr. DeCarlo." Gabriella gave a lingering, lascivious stare at the growing bulge in Enzo's tight briefs. Removing her hands from her breasts, she parted her legs in open invitation.

As his memory drifted back over the many ways Jen had plated herself for him, Enzo crawled toward Gabriella, focused on his arousal. Jen would understand that what he was about to do was nothing more than a business transaction on behalf of the DeCarlo family.

Not that he had any intention of telling her.

There was something off about Enzo the following morning. He seemed uneasy and avoided looking Jen in the eyes. When she asked if something was wrong, he'd given her some vague explanation about another business dinner he'd had to attend. He'd even shown up with bagels.

Was it possible he had some inkling about Mike Ye? She knew the Italian gangs kept tabs on Chinese gang activity, but was it at that level?

Stop it, Jen, she told herself. *That's fucking paranoid.*

If not paranoid, she was at least preoccupied with what Mike Ye had revealed to her about the hospital hit—especially what she ought to do about it. The strain of pretending not to know it was her own boss who'd put the hit on her, blamed it on the Tigers, and played business as usual was taking its toll. Other than Eddie, there really was no one Jen could trust, not even the sub-deputies and soldiers she considered loyal to her. Naturally, she was on her guard every moment of every day, and vowed to ensure Eddie was by her side whenever she ventured out of her apartment, especially on Black Dragon business. It also had her thinking even more about the future—particularly her son's.

She looked at Enzo across the breakfast bar in her Flushing apartment and opened her mouth, fully intending to tell him what Mike had told her, knowing he'd want to take his own revenge. After all, he'd been there too, and might have been killed if not for Eddie. But what came out of her mouth was, "I really don't want our son growing up here."

"Why not?" Enzo replied through a mouthful of cream cheese. "We have a good life and the support of my family."

Jen suppressed the snort of derision that fought for escape. "You mean your family's *money*? They don't even know Nicholas exists."

"You know what I mean," Enzo said. "I'll be head of the family one day. Nicholas will work his way up the business just as I did."

"Maybe I want other things for him," Jen said mildly, while her internal voice screamed *No!* with the vehemence of a Category Five hurricane. She fiddled with the deli wrapper to cover her agitation.

"You mean, you don't want him to end up like me?"

Jen sighed. Enzo was in an argumentative mood; her timing could have been better. "That's *not* what I'm saying at all," she told him, although it pretty much was. "What I'm saying is, I might want a better life for him than either of us has. Our families' way of life is dated beyond belief, Enzo. We both know that."

"We're modernizing our business model," Enzo countered. "The DeCarlo company is coming into the twentieth century."

"Oh, good, when it's almost over."

He rolled his eyes. "I'm gonna build a legacy for our boy to be proud to carry on. I'll make it 100 percent legit one day."

"Enzo, you act like little more than a common thug." The irony of the statement, in light of her part in Mike Ye's demise, wasn't lost on Jen. She shivered at the memory of his warm blood on her cold hands. *Out damned spot.* "I do not want our son to grow up to be a gangster. I have already lost my brother to that lifestyle, and I have no wish to bury my child as well."

"You honestly think I'd put my son in danger?" Enzo's pale eyes glittered with affront.

She shrugged. "Your father's put *you* in danger, Enzo."

"That's not the same," Enzo protested. "He's from an entirely different era. Things were different back then."

"Yes, I've seen the documentaries—*The Godfather* and *Goodfellas*? Classics." Jen attempted levity to diffuse the tension between them as it was rare they got time for just the two of them. Jen had packed Josefina off to the park with Nicholas so she could enjoy some time with Enzo, and she was beginning to regret that decision. Some days, she wondered if the kid was the only thing they had in common anymore. Well, that and sex.

"It's not like that." Enzo was quickly on the defensive.

"Maybe it's not, but you have to ask yourself why the hell you do what you do." The question echoed in her head, and she stifled it.

"To earn a living." Enzo really wasn't getting her point. "And to build a future for us and our son. If you weren't so controlling, you'd be able to see that."

She was controlling? Jen ground her teeth as if to stop the words that wanted to leap from the tip of her tongue. At the hospital, she'd felt connected to him and to their child, as if she and Enzo and Nicky were a family. Since then, she'd begun to fear he was too set in his ways, as if the anachronistic traditions his family clung to had dug so deeply into his soul that he would never be able to break free.

But does he even want to? That was the crux of the problem: He wanted to have a new life while keeping the old. But he couldn't have it, not until he either brought his family into it or jettisoned them. How often had he demanded her respect instead of working to earn it? If he wanted her respect, he needed to tell Papa DeCarlo about his grandson. She'd told her father, for all the good it had done.

They ate their bagels in silence and waited for the nanny to return; at least then they'd have some common ground. Jen had no doubt Enzo loved Nicholas, but he just wasn't prepared to show it in the one way that really mattered.

Jen decided it would be in her best interest to regard Enzo as she did Storm Cheung—a challenge to be met. She'd bide her time and be watchful for opportunities to act from now on. In the meantime, she would smile and pretend everything was fine.

"I'm sorry, Enzo," she said. "You're right. I'll try to be less controlling."

She did not imagine the look of blank surprise on her lover's face as she smiled and looked demurely into her coffee cup.

CHAPTER FIFTY-FIVE

June 1993

Eddie's frowning gaze made Jen feel like a naughty little girl again. Nervous, she crossed and uncrossed her legs, unable to find a comfortable position on a sofa she had bought for its comfort.

"Why now?" Eddie asked her.

It was clear he was struggling to remain professional. Jen wasn't oblivious to the change in dynamic between them since she began working with the Black Dragons, more pronounced since Mike Ye's death.

"Enough time has passed for those who know Storm ordered the hit to not suspect me," Jen told him. "And enough time for him to have forgotten what happened to Mike Ye."

Hearing herself speak Mike's name for the first time in months brought back the vivid, nightmarish memories of the gangster's death. She had lost control in a particularly horrifying way. Yes, he had relished telling her that Storm had ordered her killed. And, yes, the knowledge had stunned her to the core. But should she not have suspected it? After all, the timing of the hit made sense. The truth was, she had not wanted to suspect Storm, and the most disturbing thing about the situation, next to her shocking loss of self-control, was that Storm's betrayal had struck so deeply. Jen had mocked his vulnerability to her, yet had never considered her own.

Storm had gotten over Mike's death with dispassionate speed although he'd paid for the funeral. The guy had no immediate family, so there weren't even been any mourners to follow his casket through Chinatown, nor anyone to send money to. Mike had simply been met with an occupational hazard that was chalked up to gang tit for tat or the settling of a personal score.

Jen had left no fingerprints at the scene of the killing. The owner of the butcher shop deposited the body in an open dumpster behind a Vietnamese restaurant a couple of blocks down on Kenmare, where it was found three days later. But the body had been dined upon by rats, so the coroner could not determine the cause of death. Overall, the killing sent a mixed message at best and had increased tension on the streets.

"Would it not be best to let sleeping dogs lie?" Eddie ventured. "Mr. Cheung has been generous with you since—"

"Since he tried to have me killed?" Jen flashed her bodyguard a sardonic grin. "Sure, he's increased my take from the Flushing parlors and paid out some fat bonuses, but I've earned every fucking cent of that. Have you considered the fact it may just be to assuage his guilty conscience?"

"He has a conscience?"

She glanced at him sharply. Was that humor? "It's obvious to me that I'm not the only one playing nice and biding my time. Who is to say he's not going to try again?"

Both Jen and the Dragon leader had carried on with the charade of normality. She did it to survive; perhaps Storm did it because she was valuable to him. In any event, Jen had kept her ear to the ground with help from Eddie, Den Cha, and Gary Hu, and there was not so much as a rumbling among the ranks about Storm's intention to permanently remove her from the Dragons. But if she had learned one thing in working with the gangs, it was that everything could change in an instant.

"Things are quiet, Jen, for the first time in weeks," Eddie observed.

"Which makes it the perfect time for a pre-emptive strike," Jen said. "Storm is weak. He lost Charlie-Boy and Mike and did nothing. His executive posse is split, and he's been reluctant to deal with incursions by the other gangs. It's only a matter of time before the Tigers, or Ghost Shadows, or BTK make a play for *all* of the Dragons' territory. And then what?"

"War?"

"One we have no hope of winning with Storm at the helm." Jen stood up and wandered into the kitchen. The baby would awaken from his afternoon nap any minute, and she had his bottle to prepare. It was one of the nanny's rare days off, and Jen was determined to take some much-needed bonding time with her son. "Even those loyal to him are saying he's grown soft since Charlie-Boy died."

Eddie raised an eyebrow. "So, you think you'd be doing the gang a favor by taking out their leader?"

"Don't you? Storm should have declared outright war on the Tigers after Charlie-Boy was killed. But no, he let it slide, along with everything else those bastards have done."

Eddie wasn't about to let her distance herself from Fok's assassination. "What if he didn't move against the Tigers because he knows or suspects it was you who killed Charlie-Boy?"

Jen shook her head. "If he did, we wouldn't be here today."

"Maybe. Look, if you're determined to go through with this, I'm coming with you. Storm does deserve retaliation for trying to kill you, and you can't expect me to stand back and allow you to do something as dangerous as this alone."

Jen was hit with two conflicting reactions at once: gratitude that Eddie wouldn't abandon her to do something alone, and annoyance that he wouldn't *allow* her to do something alone. Annoyance won, if briefly. For a moment, Eddie was a stand-in for her father, Enzo, and practically every other man in her life who'd aimed to control her. She shook the annoyance away. Jen had no intention of carrying out an assassination by herself, and Eddie Sun was literally the only person she could trust to have her back.

"I was hoping you'd volunteer," Jen gave Eddie a warm, sincere smile. "I'm going to need you."

"You mean, you need my gun," Eddie replied just as Nicholas's hungry cry erupted from the nursery.

CHAPTER FIFTY-SIX

Although it was dark on Bayard Street, the air carried with it the warmth of the day, along with mouth-watering aromas from the restaurants and cafés that lit up the sidewalk with neon signs and bright, welcoming lights. It was a sure sign the blistering heat of July was on its way, when even the nights would be too stifling to enjoy a cold beer and a card game with friends out on the street.

Storm Cheung was in a relaxed mood, thanks in part to the copious amounts of beer supplied gratis by Des Chow, the proprietor of the Goldman Bar. He had enjoyed Black Dragon protection for seven years and had every reason to be grateful. For a small, hole-in-the-wall, street-side bar, the place turned more than a healthy profit and gave him a good living—all thanks to Storm's patronage.

The gang leader sat with his back to the wall; he had Stevie Lee on his left hand, nearest the bar's door. Stevie was armed with a .375 SIG Sauer, even though Storm didn't feel it was entirely necessary. This was just a pleasant Thursday night with a few close friends over a hand or three of seven-card stud. Plus, only a select few knew of Storm's weekly card game, and the bar was situated in the heart of Dragon territory—the only place the Dragon leader could really relax.

"You guys gonna deal me in?" Des Chow laughed as he deposited five bottles of frosted Bud onto the round, copper-topped table. "I need to win back my rent money from this crook." As he pulled up a chair from the neighboring, empty table, its iron feet scraped loudly on the sidewalk.

Storm laughed along at the playful slight. He and Des went back a hell of a lot of years—Des had been around almost as long as Charlie-Boy Fok and was always quick with the friendly digs.

"We're playing for quarters," Storm reminded him. "There are not enough hours left in the night for you to have any chance of winning anything back!" Finishing the shuffle with a one-handed cut, Storm dealt out the next hand.

Everyone around the table laughed at Des's expense, their merriment catching the attention of a small gaggle of bar hoppers who wandered slowly along Bayard as if it were some seaside promenade. In the semi-darkness of the street, these passersby were an amorphous human blob. Storm and his fellow players ignored them and set about the fresh beer and cards with gusto.

Two shapes separated from the group on the sidewalk—one petite and slim, the other tall and bulky. Both were dressed in black puffer jackets and black jeans, and wore dark, wide-brimmed hats. They paused as if in conversation, with the attitude of a couple trying to decide where to go next.

Stevie Lee was the first to look up. It was his job to remain vigilant—and therefore stone-cold sober—and the sudden presence of the two had him on alert. Acting on instinct, he reached a hand inside his loose-fitting denim jacket for his SIG.

The first bullet hit Stevie in his right shoulder and instantly stopped any plan he had to defend his boss. The second, third, and fourth hit Storm Cheung in the head as he reacted to the sharp crack of the gunshot. The slugs blew out his eyes and snapped his head back with such force that what remained of the back of his skull stuck to the brick wall behind him. Another two shots tore through the tepid night air and hit Stevie Lee who slumped from his chair bleeding with a pair of thumb-sized holes in his chest.

Des Chow and Storm's two remaining friends shouted in panic and scrambled away from the carnage. In their desperate need to be out of the way before the assassins turned their attention to them, they stumbled over the heavy metal chairs and fell sprawling to the sidewalk. Undeterred, and with little dignity, they struggled to their feet and scurried into the bar to peer out through the relative safety of the windows.

The street was empty, the death-dealers gone.

CHAPTER FIFTY-SEVEN

News of Storm Cheung's murder in the heart of his turf spread through Chinatown like wildfire, just as Jen had expected. She had placed a handful of choice phone calls in the early hours of the morning to members of the gang she could rely upon to get the word out that the Mott Street Tigers had assassinated the head of the Black Dragons.

Now, standing behind Storm's desk and before the dozen or so deputies who were subdued by shocked disbelief, Jen felt an exhilarating rush of power. This was her moment; she no longer existed in Storm's shadow under constant fear for her life. She was safe, her son was safe, and she found herself at the helm of a small empire. But Jen strategically stood with Eddie by her side, as his imposing presence discouraged the Black Dragons' rank and file from reacting negatively to what she was about to tell them.

"Tradition dictates the second-in-command steps into the leader's shoes upon his death, and it is a task I accept with a heavy heart," Jen told them. It was not up for debate, no matter how unorthodox her appointment to be Storm's deputy. She'd expected some dissent, especially from Storm's most loyal lieutenants, but heard only a low murmur ripple among them. It had been a wise decision to take out

Stevie Lee alongside Storm; if anyone were to question her succession, it would have been him.

"I know how most of you will feel about having a woman leader—especially a snakehead." Holding up her hand, Jen spread her fingers wide to show them all the smooth stump of her pinkie finger. "I became one of you when I *proved* I was worthy, and I have done nothing to bring dishonor to the Black Dragons." She studied the faces before her; they were still reeling from the news of Storm's death. Her timing was absolutely perfect.

"Are we to seek revenge against the Tigers?" A voice rose above the group. Heads turned and the muttering increased in volume. It was Den Cha; Jen had briefed him with the question beforehand and his timing, too, was perfect.

Jen raised both hands to quiet the voices and regain the room's attention. "If you are thinking a mere woman will not have the fortitude to strike vengeance against those who murdered our leader in cold blood, then you are mistaken."

Jen stopped short of reminding them Storm would likely have demanded restraint in the interests of not escalating the violence out on the streets. Instinct told her that to tarnish their beloved leader's name in such a way would have been counterproductive. Now that he was out of her way, it was more important that she garner the gang's unwavering loyalty and secure the Dragons' future by slaking their thirst for revenge.

"What the Tigers did last night was nothing less than a declaration of war," Jen continued. She had everyone's rapt attention at the suggestion of revenge. "We would be less than honorable if we didn't counter it with a declaration of our own."

The murmuring picked up once more, only this time there were nods of approval and a smile or two.

"We shall take this fight to the streets, to the very heart of Tiger territory. We will take the battle to them before they take advantage of our grief." Reading the room, Jen saw the bloodlust in every single set of eyes present. "The Tigers have been attacking us without consequence for far too long; it's time we make a show of overwhelming force. So, this time, we will fight them with guns and Molotovs—the time for cleavers and knives is long-past."

"We must wait for our leader to be put to rest," Ken Lo spoke up from the back of the office. He had stepped into Mike Ye's shoes as one of Storm's trusted inner circle and had only missed out on being assassinated alongside the leader by sheer luck, as he was a terrible poker player.

"And hand the Tigers the advantage on a plate?" Jen stood firm. "We must act fast, while they assume we will be in mourning. The Tigers will not expect retaliation so soon."

"How soon?" There was confrontation in Ken Lo's voice.

"Arm yourselves, then gather your most trusted soldiers and arm them, too. We'll take to Doyers, Mott, and Mulberry tonight. We will strike while the Tigers least expect it."

As the sub-deputies chattered between themselves, Jen nodded to Gary Hu. He stepped toward the desk with a cleaver in his hand. As with Den Cha's provocative question, this had been staged by Jen.

"Show us," Gary said, looking down his nose at her through narrowed eyes. "Show us you are worthy to lead." He swung the cleaver, driving the end of the blade into the desktop.

The room fell silent, with all eyes on the two standing at Storm's desk.

Jen turned to face Gary, locking eyes with him for a moment before pulling the cleaver from the wood. She saw Eddie look away as she addressed the gang. "I am asking that you forget I am a woman and remember that I am your leader. Tonight, I will be one of you, and together we will bring the Tigers to their knees once and for all."

Jen turned, splayed her hand on the desktop, and brought the cleaver down in a swift, shining arc of sharpened steel. Once again, her blood was spilled on the gang leader's desk.

CHAPTER FIFTY-EIGHT

As dusk fell across Manhattan and Chinatown's streets began their transformation from bustling commerce to relaxed Friday nightlife, Jen Mo-Li finalized her deadly preparations.

Splitting the gang into three groups of ten, she armed them with handguns and Molotov cocktails. The old ways of doing battle would be buried with Storm Cheung. They all had knives for close fighting.

"We strike at nine precisely," she instructed Den Cha and Gary Hu, each of whom she had placed in charge of a group. She would head up one of her own, along with Eddie. Despite his insistence that she lead from behind, Jen was determined to prove herself a worthy successor to the leader she'd gunned down in cold blood, and she knew that couldn't possibly happen if she chose to cower behind Storm's desk while the gang wreaked havoc on the Mott Street Tigers.

Jen checked her watch; it was almost eight thirty. She wanted to get things underway and finished. The *Morning Rainbow* would be docking in New York Harbor in the small hours, and she wanted the Tigers finished off well before then. The pain in her right hand didn't feel quite so severe as it had the first time she'd proven her loyalty to the Dragons, thanks to either the adrenaline coursing through her body or her getting used to maiming herself. Another manicured fingertip had been sacrificed for the cause, but her hands matched now. Unfortunately, the wound made handling her Glock a painful exercise.

"Den, you take the pool hall first. Gary, hit the brothel. We'll take out Jīn Bāozi before Big D even gets word what's happening in his territory." The restaurant had become a favorite of the Tigers' leader since they snatched it from under the Dragons' noses, and Jen had intelligence that he'd be there eating dinner by the time she got to him.

Looking across at Eddie for support, Jen saw only judgment in his eyes. He'd fight alongside her; that much she could rely upon, but it would only be out of a warped sense of duty and a perverse need to protect her. Eddie Sun would die for Jen if necessary, even if he disagreed vehemently with her goals and her methods of achieving them.

"No prisoners?" Gary Hu asked, fiddling nervously with the handle of the gun he'd tucked into the waistband at the back of his jeans.

"Tonight, we are not sending a message," Jen gave her answer to the entire gang. "The time for sending messages to the Tigers died along with David Cheung. Tonight, we wipe out as many of them as we possibly can and, with the gang weakened, we will reclaim our territory."

No one could doubt that the night was about avenging Storm's death and clawing back honor among the Chinatown gangs. As nods and murmurs of approval spread through the Dragons, Jen knew she had played her hand to perfection.

CHAPTER FIFTY-NINE

The Nom Wah Tea Parlor was still open and enjoying a brisk, summer night's business when the first Molotov cocktail crashed through the window. With a cursory nod of the head, Den Cha instructed someone in his cohort to kick open the tea parlor's door and hurl another firebomb into the place. It smashed against the edge of the bar and created a rapidly spreading wall of flames along the floor and bar top, sending patrons and staff to the exits.

There, Den Cha and the Dragons were waiting, eyes peeled for any Tigers who might be in attendance. There were none, so Den and his men loomed and threatened the terrified victims as they fled into the night but did them no harm. The objective at the tea parlor was to instill terror, not massacre innocent people and alert the police too early in the fight.

Jen's decision to attack the Nom Wah ahead of the pool hall was one she had not taken lightly, as it held a special place in her heart. But it was an iconic place in Chinatown, and its partial destruction would ensure news coverage after the fact, which would spread the word among every single gang that the Black Dragons were not to be messed with. As the fire within the Nom Wah Tea Parlor lit up Doyers with a flickering, crackling dance of light and shadow, a sharp, piercing whistle cut the night air, and the Dragons moved on to their next objective.

The Sum Ying Pool Hall, just up Doyers from the Nom Wah, was a poignant target for Den Cha. In the street just outside its front doors, Charlie-Boy Fok had met his end, presumably at the hands of the Tigers. Jen had placed it on her hit list at Den's request. It was also a focal point of the Tigers' territory, a place they considered themselves safe. They would learn otherwise.

Den Cha led the attack from the front. Bursting through the hall's front doors, he took down the solitary doorman with a well-aimed slug to the guy's forehead. The guy hit the floor before he'd even had the chance to reach for his own weapon. There was no longer any reason for stealth; Cha wanted the Tigers to know damn well they were under attack. That would spread fear through the gang, especially with the simultaneous attacks going on within their territory. Despite the element of surprise, the Dragons were met by gunfire the moment they marched into the pool hall. However, they quickly figured out that only two of the dozen or so Tigers within were armed with anything more lethal than knives and cleavers.

"Take them out!" Den barked at his soldiers as they spread out to take cover behind the tables. He waved his gun in the direction of the bar, from behind which two Tigers fired indiscriminately in their direction. Two of his men crawled out from behind their pool table and made their way toward the bar. Den led the suppressing fire, which kept the pair of shooters cowering behind the bar and their colleagues hunkered down behind pool tables. Pausing to smack a fresh clip into his gun, Den Cha turned his attention to the array of bottles that adorned the back of the bar. Once reloaded, he emptied all ten bullets into them. That showered the Tigers behind the bar with a cascade of shattered glass and cheap liquor.

As Den lit up a Molotov, the flame leaped high from the gas-soaked rag dangling from the bottle's neck. "Stand down!" His voice rang out above the staccato cracks of gunfire. The room fell silent. "I'm giving you all three seconds to get the fuck out!" Den held the flaming bottle aloft above the safety of the pool table, its heat singeing the skin at the back of his hand. "One...."

The two gunmen behind the bar were the first to emerge, soaked through with booze, hands held high, and a look of shameful defeat on their faces. Dropping their weapons onto the bar as they got to their feet, they stood frozen, their eyes fixed on Den Cha's hand and the burning bottle.

"Two...."

A handful of Tigers stood up from behind their pool tables, and the hall filled with the hollow sound of cleavers and knives clattering to the sticky wooden floor. Hands above their heads, they shuffled single file in the direction of Den Cha, his Black Dragons, and the exit. The two behind the bar joined them.

"Three...." Den enunciated the word with dramatic finality; the bottle in his hand was becoming dangerously hot.

The remaining Tigers dropped their weapons and scrambled to their feet. Even though they were bringing great dishonor upon themselves by surrendering, they knew they were outgunned and beaten. Not even Big D would have expected self-sacrifice against such overwhelming odds.

With all their opponents disarmed and gathered, Den Cha hurled the Molotov cocktail. The bar, its shelves, and the remaining stock of alcohol burst into flames. Then the Black Dragon turned and opened fire on the Tigers making their way toward the door. The other Dragons popped up from cover and followed suit. The Tigers at the head of the line were cut down before they could register the Dragons' misdirection. Those remaining scattered. As they scrabbled around on the floor for the weapons they'd discarded on the unspoken promise of mercy, they, too, were met with an unrelenting, vicious spray of bullets. If ever there was a defining illustration of a bloodbath, the scene unfolding in the pool hall was surely it.

A battle that left every Tiger dead, Den Cha would have countenanced, but this ruse sickened him. It went against every concept of honor he believed in to mow down defenseless young men through an implicit lie. It wasn't a battle; it was a slaughter. Orders were orders, he told himself. Their new leader had been specific in her strategy. So, as the fire took hold of the Sum Ying Pool Hall, the Dragons made sure every Tiger was dead. There could be no possibility whatsoever of any witnesses to attest to the Dragons' dishonorable actions.

A couple of streets over, the Venus Joy Spa went up in flames as well. The brothel, freshly restored following the bomb blast that had all but destroyed it only months before, bore the brunt of Gary Hu's gang as they shot out the windows and tossed flaming bottles of gasoline through the shattered glass. The parlor's front door was torched, too, with the express objective of preventing escape to the street. Girls and clients alike were thus forced to flee the burning building through the rear entrance where Ken Lo's group awaited them. Driven by blind terror, pushing and shoving one another, trampling upon those who fell with complete disregard, they burst through the back door. Most were half-dressed. Others completely naked but risking embarrassment in their panic to be free of the blaze that spread through the building with preternatural speed.

While humiliation and collateral injury were all the girls and their clients sustained, the half-dozen or so Mott Street Tigers inside the building were shot down as they escaped into the night air. Within mere minutes, no one else scrambled through the door, and the Dragons' victims lay scattered across the ground in the alleyway behind the Venus Joy. Ken Lo motioned for his comrades to ensure that every single Tiger was dead from a bullet between the eyes. As they did so, Ken ventured into the parlor, coughing against the thin gray smoke that wafted out into the night.

"Hello?" Ken's voice echoed against the faint crackle and spit of the flames eating the front of the building. It wouldn't be long before the fire made its way through the entire place. Nevertheless, Ken had to make sure no Tigers were hiding within. To leave such matters to chance would be to court Jen's wrath.

Of course, no one replied.

Ken made his way through the kitchen. The sharp cracks of pistol shots outside came to an abrupt end, which meant the Dragons had guaranteed no survivors. He pushed open a cracked door that opened out into a dimly lit hallway dotted with bedroom doors on both sides. A door stood at the far end; out from beneath it billowed thick, black smoke from the conflagration beyond. It was highly unlikely there'd be anyone alive at the front of the house. With a sudden movement to Ken's left, one of the narrow doors flew open. Ken's reflexes kicked in; he raised his pistol in reaction, his finger on the trigger.

Madam Tung Yijun fired first. She watched him fall as the Venus Joy Spa burned down around her.

CHAPTER SIXTY

Jen, Eddie, and their gang of eight Dragons hit the Jīn Bāozi restaurant on Mulberry in perfect synchronicity with the attacks on the Venus Joy and the Sum Ying Pool Hall. Jen knew Big D would have been alerted to the attack on the Nom Wah, which she had calculated would provide the perfect misdirection for the main thrust of the Dragons' assault on the Tigers and their territory.

"You should stay back," Eddie told her as they rounded the southern part of Mulberry Street. "You can't expect Big D to go down without a fight."

"Which is all the more reason for me to be here." Jen was weary of the argument. "I will not ask my people to do anything I'm not prepared to do myself." She looked around at the Dragons flanking her and Eddie as they made their way along the street.

"They would understand," Eddie pressed. "They would expect you to lead from behind because—"

"Because I'm a woman?" Jen scoffed.

"*Because* you are their heart and head. Without you, the gang would have no direction. Not since Storm's death."

"Storm would not have cowered in his office while his soldiers fought in the streets, Eddie. I sure as hell am not going to do that, either.

My place is here, regaining the territory Storm Cheung's weakness cost the Black Dragons."

Jen was pumped full of adrenaline and spoiling for a physical fight, not a verbal one. She saw this night as her liberation from years of oppression, from living in the shadows of the men to whom all assumed she owed allegiance. It was no longer about the money. Jen had more than enough of that for three lifetimes of luxury. The assault on the Mott Street Tigers on their own turf was about restitution and the righting of wrongs. Above all, it was about *power*.

The Dragons stormed the restaurant as Big D and a select few friends closest to him were being served their entrees; their large, round table all but obscured by over-attentive wait staff. Around them, no more than a handful of tables were occupied by Big D's most trusted gang members, all of whom Jen had assumed would be armed with more than cleavers.

Just inside the front door, Jen fired off the first shots in the direction of Big D's table. Her gang then rushed in behind and around her, aiming shots at the occupants of the tables about the restaurant; a half dozen Tigers went down with the clatter of shattering crockery before they even had time to register the attack. The wait staff dropped their platters and scattered, as the Dragons let loose with a volley of bullets toward Big D. But the gang leader was too fast. He dropped beneath the table, upended it in a cascade of food, plates, and glasses, then pulled his handgun and returned fire, flanked by two of his lieutenants.

Jen, Eddie, and the Dragons darted for cover. Eddie pulled Jen toward the hostess stand where the pretty young woman occupying it cowered, her head buried in her hands. Jen grabbed the girl by the shoulders and shoved her toward the front door. Sobbing, the hostess crawled away to press herself against the front wall of the building.

"Go!" Jen snarled, then thrust her gun at the girl.

"Jen, no!" Eddie barked.

The pistol bucked in Jen's hand, the bullet digging into the wall just above the girl's head, spraying her with plaster. The frightened young woman scooted to the front door and disappeared.

Jen stared at Eddie in utter disbelief. Did he think she'd meant to kill the girl? Did he think her a monster?

Focus, she told herself. And focus she did, on the gang lord hunkered behind the upturned table at the far end of the dining room. The situation evoked memories of clashing with Enzo in the restaurant ... and the passion they'd shared in the back alley and later in her bed.

She chanced a peep around the hostess stand and saw one of her own men go down, clutching at a ragged, gaping hole in his chest as if desperately trying to stem the flow of blood with his trembling fingers.

Focus.

Jen leaned a little further out and let off a volley of shots at the upended table closest to Big D's. Shards of wood tore from the tabletop as a handful of Jen's .38 slugs ripped all the way through. She felt a surge of satisfaction as screams rose up from behind the table; her shots had hit home.

The Black Dragons surged deeper into the restaurant, picking off more Tigers as they went. Their bullets shattered a tank filled with exotic fish that took up most of the back wall, sending water, glass, and gasping fish out onto the tiles.

Taking advantage of the distraction, Jen crawled out from behind the hostess counter and made her way toward Big D's table with Eddie close behind. Using the cover afforded by the smaller tables designed for romantic dinners for two, Jen went unnoticed by the Tigers, who were busy returning fire on the encroaching Dragons.

Another Dragon went down with a shocked yelp, his knee blown apart. Clutching his shattered leg, the gangster fell, wailing, to the floor. There, he rolled around in agony, until another shot silenced him.

In her peripheral vision, Jen spied three Tigers scurrying out from behind a table in the corner opposite Big D's, under suppressing fire from the table adjacent to theirs. Their intention was clear—they meant to flank the Dragons and take them out from the side and rear. Jen fought the urge to shoot; to do so would be to give away her position and draw fire. With Eddie so close behind her, Jen knew they'd spot him the moment attention was drawn her way; the man was hardly inconspicuous. Fighting alongside Eddie felt immeasurably good, despite their differences. Eddie Sun was unwaveringly on her side again, no matter what.

The trio of Tigers took down two of Jen's men closest to the restaurant's door. One of the Tigers had taken a hit in the arm, but they'd shot her guys to pieces. They'd never really stood a chance. The Dragons were down to a handful and their main egress was cut off, but Jen remained relentless in her objective, even though time was running out. She'd underestimated the Tigers' firepower and tenacity, having assumed she'd be catching them with their guards down and mostly armed with those ridiculous cleavers. If she could only take out Big D, the Tigers would fold, and the Black Dragons could claim victory.

She was almost there.

Over the clatter of gunfire, Jen almost didn't hear the pained grunt from behind her. She twisted around to see Eddie clutching at his right shoulder, his fingers rapidly turning red. Fear spurred her heart into a wild gallop, but he shook his head and mouthed, "Just grazed." He tilted his head toward the front door, indicating they should fall back.

They were outnumbered. That much was evident, but Jen refused to contemplate giving up; this was her chance to get to Big D. Should the Dragons fail, the remaining Tigers would throw up a ring of steel around him and regroup, and she would likely never get the opportunity again. Jen shook her head fiercely at Eddie and crept forward, gun in hand, the stump of her finger pulsing with dull pain that spread to her shoulder.

Behind her, to the left, another of her men went down in a hail of bullets as he attempted to gain ground. Jen crawled on her belly until she was beneath a table that still wore a relatively pristine tablecloth. It was almost level with the table Big D and two of his men were using for cover. Two or three feet more and the Tigers' leader would be in her sights.

Reaching up, Jen grasped the edge of her table and toppled it. It crashed to the floor, dumping cutlery and plates, while Jen rolled the last three feet, ending up behind a stack of chairs. Now, she could see him—Big D Dang. With cold fire in her heart, she shot at the Tigers from a prone position, her first bullet catching the arm of the Tiger to Big D's left. The man cried out, spun, and let off a trio of shots at Jen's previous hiding place. She ducked her head beneath a chair as the tabletop exploded, then returned fire. Three slugs to the guy's chest punched him out of the way, and Jen now had a clear shot at Big D.

She'd often heard the phrase, "like a deer in headlights." It perfectly described the expression of disbelief on Big D's face as Jen aimed with a steady hand and steely determination. He moved to defend himself, swinging his gun toward her, firing as he did. But the bullets dug into the wall above Jen's head. She grinned fiercely as she emptied the last three bullets in her clip into the Mott Street Tigers' general. She hit him in the arm, leg, and flank. The force of the shots knocked the gangster over, but he rolled back up and took aim at Jen, along with the remaining fighter at his right hand.

Damnit! Where was Eddie? Jen cursed beneath her breath and rolled farther, putting herself further behind the stacks of chairs. She ejected the empty clip from her pistol and scrabbled in the back pocket of her jeans for the last full clip she'd secreted there. She only just registered that the restaurant had fallen silent around her—the sound of gunfire had ceased, worryingly so. It informed Jen that she and Eddie were likely the only two Dragons left standing.

The silence didn't last long.

A rapid volley of shots hacked into the stacked chairs sending fabric, batting, and wood everywhere. Jen's thoughts went to Nicholas and the awful possibility of him growing up without a mother. Terrified for the first time that night, Jen fumbled with the full clip, her hands slick with nervous sweat, and the raw stump of her pinkie seeping blood through its bandage. The magazine slipped from her fingers and clattered to the floor. A bullet then smashed through the thicket of chairs to graze Jen's temple; the thin trickle of blood it loosed tickled her skin as it snaked its way downward. The chairs wouldn't hold much longer, of that much she was certain, and it was obvious she had no backup. Even Eddie had been silenced.

As she tried to steady herself and think of a way out, the restaurant door exploded inward, and the place filled with the chaotic roar of gunfire. The Tigers still in the room were taken entirely by surprise; they died swiftly, without knowing at whose hands.

Jen, who knew who it was, heard the voices of Den Cha and Gary Hu yelling Chinese obscenities over the din of their assault. Distracted by the sudden intrusion by twenty or so Black Dragons, Big D and the guy with him turned their attention away from Jen, which gave her the reprieve she needed to compose herself, snatch her full clip, and snap it into place. She then returned her focus to Big D. He and his companion were doing their best to return fire, but they were now hopelessly outnumbered. Jen fired off a trio of shots, taking out the last of Big D's lieutenants. She fired twice more, and Big D took two bullets, one of which grazed his neck, spraying his face with blood. Yet he refused to die. He continued shooting at the Dragons until he'd emptied his gun.

As Jen prepared to end him, one of the Tiger foot soldiers appeared from Big D's right, grabbed hold of him, and dragged him backward toward the kitchen door as bullets from the advancing Dragons ricocheted and chipped the tiles around them. Despite it all, the Tiger managed to kick open the kitchen door and pull Big D through. The Dragons responded by dashing forward, peppering the door with bullets as it swung closed.

"*Stop!*" Jen shouted so loud she tasted blood at the back of her throat.

"Cease fire!" Gary Hu instructed the Dragons, and the restaurant once again fell silent.

Jen struggled to her feet and mentally checked herself—she was lucky the only wound she'd sustained was the flesh wound to her head, which leaked blood down the left side of her face.

"We should finish them," Den Cha said with a nod toward the kitchen.

"Big D will serve us better alive now," Jen told him, "if indeed he lives."

She turned as Eddie crawled out from behind his table and was almost felled by a surge of combined worry and relief as Gary Hu helped the big man to his feet. He was missing his gun, and one arm hung loosely at his side as blood soaked through his jacket and covered his right shoulder.

"Dang will recruit more Tigers and come after you, Jen," argued Den, seemingly thirsty for yet more Tiger blood. "You must let us put him down like the dog he is."

"The leader of the Mott Street Tigers ran like a coward," Jen said with a satisfied smile. "That gives us more of a victory than killing him. He will be seen as a coward rather than a martyr, and without the respect of what remains of the Tigers and the other gangs, he'll be finished."

Jen gazed at the lifeless bodies strewn around her and thanked whichever god had looked over her that night, letting her go home to her child.

CHAPTER SIXTY-ONE

Jen awoke next to Enzo, his body warm and welcome in her bed. She'd called him as she'd left Mulberry Street the night before, with the sound of police sirens in the background. For the first time in weeks, Enzo had escaped his smothering family and made his way to Flushing in the night. The promise of raw, unbridled sex had been far too good for him to pass up.

To Jen's surprise, he'd asked about the injury to her hand and the two-inch graze on her temple. She'd said she slammed her pinkie in a kitchen drawer and ripped the nail off, and that as she reacted to the pain had hit her head on an open cabinet. He gazed at her questioningly for a moment but ultimately decided to accept her vague explanations.

"You're a very clumsy woman, you know that?" he'd teased, then added, "Good thing you're not clumsy in bed or I'd be in deep trouble."

"Have I ever been clumsy in bed?" she'd asked and proceeded to show him just how graceful she could be. High on adrenaline and the aftertaste of fear, she was also aggressive to the point of violence. But Enzo hadn't complained.

"Shit!" Enzo jolted awake and immediately squinted at the red LED numbers of the clock on Jen's nightstand; it was almost eight. "I should have been home hours ago."

"Of course you should," Jen couldn't help but sound sardonic as she watched Enzo scramble out of her bed and begin searching for the clothes she'd ripped off his body. She knew the routine by heart. On the rare nights he dared to stay over, Enzo was always up before daylight to ensure he was home before his father was awake enough to ask questions. It irked Jen that Enzo didn't see anything wrong in that; he was a grown man, for the love of God!

"Later," Enzo said by way of goodbye and an apology. "Give the kid a kiss from his old man."

Jen sat up and the bed sheet fell to expose her breasts. Enzo's eyes twitched toward them and Jen saw temptation flicker across his face. "Why don't you stay, Enzo?" Jen said in her most seductive voice; she traced a finger down along her cleavage and ran her tongue over her lips like some cheap, wanton slut. "What difference will another hour or so make?"

"Sorry," Enzo said as he picked up his shoes. "You know how it is...."

Before Jen could tell him yes, she knew damn well how it was, Enzo had high-tailed it from her bedroom without as much as a peck on the cheek. Moments later, her apartment door slammed shut.

Jen slumped back against her pillows. She figured she'd stay in bed until Nicholas stirred. He'd taken to sleeping late, and Jen was determined to make the most of it. She had much to think about now that the Dragons had asserted their dominance over the Tigers, and many plans to make.

Jen picked her cell phone up from the nightstand; she'd forgotten to charge it again. Jen fished for the charger cord and plugged the thing in. In an instant, the phone's screen lit up and informed Jen she had a dozen missed calls. A smile flitted across her full lips; word of the night's victory had spread fast. Eschewing more sleep, Jen lifted the phone closer to her ear to listen to her messages.

"You know what?" Enzo's voice startled Jen as much as his sudden reappearance in her bedroom. "Fuck the old man!"

"Pardon me?" Jen laid her phone down on the comforter and sat up again.

"I said, fuck him," Enzo replied with a broad grin. "I'm gonna take you and my kid out for breakfast, and to hell with what The Don says."

"Are you serious?" Jen was nonplussed by Enzo having grown balls. Had the previous night's sex been *that* good?

"Yeah." Enzo beamed. "So...." He waved his arms in her direction, indicating she ought to get her shapely ass out of bed.

"I guess it's an offer I can't refuse?" Jen couldn't resist. She threw back the covers and swung her legs over the edge of the bed, pausing a moment to relish the effect her nude body had on Enzo—he always looked like some horny teenager at a strip show.

"Funny," Enzo groaned.

It was with some reluctance Jen left the comfort of her bed—*their* bed—but she had no intention of wasting the moment. Naked, she made her way over to the bathroom and figured she'd push her luck and ask Enzo to get his son up and ready.

Enzo insisted on pushing the three-wheeled buggy—he always did when they ventured out into the anonymous Flushing streets as a family, and it pleased Jen to watch him playing the proud father. In moments such as these, their conflicts over Nicholas's future seemed like the plot of a TV family saga and Jen dared imagine that one day, the three of them would be a happy, normal family.

They stepped from the cramped elevator single-file and Enzo led the way to the apartment complex's front door. Jen held it open for him to maneuver the buggy through—Enzo still hadn't got the hang of opening doors with his butt—and they stepped outside.

"*Miss Mo-Li!*" A voice demanded Jen's attention.

"Do you have a statement to make?" Another voice added, and in that instant, Jen and Enzo found themselves surrounded by a gaggle of reporters and television journalists thrusting cameras and microphones in their faces.

"What the fuck?!" Enzo snarled as the buggy's progress was blocked by a heavily made-up middle-aged woman with a microphone. She was accompanied by a cameraman wearing cargo shorts and a sleeveless T-shirt; the logo WNYW emblazoned on the side of his camera. "Do you have anything to say about last night's tragedy?" The reporter thrust her mic at Jen's face, evidently expecting Jen to speak.

Jen shook her head and moved closer to Enzo. She kept her mouth closed, but her mind raced. How was it possible the press and news stations had linked her to the death and destruction of the brothel, pool hall, and restaurant? She'd gone to great lengths to cover her tracks and had made sure to keep her new appointment as head of the Black Dragons under the radar.

"Get the fuck out of our way," Enzo snarled as Nicholas, terrified by the small crowd of journalists and their loud clamoring, began to cry.

"What is your involvement with the *Morning Rainbow*, Mr. DeCarlo?" demanded another reporter—a fresh-faced young man with a deep, booming voice. Naturally, they all knew precisely who Enzo was, as the DeCarlo family was notoriously high-profile in New York, despite The Don's attempts to gain some legitimacy.

"I *said*, get the fuck out of my way." As Enzo forged ahead with the buggy, its wheels ran over feet, and its metal frame jarred against shins.

"Twenty-four dead, Miss Mo-Li," the WNYW woman insisted as she sidestepped the buggy and shoved her mic even closer to Jen's face. "And the boat has been linked to you. What do you have to say?"

Cringing away from the picture that was beginning to emerge from the questions, Jen fought the urge to race back to her apartment. To do so would mean leaving Enzo and Nicholas and fighting through the journalists who had closed in behind them; they were completely surrounded, and more were on their way.

Among them, making his way past the TV station's vans, was Eddie Sun. Walking quickly, his wounded arm strapped to his chest with a sling, Eddie scanned the growing crowd of journalists for Jen.

"How do you explain your contact information being found on some of the victims?"

"Were you aware the boat was unseaworthy?"

"How much did those poor people pay you, Miss Mo-Li?"

"Is your father involved in this scandal, too?"

Questions, questions, more questions, and as the voices became ever louder to make themselves heard, they grew less comprehensible. Jen held her hand up in front of her face, just as she'd seen countless people in her predicament do on TV. *Tragedy*, they'd said. Something tragic had happened to the *Morning Rainbow*. She had to get away from the reporters and find out for herself, but how? The sight of Eddie on the periphery of the crowd brought immeasurable relief.

"What's going on?" Enzo twisted around to face her. "*Jen?*" He jabbed at a journalist's legs with the buggy and gained a few inches. Enzo, too, seemed to be contemplating a retreat to Jen's apartment and was likely figuring out just how many heads he'd have to bust to achieve that when his cell phone rang. Enzo fished it out of his pocket and stared at the screen as it chimed and vibrated in his hand.

"Oh, God," he murmured. "It's my father."

CHAPTER SIXTY-TWO

"What the hell have you got yourself involved in, Enzo?" Vincenzo DeCarlo gripped his desk phone's beige receiver so hard his knuckles whitened. "*You're all over the fucking news!*"

Angel Corozzio sat still and silent as Vincenzo listened to Enzo's reply with a reddening face. If ever there was a time the man might blow a blood vessel, this was certainly it. The consigliere cast a sideways glance at Rico, who sat meekly beside him. His son looked as guilty as if he'd been the one caught outside a Flushing apartment with some wannabe Triad gangster and a kid who looked very much to be his. That Rico had said nothing about Enzo's double life made him complicit in deceiving Vincenzo, and that was unforgivable; *omertà* didn't apply when it came to family. He'd done little to redeem himself by giving Enzo's cell phone number to The Don, although the revelation was inconsequential given the circumstances.

"Give me the address," Vincenzo demanded, spittle foaming from his lips onto the phone's mouthpiece. It was not a request. "I'm sending a car and a lawyer over, and don't say a fucking word to any of those goddamned reporters!"

It had been Angel who'd alerted The Don to Enzo's impromptu appearance on the morning news. Reports of a freighter carrying illegal

Chinese immigrants having run aground in the early hours near the mouth of the Hudson had dominated every morning news channel. The story had even displaced reporting of the violence in Chinatown. After all, that was speculated to have been gang-related; these were innocent people, albeit illegal immigrants, which made for much better television.

Angel had eaten his breakfast to sad footage of blurred-out corpses being fished out of the Hudson. It was just another unfortunate tragedy in a world filled with tragedies, although very close to home. Angel had even raised an interested eyebrow at the mention of Ming Sen Mo-Li—he'd never had the property magnate pegged as a human trafficker. On the odd occasions the DeCarlo family and Mo-Li had crossed paths in the past, they had always found the man to be whiter-than-white. In fact, Angel had not been aware Mo-Li had a daughter until the TV reports said her name and phone number had been found in the pockets of some of the drowned Chinese who'd jumped from the boat as it went down. Then, there she was, coming out of her classy Flushing apartment and playing happy family with Enzo DeCarlo like they hadn't a care in the world.

"Don't argue, Little Enzo," Vincenzo's raised voice bounced around his office.

He kept his eyes glued to the TV in the corner as he listened to his son, his mood not lightened by the live feed of Enzo attempting to battle his way through the sea of journalists, interspersed with film clips of the rescue operation the night before and the shivering, miserable survivors being ferried to safety. All the while, at the bottom of the screen, the ticker-tape feed kept a running tally of the death toll as more bodies were hauled from the water.

Listening intently, Vincenzo jotted down the address Enzo gave him. "The car will be with you in ten—make sure you're damn well in it —and *only* you." His voice was little more than an irate snarl. "*No fucking excuses!*" To add to that finality, Vincenzo slammed down the receiver, sat heavily in his chair, and reached for the bourbon.

"Why wasn't I informed about any of this?" Vincenzo demanded of Rico as he poured himself two fingers of scotch—never mind that it had only just turned nine.

Rico shrugged.

"I *knew* Enzo was up to no good in Chinatown." Vincenzo punctuated the statement with a slug of his liquor. "He never could keep his goddamned dick in his pants ... but *this*." He waved a hand toward the TV set. "How the hell did he get mixed up with that fucking chink and her mess?"

"It's not Rico's fault, Don," Angel stepped in. Some of it *was* his son's fault, and he'd deal with that when the time was right, but he couldn't sit back and watch Vincenzo taking out his frustration toward Enzo on the boy. "His loyalties were torn—you know how that goes. Enzo is his best friend, his *brother*."

The Don nodded his agreement, although none of the anger had left his eyes. "Your son's loyalty to Enzo is as unwavering as yours is to me," he said. "But it is important he appreciates who takes care of him, who puts food in his belly."

"I'm sorry. I couldn't betray Enzo's trust," Rico spoke up. "If I had realized who he was getting mixed up with, I would have said something to you. I thought Jen was just some—"

"Chinese whore?" Vincenzo spat.

Rico studied the Persian rug. "Yeah."

"And you didn't think to tell me he'd gotten her pregnant? Or that I have a grandson I know nothing about?" Draining his glass, Vincenzo refilled it. "How the fuck do you think that makes me feel, Rico? That kid is DeCarlo blood, even if he's half fucking Chinese."

"Look, Vincenzo," Angel interjected. "This is getting us nowhere. We can deal with who is in the wrong once Enzo is away from the TV cameras and Jen Mo-Li. It's only a matter of time before the cops arrest her, and if they can cuff a DeCarlo at the same time, they're gonna think all their Christmases have come at once."

"Enzo has no part in trafficking," Rico said. "He thought she was a rent collector, not a gangbanger. He really had no idea—honestly."

The news of his son's innocence didn't sit well with Vincenzo. "Enzo is *that* stupid? He knocks up some random slut who *just happens* to be the daughter of one of the biggest real estate owners in Manhattan *and* a trafficker for the Black Dragons?" He downed his freshly poured bourbon in one. "How the hell did I raise such a *ritardato*?"

"If the cops arrest Enzo, they have nothing on him for this," Angel nodded at the TV. There, a somber-faced anchorwoman was reporting that the number of dead Chinese had risen to thirty-one and that *children* had washed up on the muddy banks of the river.

"You know that won't matter a damn," Vincenzo growled. "Those bastards will make something stick. Just look at that circus...."

For a split second, Angel feared The Don was going to hurl his glass at the TV. Instead, he filled it again.

"The cops have tipped off the TV stations so they can look good making their high-profile arrests. Do you honestly think they're going to overlook the fact that my son is associated with that woman? What about when they discover that bastard kid is Enzo's? They're gonna put two and two together, make five, and come at the DeCarlos for trafficking and negligent homicide."

Angel got to his feet. "I'm sure it won't come to that," he said with wavering confidence. "I'll have our attorneys on standby all the same."

"Just go get that idiot son of mine, Angel." Some of the fire had left Vincenzo's eyes, most likely tempered by the bourbon, and he looked deflated. "I'll make some calls and try to figure a way out of this fucking mess—and for Christ-sake, don't tell Elena she has a half-breed grandkid."

Angel nudged his son's shoulder, and Rico stood up. "We can talk about this on the way," the consigliere said. Angel had no desire to leave Rico alone at the DeCarlo house. He'd seen Vincenzo in such a foul mood before, and he didn't want to have to worry about his son's safety.

CHAPTER SIXTY-THREE

The media circus outside Jen Mo-Li's apartment came to a sudden, dramatic end as Eddie Sun muscled his way through the crowd of journalists and hustled Jen and the baby away to a waiting SUV farther down the street. A few of the reporters wound up with scraped knees and bruised ribs as the burly Chinese guy barged through them with his good arm extended to shove aside anyone who got in his way. But they were also happy to get shots of Miss Mo-Li running away.

With unfortunate synchronicity, Vincenzo DeCarlo's consigliere arrived at the same time to spirit Enzo away, which, to the sensationalism-hungry journalists, smacked of a conspiracy and had them all saying so into their respective cameras.

Back within the safety of the DeCarlo house, Enzo took a little time to compose himself before facing The Don. Sure, he'd fucked up, and there'd be no talking his way out of his mess—not this time.

"How could you not know what she was?" Vincenzo demanded to know. "Since when did you get so blinded by pussy, Enzo?"

"I just didn't." Enzo had no other reply. He'd underestimated Jen and perhaps trusted she'd tell him the truth—eventually. Her story about the injury to a second finger and her head had been suspect and should have alerted him. He'd underestimated Jen every step of the way and was even beginning to wonder if she'd somehow conspired to entrap him as part of some devious plan to further expand the Black Dragons' empire.

"You didn't check her out?"

"Jen wasn't some real estate deal," Enzo countered. "We just met and—"

"Spare me the falling in love bullshit," Vincenzo scoffed. "You're a DeCarlo, which puts you in the spotlight every time you set foot out of this house. That's one of the first things I taught you. It goes without saying you won't be seeing that whore again, even if she manages to keep her ass out of jail. Although, with thirty-one dead on top of everything else the DA is going to throw at her, she's gonna need a damn good lawyer."

Enzo's mind raced. He was beyond angry at Jen for not telling him the truth about who—*what*—she was, and for being the mother of his son *and* some special kind of monster who'd negligently killed over thirty innocent people she was smuggling into the country. Enzo didn't know how to even begin processing that one. But....

"I won't turn my back on Nicholas," he told his father.

"Who?" Vincenzo's booze-dampened brain was slow on the uptake.

"My son," Enzo replied quietly, firmly. "You can't tell me to forget about my son—your grandson. He's a DeCarlo."

As Vincenzo fell quiet, Enzo's thoughts returned to Jen. He wasn't hypocritical enough to judge her for the businesses in which she was involved, nor for the bloodshed she'd undoubtedly been party to—Enzo's dealings with the Mott Street Tigers had taught him just how ruthless the Chinese gangs could be. It was her lies that rankled the most. They'd had a kid together, for fuck sake! How the hell could she lie to his face?

Vincenzo broke his silence. "You're right, of course. We cannot have a DeCarlo left to the mercy of the chinks." The word grated on Enzo, which he figured was his father's intention. When The Don was in a bad mood, he loved to get a rise out of anyone in the firing line so he could vent his frustration. "I'll speak with Angel, and we will figure something out. That child belongs where it's safe, not with a mother who is likely to end up rotting in a prison cell or back in fucking China."

Enzo's blood froze.

That was not an option he'd even begun to consider. Should Jen flee to China, he would never see his son again, and that was a scenario he couldn't sit back and allow to happen.

———

"How did all this happen, Jen?" Eddie asked her. "You had the boat refurbished back in Fujian."

"Storm cut the refurbishment costs in half behind my back." Jen couldn't hide her anger at Storm's final betrayal—one he had hidden, costing many lives. "The *Rainbow* should never have set sail. It's a miracle she made it all the way to New York."

"If it had sunk at sea, there would have been no one left to connect it to you," Eddie observed.

She cut him a sharp glance. "Not helpful, Eddie. And why did they have my phone number on them? Did Tang Xun give it to them?"

"I think it more likely," said Eddie, "that Cheung did, don't you?"

Jen sucked in a breath at the enormity of it. Was it possible that what happened to the *Rainbow* had been intentional on Storm's part? Was it the man's way of taking her out in the most galling way possible? Fuck that. She was glad she'd murdered the bastard.

Jen rose from her couch and paced across the cramped living room of her Chinatown bolthole like a caged animal. She had begun to hate the place, but at least here she and Nicholas were safe from the reporters and the police. It had been Eddie's idea to bring them here; it would take a lot to track them, as only a select few knew about the place, and the other residents were—one and all—immigrants Jen Mo-Li had brought into the country. They could be trusted to keep their mouths shut.

It seemed inevitable that Petey would make an appearance. Less than an hour after Jen, Nicky, and Eddie had snuck in, Petey was knocking on the apartment door.

"I'll leave you to it," Eddie said as Jen let her brother in. His distaste of Ming Sen's youngest child lay too close to the surface. Jen was relieved he'd decided to absent himself.

"Nice to see you again, Eddie," Petey said as the two passed in the doorway.

Without turning his head in acknowledgment, Eddie grunted his reply and headed off toward the stairwell.

"I see Eddie's as talkative as ever." Petey wandered through to the small lounge and flopped down on Jen's couch.

"What do you want, Petey?" Jen was blunt, in no mood for her brother's games. "Is Father alright?"

Petey nodded. "He's as indestructible as ever," he replied, "but your latest fiasco did almost give him a heart attack."

"I'm so sorry."

Petey missed the obvious sarcasm. "It's way too late for *sorry*, Jen. You have brought dishonor upon the family name, more than could ever be forgiven. As if that mistake wasn't disgrace enough...." Petey gestured toward Nicholas, who was beginning to fuss in his buggy.

Jen stood over Petey, arms folded across her chest, lips pursed. "I really don't need your judgment, Petey. You need to go." She remembered with disgust the last time he'd paid her a visit, and the clumsy pass he'd made because he assumed ... whatever it was he'd assumed about her relationship with Danny.

"I mean, trafficking is one thing, but *prostitution*, Jen?" Petey said as he heaved himself up off the couch. "Has our father taught you nothing?"

"He taught me I had to take care of myself, since he didn't give a damn what happened to me as long as it didn't reflect on him," Jen snapped back. "He taught me that nothing I do will ever be good enough for him. That I would only ever be second best in his eyes—even to a fool like you."

Petey stood to face her, smiling. "I may be a fool, sweet sister, but I am no murderer."

"Get. The fuck. Out." Jen took great pleasure in seeing her weak little brother recoil at her language. She yanked open the apartment door, and all but shoved Petey out into the hallway. "Don't come here again, Petey. I don't ever want to see you."

Petey fixed Jen with the most shameless puppy-dog reproach. "We're family, Jen, and that is a bond which can never be broken, no matter what disgrace you have brought upon the Mo-Li name. I love you, Jen, and I am prepared to put my good name at risk to keep our family together."

"My son is my only family now," Jen said, and slammed the door in her brother's face.

Pressing her back against the door, Jen took a moment to compose herself. She couldn't remember a time when she'd been so close to tears. She didn't want her son to see her crying, this was a time he needed to know his mother was strong, all-powerful, and more than capable of protecting him. After a deep breath, her pounding heart slowed. Jen went to lift Nicholas gently from the buggy. Holding her son tightly, Jen Mo-Li gave in and wept.

CHAPTER SIXTY-FOUR

A SHARP, RAPID KNOCKING AT HER FRONT DOOR BROKE JEN'S tender moment with Nicholas in two. "Damnit, Petey! I told you to go!" she snarled, turning to face the door. "I am *not* letting you in!"

She'd turned to carry Nicky to his little room, when her front door burst open with enough force to slam it against the wall. Gripping her baby so tight to her chest that he bleated in alarm, Jen skittered away from the door. But the men—three of them, all dressed in dark suits—were already upon her, reaching for her, reaching for her son.

Jen screamed and Nicky wailed, amplifying her terror.

"*Be careful with the kid!*" Enzo's order made the hands retreat.

Jen whirled to find him, incredibly, standing just inside the doorway. "What—what are you doing, Enzo?"

"What does it look like I'm doing? I'm taking my son."

"*Our* son! I'm his mother, damn you!"

"And I'm his father. Nicky will be better off with me."

This was a different Enzo—one she had never met. He was solemn, even grim, and matter of fact about his purpose. She saw no trace of love or affection in his eyes; the emptiness there was devastating.

Rico stepped into the room behind him. Jen knew she wasn't imagining the hint of unease in his eyes. Her eyes swept the hate-filled faces of the three thugs they'd brought with them, and she bristled.

"No fucking way. I'm his mother. You have no right—"

"You're wanted for negligent homicide." Enzo stepped toward her. "You'll go to jail just for the boat—longer if they pin the gang stuff on you. Was that you, Jen, with the Black Dragons last night? There are rumors about a woman with them."

She opened her mouth to speak, but he waved her down.

"No. I don't wanna know. Damnit, Jen, don't you care what happens to Nicholas if the cops find you? Or the Tigers?"

Jen stepped away from him, shaking her head. "They won't find me. Not if I—"

"Run away to China?" Enzo's pre-emption hung heavy in the air between them. "I can't let that happen. The kid is a DeCarlo, and he'll be raised like one." He took another step toward her, his arms out.

"*No!*" Jen lashed out with a kick at Enzo's crotch, which he barely managed to avoid. Her foot caught him solidly on his left hip, spinning him around, off balance. Jen then twisted away and dashed for the bedroom.

"Get her, and don't fucking hurt the kid!" Enzo ordered, and Rico and the three goons set off after Jen.

Cornered in the bedroom she had shared so many times with Enzo, her back literally against the wall, Jen prepared to fight back as Rico approached with his arms outstretched to take her son. The burly trio of goons formed a wall of muscle behind Rico, behind which Enzo hid—the coward.

"Rico, please...." Jen implored over her son's piercing screams. Surely there was some grain of humanity in his father's friend.

"You can't win this, Jen. You know you can't." Rico's words were delivered in a cold monotone.

"*You're not taking my son!*" Jen screamed and aimed her fingernails at the gangster's face.

Rico pulled back as Jen's manicured talons scraped across his chin, drawing blood. This seemed to prompt the other thugs into action. They came at her as one, while she struck out with her feet, kicking and jabbing. Some blows landed, but most missed their mark as she struggled to balance with the baby in her arms. Inevitably, her lack of balance caused her to stumble away from the wall. One of the men got behind her and wrapped a bulky arm around her neck in a choke hold.

"*Get the fuck away, you bastard!*" Jen's voice came out strangled, high-pitched, but still loud enough to be heard over Nicholas's yowls. She kicked out at Enzo as he approached, but he was wise enough to stay out of range. Her bare feet swiped hopelessly at thin air. She was sobbing now, wasting the air she fought for.

"Give him to me, Jen," Enzo said.

He glanced up at the thug who held her and the arm about her neck tightened. Sparks flew before her eyes—bright gold and blue.

"What kind of life can you give him?" Enzo sounded calm and reasonable as he chanced to come a step or two closer. "I'll raise him in a safe, secure family. I'll send you pictures at Christmas and on his birthday...."

The bright motes were gone; her world had gray as Jen lashed out with the heel of her free hand and landed a punch on the bridge of Enzo's nose. Her celebration of the resulting trickle of blood was cut short by a huge, meaty hand that wrapped powerful fingers around her wrist and wrenched the arm to her side.

With a swipe of his hand, Enzo wiped away the twin trickles of blood that dripped from his nostrils. "Y'know, I was gonna let you see him once in a while, but now I think if you ever try to make contact with him—*ever*—I'll take him someplace you'll never find him."

"Dragons...." she managed to force out. He couldn't hide from the gang. *Her* gang now.

He shook his head. "Don't think so, Jen. The cops are rounding them up—the Dragons are finished. The families still have clout in Chinatown, Jen, remember that." Enzo took hold of his son, whose little face was bright red, his screams hoarse, and eased him out of Jen's grip.

Jen tried her best to struggle, but the fire in her lungs and agonizing fog in her brain were all-encompassing, and the fight drained away as Enzo's goon squeezed the life from her. She tried to protest one last time as Nicholas was torn from her arms, but no sound came out. As she saw her son being carried away by the man she had once loved, Jen Mo-Li blacked out.

CHAPTER SIXTY-FIVE

Vincenzo DeCarlo contemplated his wife as she fussed and cooed over their grandson. Considering that she'd been entirely unaware of his existence when Enzo had brought him home a little less than two hours ago, she had already taken the kid to her heart.

"That Chinese woman needs to disappear." Vincenzo closed his office door and turned to his consigliere. "She's too dangerous."

"We've taken her kid," Angel countered. "And every goddamned cop in New York is looking for her. Surely that's enough? Hell, Enzo could point them right at her."

Vincenzo eased himself down into his executive chair. "As long as she's alive, she might come for the kid. I can't afford to have Enzo looking over his shoulder the rest of his life. It'll make him nervous and sloppy, and that's bad for business."

"Is this you getting sentimental, Vincenzo?" Angel ventured with a wry smile. "You finally have a grandchild in the house and it's making you soft?"

Vincenzo cracked a smile. "The kid's half-Chinese, Angel," he said. "But he's half-Italian, too. He's also a DeCarlo, and Enzo's kid, and that makes him useful. Like I always say—"

"Business is business. Yeah, I know." Angel hovered over the couch by The Don's desk, as if unsure he was welcome to sit. "But killing Jen Mo-Li? What about reprisals from her family? Or the Black Dragons?"

"Her family has been on a slide since the eldest son died, and most of the Dragons will be incarcerated—or dead—before the end of the week. Our only real threat is from Jen Mo-Li herself."

"If she goes back to China—"

"She can *return* from China."

Angel seemed to shrink a bit, his shoulders slumping ever so slightly. "Are you giving the order?"

"I am."

Angel nodded. "I'll have Rico take care of it."

"Are you sure that's wise?" Vincenzo asked him.

"My son can be trusted to do the job well. He's Enzo's friend; he'll do what's best. Think of it as his opportunity to redeem himself."

"Very well," Vincenzo conceded. "Have it done by tomorrow. I'll make sure the cops don't look too hard for the woman until then."

He eyed the nearly empty bourbon decanter on his desk, wishing he'd never promised his wife he wouldn't drink until five. *Fuck it.* He emptied the decanter into the lead crystal glass that sat by the phone on his desk.

Hell, it was five o'clock somewhere, right?

She'd called Eddie back to the apartment the instant she'd regained consciousness. Enzo was gone, of course, along with her son. Her heart was empty, hollowed out by grief, but Jen knew there was no time for weeping and feeling sorry for herself. Her one and only goal was to get her son back.

"We will take on *all* the fucking Italian families if we have to," Jen told Eddie and the handful of Dragons he'd mustered. Of them, Den Cha was the only deputy there. Gary Hu was languishing in police custody on charges relating to the attacks on the Tigers' territory the night before.

Eddie shook his head, his grim expression leaking sorrow. "It's over,

Jen." He spoke softly, firmly. "The Dragons are finished. We have nothing left to fight with."

"Bullshit, Eddie," Jen spat. "They took my son, and we're going to get him back. We have guns and men . . . I say we fight."

She glanced down at the coffee table in the center of the room, and the meager array of handguns assembled there. Surely the gang had more weapon caches in the city. If not, she'd find a way to acquire more, even if it meant buying from the other gangs; they all had their price.

Eddie's bullheadedness was unrelenting. "We need to get you on the first boat to China. The airports will be sealed tight by now, but there are captains at the harbor who won't ask questions—for the right price."

"I *won't* go anywhere without Nicholas," Jen repeated for the umpteenth time. She looked around at the weary bunch of men in her cramped living room. "And you are *all* obliged to follow my orders." She held up her hand, displaying the fresh stump of her finger. Wrapped in a clean bandage, it still oozed blood.

"No, Jen," Eddie insisted. "I'll get you back to China, and you can take some time to regroup. You can come back for Nicky once the heat dies down here. We can't fight the Italians."

"No, *Eddie*. I am sick of your insubordination. Do you dare stand there in *my* home and openly defy me? In front of my men?"

"Jen...." he said, and the soft, sad, expression in his eyes broke her anew.

Snatching one of the Glocks from the table, Jen pointed it at him. "You will do as I order you to do," she growled. "You *all* will." She scanned the room and saw the creeping distrust in everyone's faces ... all except for Eddie. She had expected to see fear, but no; the sorrow had only grown deeper.

He took a step toward her, his hand outstretched. "You need to give yourself time to think about your next move. Don't rush into a war you can't win."

This was the *et tu* moment she'd hoped would never come. "I never thought you'd betray me, Eddie. Not when I need you."

"I am not betraying you, Jen. Nor would I ever. I'm trying to save you." Eddie took another step toward her. "Now, give me the gun."

"I don't need saving, damn you!" Jen spat. She fired.

The bullet caught Eddie square in the chest, punching him backward against the door frame and spraying blood into the air. Jen felt it patter on her face like warm raindrops as she watched him slide to the floor, leaving a crimson banner to mark his descent. His eyes were open wide with shock and betrayal and that horrible sadness she so hated. And then, his life bled out and they were just open.

Jen, numb, had no idea how she'd come to be on the floor. What in the name of God had she done? She hadn't meant to kill him, had she? Surely not. Not Eddie! She felt someone lift the gun from her hand—she thought it was Den—and she crawled on her hands and knees to Eddie's side.

"Eddie...." she said, reaching for him. Her hand touched his shoulder, and he slumped sideways into her arms. She laid her cheek against the bald head, already cooling, and let out the tears she had been denying herself for so long—tears for Danny, for Enzo, for Nicky, for Eddie, for her own sense of self. She would relive this, she knew, whenever she closed her eyes or sat in silence. She would hear the shot, feel the spatter of blood, and see that look on Eddie's face as his life fled.

That look. She knew that look would haunt her nightmares.

When at last she opened her eyes again, the Dragons were gone. For the first time in her life, Jen Mo-Li was completely alone in the world.

CHAPTER SIXTY-SIX

It was as a woman with nothing left to lose that Jen Mo-Li walked into the offices of Jonathon "Big D" Luen Dang, carrying only a suitcase.

"You are either courageous beyond belief, or incredibly foolish to come here," Big D said as Jen was frisked and escorted to the chair opposite his by a pair of thickset bodyguards. They stood on either side of her, guns drawn, as if waiting for the slightest reason to end her life. "I am unsure which." He winced as he sought comfort in his padded chair, the bandages swaddling his wounded body visible beneath his thin white shirt. An IV drip stood beside the chair, feeding medication into the Tiger lord's veins.

"Both," Jen told him without humor. "I need help, and if you kill me, that will be help enough." She studied the gangster's eyes but was unable to read him.

Big D returned the scrutiny. "You have waged war on me and my people. You tried your very best to kill me just last night, and now you ask for my help?"

Jen didn't need the man to point out the irony of her situation. Less than twenty-four hours ago, she had been riding high on her victory over Big D and the Tigers and had delighted in watching him scurry away wounded and scared. Now she was relieved she hadn't killed him.

"It was ... business," she said.

"You have all but put a stop to *my* business, Ms. Mo-Li. You destroyed my commercial interests, murdered my people, and brought great shame upon me." He rubbed at his heavily bandaged shoulder, grimacing in pain. "But I understand you have lost far more than business interests."

"My son."

"The Italian family has him?"

Jen fought against the tears that had been all too frequent since Enzo had taken Nicholas. "I have no means by which to get him back. All I can do now is run."

"Run where?"

"China. Fujian Province."

"Will you return?"

Jen shrugged; she'd barely given that any thought since Eddie died. "For my son. One day."

Big D looked pensive. "Why should I help you, Miss Mo-Li? What is stopping me from putting a bullet between your lovely eyes right here and now?"

Jen was surprised the gangster's unveiled threat didn't frighten her; death did seem a viable path out of her predicament. "Nothing. But I have money. I can pay for my passage."

"How much do you have?"

"Eight million."

His eyes widened. "American dollars?"

Jen nodded. Although she could count on her U.S. accounts being frozen, she had money in several offshore banks she could call upon at short notice should the need arise. "You can have it all if you can get me on a boat tonight."

Big D frowned thoughtfully. "That's short notice. Although we do have a ship leaving port in the morning."

"You can expedite its journey for $8 million."

"I suppose I *could*."

Jen knew the man was playing with her, enjoying the cruel twist of fate that had put her in his power. That was fine. Let him have his fun; she'd seen the greedy gleam in his eyes at the mention of her money. For that amount, she suspected he might send his ship out with only her aboard.

"You could use the money to rebuild your interests," Jen stated the obvious, more to break the silence than anything else. "The Black Dragons are done. Chinatown is yours to take."

"I want the money upfront."

"Give me a phone and an hour, and you'll have all of it. And thank you."

"There's no need to thank me—it's business, nothing more. Will you need time to gather your things?"

Eddie's face, the look in his eyes, arose to haunt her. "I have everything I need right here." She prodded at the suitcase with her foot.

Big D addressed his soldiers. "Give Ms. Mo-Li an office and a phone. She has an hour, and then we leave for the harbor, with or without her."

The two Tigers ushered Jen out of Big D's presence and into a small, well-furnished office. There, she was given access to the phone she needed to make the calls that would allow her to escape.

Big D's silver Ford Explorer, chosen for being inconspicuous, pulled out of Mott Street precisely an hour later with one of his soldiers driving and the other following at a short distance in a green Mountaineer.

Jen was safely ensconced in the Explorer's back seat. She'd transferred most of the offshore money into a holding account for which she would provide the details and passwords once she was safely on the boat and heading away from New York. Trust was rare as hen's teeth between rival gangs; she wouldn't have been surprised if the gangster hadn't thought to make good on his suggestion of a slug between the eyes the second he had his hands on her money. At least she'd get herself safely on the boat, after which she'd take her chances.

It was growing dark when they reached the harbor, so dark Jen couldn't make out the name of the ship Big D pointed out as his. All that mattered was that thiswas her only way of escape from America and New York's zealous law enforcement. It also meant she would soon be thousands of miles away from her son, but what other choice did she have?

"This is where we say farewell, Ms. Mo-Li," Big D announced with little ceremony. "You have some information for me?"

Jen had memorized the account details since she was neither dumb nor inexperienced enough to have them written down and about her person. "Do you have a pen?" she asked Big D.

He did, and she recited the account details for him, which he wrote on a twenty-dollar bill. With that done, Jen slid out of the car and retrieved her suitcase from the trunk.

"The captain is expecting you, Ms. Mo-Li," Big D said by way of a goodbye.

With a heavy heart, Jen closed the door, picked up her suitcase, and watched as the gangster's car pulled slowly away. That her life had led her to the dockside of New York Harbor like so many of her clients in the past was cruelly ironic. Dare she hope she could turn things back around in Fujian and return to reclaim her son?

The sound of screeching tires jolted Jen from her reverie. Spinning back toward the entry to the docks, she saw a low, black sports car hurtling toward her. The suitcase fell from her hand. With nowhere to run, she could only stand there, frozen, expecting to be run down. But the car slowed to a stop as it pulled up beside her. A tall, thin man unfolded from the driver's seat.

"Rico?"

"I'm sorry about this, Jen," Rico said and raised his hand to point a gun at her head.

"Why?"

Rico offered a pained smile. "We both know why," he said with genuine sadness. "The Don half-blames me for you and Enzo 'cause I looked the other way."

"I'm leaving the country. You could just *say* you did ... *this*." Her eyes went to the gun, a sleek, black pistol.

"*This* is how I redeem myself. I can't lie to Don DeCarlo." His finger slid to the trigger.

"Rico, please...."

Gunshots suddenly rang out, echoing from the facades of warehouses and the bluff hulls of docked ships. A muzzle flashed from Rico's pistol, and Jen felt the mule-kick of a bullet in the bicep of her left arm. The force knocked her off her feet and she hit the ground hard, vision blurring, ears ringing.

Rico collapsed beside her with blood spilling from his mouth, and for a moment, they lay face-to-face, sharing pain and terror. Gurgling, fighting for breath, Rico looked into Jen's eyes and pushed out a series of words that, at first, made no sense to her.

"Your brother ... not Tigers ... Enzo."

"Enzo?" she murmured, not understanding.

He coughed and spat blood. "Killed him. At Xi's bar. Can't lie to you, either, I guess."

Enzo. No, no, not....

The sound of hard footfalls caused Jen to curl herself up into a tight ball as blood soaked her clothes. In her hazy vision, she saw the dirty green Mountaineer parked at the end of the empty dock, and then Rico dragged away from her by his feet, his gurgled protests filled with Italian expletives.

One shot, another, and Rico fell silent.

Doing her best to ignore the agony in her arm and the chaos in her head, Jen moved to get up off the ground.

"Stay dead for a minute," said Big D's voice from above her. "We need to be sure he was alone."

Cradling Rico's horrific revelation, Jen wondered if she wouldn't rather stay dead forever. As Big D and his two soldiers probed the shadows around the dock, guns drawn, she glanced over at the dark shadow that was Rico's body. Had Enzo sent him to kill her, or had his father? Rico had mentioned not being able to lie to The Don. Either way, Enzo was going to be devastated at the loss.

A brother for a brother. Good.

"Can you walk?" Big D returned to her side.

Jen nodded and allowed him to help her to her feet. Big D had one of his guys pick up her suitcase and between them, they walked her toward the waiting ship.

"We'll take care of this," the gangster said, gesturing at Rico. He delivered Jen to the gangplank before he spoke again. "We'll make sure that, to the DeCarlos, you are dead. That way they won't come looking for you."

Weary, and in pain, Jen took her suitcase from Big D's soldier and made her way onto the freighter.

CHAPTER SIXTY-SEVEN

Jen Mo-Li sat alone, her throbbing arm in a sling, in the dingy, rusted cabin in the bowels of a vessel she'd not even caught the name of. Other than the crew, Jen was one of only a few people aboard the ship. It would return in three months or so, filled with young, hopeful Chinese people, all eagerly anticipating the beginnings of their new lives in the free world.

If only they knew.

She'd been lucky. Rico's bullet had gone straight through the flesh at the top of her arm; it would leave a pair of scars, but there would be no lasting damage. The captain, a pleasant young man with more competence than her own Captain He, had patched her up using the boat's well-stocked first aid kit. Apparently, he doubled as the ship's medic to keep costs down.

Jen had tossed her bloodied shirt into the river and replaced it with a shapeless, brown, long-sleeved shirt from her suitcase—she'd not had much to choose from at her Chinatown apartment, and she dared not show her face in Flushing. For once in her life, Jen didn't care too much about how she looked. There was no one to see her, no one to judge her appearance.

Big D had taken her ID and cell phone, so the mighty Jen Mo-Li was a nobody, as anonymous as the multitude of Chinese people she'd smuggled into America with names she had chosen for them.

Jen eased herself back onto the hard, lumpy mattress of the bunk that was to be her bed for the next month or so until the boat docked in Fujian. By then, her new pregnancy might be showing.

She closed her eyes, caressed her belly with her good hand, and thought of the son—and the brother—who'd been torn from her life by Enzo DeCarlo.

ABOUT THE AUTHOR

Who am I? I sometimes find it hard to answer this question. It depends on what hat I'm wearing that day, what setting I'm in, or the venue I may be attending. I'm Dr. Vince. I'm an international financier, investing in stocks, real estate, people, and businesses. I was a CEO of a private equity fund in Hong Kong. I've operated my business throughout the Asia Pacific Region in amazing locations such as Indonesia, Singapore, Thailand, China, Japan, the Philippines, Hong Kong, and Korea. I helped executives and businesses raise billions of dollars in capital while making a small fortune for myself. But this is all the boring stuff I do. I am a Professor in the School of Business and Accounting at Monroe College. I love mentoring and teaching. Helping young people achieve their goals, and showing people how to make their own dreams a reality is what I'm meant to do with my life. This is the rewarding and satisfying stuff I do.

I have a Doctrate in Business Administration with an emphasis in Leadership, Decision Making, and Behavior. I also hold an MBA and a Master's degree in Innovation & Entrepreneurship. I'm passionate about writing, telling stories, and creating content. I want to bring a reader into a world that captivates them, makes them laugh, scares them, and gives them a brief moment to forget about everything else. I've always been enamored by great stories and even more so with great movies. Yes, I love Star Wars, The Lord of the Rings, The Matrix, and other great sci-fi movies. I'm a kid in an adult body. But a great Suspense/Thriller, Mystery, or Drama also keeps me glued to the screen.

Yes, I cried during Charlotte's Web, The Notebook and so many other tear droppers. Who hasn't? Maybe I'm a hopeless romantic or just a sensitive soul. I guess you can say that I get moved by a great story. I am a member of the Writers Guild of the East. I'm passionate about film and attended the New York Film Academy as well as the Hollywood Film School to learn how to film my stories.

To sum me up, I'm a dreamer who never stops dreaming that the impossible is possible. I use my real-life experiences and adventures in all my novels. I've lived in 11 countries and 16 cities. I've interacted with gangsters, CEOs, scammers, and market manipulators as well as many wonderful people from beautiful cultures. I've loved, I've been heartbroken, I've climbed the mountain of success only to come tumbling down twice. I've learned a lot and experienced even more chaotic, often crazy things in my lifetime. I want to share these experiences with you. The good, the bad, the ugly. The full and very interesting me. Enjoy! For more information or to contact the author, go to: VincentdeFilippo.com

Made in the USA
Columbia, SC
06 September 2025